Praise for Cathi Hanauer's "vivid" (*Cleveland Plain Dealer*) novel,

GONE

"Gone asks the question many long-marrieds barely dare to contemplate: What would you do if your husband left to drive the babysitter home and just never came back?"

—*O, The Oprah Magazine*

"A clear-eyed vision of what is gained and lost in a contemporary marriage when the wife and mother begin gaining power outside the home."

—*Vanity Fair*

"Hanauer's portrayal of Eve as a woman who has no choice but to muddle through and do the best she can will resonate with many women. Hanauer delivers a novel that is rich with relatable characters, realistic in its approach, and highly readable."

—*Kirkus Reviews*

"Lose yourself in Cathi Hanauer's *Gone,* the tension-filled tale of a woman who becomes a single mother when her husband vanishes after driving the babysitter home."

—*Shape,* chosen as one of "Summer's Best Reads"

"Rings true with emotional clarity; [Hanauer's] eye for detail and ear for conversational patterns lends credibility to this stark family drama."

—*Publishers Weekly*

"This compelling read about marriage, identity, change, and adaptation nicely examines, from both the male and female lens, how marital expectations and roles may need some tweaking when life throws its curves. A smart, modern read that is relatable and engaging."

—*Library Journal*

"The most beautifully crafted novel I have read in a while."

—*The New Jersey Star Ledger*

"If you're looking for more than fluff and folly, Hanauer's novel delivers. At its core, though, it remains a simple, beautifully told story about a marriage, love, and what remains when one partner has gone."

—*The Florida Times-Union*

"For all its turmoil, Gone is also about redemption and the lasting power of love, even if it means redefining relationships. And Hanauer leavens the story with humor."

—*Daily Hampshire Gazette*

"Compelling reading. . . . One you'll have trouble putting down."

—*Concord Monitor*

"Cathi Hanauer is a great chronicler of modern love and life, who has created, in the pages of *Gone,* the beautiful, intricate story of a beautiful, intricate marriage. This novel will resonate with anyone who has ever been married—which is to say, it will resonate with anyone who has ever struggled to reconcile love against ambivalence, loyalty against the lure of solitude, and domestic fidelity against the call of the open road. You will see yourself in these pages, and your heart will open wide."

—**Elizabeth Gilbert,** *New York Times* **bestselling author of** *Eat, Pray, Love*

ALSO BY CATHI HANAUER

Sweet Ruin

My Sister's Bones

The Bitch in the House (editor)

Gone

A Novel

CATHI HANAUER

Washington Square Press

New York   London   Toronto   Sydney   New Delhi

WASHINGTON SQUARE PRESS
A Division of Simon & Schuster, Inc.
1230 Avenue of the Americas
New York, NY 10020

"A Marriage," copyright © 1987 by Michael Blumenthal, from *Against
Romance: Poems*, by Michael Blumenthal. Used by permission of Pleasure Boat
Studio: A Literary Press. First published in 1987 by Viking/Penguin.

Lyric excerpt from "Hurt," written by Trent Reznor. All rights reserved.
Reprinted by permission.

First Washington Square Press trade paperback March 2013

WASHINGTON SQUARE PRESS and colophon are trademarks of
Simon & Schuster, Inc.

For information about special discounts for bulk purchases, please
contact Simon & Schuster Special Sales at 1-866-506-1949 or
business@simonandschuster.com.

The Simon & Schuster Speakers Bureau can bring authors to your live
event. For more information or to book an event, contact the Simon &
Schuster Speakers Bureau at 1-866-248-3049 or visit our website at
www.simonspeakers.com.

Designed by Jill Putorti

Manufactured in the United States of America

10 9 8 7 6 5 4 3 2 1

The Library of Congress has cataloged the Atria edition as follows:

Hanauer, Cathi.
    Gone : a novel / by Cathi Hanauer.—1st Atria Books hardcover ed.
        p. cm.
1. Self-realization in women—Ficiton. 2. Married women—Fiction. I. Title.
    PS3558.A459G66 2012
    813'.54—dc23
                                                        2012016486

ISBN 978-1-4516-2641-4
ISBN 978-1-4516-7674-7 (pbk)
ISBN 978-1-4516-2642-1 (ebook)

To my mother, Bette Hanauer,
whose love of books and reading
aids, fuels, and inspires me.

And to Wendy Osborn,
for listening and for saying all the right things.

But come now, stay with me, eager though you are for your journey.

—HOMER, THE ODYSSEY

Part One

1

THE TREE—a towering sugar maple on the strip of grass between sidewalk and street—had been dying for years, and now, out her living room window, Eve Adams was watching two men take it down. Or one man, really: the younger one, his dark hair pushing out below his hard hat, the rim of his boxers peeking from the waist of his jeans. He had shimmied up the trunk an hour ago, all leather straps and ropes and work boots, while the older guy, cigarette glued to his lip, held the lines that guided the pieces of tree to the ground after the boy detached them. (He *was* a boy, Eve thought; nineteen or twenty if he was a day.) After securing the rope around the next section to go—first the branches, long and unwieldy; then the trunk, massive and contained—the kid would rev his chain saw and cut with precision, a surgeon amputating a limb, until the wood fell away, hitting the ground so hard that Eve literally felt the earth shake. A thrill would shoot through her, briefly dislodging her mind's contents until all that remained, other than a hint of sadness for the tree, was awe and wonder. She loved watching men cut down trees. Especially when, as now, there was a sapling nearby that would thrive without its expiring ancestor to steal its sunlight and root space.

But the final thrilling moment she could afford to watch ended, as all moments must, and now—Monday morning, just past 8:35— Eve's dark thoughts flooded painfully back. Eric was gone. And while other women's worlds might go on hold when their husbands ran away with the babysitter, she did not have that luxury. For one, there were bills to be paid, bills piled on the desk awaiting money that very well might not yet have been earned. For another, her clients were counting on her, and she would not abandon them just because Eric, as all signs seemed—unfathomably—to indicate, had done just that to her, not to mention to the kids. One family member indulging in some wacko retro-adolescent Jack Kerouac escapade was more than enough. She grabbed her purse and files and hurried out to the car, snapped on her seatbelt and turned the key. But checking the rearview mirror, she paused to look at herself for the first time since she'd dressed to go out, with Eric, on Saturday night.

Admittedly, her face was not exactly the one he had married sixteen years ago. Her eyes were puffy pillows with purple crescent moons underneath (though this she blamed at least partly on her lack of sleep the past two nights). Worse was something she'd noticed only this year, in not just herself but other women screeching into their forties: that slight loosening and drooping of the skin, like a cake not fully baked. Eve forced herself to sit up straighter. At least her irises were still bright blue—even age couldn't steal the color from those—and her cheeks had always held a rosy year-round glow. And she'd dressed well today: black pants, crisp white blouse, red stone choker made by a friend of Eric's. She shook out her hair, which she hadn't had time to dry, having driven eight-year-old Danny to school (and, okay, taken time to watch the tree men). Eric had been driving him lately when she had morning appointments, and she'd gotten spoiled by it, she realized. Well, she'd just have to get *un*spoiled now.

She put the car in reverse, turned the heat to full blast, and pulled none too slowly away from her house and around the corner. This morning's very early phone calls, to the police and to Visa, had yielded two obnoxious new pieces of information. First, the babysitter, Dria, had still not been seen or heard from by her housemate or at the library, where she worked. And second, two tanks of gas and a hotel room in Pennsylvania had been charged to the credit card Eve and Eric shared ($62 for the hotel—at least he was traveling cheap). Clearly he wasn't lying in a gutter, as she'd worried sick about all yesterday and last night. In fact, she had told the police, once she'd regained her composure enough to talk, to leave it alone at this point—not, they'd made clear to her, that they could do much anyway if he was away by choice. Still, she was not one to chase a husband who didn't want to be home. After all, she had enough to do managing the lives and household of the three family members, herself included, who remained.

Danny, anyway, had seemed fine with the explanation she'd provided last evening, casually, at Burritoville—this before she knew anything, really, but she'd had to tell the kids something, and why worry them before there was reason to? "Daddy's gone away for a little while," she'd said, after they were settled at the tiny terra-cotta table with their food and utensils and drinks. "He needs some space and time to collect himself and replenish." She forked grilled chicken salad into her mouth, even though she couldn't imagine swallowing it. "He'll be back soon," she'd added, then wished she could reel the words right back, because honestly, she had no idea.

The boy had listened, nodding thoughtfully, politely chewing his bean and cheese taco, his ears protruding like perfect little jug handles, his eyes an impossibly pale blue against his even paler white skin, which was just starting to produce the smattering of spring freckles that appeared, regardless of sun, like a perennial plant. Fourteen-year-old Magnolia, predictably, was more belligerent. "What do you mean *space and time to replenish*?" she'd demanded, pushing her mop of black curls out of her face, then shaking it back to exactly the same place so she could hide behind it. "Did Daddy *tell* you that? Did he legit say those *exact words*?"

"No," Eve said patiently. "He didn't actually tell me anyth—"

"Then how do you know?" she'd yelled. "How can you possibly know what he needs or why he left?" She'd stood up, leaving her quesadilla, along with the two extra sour creams she'd ordered, and stormed off to the bathroom, yanking down the overly large sweater she wore lately to hide the ample new curves on her suddenly towering body. Eve and Danny glanced at each other, then went on eating, or at least trying to. When Magnolia came out nine minutes later—Eve had already put the quesadilla and sour creams into a take-out container—it was clear she'd been crying. "Oh, sweetie," Eve said, instantly filled with sympathy. "Don't worry. It's okay."

But even as she'd said that, Eve thought it was anything but. At that point, all she'd really known was that Saturday night, after what she'd thought was a lovely, wine-filled dinner out to celebrate her first and likely only book—*Feast on This: How to Eat Right, Feel Good, and Look Great in a Time of Nutritional Chaos*—going into a small second printing, Eric had gone to drive Dria home and hadn't returned. Calls to the police had yielded nothing—no reports of nearby violence or wrongdoing, no local accidents. A call to Eric's cell phone revealed only that he'd left it on their kitchen counter. (He had always hated the thing; took it places only when Eve insisted.) Calls to Dria's cell went unanswered, voice mails to her unreturned, and if Eve had had to hear the girl's voice say, "I can't answer right now, but have a beautiful day!" one more time, she might have gone ahead and slit her wrists. And after contemplating and deciding against calling Eric's mother, in Arizona— why worry Penelope, or humiliate herself, until she was sure he wasn't hiding out locally?—Eve had floated through the rest of the weekend in a fog of alternating panic, anger, and even optimism. Maybe he'd somehow gotten inspired and was off creating the brilliant sculpture that would restore his career to its former success, and their bank account to its former robustness! Until this morning's calls to Visa and the police set her straight.

"I'm not *worried*, Mom," Magnolia had shot back in the restaurant last night. "God, if he's rude enough to leave without even taking his phone or telling us where he's going, why should I worry about him?" Eve knew her daughter *was* worried, of course, but still, she'd felt a secret stab of righteousness at Maggie's words; that's exactly what Eve had been thinking too. "Anyway, that's not what I'm upset about," Magnolia added.

"Well—will you tell us what you're upset about?" Eve had said. "Maybe we can help you."

"Yeah, I guess my eight-year-old brother has a lot of insight into fourteen-year-old relationships," Maggie snapped.

Eve had thought then of a riddle another mother recently told her: *How many teenagers does it take to screw in a lightbulb? One: She holds up the bulb and waits for the world to revolve around her.* "Do not take this out on your brother," Eve had said sharply, but Danny just looked away. "And you may not speak to me that way either, Magnolia. Apologize!"

"Sorry," Maggie said, ungenuinely, but then her eyes filled with tears. "I'm really sorry, Mom. Sorry, Dan man. I'm just—I had a stupid, sucky day. Can we go now, Mom? Please?"

She had been struggling, Eve knew—her strange new body, the veritable tsunami of hormones that washed over her every day— and though Eve was sometimes truly stunned by the rage and snottiness that spewed forth from her daughter's mouth, she also, like other mothers she knew did their own ill-mannered teen offspring, cut her mountains of slack and forgave her the second she was remotely contrite. Plus, the girl was funny as often as she was rude, and Eve loved a good laugh. *Laugh at life or life will laugh at you,* was the motto she tried to live by.

Anyway, Magnolia had seemed better this morning, eating her grapefruit and oatmeal (piles of sugar on each) and even bantering a little with Danny. (*"Hey, Dan, my main man." "Hey back, my main Maggot."*) One less thing to worry about. Not that Eve actually would worry anymore about Eric, now that she knew what the hell he was up to. At the thought, she turned a little too fast onto Main Street, passing the beloved, if almost obsolete, Bramington video store and the slightly seedy piercing place; the recently arrived handmade organic chocolate shop and cozy Bramington

Books and the newest restaurant, Dharma ("locally grown lacto-ovo vegetarian fare"), which had replaced Angelo's Ristorante in her western Massachusetts town, known for its diverse population of artists and musicians, lesbians, aging hippies, earnest trust funders, and recovering (and nonrecovering) alcoholics, drug addicts, and transients. Around the corner, past Nirvana Yoga, which succeeded George's Gym, and Bramington Kung Fu, where Danny practiced, the soon-to-open franchise porn shop had its usual line of women—mostly large and middle-aged, sporting frizzy graying hair and caftans—protesting its opening ("Porn hurts men as well as womyn," one's sign said), while nearby, three scruffy guys in jeans and work boots posed with their sign: "Honk If You're Horny!" They waved and smiled at Eve as she drove past (in a chorus of honks and cheers from several cars), and she might even have smiled back—*Laugh at life* and all that—if she hadn't been so pissed off at Eric.

She pulled onto the highway, accelerated to 70, and set cruise control, then dug blindly for her cell phone. Normally at times like this she called Eric, interrupting him in his studio to update him: where she was going, what they were having for dinner, what activities the kids had today. She'd talk and talk, filling up the space, the miles, while he laughed or said "Uh-huh" or told her some news about the world (another country gone to war, another male politician who'd had some career-ruining affair) that she wouldn't have known otherwise, having pretty much given up reading the paper after Danny was born. (It was all she could do to get through her e-mail, her nutrition journals and e-Blasts, and the occasional novel.) Of course, she probably could have turned on the radio and heard the same news, but it was much more fun to hear it from Eric, who would explain the history of the war or, in the case of lighter news, sometimes editorialize for her in a funny way.

But today she obviously couldn't call him. And her hands were trembling again: one on the wheel, the other holding her phone. Annoyed, she shook them out, one at a time. She took some deep breaths—in through the nose, out through the mouth, the one thing she'd retained from her brief yoga phase—then turned on the radio, loud. Both NPR stations were in the midst of fund drives. After flipping around a bit (rap music, or hip-hop, whatever kids called it now, rude and tuneless, featuring hos and bitches and lady lumps and sluts and junk in your trunk, jizz in your pants, dicks in yo face, dicks super size, dicks that need no introduction), she turned off the radio in disgust. She glanced at her hands—good, all better now—then, after checking traffic, opened the phone again and dialed her best friend, Loretta. The voice mail came on. "Hey, it's Howard, Loretta, Ben, Josh . . . and Edie, born 1/25!" said Loretta's voice. "Leave a message, but I'm not making any promises."

Eve hung up. She had sent Loretta a long e-mail yesterday and hadn't heard back—no surprise, given that her friend had a seven-week-old—but still. Eve missed the daily, if not hourly, e-mail they'd shot back and forth for, what, almost two decades now? Since graduate school, anyway—even after Loretta married Howard just over a year ago. In the e-mail yesterday, Eve told her she had both good news and bad. The good was that her book was actually selling, at least enough to earn out her small advance and maybe even make some royalties eventually. The bad was that Eric seemed—ha-ha!—to have left her. "At first I figured, *Oh, something probably just caught his eye for a sculpture,*" Eve wrote. "A dilapidated pile of wood, or some half-melted snow-man. I imagined him standing in the dark analyzing angles and shadows—and *Good,* I thought, maybe he'll actually *make* something this time. Even later, when I woke up at 3:00 AM and he still wasn't home, I told myself to relax, he's probably just at the studio." But later, Eve told Loretta, she had gone to the studio and found it dark and locked. No Eric.

Now she wanted to update her friend. He really was on the road with Dria, going west! All evidence pointed to it. "Can you believe it?" she would say, attempting a laugh. "I've become the worst sort of cliché." And Loretta would know exactly what to tell her.

With a sigh, Eve dropped the phone back into her purse. She glanced at the files on the seat next to her, which she hadn't had the time—or the wherewithal, anyway—to review in the chaos of the weekend. Maybe at a stoplight she could take a quick look. Otherwise she'd have to wing it. That would be hardest with her first client, Michael Cardello, since he was the most at risk of the three. She remembered now that she had planned to call her old New York boss over the weekend for advice. (That, like everything else, had fallen away after Eric didn't return on Saturday night.) The middle client, Keisha Williams, was new, and the third, Nancy Kalish, was easy; she seemed to keep Eve coming purely for motivation to stay at her current weight, if also to catch each other up on both of their lives, which was just fine with Eve. In fact, Mrs. K was her oldest client; she'd been her first serious case when Eve went out on her own, and Eve would be forever grateful to her for that.

She sped up to pass a dawdling car, then reset cruise control. In fact, she sometimes wondered if she'd have made it on her own if it weren't for Nancy Kalish, especially since it was so much simpler and more prescribed to just work for a company—or had been for a long time, anyway. Eve had come first to New York, fresh B.S./M.S. dietetics degree in hand, to work at the original of the now ubiquitous Beardsley Nutrition Center, on East 34th Street, and she had been happy there for years, embracing the center's philosophy of "nutritionism" and food innovation: the idea that the public needed someone—a whole industry, in fact—to help it eat right and to continually create new foods, bars and drinks, supplements and extracts. She had worked there full-time and then switched to the center up here (conveniently, there was one just twenty minutes away) when she and Eric, whom she'd met along the way, departed Brooklyn; Williamsburg was getting more expensive as the well-off hipsters swarmed in, and Eric had been established enough at that point to leave the city and buy their house here.

When Magnolia was born, Eve promptly quit to raise her full-time, a decision Eric had happily supported. And when Maggie was

two and Eve wanted "a little something outside the home," Beardsley took her right back, first to fill in now and then for a woman
on maternity leave, then to stay on for fifteen or eighteen hours a
week. The job paid little, but back then, with Eric doing so well
(and working nonstop), Eve needed flexibility more than income.
And the women at the center, most of whom had children and also
worked part-time, understood if you had to e-mail your work from
the Happy Tykes hallway or fax it from the pediatrician's machine.
They covered for each other flawlessly, no questions asked, and for
years it worked perfectly for Eve. (They'd graciously given her a year
off when Danny was born, and another to ease her way back up to
fifteen hours.)

But when Danny was three or four, something distressing happened: Eve found herself questioning the center's philosophy. She
didn't want to. Why rock the boat when the boat was a cushy yacht
with a complimentary bar? But she saw the country getting fatter and
fatter, and not just the people who wolfed cheese fries and Big Gulps
and tubs of buttered popcorn, but the ones who followed the advice
of people like her and her colleagues: low-fat diets, energy bars and
drinks, chemical substitutes replacing real food. Her clients were hungry, so much that they couldn't help but gorge—on food low in fat,
yes, if not downright devoid of it ("Nonfat cookies, doughnuts, cream
cheese, sour cream!" their packages screamed), but loaded with sugar
and carbohydrates and preservatives instead. They lost weight at first,
but they gained it back, and then some. And in the meantime, along
with the rest of the country, they got cancer and diabetes and heart
failure.

Worse, new studies constantly appeared that completely con-
tradicted earlier ones, many of them funded by the very industries
they came out advocating (tofu makers insisting on the virtual necessity of soy; dairy marketers who could "prove" that calcium reduced menstrual cramps), and some downright alarming, like the
one that linked grapefruit to breast cancer. The media loved it, of
course—Who wouldn't pay money for the story that their favorite,
formerly healthy breakfast food would have them in the hospital

on chemo any minute now?—as did the center, since they were quoted prominently as the stories broke. Eve and her colleagues were expected to get behind the studies, as well as to enthusiastically embrace and tout each new miracle food. One year it was folate: it did this, it did that, it prevented birth defects, which was all well and good until suddenly it was added to bread, to multivitamins in megadoses, to breakfast cereals and bars, the products now marketed on its presence—"Folate-enriched snack cakes, frozen pizza, cookies!"—right up until they discovered that too much causes cancer. Oops.

But no matter, because by then, they were on to lutein: great for the eyes, for the skin. And then fish oil, and then flaxseed, and then chocolate, of all things, and its "antioxidants." Her clients, who were overweight already, were stuffing their fridges with pounds of Godiva chocolate and cases of red wine in between the Balance Bars and PowerBars and soy bars and "yogurt"-covered everything (which, Eve knew, often had little or no yogurt in them). Their drawers were filled with bottles of quercetin and resveratrol and grapeseed extract. Meanwhile, and despite also having fancy gym memberships and working out hard and often, they got bigger and fatter—and not just her clients, but everyone else too, many of whom were taking their cues from people like her at Beardsley.

It was a culture of fear and constant change and insane complication, she realized, one the industry needed to propagate to keep itself from becoming obsolete. But whenever she mentioned it to anyone at the center, they looked at her like she was nuts. So she turned to alternative magazines and Web sites on her own, which tended to add the environmental element: low-carbon footprint, organic only, meat is bad bad bad, not just for the animals (who are, of course, horrifically treated), but for the environment, for the planet. For a while she bought into that, and even got a little crazy with the whole thing: the vegans, the gluten intolerant, those who claimed milk is no more than cow pus from the ever-infected udders of machine-milked cows, those who believed in only local and hormone and antibiotic free, in not eating fish that was overfished. Really, what could you eat anymore? She got the kids off dairy and onto soy before reading that soy caused children to develop too early; she had them taking a multivitamin and an overpriced vitamin D until she read of "mounting evidence" that a vitamin taken separately from the food it occurs in does "absolutely nothing."

At that, she had screamed and thrown the magazine across the room. She was so sick of reading contradictions, of having to start over every year believing that all the supposed good things—the things she'd worked hard to prepare and coax on the kids—were now dangerous and bad. She was sick and tired of worrying about food. She liked food, and she liked to eat, and she wanted to just *eat*, for God's sake. And she wanted to help other people learn to eat in a way that was pleasurable yet wouldn't make them fat and sick and desperate and hysterical and neurotic.

She thought of the way her mother, pragmatic and unhistrionic, had taught her to eat: wholesome, tasty, home-cooked meals, neither too little nor too much; a treat here and there—a *real* treat, as opposed to something devoid of sugar or fat free. And then she got an idea. She found a pad and wrote on the top: "Eve's Simple Ten: ALL You Need to Know and Do to Eat Right, Feel Good, and Look Great. She contemplated for a second, biting her pencil, then wrote:

1. Eat a variety of foods, in sensible portions.
2. Exercise for at least an hour a day when possible. (A brisk walk is fine.)
3. Avoid anything that says "diet," "low fat," "reduced," or "lite."
4. Realize that if it seems too good to be true, it probably is. (There's no such thing as a healthy doughnut. Which is not to say you should never eat one.)
5. Walk when you're able to. Including taking the stairs.
6. Don't skip meals, especially breakfast, or go to bed very hungry.

7. Cook at home when you can. When you can't, order the smallest size. If it's still more than you really need, have only half or a third.
8. Don't substitute a packaged bar or a drink for a meal.
9. Eat an apple every day.
10. Treat yourself to something you really want. But not too much of it.

Voilà, she thought, and she tossed the pencil back on her desk.

The next morning, she brought the list to her director, Marge, who glanced at it agreeably. But her brow furrowed as she read. "It goes against a lot of the things we advise," she said. "We sell our own low-fat packaged meal bars, after all. And we believe in sugar substitutes, which many people would say are 'too good to be true.' After all, look how much less sugar people are consuming since Splenda appeared."

"But they're not losing weight," Eve said. "They're getting fatter. And in three years, Splenda will likely go the way of aspartame, and saccharin before, and be found to cause cancer."

Marge smiled politely. "Everything causes cancer."

Eve blinked. "But not when people are thirty, or even forty-five. My grandparents lived on cheese and sausage and fruit, and they lived until their nineties. They died of natural causes."

"Sausage? We could never advocate sausage." Marge wrinkled her nose, then discreetly adjusted her bra strap. "Though, actually," she said, after a second, "I think I did just read that Beardsley is developing a fat-free breakfast link."

So Eve decided to start a little business on the side, one in which she could try out her Simple Ten and see how far she got. Calling herself a nutrition and weight-loss coach, she would visit her clients to advise about diet and lifestyle, with an emphasis toward taking off weight. Then she'd be available around the clock, or as close as possible, to answer questions and give moral support. In return, clients would sign an agreement saying they would stick to the

Simple Ten. If they didn't lose weight and keep it off, she'd refund
their investment.

It was risky, she knew—she had no idea whether it would work—
but she put up flyers around town and crossed her fingers. For two
weeks, nothing happened. Then she got a client, a thirtyish coke-
head named Regan who had no apparent interest in changing her
diet (which seemed to consist of Diet Pepsi, Smartfood popcorn,
and Grand Marnier) or in breaking her drug habit, but did want
to talk to Eve, shrink-style, about the string of addict boyfriends
she was sleeping with. Regan employed Eve daily; Eve would rush
to meet her in the hour between finishing at Beardsley and picking up Danny at preschool. *What am I doing?* Eve thought on the
fifth day of spending her lunch hour with this strung-out nutcase.
She knew she should be compassionate—and the extra money was
most welcome by then—but she missed having time to do errands
and, okay, leaf through *People* magazine at Stop & Shop, and after
a week of Regan, she'd had it. *You'll just have to continue to advocate what they say at the center,* she told herself as she drove around
town and sadly removed her signs. Eric's work had fallen off too
much for her to quit without something else. And she'd never find
another part-time job with enough flexibility to be home whenever
the kids were.

That night, as she picked up the crumpled pants and random
socks from Danny's floor, her phone rang. It was Nancy Kalish. She
had seen the sign at the library, she told Eve, and was intrigued. She
had been a "big girl" all her life, but lately had gotten downright
obese; she chuckled as she said this. She had tried "literally millions
of diets" and always just ended up heavier. She was done with diet-
ing, she said. But she was always open to ideas. Maybe Eve could
help her.

Nancy Kalish didn't get thin—she wasn't built for that—but
she did lose thirty pounds in six months, twenty-three of which
she kept off, with a lot of hard work and counsel from Eve. She
was thrilled. At sixty-six, she was wearing clothes she hadn't worn

since college. Her blood pressure dropped, and her doctor, who was heavy himself, asked for her weight-loss tips. Nancy no longer was constipated or had indigestion (due, Eve was sure, to no longer drinking coffee with nonfat nondairy creamer and four Nutra-Sweets per cup all day long). At year's end, she gave Eve three crisp hundreds inside a card that said "Happy Hanukkah to My Guru!"

Newly renovated, Nancy asked if she could introduce Eve to her friends, most of whom also had "a few extra pounds it wouldn't kill them to lose." Thus began the self-named Big Bad Bubalas, a monthly group of women, led by Eve, who for years had done all the "right" things—eaten nonfat yogurt and put nonfat margarine on their fat-free, sugarless oat bran muffins—only to find their hips and stomachs expanding, their bra sizes and number of chins increasing along with their appetites and blood pressure. This led them to feel duped and disgusted, which led them to give up and shovel in lasagna and chocolate cake and greasy, delicious garlic bread in staggering amounts. At the end, tubbier than ever, they slunk back, panicked and humiliated, and restarted their diets.

Eve ran the BBB sessions the first Tuesday evening of each month, alternating at the homes of Nancy, Reenie Stedman, and Gracie Flynn. The women liked her, she knew, because she wasn't puritanical and she wasn't anorexic. (And she liked them—not surprisingly, as many of them were Jewish, and she liked most Jewish people she met. She thought this must be because she had a thing for their culture—the passion, the love of food, the gushiness and bluntness, the talking and whining—though, interestingly, the half-Jew she'd married talked less than anyone she knew. But she made up for that herself.) She never forbade a muffin or a spoonful or two of sugar in coffee, only suggested they start with a *quarter* of the muffin—"since most muffins are basically cake without the icing," she told them—and then walk around the block and see if they still really wanted another quarter or could get by instead with an apple, a banana, or a nice cup of apricot tea.

Of *course* they could have chocolate, she told them, as they squealed with delight, *but*: they had to have a healthy meal first, because otherwise they'd eat too much of it. So they made big, lovely salads, not too heavy on the dressing ("And please," she begged, "*real* dressing, not that 'lite' crap"), and slices of whole-grain bread. Though if they hated whole grain, no biggie, just have white; no one was gonna die from a slice of Wonder bread now and then, just *realize what you're eating.* ("Read the ingredients, for starters. All twenty-three of them, including potassium bromate, which causes tumors in rats, and alpha amylase, which is often derived from swine pancreas. Yum!") And a slice of cheese, or a handful of nuts— "a *hand*ful, not a bagful"—or a slice of lean meat on the bread. Fill up on all that, because "the trick to not overeating," she told them again and again, "is not letting yourself get too hungry." And then, when you're good and full and maybe craving a nice little sweet, have your chocolate—a square or two, not the whole bar. Savor it as the delicacy it's meant to be rather than wolfing it like a feral animal. (They laughed at that one; they loved it when she made fun of them.) Awareness, moderation, simplicity: that was her message. And compromise without complete sacrifice. "Meet your body halfway," she told them. "Never ignore your desires. But be aware of your needs."

And have *fun.* Yes, she told them, they did have to exercise— humans were not bred to sit at screens and steering wheels all day, believe it or not—but neither did exercise have to be some horrible thing that involved jogging till you barfed or staggering through ninety minutes of boiling hot yoga or some god-awful step class. That was fine if you *liked* those things, but if not, hey, watch *Law & Order* while skipping rope, or take a walk with a friend. So they picked each other up at 7:00 AM and trotted faithfully around the neighborhood, Geri's white sneakers gleaming, Winnie's coiffed yellow hair bright as the icing on a butterscotch cake. Soon a couple of them also wanted personal counseling, moral support, menus, and recipes.

Eve didn't love giving the specifics; she wasn't a recipe person herself, just threw good food in a pan with olive oil or butter and whatever herbs she had growing that year. But she aimed to please, so she bought a cookbook or two and found some recipes she could share. The women were thrilled, thanking her profusely, showing up week after week. It amazed her. So much of what she told them seemed like simple common sense, but to them—many of whom had been on diets since they were children—it was revelatory. Almost immediately, they ate better and felt better. Most of them lost weight, some a lot. And most, with her help, kept it off.

At first, Eve was high as a kite. But her work, which used to fit easily into the hours when the kids were at school, now spilled over into nights and weekends, since afternoons and evenings, as always, were spent grocery shopping, getting the kids to doctors and dentists and haircuts, and cooking dinner for the four of them. Soon she was tired and stressed out, not to mention resentful about doing household things she used to not mind or even to like. But she didn't want to ask Eric to come home and help out because, well, if he couldn't see for himself what was needed, she wasn't about to spell it out for him! And anyway, who knew if he was just on the verge of pulling out of his slump? So no. She would handle the home front, as always, just as he'd always handled the bulk of the income earning. But after briefly consulting him for approval (which he gave immediately; he'd always encouraged her to do whatever she wanted work-wise), she quit her job at the center and took on a little more personal counseling, working it around the kids' needs. It was a gamble, but it worked, and soon she was making as much as she had part-time at the center—which, for the first time ever, was almost as much as Eric pulled in that year.

That's when she'd gotten the idea to do the book. It took her six months to write—the information was all there, waiting to spill from her brain onto the page—and another year of much harder work with her editor to get it to sound good and make sense, since she'd never been much of a writer. But now, miraculously, here it was, in bookstores. Eve still couldn't believe it. And she owed Nancy Kalish, who had called this train into the station and walked Eve right onto it.

*   *   *

Eve would have to thank her again later. Now, though, she pulled into Michael Cardello's neighborhood, two towns over from her own, passing blocks of small but tidy houses filled, Michael had told her, with Irish and Italian Catholics, some of whose children—particularly the wealthier, more progressive, or less straight and narrow-minded—had grown up and moved to Bramington. She passed a woman talking on a cell phone while absently pushing a toddler on a plastic swing dangling from a tree, and then, a few houses down, an elderly man sitting in a lawn chair, towel draped over his shoulders, while a younger man stood behind him cutting his hair. She drove onto Michael's block, parked on the street, took a deep breath, and got out.

Michael's wife, Diane—a smiley brunette in white nurse's pants and shoes and a light leather jacket—answered the door. "Good to see you," she said, ushering Eve in. "I wish I could stay, but I have to get to work. Isabella is plugged into a *Sesame Street* video. Hopefully she'll stay out of your way. James will be home in an hour. A car pool is bringing him." She glanced toward the kitchen, then lowered her voice. "I'm trying to set up more of that, since it's so hard for Michael at the school—the halls are crowded, and the kids' cubbies are tiny. He can't get around there, he blocks the hallway, and I honestly worry he'll trip on a kid or fall onto someone. Plus, he can barely fit into the car anymore to get there. And of course he feels awful about all of it." She pulled one thumb, cracking the knuckle, and then the other. "He's not doing well this week," she said. "He's lost control twice with the eating, and it's worse each time. I really don't know what to do anymore. Neither does he. It's—it's horrible, I have to say." Her face wavered, as if she might cry, but she composed herself. "Anyway," she said. "I hope you can help."

Eve nodded, feeling tense, wishing again she'd called her old boss. Really, she was in way over her head here. The family had already tried the standard routes their insurance plan allowed—their primary care physician and a psychiatrist. They had even paid for a hypnotist. Still, they got nowhere, and bills they couldn't afford had added up. Michael hadn't liked the psychiatrist, and Eve, having spoken to him once, could see why. So he'd stopped going. As a last resort, the Cardellos had called Eve a few weeks ago, after a friend recommended her. But she hadn't made much progress either. Not that that surprised her; her job was to educate and hand-hold, and Michael was probably ill beyond the sort of help she could provide. As for the hand-holding, she was trying, but . . . "Don't worry," she told Diane, disingenuously. "I'll talk to him."

She found Michael in front of the stove, his massive form cloaked in tent-sized jeans and an enormous black T-shirt, blocking the oven and all four burners. He turned to Eve and smiled, holding out his hand. "Thanks for coming," he said, and his huge hand, warm and slightly sweaty, engulfed hers. "Would you like coffee or tea?" He wheezed when he spoke, as if the effort of talking, if not simply standing, left him out of breath. At slightly under six feet tall, Michael weighed, he had told her, close to 500 pounds, with a body mass index in the 70s. Normal weight for a man his height, she knew, was below 200 pounds, with a BMI of less than 25. He was what her industry termed "super morbidly obese"—a BMI over 50—which put him at risk for everything from heart disease to diabetes (both of which Eve suspected he already had, the latter doing daily damage to his eyes, heart, kidneys, and nerves), as well as osteoarthritis, acid reflux, sleep apnea, and more.

In fact, at their last visit, Michael had told Eve about his problems with sleep. When he lay down, he had trouble breathing, since his huge stomach hindered the function of his diaphragm. On the nights he was able to breathe well enough to fall asleep, his throat often became constricted and eventually blocked, and he'd stop taking breaths. This, of course, woke him again—not always consciously, Eve knew, but Diane had told him, when she slept in the room with him (rarely anymore, due to his snoring and fidgeting and size; he mostly slept on the living room carpet now, for the sake of both Diane and the bed), that he'd startle awake and doze back off. This went on all night—sometimes as often as twenty-five or thirty times an hour. He was exhausted in the morning—exhausted all the time, really—but it was hard to know how much of that was the sleep apnea and how much everything else: the overeating, the stress, the effort of simply functioning at that weight.

"Tea would be great," Eve said, answering his question. She smiled. "Thanks."

He poured two mugs, and they sat. Michael used a special bench—his weight would likely break the chairs—and he sat several feet from the table because his legs no longer fit under it. Eve wondered what he did about eating meals with his family. But then, she didn't think he ate most of his food at mealtime anyway. Michael was a binge eater—had been all his life, he'd told her when they met. But in the past four years—since James was born, and then Isabella eighteen months later—it had gotten much worse. Before the kids, when he'd had more sleep and time to walk a little, he had kept it somewhat under control, but once he became a parent, it had all gone to seed. Then, to top it off, last year he'd lost his job as an associate editor at the city paper. They had told him they were eliminating the position, but a few weeks later they'd hired someone else.

When Michael found out, he was destroyed. He had loved his job and was good at it, but his weight, he knew, had become a real problem. He couldn't fit at his desk, and he overwhelmed the staff room when they went into meetings—not just his size, but also his odor. He showered every morning, but just the effort of getting to his office made him smell by 10:00 AM, no matter how much deodorant he used. He barely fit into the stalls in the bathroom, and he blocked the hall when he walked down it. It was a respectful, humane office, with several employees with special needs, but Michael's presence, even though he had good friends there, had become increasingly uncomfortable for much of the staff. After they fired him, they had given him some writing and editing to do, freelance, from home, but the new work paid much less and isolated him from longtime friends. It also left Diane with no choice but to go up to full-time at the hospital, where she was a pediatric nurse; they needed the health insurance, not to mention the money. Michael, now home all day, took care of the kids when she wasn't there.

Eve knew that Michael deeply loved James and Isabella, but he was limited in what he could do with them. He could barely bend down to walk with them, let alone run and play; he couldn't sit on their beds to read to them, worried he'd break the furniture. There were few places he could take them. And the combination of caring for the kids while trying to work from home, along with the humiliation of losing his job, had left him tense and unsettled—which, of course, had led to more binges.

"So, how are you?" Eve asked, blowing at her tea.

Michael took a deep breath, and Eve smelled his body odor and the soap-scented powder he used to cover it, his slightly sour breath and the spearmint tea he attempted for that. He held his mug on his massive lap, where it practically disappeared into the folds of his shirt-covered flesh. "I could be better," he said.

Eve nodded. "What's happening? Are you sleeping?"

"No. But really, that's the least of it." He paused for a few seconds, perhaps trying to decide where to start. "I'm completely out of control," he said. "I think—no, I *know*—it's the worst it's ever been. And it's getting harder to hide it from James. He's starting to catch on."

Eve nodded again, wondering what the hell she could do to help him.

"About a week ago, Diane was at work one night," he said, "and I felt a binge coming on. I had eaten a normal breakfast and a normal lunch, so it's not like I was starving. And I tried all the things—deep breaths, meditation . . . whatever. None of it worked, as usual. I couldn't stop the cravings, and I couldn't handle them. It's like—how can I explain it?"

"You don't need to," Eve said gently. "I know it's not in your control."

He nodded, looking grateful. "It was around 8:00 at night, maybe 8:30," he said. "I should have been putting the kids to bed, but I knew that once I did, I'd be trapped here. Not that I'm not anyway, to some extent, since I can't really drive anymore." He shook his head. The cat wandered in, a little calico, meowing loudly. Michael put his mug on the floor and snapped lightly to summon the cat, who jumped into his lap.

He scratched gently behind her ears. "Anyway," he said. "So, I decide we're gonna take a walk to the grocery store. James is all excited, you know, like it's a big adventure." He smiled sadly. "I put them into their coats. It was freezing out. I put them in the double stroller with some blankets, and off we went—me knowing, of course, that if James told Diane, she'd kill me."

"How far is the store?" Eve asked.

"Quarter mile or so. Which is just about my limit these days. So I get us there, and I put the kids in a cart—Jamesey is helping me with Bella, we finally get into the aisles. I'm sort of insane by this point, just dying to get some sugar, anything. I wheel them around, and I get ice cream, and cookies, and popcorn, and cereal—all the usual junk—and James, who'd never paid much attention before, turns to me and says, "Daddy, who are all those treats for?" I felt so guilty and pathetic, and I couldn't really think by that point, so I did the stupidest thing on earth, I told him the truth. I said, 'It's for me, buddy.' My God. What the hell was I thinking?"

"You were trying to be honest," Eve said.

He shook his head. "Idiotic, that's what it was. So Jamesey says, 'Why do you get to have all those treats and we don't?' And I said, 'Well, James, it's because I have a problem, and I'm trying to work it out, but I don't really have it under control.' I said, 'Do you see how big I am?' and he said, 'Do you mean fat?" and I nodded and said, 'Yes. Fat. Well, I'm like that because I have a disorder, an eating disorder, and the thing in my brain that helps me stop eating is not working right.'" On his lap, the cat purred loudly. "I swear, Eve, I don't know what I was thinking, telling him all that," he said. "But I was out of my mind that night."

"That was okay to tell him," Eve said, going with her gut. She would have to find a shrink, too, to consult with about this, if not one who would actually go to his house. But who would do that? And Michael couldn't afford it even if she did find someone.

"Well, predictably, James says to me, 'Daddy, I have that disorder too!'"

Eve smiled, and he smiled back, funny as it wasn't.

"Then he says, 'And Bella too! She has it too! So can we get some ice cream?'" So I say, 'Listen, James, you don't have this disorder, and I pray to God you never will. But it's not a disorder to eat ice cream, and of course you can have some. We'll go home and all eat ice cream, and then you have to go 'nighty.' And he says, 'And brownies?' because he sees I have a box of brownie mix. So I said—in a stunning act of sacrifice, I might add, though only because I knew Diane would kill me, she's so nervous about the kids around all that crap—I said to him, 'You know what, James? Let's put back the brownies and all this stuff, and just get ice cream. And we'll each have one small bowl, because that's the healthy way.' And he says, 'Okay, Dad.'"

He sighed. "Poor sweet kid. Do you know, he told me one night that I smell like stinky shoes? He wasn't saying it to be mean, just matter-of-factly. He doesn't even know how to be mean. Well, he'll learn. He also told me his friend's big sister said I'm a cow, and he asked me what she meant by that."

Eve shook her head.

"Anyway," he said. "So that night, I'm thinking, how can I get more of this stuff out of here without him seeing, because I know the mere half-gallon of ice cream isn't gonna do the trick. So we go around and put everything back, but when he's not looking, I sneak the brownie mix down my pants." He looks at her. "I stole it, Eve. I've never done anything like that." He was sweating, and panting a little, and his face had turned red. Eve felt a flutter of panic. What if he had a heart attack? She had learned CPR at some point, but that was years ago.

"So we buy the ice cream," he continued, after a minute, "and I steal the mix, and we go home—no easy task, I can barely fit through the grocery checkout. I can barely walk anymore, my feet and knees are so sore. At home, I'm trying to take off the kids' coats, I can't even breathe. I get out some bowls, and Jamesey says, 'This is the one mommy uses,' and he gets out a different one, and then he says, 'She gives us one scoop each. Here's the scooper.' And I realize that he's nervous to have me feeding him this—like maybe, you know, if he lets me feed them, they'll get this disorder, too, or somehow look like me.

"But I give them each a scoop, and I give myself a nice little scoop, too, just like theirs, and we all eat them up, and then I put them to bed—not calmly, I'll add, because I was desperate to get back downstairs—and when James asked me to read him a story, I snapped, which was maybe the worst part of the whole thing." His eyes teared up, and he blinked them clear again. "Once I've got them in bed, I go down and eat the rest of the ice cream, which takes about ten seconds, and then I make the brownie mix and eat half of it raw while the other half is in the oven, and then I eat the oven half, which is still mostly raw. At one point James called down, and I yelled up at him to go to bed. I never yell at him. But it was ten by then, and Diane was due home in an hour, and I was panicked because time was running out.

"So I finish the brownies, and I want more, of course, but I can't go out, I can't leave the kids. So I start scouring the house. And there's nothing much in the way of sweets, because I eat them as fast as she buys them, not that she buys much anymore. But I make the rest of the eggs in the fridge, maybe eight. There goes our breakfast. I scramble and eat those, and then . . ." He stopped.

Eve's heart was in her stomach.

"I ate whatever I could find," he continued, after a second. "The hot dogs—a whole pack, raw. All the cereal in the house. All the bread. I found a lasagna in the back of the freezer, something Diane was probably saving for a quick dinner. I microwaved it for as long as I could stand to, then ate it half frozen. I wanted sugar after that, so I scoured the pantry, and I found an old, stale box of teething biscuits that had been Isabella's, or maybe even James's. I ate it."

She swallowed. "And then?"

"And then I was done. I'd eaten pretty much everything." He shifted on the bench. "That's about it, I guess. But it was horrific. That's the worst I've ever felt, and not just physically. Diane came home and—"

Eve waited.

"I was in tears. I told her, 'I'm so sorry, I'm so, so sorry.' I told her I couldn't control myself, and I don't know what to do. I told her that if I wasn't a Catholic, I'd have killed myself by now, and I may still. I mean, merciful God, right? He's really looking after me, let me tell you." He laughed bitterly. "Diane forgave me, more or less, or at least she tried to. She's as sympathetic as anyone could ever be, but she's losing patience with me. Like they did at work. There's only so much you can forgive in a person." He let out a breath through his lips. "So of course I was sick all night. I didn't throw up, because I never throw up, as you know."

Eve nodded. He had told her early on that vomiting terrified him, to the point that he'd trained himself never to do it. Whatever went in had to stay in—or come out the other end.

"But I was sick in every other way," he said. "I'll spare you the disgusting details. After a while I couldn't bear to stench up the house anymore, so I went outside. But I couldn't walk around out there, because my feet and knees couldn't take it. So I just lay down on the grass, which was cold and wet, and I stayed there. All night. I lay on my lawn, burping and freezing and doubled over with pain. It was the worst night of my life."

Eve reached out and took one of Michael's hands; the other still cradled the cat, now asleep atop his stomach. "I'm so sorry," she said.

Michael nodded. After a few seconds, he let go of her hand. "I can't go on like this, Eve," he said. "I really—I would rather be dead. I hate myself for saying that—how can I even *think* that when I have two little kids? But I swear to God, I can't live like this anymore."

"Of course you can't," Eve said.

"So what can I do, then? How can I stop this?"

She sat still for a good thirty seconds, racking her brain. Finally, and with great relief, she said, "Have you thought about bariatric surgery? Gastric bypass?" It was a last resort, true—a difficult, unpleasant operation and recovery. But Michael was ready for a last resort. And it had a better success rate than anything else for dramatic weight loss and maintenance.

But he was shaking his head, looking terrified. "I can't afford it," he said quickly.

"Most insurance will cover it if your BMI is over a certain number," Eve said gently. "You just have to show that you've tried and failed at other weight-loss methods."

"But you throw up," he said. "Right? They make your stomach really tiny, and if you eat more than a few crumbs of food, you throw it up." He was breathing hard. "I couldn't do that."

Eve stood up. "Listen," she said. "Before you say no, let me find out more about it. I'll call you in a few days and tell you what I've learned, and we'll talk about it. Okay?"

Michael nodded, but he didn't look happy.

"In the meantime," Eve said, "if you feel a binge coming on, will you call me?"

He nodded again, but she knew he wouldn't. He never did.

Michael stood then too, setting the cat down as gently as he could with his heft. He held out his hand. "Thank you," he said, but he looked completely unsettled now.

Eve shook her head. "Don't thank me," she said. "And do me a favor? Don't pay me yet either. I didn't do a thing today but listen, and I wasn't as prepared as, as—"

He raised his eyebrows, watching her.

"—you know. As I'd have liked to be."

Michael smiled now, the anxiety momentarily disappearing. "See, you're like me," he said. "Overly moral. Lucky for you, I'd never let you walk out of here without pay. Then you'd have the moral upper hand." He reached for his back pocket, extracted his wallet. "Please," he said, holding out some bills. "Just to have someone make me feel like they care is worth ten times this."

Eve frowned. She felt lousy about the way the session had gone, and she knew she didn't deserve that money. But her next client was pro bono, and then there was just Mrs. Kalish. She had to go home with something. And mess or no mess, Michael had a spouse out there working—a spouse who would come back at the end of the day.

She reached for the cash. "Thank you," she said, and then, "I'll call you. Don't worry. We'll figure this out."

He nodded. "Thank *you*," he said.

2

IN THE CAR, rushing now, Eve tried to follow the MapQuest directions to Bloomfield, where her next client lived, even without fully trusting them. Eric was the one who could navigate streets, in real life and online. Big help that was now. She turned left, hoping she wasn't getting lost, passing a nail salon and abandoned storefronts, plywood standing in for former doors, graffitied in lime green and black. In front of a convenience store, clusters of boys and men stood about, arms folded or punching keys on a phone or holding a boom box or a leash that led to a pit bull or rottweiler. So different from Michael Cardello's town—and from her own, full of dreadlocked kids with hackey sacks and friendly vagrants holding signs ("Will Answer Questions For Food") and, other than the occasional fiddle or saxophone prodigy or young boy band on their way up, street musicians with out-of-tune guitars loudly competing with each other, "Bad Bad Leroy Brown" on one corner, "Que Sera Sera" on the next. And everyone either too liberal and PC or reserved in that old New England way to tell them to please tone it down. Here, the music came prepackaged, loud enough to shake the street. A couple of the men—hefty dudes in big jackets, pants slung low— glanced at Eve as she drove by, while others looked bored or antsy. There were no women, and not, she thought, many signs of joy in the men—but then who was she to judge? It's not like her life was so perfect. She found the address, parked, and got out.

A tall, very top-heavy teenage girl opened the door and stared at her bluntly. She had large features and straightened shoulder-length hair, and she wore dark stretch jeans, flip-flops, and a big green sweatshirt. She held a pink-blanket-clad bundle casually, like a football, in one arm. "Hello," Eve said. "I'm Eve Adams, the nutritionist Sue Feldman sent. Are you Keisha?" The girl nodded and moved aside, and Eve stepped in.

The house smelled vaguely like cooked food—spices, meat—combined with something chemical, like the protective coating on a new carpet or chair. Keisha led Eve past the living room, a pastel-colored playpen dominating the small space between the overstuffed furniture and a large flat-screen TV, which was blaring out a courtroom show. In the kitchen—the battered beige linoleum scrubbed clean—Keisha, still holding the baby in one arm, sat at a bright yellow table that had pieces missing from the sides, exposing fiberboard underneath. Eve sat down across from her and smiled. "Boy or girl?" she asked, though it was obvious; the blanket was pink.

"Girl." Keisha raised the baby slightly to be viewed. She had gorgeous brown skin, a few shades lighter than her mother's, and tiny pursed lips. She wore a pink headband with a bow.

"She's beautiful," Eve said, already wishing she could hold her.

"Thank you," the girl mumbled.

"What's her name?"

"Amani."

"That's lovely. And how old is she?" Eve knew this answer already, too, as Sue had told her, along with the details. Keisha, who'd recently turned sixteen, had gained eighty pounds in her pregnancy, topping off the forty or so she'd put on last year, her sophomore year of high school. She was a junior now, and both she and her mother (apparently no fathers, neither Keisha's nor the new baby's, were in the picture) were determined she graduate; she had decent grades and showed up regularly, which was more than many of the other kids at her school did. Sue—Keisha's guidance counselor and an acquaintance of Eve—was worried, on top of everything else, about the girl's weight. She thought that even one or two visits from Eve might help, and she'd set up the appointment for them to meet and given Eve the information.

"Five weeks," Keisha said, answering Eve's question.

"Great. And how are you doing so far?"

Keisha shrugged. "Fine. My mama mostly take care of her, so . . ."

"She takes her to work with her?"

Keisha nodded. "She babysit, next town over. The lady she sit for say it's okay, so . . ." Her voice trailed off again.

Eve nodded. "And you've been back to school now, and work, for—two weeks?"

The girl scratched her head. "Three," she said.

"So you went back when, let's see, the baby was . . ."

"Twelve days."

"Twelve days! Oh my."

"My boss say that's all I can take from work or I lose my job, so . . ." She shrugged again.

Twelve days after giving birth to Magnolia, Eve recalled, she was still barely functioning beyond feeding the baby, whom she nursed on demand—basically nonstop around the clock. Thankfully, Penelope, Eric's mother, had come and taken over the house so that Eve could sleep when the baby slept and recover from the delivery. She remembered her episiotomy still burning at the time, her breasts leaking all over the place. She looked at Keisha. "So you probably weren't able to nurse her at all before you went back."

"I did. For a week in the day. After that, mostly just at night."

"Really? Great! And so—you still nurse her at night, then?"

Keisha nodded, looking down. "She don't wake up much. One, maybe two time a night."

"That's great, though!" said Eve. "That's excellent. That breast milk is so, so good for her. And it's good for you too. Breast-feeding will help you take off the weight."

The girl didn't respond, and Eve wondered if she was sick and tired of little white women telling her what she should and shouldn't do. "So," she said, taking the zeal down a notch, "I'm guessing that between school, the baby, and your job, you probably weren't able to write down the stuff I asked, but that's okay. We can always—"

"I did it." Keisha stood up partway, her large body almost engulfing the baby, and pulled a folded paper out of her back pocket. She held the child, Eve noticed, as nonchalantly as if it were a sack of flour; no fancy Snuglis or BabyBjörn carriers for this new mom. Eve herself, as a new mother, had been afraid of dropping her children, at least at first, and by the time that fear had gone, the babies were bigger and harder to hold. The carrier made it much easier. Plus, she could get things done while she held them—make dinner or check her e-mail—when she stood. Though Keisha seemed to be getting plenty done too.

Eve took the paper. In tiny, neat handwriting, the girl had kept an immaculate food journal for the four days since they'd spoken. "Wow," Eve said. "This is *really* good, Keisha." She scanned it quickly. She had decided beforehand that she would do a much abbreviated first visit with this client, both because the visit was likely pro bono (Sue was trying to get her something, but . . .) and because she wasn't sure the girl would do any of the things she suggested anyway. She would start with a few small tips and see if they got anywhere. "I can tell you one thing right off that will help you a ton," she said, looking up. "You need to eat breakfast. That's your most important meal of the day."

Keisha nodded, her eyes focused on the table.

"Breakfast is like fuel," Eve continued, switching to autopilot. "Not just for your body, but for your brain too. So trying to function without it is like trying to drive your car without gas. You might get a little ways down the road, but then you'll slow down or stop. You'll be groggy, you'll lack energy, and later you'll overeat. Here, for example." She pointed to one day that Keisha had had three pieces of pepperoni pizza for lunch. "If you eat breakfast next time, you might be able to limit your lunch to only one slice, especially if you add a glass of milk and a vegetable or fruit. Now that's a pretty healthy lunch. Especially if you're willing to lose the pepperoni." She smiled.

Keisha nodded again, still staring at the table. In the other room, Judge Judy was yelling at someone. "Now, I know it's not easy to find fruits and vegetables at school," Eve said, as if she had a captive audience. "So it's good to bring an apple or a banana from home if you can. Maybe also a little bag of carrots or peppers or green beans, which are not bad with a little salt on them."

Keisha still wasn't looking, but at least she nodded at the right times.

"So, okay. Here's another thing." Eve pointed to the sheet. "You had a large soda with the pizza, right? This will probably make you want to kill me—" She looked at the girl for a smile, but received zilch. "But if there's just one thing you could eliminate from your diet and do every part of your body a favor—teeth, blood, bones— it's soda."

The baby made a noise. Keisha ignored her, and she stopped.

"Now, I know a small milk is as expensive as a big soda, and it might not taste as good to you at first. But your body needs milk right now." Eve explained why—the calcium, the protein. Keisha nodded, and Eve went on. "Let's talk breakfast. What kinds of food do you have here?"

The girl shrugged.

"Do you have eggs?"

Another shrug. "On Sundays."

"But not during the week?"

She shook her head. "My mom leave at 6:15. She don't have time to cook in the morning. She get breakfast on the way to work. And I get free lunch at school, so . . ."

"Is that where your mom is now?" Eve asked. "At work?"

Keisha nodded. "Her friend bring Amani home, 'cause she get off earlier. Then I watch her till Mama get home again. Then I go to work, seven to midnight."

Eve refrained from shaking her head like the patronizing, over-sympathetic, privileged white person she was. "You work at McDonald's, right?" she said.

"Bigger Burger," Keisha corrected.

"Oh, right." Eve took a breath. "What else do you have in the house? Cereal?"

Keisha got up with the baby, opened a cupboard, produced a box of Cocoa Krispies.

Eve smiled. "It's not soda, at least. And if you add milk, you get protein. Do you have milk?"

Keisha opened the fridge. Large containers of store-brand cola, a couple of take-out containers, a box from KFC. She shook her head no.

Eve thought of her own fridge, packed, as it almost always was, with fresh vegetables, fruits, cheese, milk, and lots of leftovers. She was obsessive about having certain items on hand, replacing them even before they ran out: not just bananas, carrots, and apples, but her favorite dark chocolate, her favorite red wine, sparkling water, salad dressings and teas. She kept a detailed list for food shops, and if Eric used up something without putting it on the list, she gave him hell. It was the least he could do, help her update the list, when she did all the shopping and cooking. She bet he missed her now, wherever he was. Or at least missed her refrigerator.

Keisha closed the fridge door and stood there, not unlike a large tree, except with a baby stuck to her arm. Eve looked at her a moment, thinking, then glanced at her watch. She still had an hour until her next client. "Do you have a little time now?" she asked.

"I have work at four," Keisha said.

"Let's go food shopping. I'll have you back in a half hour."

Ten minutes later—Eve made Keisha sit in back with the baby, as the girl didn't own a car seat, and she drove about three miles an hour—they were walking down the aisles of the nearest grocery store, the baby asleep on her mother's arm. Eve picked out items, explaining why she was buying each one: low-fat milk, orange juice, eggs, butter (Eve didn't believe in nonfat cooking sprays), whole wheat bread (not easy to find, but she located a loaf in back of all the whites), apples and bananas, baby carrots (there were no peppers, cucumbers, or green beans), store-brand turkey breast, and sliced cheese. Peanut butter, jam, sandwich bags. For cereal, they picked out store-brand whole wheat flakes, lightly sweetened, and a large box of Cheerios—"One is oats, one is whole wheat," she explained. "So they won't turn to sugar in your blood as fast as Rice Krispies or Corn Flakes, which means they'll make you feel full longer." In the pharmacy aisle, miraculously, Eve found a bathroom scale—not cheap, but she wanted the girl to see her progress if she stuck to the plan. At the checkout, Eve charged it all on her Visa. Eric was charging hotel rooms, after all. Plus, it would make her feel a little better about her incompetence with Michael today.

Back at the house, the baby was finally starting to fuss—something that seemed to bother Eve far more than Keisha. Eve carried in the groceries while Keisha lay the baby on the kitchen table and unrolled her from the blanket, revealing a pristine white dress and shiny pink shoes on her thumb-sized feet. *My God!* Eve thought, wondering how this girl's mother possibly afforded everything—diapers, clothes, formula, baby equipment, plus the house and the heat and everything else—on the pay of a nanny and a part-time teenage fast-food worker. No wonder they had nothing to eat. The baby was screaming now, her mocha face tinged with pink, and Keisha set about making a bottle from a can of powdered formula, neither glancing back at the baby nor appearing to rush.

Eve bit her lip. When her own babies had cried—especially Magnolia, whose cry even then was loud and angry—her breasts had turned on like faucets, and she had raced around doing anything to stop the wailing. She had never just "let the baby cry," as some experts advocated, though, of course, you had the equally vehement "there's no such thing as spoiling a baby" experts. Eve tended toward that lobby, figuring that if her babies' cries had such a physical and mental effect on her, they must be designed to make her snap to. She'd held and burped and changed and fed on demand, and then, when Magnolia became a toddler who demanded her way or freaked out, thought, *I've ruined her forever.* And so it went, until Danny came along and, with just the same treatment, was the most agreeable child on earth.

Eve thought about how, when she'd woken on the couch two days ago, the morning Eric hadn't returned—her head throbbing with hangover and fear—Danny had been sitting at her feet, a skinny boy in green pajamas mangling the newspaper as he attempted to read the comics. He didn't ask her why she had slept downstairs, why she was still dressed, why she looked, she was sure, like a truck had run over her face. He just sat there, clearly wanting to be close to her, and fighting the paper, his bony white arms flailing about, until finally she said, "Do you want me to fix that for you?" He nodded, and she'd folded it neatly and handed it back, and then he'd read it intensely, either not noticing or not caring where the hell Daddy was, until suddenly, as if he'd just thought of something astounding, he let the paper slide down to the floor and said, naked blue eyes alight, "Mom, you know what? Harriet Tubman wasn't even a *boy*! He was a *girl*!" She wanted to bury him in kisses, eat him alive.

"Do you want me to hold her?" Eve couldn't bear the wails anymore.

Keisha shrugged her big back without turning around. "If you want."

Eve washed her hands, dried them on her skirt, and snatched up the baby. My God, was she small! Like a mini football. Had her own kids ever really been this tiny? She lay the baby carefully on her shoulder. "Shh," she whispered, and she walked in small circles, jiggling the baby until the cries subsided. She hoped that Keisha was taking notes, seeing how to soothe the poor thing.

When the girl was ready, Eve handed her the baby, and Keisha stuck her on one arm, as usual, and, with the other hand, plugged the bottle into her mouth. Immediately the baby sucked away. Keisha watched her, expressionless. She was standing—as if it didn't occur to her to sit down—and Eve pulled a chair over behind her. "Sit," she said.

Keisha sat, her heft making a midget of the chair.

"She's a good eater," Eve said, watching the baby. With a sigh, she peeled her eyes away and began to put the groceries in the pantry and fridge. She folded the bags, then brushed off her hands. "So," she said. "You should be set for a little while, at least."

Keisha nodded. She was looking at the baby now, Eve was happy to see. But she glanced up for a moment. "Thank you," she said.

Eve smiled. "You're welcome. So here's what I'm asking from you in return. I'll write it down." She fished her monogrammed pad and a pen from her purse. "Number one, eat breakfast every day—orange juice, milk, and one of the things we bought, eggs or cereal or at least toast. Number two, bring a fruit and a vegetable to school for whenever you feel hungry. That's why we bought the carrots and baggies." Keisha nodded, and Eve said, "Third, make a sandwich and eat it before work, so you're not tempted to eat the stuff there. If you have to eat there, have a hamburger or cheese-burger—just one, or even a half——and your carrots or apple with it. Skip the fries." She looked at Keisha, but got nothing this time. "Last thing," she said, "and this will be the toughest. No soda. I won't ask you to promise, because I know how hard it will be."

"That don't sound so hard," Keisha said.

Eve laughed. "Well, it's a big change. And change is always hard." No response.

"Okay, then!" Eve said. "I'll call you in a few days, and we can schedule something for a week or two, if that works. Or call me anytime if you have questions." She put her business card on the table. "Bye," she said. "It was nice meeting you and your beautiful daughter."

She showed herself out and back to her car. At least she had tried. And at least she was *here*. She could be sitting home obsessing over her missing husband. She wiped her hands (which were suddenly sweaty) on her pants, then flipped on NPR, turning it loud enough to drown out her thoughts. She listened attentively to the fund drive until she reached the exit for Longmont, Mrs. Kalish's town.

She pulled off and began the scenic drive through the wind-ing hills of the wealthy enclave, one big, immaculately landscaped home more beautiful than the next. Lawns sparkled like emeralds; cherry trees, which would soon be in bloom, were perfectly manicured giant mushrooms. Saabs and BMWs gleamed behind electrically sealed, burglar-alarm-protected garage doors, Eve knew, just as the people who drove them glittered, expensively dressed and lotioned, inside the houses. The Kalishes had a classy Tudor with an outdoor pool, a game room "for the grandchildren" (so far they had two—one a toddler, one an infant), and a darkroom; one of her sons had been into photography before he became a radiologist, following in his father's footsteps. Eve walked to the doorway, files in hand—might as well *look* professional, at least—and rang the bell, listening for the clack of heels on hardwood floors. The door opened, and Mrs. Kalish, a wide-faced woman in black pants, a cranberry sweater, and bright lipstick, rushed to hug and kiss Eve. "Come on in, come in," she said. "I'm so glad it's our day. Here, give me your coat. How are you, sweetie?"

Eve relinquished the coat. "Not bad," she said, almost happily. "And you?"

"Don't ask!" Mrs. Kalish waved her hand in the air. "I've been craving cream puffs all week after seeing someone eating them at the bakery—tiny little thing, just like you, probably has the metabolism of a fruit fly or hummingbird or one of those creatures who has to eat every second just to survive." She laughed, then motioned Eve toward the kitchen. "Come, let's have tea. It's freezing out there. I don't know why we don't give in and move to Boca already with everyone else, but Seymour won't go." She glanced down the hall, then whispered, "I'm not ready either, but don't tell him, I like to make him think he owes me. Anyway," she said, loudly again, "I let myself have one little cream puff—oh, I can't lie, two—but they were small. Ish. And I knew you'd say that was okay, to go ahead and have one rather than deprive myself and then have ten later. Right? But honestly, Eve, the only thing stopping me from having ten *right then* was knowing I would see you today. I couldn't bear it if you saw me with even one more chin." She grinned, merry as ever. "Plus, the grandkids are coming next week, and . . . oh well, I should shut up already. Chamomile or your new favorite, twig tea? I finally found it at that health food place near the highway."

They had arrived at the kitchen, where the kettle was screaming. Eve chose a tea, and Mrs. K placed the two mugs on a tray that contained a silver dish filled with sugar cubes and a tiny pair of silver tongs.

Eve smiled. Mrs. Kalish always made her tea and always presented it this way, half elegant, half motherly, chatting nonstop the whole time. Eve supposed all this yapping might get old for some people, but she personally found it comforting. Her own mother, Florence, who now lived in Georgia with her sister, Aunt Fay, was the antithesis of Nancy Kalish: reserved and quiet and Catholic. Her father, for his part, had been genial but also somewhat formal. Eve spoke to her mother once a month or so and saw her rarely; Florence didn't like to travel, and since she didn't ask for the kids to come down anymore, Eve didn't go to the hassle and expense of taking them. She and her mother got along fine but had little in common. Both Florence and Fay were involved with the church and had an active social life through that. And Eve's childhood hadn't been unhappy; it just hadn't been jolly or fun. Mrs. K, in contrast, struck her as both, not to mention passionate.

That, Eve thought, following her client into the living room, was one of the things she'd loved about Eric at first too—his passion. His, of course, came out mostly in and through his art: the way he'd work all night on a sculpture, not stopping even for a drink or a bathroom break; the way the pieces looked at the end, triumphant and almost living and breathing, as if he'd transferred an actual part of himself—his emotions, his lifeblood—into them. Or the way he held her face and looked at her, really looked, as if he saw something she herself couldn't even see. She loved when he looked at her like that, though usually, especially after the first couple of years, those looks were reserved for his work. Usually, it seemed to her now, she was the one looking at him. Well—until the kids, anyway. Then he looked at his work and she looked at the kids. But that had worked too. Or at least she had *thought* it was working.

Mrs. Kalish placed the tray on the coffee table, and they sat on the couch, sipping, talking, paging through photo albums of the grandchildren. Mrs. K was an avid watcher of mainstream TV news, which is why she was so up on every trendy, headline-generating new food study, be it that raspberries reduce cancer (all those antioxidants!) or, a year later, that raspberries *cause* cancer (all those pesticides!); that eating vegetables fights Alzheimer's or, a few months after, that there's no correlation whatsoever. She wanted to talk about them all, to have Eve help her make sense of them, and Eve was happy to oblige. Finally, when their hour was three-quarters over, Mrs. Kalish said, "So, what do you think, Eve? Any tips to help an old fatty stop craving cream puffs?" She sighed with joy. "Even the *words* make my mouth water."

Eve smiled. "Try baking something halfway there," she said. "Still sweet, but not quite so indulgent. Those pear sunflower muffins, or oatmeal raisin cookies. When they're done, put them all in the back of the freezer except for one or two, then sit down in another room to eat those—after you have your apple, of course." She smiled again. "Eat them slowly, enjoy them, maybe with a big cup of tea. After that, if you still want a cream puff? Go get one. But *one*. Not fifteen. And then take a walk." She looked at Mrs. K. "Are the women still walking?"

Nancy nodded solemnly. "Absolutely. It was icy on Saturday, so we walked in the mall. Well—Winnie couldn't go, because Herb had the urologist, and Grace had the periodontist, and Sylvie's grandchildren were in. But the rest of us went. And let me tell you, even at 10:00 AM, that place is swarming with girls in those tiny little tissues that pass for clothes they wear now." She shook her head. "Nothing like fifteen-year-olds to make you feel like you should hang it up and eat yourself to death while you can still roll yourself to the food court."

Eve laughed. "Well, I have something to help. See what you think." She reached into her bag and pulled out a pomegranate; she had bought it at Whole Foods on Saturday. *Saturday, back when she had a husband.* "A new fruit for your weight-maintaining pleasure," she said.

Mrs. Kalish picked it up to examine it. "Fantastic," she said. "What is it?"

"A pomegranate."

"You're kidding! That's what they look like? I've had the juice, but . . ."

"Right. Everyone has pom juice now, and pom juice pops, and pom gelato, and whatever else they can think of to put it in. The fruit, on the other hand, has been around for a long time—though admittedly not in Massachusetts in March. We can thank Whole Foods for that too. Come, I'll show you how you eat it."

In the kitchen, Eve demonstrated how to cut the fruit in half and soak it in cold water to get the seeds to sink while the pithy parts floated to the surface—seeds that you eat slowly, one by one, reveling in their sweet tartness. "It's healthy, it's natural, it's low in fat and calories, and it's a pain in the ass," Eve explained, "which means that instead of focusing on avoiding cream puffs all day, you can focus on preparing your pomegranate. Here, taste."

She held out a few gel-covered seeds, and Mrs. K popped one in her mouth. She chewed, swallowed, smacked her lips, then nodded and reached for another. "'*Your shoots are an orchard of pomegranate,*'" she quoted, chewing. "That's from the Bible. Can you believe I remember that? I learned it about a hundred years ago—in Hebrew school, I think—yet I never tasted the actual fruit." She smiled at Eve. "Just when I think you can't possibly teach an old dog new tricks, you pull another one out of your hat."

Eve waved away the praise, then began to clean up the mess, scooping the seeds onto a plate. "I'm in these places anyway," she said, throwing the deep red rinds in the trash, "shopping for the kids and—" She started to say Eric, then stopped.

Mrs. Kalish was watching her. "Oh, leave that, leave it," she said after a moment, "I'll get it later. Come, talk to me before you go, I haven't even asked about *you*! How are the kids?" She took Eve's cold hands in her plump warm ones and led her back to the living room.

Eve sat in a chair, withdrawing her hands (though not really wanting to). She took a deep breath. "Magnolia's not such a kid anymore," she said. "Though emotionally, she seems to have regressed to the terrible twos. She's fourteen, so . . ."

"My God, *fourteen*, already?" Mrs. K shook her head. "I remember that age. Becky and Seymour used to fight. Oy oy oy, did they fight." She settled heavily on the chair facing Eve's. "What's she like now? You haven't brought me pictures in forever! Does she look like you?"

Eve shook her head. "She's dark, like her father. Tall like him too. Very suddenly, actually: she grew eight inches this past year. Towers over me. And most of her friends. Even over most of the boys, unfortunately."

The older woman nodded. "Rebecca did that—shot up like a weed. Any boyfriends yet?"

"She was in love with a boy forever. And he with her too, I think. But it looks like he's moved on now."

Mrs. Kalish clucked. "Poor girl."

"I know." *Oh well, lots of fish in the sea,* Eve was tempted to add, but the truth was, there really weren't many fish like Nate. For years, he and Magnolia had been the closest of friends. Until last spring, in fact, he had come over for hours at a time, his floppy bangs obscuring his dreamy brown eyes, his voice breaking all over the place. They shot hoops in the driveway, or she played violin and he air guitar, or they lay on the lawn in the sun and talked about which teachers they loved or hated, what they wanted to do when they grew up. Nate wanted to be a chef and a writer, Maggie a classical violinist—this before she quit violin three months later and he dumped the school paper to go out for Bramington High's football team. Sometimes they kissed—Eve saw them out the window or while she was pulling weeds from the garden—but, naive or not, she truly thought it seemed purely affectionate and sweet, not heavy or sexual or aggressive. Magnolia adored him. And Eve found their relationship remarkably mature for two kids.

And then summer came, and one day—it seemed that way to Eve anyway, that it happened pretty much overnight—the awkward boy with the floppy bangs and the half-girl voice was gone, replaced by the sort of brand-new man you might see, say, reclining on a billboard for Abercrombie & Fitch, jeans unzipped. Off he went to high school, freshly formed pecs and abs rippling, and there were the girls, milkmaid beautiful, upturned noses and creamy peach skin, lined up waiting for him. He chose Mia first, Mia of the waist-length blond hair (even as Magnolia's hair exploded into curly black fusilli—curls that would be brilliant someday, when she knew how to fix them, but for now were a mess she half hid behind and half fought off with straighteners). And then Sasha, and Brie, and so on. Eve would see him walking past their house, his arm around some beauty, his hand grazing her waist, both of them flushed and laughing. The girl would lean in to kiss him, and he'd kiss her back, not even acknowledging Maggie's house, not even noticing. Eve would pray her daughter hadn't seen them go by. But she had, of course. She never missed them.

"And your boys?" Mrs. K leaned forward to ask. "How's your little one?"

"Danny? Oh, he's still easy and sweet. Still lets me have as much love as I want." She smiled, even though this wasn't entirely true. Recently, in fact, she'd taken to stealing his affection when he was defenseless: moving in like a vampire when he was asleep to sniff his sweet, musty hair, or, the other day—the day before Eric left, she knew now—planting a smooch on his rail-thin white neck as he stood at the stove stirring butterscotch pudding. He'd slapped her away, laughing but also annoyed, and she couldn't help thinking that just a few months before, he'd have giggled and collapsed into her. Now, it was unpredictable. Some days yes, some days forget about it.

"He's still better?" Mrs. Kalish asked, sipping her tea. "His health holding out?"

"It is." Eve rolled her eyes skyward in thanks.

"Thank God." The woman put a palm over her heart. "You must be so relieved."

Eve nodded, though "relieved" didn't begin to describe it. Danny had first gotten sick when he was six, complaining of a stomachache one afternoon and becoming violently ill by that night, throwing up twelve or fifteen times before the morning. He was better the next day but sick again the day after that, and that was the beginning of a cycle that went on and on: a few good days and then a bad one or two, for weeks and then months, then a year. There were doctors—their beloved pediatrician, Dr. Hamilton, and a child psychiatrist, and the gastroenterologists, in both Bramington and, later, Boston—and then the tests, a camera down his throat, X-rays that required drinking a bucket of barium, swallowing radioactive scrambled eggs so they could be tracked as they were digested, and on and on, each test coming up empty, discovering nothing. Finally, fed up, Eve refused further testing and set to work at home, changing his diet (to gluten free, lactose free), his schedule, his drugs, his evening routine. She pulled him from his activities, which he could barely do anymore anyway, gave him herbal teas and warm baths and tinctures from the health food store. Anything she read about or someone suggested, she tried. It would work for a day or two, or their wishful thinking would make them believe that it had, and then she'd be carrying him through the grocery store doubled over in pain, or the school nurse would call and say, "Come now, right away. He's lying on the floor unable to get up."

Eric, she had to admit, had been amazing during that time, leaving work to take Danny to the tests she couldn't bear to watch, reading him stories or just lying with him for hours until he fell asleep, curled up in pain. It was their new life, it seemed, Eve's and Eric's: one healthy kid and one sick, possibly for life. They were adjusting. What choice did they have? Time marched on. But one day, after eighteen months and four days of stomach pain and a month of antibiotics to cure a double ear infection followed by pneumonia—the latter two likely caused by the absence of stomach acid that resulted from the various drugs he was taking for his stomach, some mainstream, some alternative, some prescription, some over the counter—one day, Danny was cured. Not only had his fever and coughing disappeared, but his stomach pain too. Gone, like a light switch turned off—or back on. He ate well and threw paper airplanes at Magnolia and jumped on his bed and went back to kung fu. Skinny as a skeleton, gaunt as a Holocaust victim—Eve couldn't get the peanut butter and pancakes into him fast enough—but healthy, happy, *normal.* It was a miracle.

A miracle, or maybe just antibiotics. With the help of Dr. Hamilton and the team of online mothers who'd gone through similar ailments with their own kids, Eve decided it had been an intestinal infection that hadn't shown up in the tests, seemingly cured by azithromycin and amoxicillin. Though who knew? Maybe someone up above had been looking out for him, or maybe it was simply another phase of life, for Danny and for all of them. He wasn't meant to be sick forever, she reasoned one night, and only then did she allow herself to realize how terrified she'd been. Escaping into the shower, she'd cried and cried, tears and soap and water washing down the drain, washing away fear to make room for relief. She'd been handed a gift, she knew: the return of her happy boy. It was the greatest gift she'd ever received.

Mrs. K was nodding, smiling. "And Eric? Any new success with his work?"

Eve froze. *And now it's Eric.* For a second, she wished she could tell Mrs. K everything.

"Well, I'm sure it will come," the woman said after a moment. "You can't force that sort of thing, can you? It must be very difficult to— Oh! I can't believe I almost forgot! I need you to sign your books. I bought eight more, for the nieces and a few friends." She rushed out and returned with a stack of Eve's books and a pen.

"Oh!" Eve attempted to smile. "You shouldn't have bought so many."

"Sweetie, don't kid yourself, I didn't do this for you. I've been spouting your theories for years. Now finally everyone can see them all written down. Sit, I'll hand you the books, you sign. Seriously, I'd weigh six hundred pounds if it weren't for you. I'd be on the grapefruit diet, then Scarsdale, then Atkins, bingeing like a starving lab rat in between."

Eve laughed a little. "I doubt that, somehow."

There was a sudden stomping, and Mrs. Kalish's husband, Seymour, burst red-faced into the room. "Where the hell'd you put my screwdriver, Nancy?" he yelled. "The damn den TV broke again." He hitched up his pants on his skeletal frame, exposing black wool socks and white Keds. He was a tiny man—a retired radiologist, Eve knew—with still brown hair that stuck out like wires all over his head and huge bottle glasses that made his eyes appear enormous.

Mrs. K waved at him. "For God's sake, Seymour, you're gonna give yourself a coronary. Juanita probably moved it. So switch to another TV. Did you say hi to Eve? She brought me a gorgeous pomegranate. If you're nice, I'll let you taste the seeds."

"The *seeds*? What do I look like, a bird?"

Mrs. Kalish laughed, and Seymour smiled, looking pleased with himself. He turned to Eve and raised his bushy eyebrows. "Hello, Eve," he said. "Nice to see you. I'm glad you take such good care of my wife. Maybe you have some idea where my screwdriver is?"

Eve smiled, genuinely now. "Sorry, Dr. Kalish, but I can't even keep track of my own—"

"Well, your house could hardly be worse than this one." He turned and walked out.

Mrs. Kalish rolled her eyes. "Ignore him. He's like a giant chihuahua, all bark and no bite. And watch, he'll be back here in— upp! Here he comes."

Seymour stomped in again, screwdriver in hand. "I found it," he said, looking not at all sheepish. "It was on the wrong shelf. Would you tell that damn cleaning girl not to touch my things, please? What the hell's she cleaning back there for anyway? Next thing I know you'll have them pouring Clorox down the chimney."

Mrs. Kalish laughed again. "Seymour, *enough* already! Go! Leave us in peace."

He stalked out, yelling, "Good-bye, Eve. It was a pleasure to see you again."

"He obviously never should have retired," his wife said when he'd gone. "He's been nothing but miserable ever since. Thank God for the *Globe* and the *Times*, so he can channel at least some of his energy into writing letters to the editor. Never have you seen so many unprintable missives come out of one man's computer.

Calling this one a moron, that one a cretin . . ." She grinned, then sighed. "Ah well. We've had a nice life together. I can't complain."

Eve nodded politely, though she couldn't imagine living with someone who stomped around like a two-year-old. "Oh—I have to go," she said suddenly. "Danny will be home soon, and Magnolia's not always there to—"

"Oh! Go, go! Go home to your babies. Here's your coat." Mrs. K began bustling around. "And here, here's this." She plucked an envelope off a table nearby and handed it to Eve. "I added a little extra this week, because—"

"Oh—no!" Eve said. "I'm giving it back. You pay me too much already."

"Don't you dare. You bring me things, and I don't want it coming out of your pocket. That's absurd. I'll see you in two weeks."

She leaned in for a kiss, and Eve envisioned a pair of bright pink lips smack on her left cheek—a vision she confirmed when she got in her car and looked in the mirror. She smiled for a second before gently rubbing them off and getting back on the road. All of her clients should be as easy and generous as Mrs. Kalish.

Eve turned a corner and thought about Keisha—time would tell if Eve could do anything for her—and then about Michael. Immediately, the relief she'd felt after suggesting bariatric surgery disappeared, replaced by sadness and a deep sense of dread and unease. She should have thought of gastric bypass for him weeks ago—or at least before she'd gone there today, so she could have read up on it and presented it properly, as a viable option. She should have been better prepared. For the first time, she wasn't doing her job as she should be—partly, yes, because her clients had become more challenging, but also because her head felt so full of everything else right now. *What kind of man walks out on his wife and kids without even telling them?* she thought, and she tried to call up the anger she'd been feeling since Eric left, but this time what came was a literal ache in her chest. Why had he gone? What had she done? She couldn't think of anything, though neither could she think of anything she'd done all that right. At least, not lately. Mostly, she had done what needed doing: kept the house and kids afloat, increased her workload when he wasn't earning enough. The anger began to seep back, and it was a relief. How dare he fault her for that? He was lucky to have her!

She reached for the CDs, but there was nothing she felt like hearing. She thought of a tape she used to play whenever she felt bad—a bunch of sad, croony songs that at least let her revel in misery. But, of course, you could rarely play a tape anymore (this car didn't even have a cassette player), and she had no idea how to get those songs onto a CD. *Another male thing,* she thought, thinking of the racks of disks in Eric's office—though now, like everyone else (or at least the men and the kids), he downloaded songs straight off the Internet. Well anyway, a CD of those songs wouldn't have felt right. It was from the era of tapes. Kirk Holdermann had made it for her.

Kirk Holdermann. God, how long since she'd thought about him? Eve pulled into the right lane to escape a relentless tailgater (an SUV with a bumper sticker that said "Coexist"). Her love with Kirk simply had not been the kind that was made for this world, or at least not for a pragmatic, realistic person like herself. *And he knew it too,* she thought. *Long before I did.*

The sky was overcast now, muddy clouds having rolled in from somewhere. Eve took off her sunglasses and dropped them on the seat. She had met Kirk in her twenties at a party thrown by a colleague; she literally had felt something move deep inside her the instant she'd laid eyes on him. He'd noticed her too, and they'd both looked away, and then back. Within minutes, it seemed, he'd ditched the women he'd come with and he and Eve were in a cab together speeding toward his place on Prince Street. They'd slept together immediately, and then again, nonstop, for the remainder of the weekend. When she left—on Monday morning at five, heading back to Brooklyn famished, bleary-eyed, her entire lower face scraped raw from his scruff, wearing a pair of his baggy sweatpants—it was like pulling off a Band-Aid, and they got back together again the second they could, him coming to her Brooklyn apartment this time, staggering up the filthy stairwell calling her name as if she were Adrian in *Rocky* or Katharine in *The English Patient.* For three months, they barely took their eyes or hands off each other, abandoning meals at restaurants and seats in stadiums just to rush home to bed or, let's face it, the kitchen counter or a filthy carpet. They had nothing in common, nothing whatsoever to say to each other, but they turned each other into hungry animals who were restless and desperate until they were pressed together, breathing in each others' hot, blood-flushed skin.

Not that he smelled particularly good. He worked—temporarily, he told her—at a fish market far downtown owned by a distant relative, and he smelled like the sea and fresh fish, or sometimes just fish period. It was disgusting, really. But she was riveted to him: to the pulse in his hands, the smoky eyes that seemed to pierce right through her like an electric current. It was chemical love, addictive love, pure and simple. It wasn't fun. In fact, it unhinged her. She felt not happiness, but lust and frenzy and a mild state of panic that this would ever end. And it did, of course. "I can't do this anymore," he'd told her one day, just after they'd finished a bout of phenomenal sex. "I can't eat, I can't think. My friends think I'm using. I'm not kidding, they want to do an intervention. I can't even go to the gym anymore. All I can do is think about you and fuck you. It's not good. It's not healthy."

"So what are you saying?" Her heart had slid down her body and out, disappeared through some terrible, invisible drain.

"I'm addicted to you," he said. "And I need to break it."

It was over as fast as it started. Eve buckled for a while, then swore off men, and then, when that got boring, dusted herself off and began dating again, and that's when she met Eric. And that love was so different; it made her feel not desperate and full of icy, gut-clenching fear, but happy and competent—elated in a grounded, grown-up way. Eric needed her and loved her. And Eve loved taking care of him, as if he were the younger sibling she'd never been blessed with. Cooking for him, folding his clothes, straightening his home . . . all those things modern wives were supposed to resent. They made her feel relevant and lucky and happy, not least because, in doing them, she freed him up to create his sculptures, and she felt a part of that too.

And oh, how she loved his sculptures! Vibrant, often ecstatic figures—gymnasts and runners, thinkers and dreamers—they exuded, at their best, a perfect balance of rapture and pain that made her suck in her breath. There was fire in their faces and forms, as if Eric first created life in the curved, brawny bodies and then edged them slightly beyond, until they seemed to burst with emotion and longing. Not everyone loved them, she knew; a critic had once called them "skeletal" and "painful to look at," adding, "In his work, I'm distracted by details that are contrary to what I think he's trying to achieve." *Fair enough,* Eve had thought at the time, but, well, she disagreed. To her, life's most intense moments and emotions were embodied in the little bronze pieces, and she sometimes imagined that, alone in his studio at night, they woke up to twirl and dance, gallivanting until they heard a key in the lock and quickly took up their poses again.

In their early days together, hers and Eric's, she would go to his studio and watch him for hours, his face lined with concentration, eyes alight even when he was exhausted, forearm muscles tensed as he molded the clay, carved away at the wax, lifted the vat of fiery molten bronze. He'd lose himself in the work, and she, in turn, in *him*—and in the metal and melted wax smells, the dark, sooty hues and the low-buzzing, overtly sexual energy of the place. She'd loved being Eric Knight's girlfriend and, later, his wife. When she thought about it, she couldn't believe he'd picked her. But he loved her. She knew he did. He wasn't romantic, but then, neither was she. And after Kirk, the last thing she needed was romance anyway, if you could even call what they'd had romantic. (Frankly, it was more like a crack addiction.)

In bed, Eric was exactly like he was in the studio: firm and possessive and intense. He knew exactly what he wanted and also, somehow, exactly where and how to touch her. With Kirk, she hadn't even felt her own body, so overwhelmed was she by *his* body, by his presence. With Eric, it was a back-and-forth. As with the clay, the wax, and eventually the bronze, he studied her, figured out what she wanted, and then gave it generously, getting his own pleasure in the process, asking almost nothing of her except that she allow him to know and possess her.

Beyond the bedroom and his studio, their partnership worked just as well. He was quiet; she talked. He was withdrawn and solitary (saving his fire, she knew, for his work), and she was social—or social enough, anyway. She was bubbly and dramatic on the surface where he was calm and soothing, able to put both of them to rest—though inside, especially as time went on, he roiled and reeled and agonized, something he had always been able to channel into his art but now, with his art not really happening, he seemed to be stuck with. In contrast, Eve, watching her babies get bigger and smarter and more adroit, felt—other than during Danny's illness, which had been a setback—more confident by the year. *If I can do this, why can't I do that?* she would think, or *If someone else can do it, why can't I?* And she launched her business and wrote her book, trying not to think too hard about any of it as she went. "Too much thinking ruins doing," her mother had always said, and as different as Eve considered herself from her mother, she agreed more or less.

And anyway, if she stopped for too long to think, she'd have had to acknowledge the one time she'd failed Eric, or at least betrayed him, and that was with Kirk. Kirk, whom she hadn't heard from for several years after he dumped her like a wad of gum he'd finally scraped from the sole of his shoe. And then one evening—she and Eric had been married almost two years, had lived in Bramington for just over one—the phone rang, and it was Kirk.

"Eve?" he said, and she felt a stab somewhere deep inside. Her groin, probably. "Eve," he said again. "This is Kirk."

"Oh. Hello," she managed.

He was in Boston for a night and had heard she lived in western Mass. Did she want to meet halfway for a drink?

"No," she said.

But he pushed it, of course, and in the end, she gave in; he had always called the shots for them. And really, what was the harm? She was married! Plus, she knew Eric wouldn't care; he wasn't the jealous type, not that he had a reason to be anyway. But he also would be gone for hours, maybe even all night. He had a show coming up in New York and had been at his studio nonstop. Eve didn't mind. He was brilliant, a rising star; he was literally building a future for them. When she walked around town, people whispered, "That's Eric Knight's wife!" She reveled in it.

But she did get lonely sometimes. And a drink with Kirk was something to do. So she showered and put on a flowing skirt and a tight red tank top and left Eric a note, on the rare chance he got home before she did, that an old friend was in town and they were grabbing a drink. Then she drove to the bar Kirk had picked, knowing she looked good (she had lost some weight since he'd known her, was exercising—the whole thing) and wanting him to see that, the bastard. She parked the car, freshened her lipstick, and walked into the place, shaky on the high heels she'd worn. He was sitting at a table, looking exactly the same. When she saw her, he stood, and his eyes raked her body, grazed her eyes, settled on her mouth. "Eve Adams," he said, and she saw his face flush with heat. "Oh, man," he said softly.

Nothing had changed. Not one thing. That same force that had always been there between them caught her and pulled her in like an undertow, shook her up and slammed her straight back into another wave and then deposited her, splayed, on the beach. "I have to go," she mumbled, turning to leave. "This was a mistake." But he came toward her and touched the back of her shoulder, and her blood went hot too, just like his.

"I'm *married*!" she pleaded, and she stepped away again, but her voice faltered, and he caught it. He moved in once more. "That's good!" he whispered, close to her ear, and he brushed her hair back with one hand, his fingers grazing her shoulder. "That's so good, Eve. I'm so happy for you." He guided her around, and this time, his eyes started on her mouth and flicked up to her eyes. "Let's just talk a little," he murmered. "Have one drink. You drove this far. I don't want things to end the way they did."

So they had bourbon, which he ordered without consulting her, and she, in a daze, sucked it down, followed by another and half of a third. And then they fell into his car, and there it was again; insert needle, push syringe, fly away. Hours later, when she made it home— lips swollen, clothes disheveled despite an attempt to pull herself to- gether—Eric was sitting in a kitchen chair, drinking a beer. He looked at the clock—4:16—and then at her, and she knew that he knew.

"It was nothing," she started to say, but she burst into tears. She had never been able to lie, and she didn't want to anyway. She had failed as a wife—failed in one of the most fundamental ways. And she wanted to pay her penance, whatever it was.

"Eric . . ." she sobbed.

He shook his head. "Is it over?"

"Yes!" she said. "I swear! It was never even—"

He raised his hand to silence her, then stood up. "Then I don't want to know. Just—don't tell me." He walked out of the room. A moment later, she heard him start the car and drive away.

But he only went to his studio, and he was back the next day, though he never mentioned the incident again. And that, it turned out, was her penance: living with herself and the knowledge that she'd done that to him.

Even now, years later, she thought about the whole thing with shame and regret. And part of her had always wondered if she might somehow pay for that mistake. Not that Eric was vindictive; she didn't think he was the type to keep score. But now, she won- dered if he just might have taken that Get Out of Jail Free card and finally cashed it in.

Outside, it had begun to rain—a cold, purple storm, ugly and bleak. Eve fumbled with switches until she got the car wipers right, then fumbled more, in the glove compartment this time, trying to find a tissue. "Shit!" she said, giving up and wiping her nose, her eyes, on her sleeve.

She glanced once more at the clock, then accelerated hard. She couldn't wait to get home. She felt an almost desperate urge to be in her house with her children. She pictured them bursting in from school, faces red and cold; imagined how she would embrace them, feel their hearts beat through their skin. The image made her tremble. She needed to be with them right now. And they needed her too. Even if, at this point, they might not exactly want her.

3

IT WAS FUNNY, Eric thought—as in, it wasn't actually all that funny—how you could fit into one category all your life, and then, with just one little sexual act, you ricocheted into another. You were a virgin, and then you were a . . . well, whatever they called people who weren't virgins these days. Or you were a faithful spouse, for years or decades, and then, suddenly, you were an adulterer. A few minutes of your time, a bodily fluid or two exchanged, and *slam*: the door to that old room shut tight, and there you were in a whole new ballpark.

Driving the RAV4 west with this sleeping girl next to him, Eric wondered yet again whether what happened last night made him an adulterer, and then, once more, was annoyed at himself for the thought. Of course it didn't—thanks, he might add, to some spectacular restraint on his part. If anything, he should hand it to himself.

But maybe that wasn't the point: what constituted adultery and what didn't, where you drew the ridiculous, nebulous line. Maybe what he was doing *now* was the crime: driving farther and farther away from his children, his home, and his wife, without having told any of them he was leaving. Not whether he was an adulterer (or not), but whether he was an asshole.

He glanced out the window. Brilliant blue sky, after a dubious sunrise, silver and gunmetal gray. He preferred the gray; bright sun smacked of cheerfulness, something he did not traffic in, and most days it made him feel guilty for working inside, as if he were refusing some sacred offering. *But you're* not *working now*, he reminded himself. *You're* not *inside*. He checked his speed limit, made an effort to slow down. On the roadside, yellow flowers poked through the snow like explorers, intrepid or desperate. *Okay, so you're an asshole*, he concluded, and for a second he hung his head. But he felt his hands on the steering wheel, his foot pressing the gas, and he allowed himself a moment of happiness. He used to love road trips; had gone any time for any reason, driving for days, pulling over when something caught his eye and spending hours, sometimes, observing it. This sort of thing fueled him. *So maybe that's part of the problem*, he thought. And if so, maybe this was part of the solution. And they'd all benefit if he could work again.

The thing was, he had to take another piss. A bottle and a half of wine and countless hours of driving could do that to a person, even though he'd already stopped once, to sleep for a couple hours on the side of the road. And his back felt like someone had stuck an ax into it. But the girl was still asleep—had been since minutes after she'd gotten in the car—and he wasn't about to jeopardize that by stopping. Really, what would he possibly say to her when she finally woke up?

Then again, judging from last night, this girl, this woman—like all the other women in his life—would likely do the bulk of the talking. Dria. The kids' babysitter, though not the usual teenage variety; this one was well beyond high school, twenty-one, maybe twenty-three. Both times they had talked, she'd been looking at his piece on the large shelf above the kitchen sink as they waited together for Eve to finish getting ready to go out. "Did you actually *make* that?" she'd asked the first time, after minutes of inspecting the sculpture, bending to see the bottom, the sides. Her eyebrows were raised, eyes adorably wide, mouth slightly open with what he'd taken to be—or hoped was, anyway—joy and surprise.

Indeed he had made it, though years ago. Shortly after he'd met Eve, in fact. Unlike most of his sculptures, which were figures in motion, this one was a young woman crouched with her arms around her knees, but with one eye sneaking a glance up and out—protected, but also not averse to a little fun. *The Contradiction*, he'd titled it, and he'd given it to Eve on their first anniversary.

"How *did* you?" Dria asked. "I mean—what exactly is the *process*?"

Eric noticed bone structure, the shapes and contours of things, and he had noticed Dria's then—the high, wide cheekbones, the small but well-defined chin, both of which helped make her paleness and gauntness seem interestingly fragile rather than just anemic or anorexic. He didn't think she really wanted to hear the long and laborious recipe for making this sort of bronze sculpture, but he found himself giving her an outline. You start with a sketch of your vision, and then you build it out of clay and create an armature, a support that holds up the clay. You form the details—eyes, fingers, ears—and then make a rubber mold of the sculpture and pour hot wax inside to make a hollow wax casting. When that dries, you return it to its original form and texture, smoothing out irregularities, perfecting details. "Chasing," this refining is called, and it takes time, since any flaw or imperfection in the wax will be transferred to the bronze itself. He paused. *Could she actually want to know all this?*

"Then what?" she said, and he wondered which of her parents had that upside-down triangle face, those oval eyes. Her complexion wasn't perfect—she had a zit here and there, doubly apparent on her milky white skin—but at her age, that was hardly surprising.

Well, he told her, then the wax casting is coated with layers of slurry and silica, each coat needing to dry in between. This gets baked in the de-wax oven, where the original wax bleeds out, leaving an empty ceramic shell mold. That's what you pour your molten bronze into. Heated to 2,100 degrees. A little of this, little of that—crack off the mold once the bronze hardens; sandblast and chase it again; buff paste wax onto the still warm piece to perfect the patina and form a rich, gorgeous glow . . . and there's your *Contradiction*. Or your *Dancer One*, or *Dancer Two*, or whatever you had sketched, exactly true, if all goes well, to your original vision. Repeat the process five or six times, and call your dealer to send up the truck.

And a few weeks or months later, depending whether they'd been waiting on you or not (and they always were, back in the days of the early dancers), there was your show: the sparkling white room full of your creations, bold and gleaming and virtually alive. Because that's what he loved so much about bronze, he told her— the way you could take the metal to its limit and actually make the figures move, or at least appear to. And once they were set up—splitting the air with their perfect arms, leaping the ground with their muscular legs—the people came, pretty New Yorkers in stylish clothes, swarming and gushing and, if all went well (and it always did back then), writing out hefty checks to Liza, the gallery owner, which turned into smaller but still quite substantial checks for him. Checks that bought him and Eve, and eventually baby Magnolia, meals out and trips to beautiful places and even the house, all with plenty left over for a dry spell: a year, two years, even three.

Not that he told the sitter all that; he stopped at the part about why he loved bronze, because it was so fluid, so free.

"Wow," the girl said, as if she truly cared. "That sounds fascinating."

He nodded. It was, thanks. When it worked.

And did he really need to tell her he hadn't gotten past the sketch stage for, oh, two or three years—and not a whole lot beyond it for another two or three before that? That he would start to build an armature and suffer such staggering self-doubt that he would stuff the thing in a corner with a drop cloth over it and then sit for days in a funk of panic and despair? It didn't matter how often he recited the Henry James quote he'd kept in his mind since he was twenty years old, about how "we work in the dark" and "we do what we can," how "our doubt is our passion, and our passion is our task" and "the rest is the madness of art." It made him vaguely ill to even think about it. But here was this girl taking an interest in it, in him. "Maybe I could come see you work sometime," she'd said. "If, you know, it wouldn't ruin your concentration."

He nodded. He didn't think she meant it—people said things like that, they were being polite—but hey, at least she had asked.

"Because I'm trying—I mean—I'm trying to figure out what to do with my own life," she'd added, and then laughed and covered her mouth with her long hand, which, he noticed, featured a ring on her thumb and short, chewed-off nails, painted black. "I know that sounds retarded," she said. "But the one thing I was ever really good at was drawing. I actually won a contest once, in middle school. And I've always loved to sketch—flowers, bumblebees, the kitchen phone . . . anything! But my mom couldn't afford to put me in classes. I never lost the itch to create, though. And lately it's been really intense, probably because my boyfriend left, but whatever, that's over. The point is, I've been trying to immerse myself in all kinds of art, and I want to take classes, but I'm not sure what to take. Maybe you have a suggestion?" She looked at him and blinked her big saucer eyes while he tried to think of something. (She could always take *his* class; it was for more accomplished sculptors, of course, and it wasn't cheap, held as it was at the Bramington Arts Center, but perhaps he could get her some sort of scholarship or just sneak her in?) "Anyway, your sculptures really move me," she said. "I've seen some other ones you made too. I Googled you."

He smiled. She was funny, this girl. And he didn't really mind the incessant talking; it was par for the course. Growing up with his mother and two older sisters, he had barely gotten in a word edgewise. But then, words weren't his strong suit anyway. And shit, she had Googled him! If she wanted to talk about that more, well, go right ahead, sweetheart.

"Don't get me wrong, I'm not saying I could ever *do* something like that," she said, looking doubtfully at the sculpture now. "It's just—I don't know. Maybe we could barter sometime. I could babysit Danny for free, and you could show me your studio and what you do."

"Sure," he'd said, though he'd wondered what the hell he'd show her. It wasn't like there was a lot going on there right then.

Anyway, the studio visit hadn't happened, perhaps because Dria hadn't babysat for them for a long time. Magnolia had gotten old enough, or maybe they just hardly ever went out anymore, with Eve's book getting ready to be published, and then actually appearing, and then the interviews—mostly local, small scale, but still, radio and newspaper. She ran around like a chicken with her head cut off all the time now. But last night, finally, he had taken her out, or at least gotten her to agree to come out with him (because really, to what extent does a married man "take out" his wife, especially when she's outearning him?). He'd chosen the restaurant—Le Jardin, best place in town—and made the reservations. All Eve had had to do was call the sitter.

At the table—cherry red candle, three pale yellow tulips, classy and elegant—they'd had two excellent bottles of wine, each of them choosing one. (Admittedly, he drank more than his one and she less than hers, but, well, he was bigger, and anyway, they liked it that way.) As they drank, washing down their grass-fed beef tenderloin and locally raised rack of lamb, their caramelized parsnips and radicchio and endive, she talked about her book and then about an interview she'd just done for a Web site, which she thought had come out okay. And then she talked about the kids—how Magnolia was more difficult these days, so up and down, and how upset she was that their daughter had quit violin—though maybe, hopefully, Magnolia was just taking a break, Eve rushed to add. And how she still worried about Danny's health, even though he was fine now, thankfully, *thankfully*—but what if that whole year he was sick had some sort of negative effect in the long run? She'd talked, and he'd listened. Again, par for the course.

And again, not that he minded. She'd been animated and happy, her lips pink, her eyes sparkling, her hair radiant. Had she lightened it recently, or had he just not looked at her in a long time?

But he found his mind drifting back to the conversation he'd had with Dria just before they left for the restaurant, probably a full year after their first discussion, once again in the kitchen waiting for Eve to come down. "Wait," the girl had said suddenly, after again examining *The Contradiction* for a long time. "Wait a sec. Is that *Eve*?"

It hadn't really been Eve when he'd started the sketch, but it had evolved that way as he worked, as he'd fallen more and more in love with her: her sunny outlook, her innocently sexy smile, her only-child bossiness that was sometimes stopped midsentence by a flash of almost tangible insecurity. So by the end, there *was* a clear resemblance to Eve, if you looked for it. "Yes," he said to Dria, to simplify.

The girl shook her head. "That's amazing. Just amazing. How lucky is she to have someone make something like that for her? Holy crow! I can't even imagine."

She *was* lucky, Eric had thought at their dinner, as he made his way through the Malbec, the empty Shiraz bottle already whisked away. They both were lucky back then when he was making sculptures day and night. Eve had adored what he was doing, and—through it, or because of it, or maybe just as part of it—she'd adored *him*. And he felt the same about her. Of course, she was pretty and sexy (the curves, the tight, perky butt . . . she wasn't a dancer, but could have fooled him), and she knew her ass from her elbow, cracked him up—the list went on—but also he loved the picture of himself reflected in her eyes. And did it really matter how much of his love was one of those qualities and how much all the rest? Love was a batch of ingredients anyway: a few parts this, a few parts that.

Eric glanced at Dria. Still dead to the world. Back then, before the babies and even for a while after Magnolia arrived, Eve would call him when she was almost done making dinner and tell him to come home. As they ate some amazing meal she'd prepared, healthy and delicious, often while holding baby Maggie, she'd ask him what he'd done in the studio, how it was going, and he'd tell her about the new sculptures—*Dancer Four, Dancer Five*, he was doing the dancers back then—and she'd listen while he answered her questions and they ate, she simultaneously feeding their funny, stormy daughter, spooning peas into her open pink square of a mouth, which the baby spewed right back out, making them laugh. Eve told him about their day, what new things Magnolia had done, where they'd walked in her stroller. He'd basked in it. Taken it for granted, even; never dreamed it would one day be all in the past.

But in the years after Danny came along—the fragile second-born, first a bony red tree lemur perched against his mother, later a thin, pale, precocious towhead—something started to shift. The change was threefold: The world was changing, his art was changing, and their home life was changing, all at once. Nine/Eleven happened, and Afghanistan and Iraq, and teenagers went off to die in combat, and the rich got richer and the poor poorer even as the middle class headed like lemmings toward the edge of the cliff. Which of them would fall? Hurricane Katrina struck, and the nation tuned in to nonstop live coverage of desperate people on rooftops left to die, children forced to abandon their pets, old men floating, dead and bloated, among rubble down flooded streets. Americans got more anxious—global warming! overpopulation! gas crisis! recession!—and Eric was right there with them. And suddenly, or it seemed sudden anyway, he couldn't make his beautiful, ecstatic art anymore: couldn't conceive of new pieces and couldn't even make the ones he was already working on work. *Dancer Seven*, for example. With *One* through *Six*, he'd known exactly what he was doing, and his hands went along with his vision like obedient little girls, chasing and molding until the sculptures were executed exactly as conceived. But with *Seven*, he couldn't get the pose, couldn't make the sculpture look convincing. Had to keep starting over until finally, disgusted, he trashed the whole thing, telling himself, *Okay, okay, maybe there were only meant to be six.* A half-dozen dancers was fine, an impressive series. But it was the first time he'd had a vision and couldn't render it.

He had thought it was probably because he was thinking too much: analyzing the fucking art to death rather than just doing it. But he couldn't help it. Sculptures of people embracing, dancing, reaching up in rapture . . . they seemed wrong, suddenly—superfluous, irrelevant, even absurd, in these times of sadness and pain and humility. It was a time to embrace the disquietude, not ignore it; to accept and let it inspire him, take him to a better, smarter place. "We cannot mature and be fully creative by burying or displacing anxiety," he remembered some philosopher, probably Kierkegaard, saying, "but only by moving through it." He believed this and felt his art should reflect the times. But he couldn't figure out what it should be or how to get there.

He had thought he had it with *The Runner*, but in the end, that was probably the real breaking point; even now, it was like one big ugly metaphor. He had started the piece, after being inspired by a marathon, when Danny was two or three, and early on it was free and exultant, like all his work—limbs expanded, muscles gleaming, thrill and victory on the man's radiant black face. But he couldn't leave it alone. It felt too much like his past stuff and a time that was gone, and also somehow not done yet, not what the piece was trying to say. He kept thinking of the words of a teacher he'd once had for a clay sculpting class: "The clay is 10,000 years old; it knows more than you do." He would see that bumper sticker, so common in his town particularly among angry young women—*Oh, Evolve!*—and feel it was speaking directly to him. The sculpture felt contrived now, juvenile and cheap.

So he went back to work on it, even though Eve had already given it the thumbs-up. But she was tired that day and hadn't really wanted to come to the studio. Magnolia was having a bad week, she told him, and even Danny was cranky, and she wanted to get them fed and to bed. But he'd begged her, so anxious was he to show it to her, to see through her eyes what was there. So she'd dragged the kids over, Danny's little blue sweater stained with snot and tears, and she'd told him, over the kids' whining and fidgeting, that she loved *The Runner, loved* it, call Liza to send for it, right away. But he couldn't believe her this time. She probably just wanted him to sell it, even if it wasn't a great piece—he'd worked for a while on this one after *Dancer Seven* failed—and he thought, too, that she was saying what he needed to hear so he'd let her go home.

But selling the piece if it wasn't right was a cop-out. He couldn't do it—or wouldn't, anyway. So once more, he went at the sculpture, changing it a little each day. The next time he showed it to Eve, she had stopped by to bring Eric a jacket, after he'd told her the building's heat was out. "Can't you leave a spare jacket there?" she'd asked him, irritation in her voice. "Not that I mind dropping one by, but—oh forget it, it's fine, I'll be there." Now, the runner's face had lost the joy and taken on intensity and pressure, the limb muscles were knotted and strained. Eve had looked at the revised sculpture and raised her eyebrows and nodded, told him the changes were "interesting" and "exciting," which he took as code for "hideous" and "pathetic." He thought she hated it, and that made him feel physically sick. But he couldn't stop by that point; he had a new vision now, was working day and night to execute it.

And by the time Eve made it back weeks later—somehow solo this time; the neighbors must have been watching the kids—the runner was bent over, clutching his gut, his face showing excruciating pain. Eve smiled when she saw it, and he thought he saw a hint of her earlier adoration of him, and he wanted to reach out and grab it and hold on. "It's fantastic," she said, and this time he thought maybe she was for real. "Breathtaking. So dark. What do you think Liza will say?"

He frowned. Liza didn't love dark art, nor did her clients. She would say, as she'd said once before, about one of his very early pieces, "I hate to tell you this, Eric, but rich people don't want to put depressing stuff in their houses. I can try, but . . ." And she *had* tried, and she had been right: no one bought it. And though the world, it seemed to him, had changed dramatically since that point, he wasn't sure people's taste had. If anything, they wanted *fewer* reminders of the hellish time they were going through. They wanted cheap, dumb entertainment to make them forget it completely: TV shows featuring buffed-out bachelors choosing from a handful of surgically altered "bachelorettes," people on islands eating maggots to win a million dollars, or the Internet and You-Tube, where you never had to look at anything for more than four seconds before you clicked onto something new and even more inane. So he never sent Liza the agonized runner either. He needed more sculptures first, he told himself—at least four more to make a show.

He had eked out a few after that, pieces he sold purely on the basis of his reputation, but most of his income in those years (first substantial, then less so) came from work he had already finished and from the courses he occasionally taught at the Arts Center. And then he'd been dry. He'd start something, and he'd get blocked. Eventually Liza and his other contacts stopped calling. He was off the "It" list. Knowing this, he'd wake in the night in a cold sweat, hyperventilating. He couldn't wake Eve—she was up half the time with the kids anyway, nursing Danny, changing Maggie's wet sheets, later dealing with Danny's stomach pain. If he offered to help, she said no—sometimes even with annoyance, as if he were invading her turf. "You sleep," she'd said to him once, "so you can work tomorrow." *Work*, he knew, meaning "make a living."

But she had accepted his help when Danny had the medical tests, because she simply couldn't handle it: the endoscopy, where they put a tube down into his stomach, the MRI, where they shot him up with dye and rolled him through a tube . . . Eve couldn't be in the room, couldn't even bear to think about it. It was Eric's moment as a parent—finally!—and he valiantly stepped in. Not that Danny exactly needed him, compliant and easygoing as he was. But Eric held his hand, distracted him and tried to answer his questions. He read to Danny when he didn't feel well, bathed him when Eve asked, took him out for lactose-free ice cream or gluten-free cakes . . . whatever diet Eve was trying that week, desperate to get him relief.

Eric loved it. Getting a sense of his weird, lovely son, who could recite funny scenes from a *Simpsons* episode after watching it two or three times, who listed, by memory, the side effects of drugs he'd seen advertised on TV: "Blackouts, temporary blindness, anal leakage, erections lasting more than four hours," he'd say, in his high little voice, and Eric would laugh harder than he had in a year. The kid was hilarious. Eric relished hanging out with him. That's when he'd built the shelf and the mini train track on the wall just below the ceiling in his room. Danny could create Lego trains, with tiny Lego people inside, that rode the train, remote operated, around the track, around his entire room. The boy was thrilled. Eve, too, was pleased—though she also was busy researching Danny's illness, obtaining his medicines, scheduling his doctor's appointments, and, of course, taking care of Magnolia, not to mention working part-time at Beardsley.

Danny eventually got better and moved on to other things: Rubik's Cubes, Bionicles, Wii. The track was still there, one or two old Lego trains abandoned on it, reminding Eric, when he needed reminding—when Danny squeezed between him and Eve in their bed and the two of them, Eve and Danny, snuggled like long-lost lovers—that he had done that for his son at a time when his son needed him; that, at least for those few months, he had been a good—no, an *extraordinary*—father.

Meanwhile, Eric slogged back to work, trying to hold on to the inspiration he'd felt building the train track, hoping it might somehow transfer into his next piece. But after more days of staring at his studio walls, shooting down every idea that came to his head, he realized he wanted to spend some real time with Magnolia too—maybe also build something for her. So he invited her out to lunch (she picked Chummy's; a toddler one table over actually vomited onto his plate while Maggie, oblivious, wolfed her fries, and Eric tried to choke down his honey cheddar jack meltwich), and then he took her to his studio and asked her what she'd like him to make. She answered right away: a replica of Duchess, their cat who had died the year before. He made it in days, along with a small, simple sculpture of a girl playing the violin that he gave to her at the same time.

Interestingly, he had always felt a bit more connected to his daughter than to his son. He had read to her as a child (till she grew old enough to read to *him*, which he preferred), and for a brief while, right after Danny was born, he had spent endless hours taking her off Eve's hands—to the movies, the playground, the local zoo full of injured and rescued animals—and she had actually chosen him over her mom. Those days were long past, but that didn't mean they couldn't reconnect. So now, he took her bowling, on bike rides, even horseback riding—all the stuff Eve had no interest in or had gotten plain sick of over the years. He put up the basketball hoop and taught her to play knockout. Best of all, while he worked on the sculptures, she came and sat in his studio, telling him things about her friends, her teachers, that neighbor kid Nate. Sometimes she complained about her mother—she was almost adolescent, after all—and he listened, amazed she would confide to him about Eve. Once or twice, she brought her violin over and played for him, and he marveled at how accomplished she'd become. When he finished the sculptures, she hugged and kissed them, and then him. "Thank you!" she said, and he wanted to thank *her*. It had been so nice to have her here all these days, and to be working on something he could pull off without feeling bad.

But it all changed after that, as fast as his ideas went from brilliant to bad. Magnolia was a teenager, off with her friends, embarrassed if he or Eve came anywhere near her. He forgave her, of course—he'd been a bit of a wild card himself as a teen—but meanwhile, Eve and Danny were a happy team of two, sharing jokes, holding hands, off to kung fu or piano lessons. So Eric turned back to his work. And what he saw was a lot of nothing.

Now, he leaned back in the driver's seat, attempting to take the pressure off his back or his bladder (he'd take either one, at this point). He had tried so hard to work that year. Tried and tried, and ultimately failed. He hadn't made sculptures. And if he were making them now—he knew this for sure—he wouldn't have to leave, and wouldn't want to. He wouldn't have to be an asshole.

Without thinking, he veered off the highway at the exit immediately upon them. He drove until he saw a gas station, then pulled in and parked, waiting for Dria to wake up. But she stayed asleep. He knew she wasn't faking because her head lolled back, mouth wide open, a pose any woman—even a baby woman like this—wouldn't assume willingly. Maybe it was the pot. It had done a number on him too, and he was no novice when it came to smoking weed—though okay, he had drunk a fair amount too. He got out of the car, closed the door gently, and locked it.

Pumping the gas, grateful for the cloud or two that had surfaced to block the bright sun from his face, he tried to piece together everything that had happened after his dinner with Eve the night before. When they got home, Eve had asked him to drive Dria, and though he didn't really see why the girl couldn't bike—she had biked over, after all, and she was probably safer on a bike anyway than in a car with him, tipsy as he was—he obliged. Eve was the domestic boss, just like his own mother and sisters had been, and, as with the talking, he liked it that way; it freed him up to think about other things. Plus, maybe Dria would tell him she'd Googled him again. He'd loaded her bike in the car, slammed the back door, and come around to his seat, Dria folding in next to him, smiling.

She seemed to want something from him; he felt that whenever he was around her. He blinked through the windshield to clear his wine-addled brain, then began the short drive to her house. She wore a teensy black skirt, and her long white legs (creamy and smooth; no zits, like the couple or three on her face) extended out from under it, slightly spread on the seat. He saw them with his peripheral vision. Was that a tiny tattoo on, of all places, the inside of her upper thigh? A butterfly, maybe, or some other insect? He couldn't turn and look, obviously. Her thick cardigan came down over the top of the skirt, but after a second, she shoved it off, and then her arms dropped out of her tight black mini T-shirt, like two milk-dipped dowels. That's when he caught the second tattoo—a black widow spider, it looked like—on the inside of her right wrist. He thought he could see a rim of skin between the bottom of her T-shirt and the top of her skirt. Again, he couldn't really look, but her stomach seemed flat, almost concave; she was like a stretched white Gumby. He personally liked some curves and even a little nicely placed fat—like Eve, actually, petite and shapely and real. Still, he was finding it hard not to respond to this display of young female flesh, skinny or not.

"Are you hot?" he asked, not realizing the connotation until the words were out, at which point he felt like a big idiot; see, this was why he kept his mouth shut. He reached to turn down the heat— Eve always had it cranked—but Dria shook her head. "It feels nice, actually. I'm so cold up here half the time. New England, brr." She shivered but didn't pull her sweater back on.

"Where are you from?" he asked after a moment.

"Arizona. Little town called Hatback."

He nodded. *My mother lives in Tucson,* he started to say, or at least thought about saying, but she spoke first: "I've been out here almost three years." She paused, as if waiting for his question, then said, "I came up with my boyfriend. He was a musician. *Is* a musician, I should say. I mean, he still is. He's just not, you know, my boyfriend now." She laughed once. "That lasted about five minutes. Oh well. But whatever, I'm over it."

Eric nodded again, and Dria shifted on her seat, then sighed. "Your son is adorable," she said. "I swear to God, I'm in love with that kid. He's so unusual. The things he says." He felt her look at him, study his profile as he stared out the window. "He looks like you," she said. "People probably say he looks like Eve, right? Because of his coloring? All that blond and all. But I think he looks like you. Something in his expression."

"Thanks," he said, wondering if that was the right answer. Was that a compliment? He never knew, though he took it as one.

"And the way he builds Legos! Oh, and he showed me that train track you guys built. Coolest thing." She shook her head. "He's an artist already. You can tell."

Eric hoped not. Not that he necessarily wanted the kid to be some Wall Street tycoon, but there had to be some middle ground between that and himself, didn't there? A doctor, maybe. Though they didn't have an easy time either these days, with malpractice suits, insurance companies calling the shots, patients who couldn't afford to pay what they owed. But something where he was using his brain to do something for humanity, yet didn't have to rely so much on being creative, *inspired*. And productive. Always producing.

"I wish my father had done that stuff with me," Dria said. She looked at Eric. "My mom divorced him when I was seven. He got remarried right away, had twin boys with the new wife a year later, and—well, that was the end of me." She laughed lightly. "I mean, I got over it and all, I was fine, but I think it probably messed me up big-time in the relationship department."

"My father left too," Eric said, surprising himself.

"He did?" Dria looked at him happily. "How old were you?"

"Two."

"Oh, man. That's so sad."

He shrugged. "Not really. I had my mother and sisters. I didn't really know him, so I never had a chance to miss him."

"But you probably did on some level. I mean, maybe not consciously, but you must have felt his absence. I mean, when other kids all had fathers . . ."

"Well, I was raised in some pretty untraditional places. Berkeley, Tucson, Portland. So not everyone had fathers, really."

"Maine or Oregon?" she asked.

"Oregon."

"Nice! How come?"

He shrugged again. "My mother liked new beginnings, I guess. This is your house, right?"

"Yeah. If you don't mind pulling up the driveway, I can go in the back door."

He did as told, then put the car in park but didn't cut the motor.

"Maybe you missed your father, but you don't know it because you channeled that into your art," she supplied. She didn't seem to be making any move to get out of the car.

He shrugged once more. "Maybe."

"Maybe it was that loss that made you an artist."

He looked at her. "Maybe. Who knows?"

"Well, you're lucky," she said. "You're lucky you figured out how to deal with your pain. Even to use it to make something beautiful! I wish I could do that. I feel like—" She looked at the ceiling, then down at her chewed-up hands, then at him. "I *feel* like an artist. I really think I am, but I haven't figured out what kind yet."

He smiled. She was young, but genuine, at least. And she had a point. He knew people like that, creative people who floundered around—sometimes their whole lives—trying to figure out what to do. He did feel lucky to have come upon his passion early in life, even if that passion was failing him now. At least he knew what he was *supposed* to do. "You'll figure it out," he said, and then disgusted with his shallowness, thought, *Why don't you just shut up, instead of saying something trite and insincere?*

"I hope," she said. "I mean, the library is a nice diversion for now. And it's a job, right? But it's not like I'm gonna make a career out of being an arts librarian in Bramington, Mass. It's too cold here, for one thing. And I don't mean just the snow." Again, she waited, then went on. "The people here, they pretend to be warm and welcoming, but I sometimes feel a little, I don't know, *judged* or something. You know?" She looked at him hard, almost begging him to differ. "Not by everyone, of course. There are tons of great people here—like you guys! You're a beautiful family! But some people up here really don't welcome anyone new or different. They love to act like this place is so diverse, but in the end, it's just like everywhere else." She sniffed. "Not that I wouldn't take it over Hatback, Arizona," she added. "Down there, you say you're a Democrat, let alone a feminist, and you get your ass shot with a semiautomatic assault rifle."

He laughed, and she smiled, her face opening up. She was like a different person when she smiled, face bright and round as the moon. But after a second, it deflated again. "I just think there's a lot of defensiveness here. People seem defensive. Don't you think?"

"Maybe they're just afraid." He wanted to stick up for this town, which had been good to him since he arrived—good to all four of them. In Brooklyn in his twenties, everyone had been hungry, with nowhere to go but up; people had nothing to lose. You could sleep with your neighbor, create a new drug, make art with condoms or tampon applicators, and people not only wouldn't bat an eyelash but might even slap the "brilliant" label on you. But in a crunch, they were all on their own—a bunch of islands secretly trying to attach to the mainland (whatever that was) without losing themselves in the process. Here, people were already attached. They had families, houses, dogs. Things to protect, things to lose. And if sometimes it was themselves that got lost in the process, well, that was only part of the—

"Yes!" she said, interrupting his thoughts. "I'm sure you're right. I mean, no one's judgmental from birth, right? We all get it from somewhere. Our parents, probably. 'They fuck you up, your mum and dad. They do not mean to, but they do.'" She looked at him. "That's from a poem. By Philip Larkin."

"I know," he said.

"You do?"

He smiled. "That poem is pretty well known, I think."

"Oh! And here I was all convinced I'd, like, *discovered* it." She laughed, then covered her mouth with her hand. "Oh, man, I'm so tired," she said after a second. "I haven't slept in days. I have wicked insomnia." She smiled. "*Wicked.* I love that. Such a New England word."

"Straight from the witches," he said.

They sat for a moment in silence. He wondered why she didn't get out, and then, "Oh!" he said. "I need to get out your bike."

"Oh. Right." But she still didn't move, and he realized he didn't really care. He didn't mind one bit sitting here, listening to her talk, pleasantly buzzed—oh, okay, stinking drunk—as he was. Eve was probably asleep already anyway; she'd probably climbed into bed the minute he left to drive Dria home. She had told him once that when he wasn't there (rarely, these days) she slept sideways in the bed, her legs splayed luxuriously across his half. He pictured her like this now, covered in blankets up to her neck, her hair a messy bird's nest on top. He liked watching her sleep; it was one of the few times she still seemed vulnerable. Sometimes he stole a kiss, if he had access to any actual skin, but one time he'd woken her up and she'd been completely pissed off. She hated being woken unless it was by the kids. In the early years, of course, she'd welcomed him into bed anytime. But after the kids were born, especially Danny, and she'd gone back to work, she couldn't afford to be tired, she said. He understood. Or at least he didn't protest.

His eyes wandered out the window until he caught sight of a tree and tried to make sense of it in the moonlit dark. It was naked, still—no leaves yet—and not unlike a human skeleton in some ways. Maybe he should try some nature sculptures. He could juxtapose a tree with a sculpture of a human reaching up—maybe point out the similarities. Or would that be completely amateurish, something a kid would do in the first year of an M.F.A. program?

Dria was rooting around in her purse. "Hey, want to smoke this with me?" she'd said, producing a joint. "Because I so don't feel like going in yet. I mean, I know my housemate will be sitting right there. She's *always* there. And I'm sorry for saying this, but I really can't stand her. Do you mind if I light this? Here, I'll open the window."

Eric looked at the joint. She probably shouldn't light that here, but the truth was, he wouldn't mind a hit or two himself. He nodded a go-ahead, and she lit up and inhaled. "Why can't you stand her?" he asked, for some reason actually interested.

"Well, for one thing, she doesn't need to make a living." Dria blew out the smoke slowly. "Her father sends her a thousand dollars a month. *A thousand dollars!* That's more than I make working nearly full-time! *And* he bought her this house."

Eric nodded, sympathizing. There were lots of well-heeled kids in this town. But he didn't envy them. Dria held out the joint, and he took it and inhaled. *It's good to have to make money,* he thought, holding his breath. It gave you a sense of purpose, led to a sense of accomplishment.

And that was part of the problem, of course. He blew out the smoke. He wasn't even teaching this semester. In a last attempt to fire himself up to produce, he had taken the semester off. And it had worked—for a moment or two. He had started something early in the new year: a girl with one foot on a balance beam, the other in the air, taking a step. She could fall or succeed, he'd thought, and, briefly, he'd liked it. And then he hadn't; it felt trite and juvenile. Just the other day, in fact, he had covered it up and shoved it in a corner.

"Not, you know, that I don't like anyone with money," Dria said. "I mean, that's not why I can't stand Julia. And I did ask myself that, just to make sure I wasn't being, you know, uncharitable. But that's not why I dislike her. It's more just—"

He took another hit of pot, then passed back the joint.

"She goes to hot yoga incessantly, for one thing," Dria said, taking it. "She takes fourteen classes a week. Ninety minutes a class. Once she actually went three times in one day." She dragged on the joint.

Eric laughed. "Really? Wow."

"And in between, she just eats cashew butter, drinks bottled water, and takes showers. She has to, because she burns so many calories in the class." She exhaled the smoke out the window. "The room they do it in is stifling," she said. "I tried it once, and I almost passed out." She looked at him quickly. "I mean, not to judge. It's not like I think I'm better. But—what is the purpose of that life? You know? What is her purpose?"

"What's anyone's purpose?" Eric asked, before he could stop the words. God, was he tired of being a downer. He knew it got to Eve too. Her eyes would glaze over when he said something like that, or she'd jump up and start cleaning things.

But Dria only nodded. "I used to think the purpose of life was just pleasure," she said. "Not pleasure where anyone else gets hurt, of course. First do no harm, and all that. But I mean, that God put each of us here for a limited amount of time, and our job was to make the most of it. That it was almost a sin *not* to really enjoy it. But you know, watching Julia, I think there has to be more than pleasure, if that's even what you get from yoga. There has to be more than even—I don't know—inner peace." She looked at him. "Don't get me wrong. I wouldn't mind a little more inner peace myself." She laughed. "But eventually, you have to *connect* with something. With some*one*, I should say. With the *world.*"

He nodded. He saw her point, actually. Or at least, it was fun to think about it. How long since he'd had an existential conversation? Since he'd thought and talked about the meaning of things, as opposed to logistics and specifics: where they had to be, who would do what. Or someone's work. Eve's, these days. He was happy to do it, of course; she'd certainly done it for him all those years. But it was nice to step back a moment, to think about the *why* of things.

"Anyway, you already do that, with your work," Dria said suddenly. "You already connect." She turned so her entire body almost faced him—no easy task, with those legs. "I mean, you look at life and find the meaning, and then you put it into your work for others to see too. You teach people. You add meaning and beauty to everyone's life."

He had to work not to laugh. *Don't idealize artists*, he wanted to say. *We're only narcissists and obsessives.* But why burst her bubble? Or his.

"Do you know," she said, "the first time I saw that sculpture in your kitchen, I actually went home and cried? The idea that someone would take that much time to find the essence of another person, and then more time trying to—what's the word? Not *articulate* it, obviously, but—whatever the sculpting equivalent is."

He laughed, a little embarrassed now. "Well, thank you. That's— I'm flattered. I should probably get home, though, before it's too late. Thanks for the pot. Here, let me get your bike out." He jumped out of the car, closed the door behind him.

But when his feet hit the ground, he had to stand still a moment.

Damn, he would feel all that wine tomorrow. And the pot hadn't helped. Still, when had he become such a lightweight?

He stepped to the back of the car and took out the bike. Did she want him to put it somewhere?

And then there she was, outside, almost right next to him.

She was so tall; really, only a couple of inches shorter than he. And why was she standing so close? He could smell her perfume, or shampoo, or whatever it was. She took a final drag of the joint, then dropped it and tapped it out with her shoe. Then she leaned back against the car and glanced up. "Oh, look at the moon," she said, dreamily. "It's so low and bright. I wonder why we see it as such a perfect circle when clearly it's not. I mean, is it that our eyes are playing tricks, or . . ." Her voice tapered off.

"It's a blue moon," Eric said.

"Sorry?"

"The second full moon in a month. That's what that means." Danny had taught him that, just yesterday.

"Cool." Dria stared up, silent. "I miss my mom," she said after a minute. "She loves the moon! My middle name, Selene, means 'goddess of the moon.'" She smiled. "I wish that was my first name. But no, I had to be named after my father. Alex the asshole."

"You could just *use* your middle name," Eric said after a moment. "I did."

"You did?" She looked at him.

"Yeah. My first name is David."

"David?" She laughed. "No way!"

He smiled. "Why is that funny?"

She laughed again. "No, it's not that the *name* is funny, it's more . . ."

She was watching him. Her smile faded a little, which only made her eyes bigger and rounder. "You know," she said finally, "I just think you're so great."

He laughed once, embarrassed again.

"And I wish . . ." She sighed, then shook her head. "I'm sorry. I just miss my mom."

He nodded, not knowing what to say.

"I think I'm just, I'm so lonely right now. And I don't think she's doing well. She doesn't sound well when we talk on the phone. She has cancer. She was in remission for a while, but I think it's back. But she won't tell me, because she knows I can't afford to fly there." She looked up, blinking several times fast. "Plus my stepfather doesn't want me there anyway," she said, gazing at the ground now. "He's another grade A loser. My mom hates him too, but she pretends not to, because then she'd be out on the street." She frowned. "I just wish I could go see her."

Eric shifted on his feet. He really should get home. But he felt sorry for her. It sounded like a shit situation.

"And being around you," she said, and she looked at him again, "I don't know why, but it makes me feel better. I know that sounds stupid; I mean, you don't even know me, and you're so much older and all. But you help me. Just doing what you do, being who you are. And I need that right now, because I really, I just feel so alone, and so sad."

He was listening. *Poor thing,* he thought, and his head spun, stars swirling by.

She turned to him and stepped closer, big eyes fixed on his. "You're such a beautiful person," she said. "I really want to thank you." She opened her arms and reached out to hug him.

Okay, he thought, and he opened his arms, let her in.

A second passed, then two. She held him, her body pressed against his, and he smelled her neck, her lemony hair. *It's a hug, for God's sake*, he thought, but her breath was warm, her backbones there under his hands. Was that a murmur in her throat? His blood begin to pulse.

He pulled back suddenly, stepping out of her grasp.

But she was looking at him, smiling. "Thank you," she said, and she leaned in and kissed him, her lips smack on his.

The thing about married sex, he thought blurrily, was that after a certain point, you never got to kiss like you meant it. He and Eve kissed, sure, but it was more of a prelude to sex, which was, frankly, a prelude to sleep, then to getting out the door in the morning. And after a while, you could just skip the kissing altogether. It was sad. People thought it was always the women who wanted to kiss, but that wasn't true. He loved to make out. He missed it.

Dria eased her lips off his, smiled, and leaned in again. She opened her mouth a little this time, and he opened his to meet hers and felt her tongue tease his lips. A tingling tug at the base of his spine. What was that taste on her lips? Watermelon, maybe. Lip gloss or pot gloss or whatever you called that stuff, something young and vaguely vile yet utterly—

But no. He pulled away, though not without considerable effort. He stepped back and put up his palms. "Dria," he said.

Her hand flew up to her mouth, and her smile disappeared. "Oh my God," she said. "I am *such* an idiot." She slapped her leg. "I always do such stupid things with guys. I am *such* a loser."

"It's okay." Eric reached out to steady her arm. "You're not a loser. Don't say that."

"I am!" She wiped at her eyes, smearing mascara all over her face. "Listen, I'm going in now," she said. "Thanks for the ride. And for, you know. Everything."

He watched her stumble around the bike, which she dropped on the driveway, and walk quickly to her back door. Under the light, her legs long white stalks, she fumbled in her purse for her keys. "Fuck!" he heard her say.

The moon was radiant overhead, alive and inviting. He thought of his mother: kneeling to clip snapdragons from her garden, floppy sunhat, smile underneath. In five days—six at most—he could be at her house. "Dria!" he called.

She turned from the door, her thick sweater hanging off her shoulders.

"Do you really want to go see your mother?"

She cocked her head. "Sorry?"

"If you could get out to see your mom right now, would you go? Could you leave?"

She took a step toward him. "What do you mean?"

His head was still spinning, but suddenly he felt good. Full of purpose and clarity, for a change. "My mother lives in Tucson," he said. "If you want to go to Hatback, I'll take you. But I couldn't get you back here. And we'd have to leave now."

She stared at him for a few seconds. And then her face broke into a smile, and she screamed and jumped up and down. "That's crazy!" she yelled. "Are you kidding?"

He laughed. "Shhh! Don't wake your roommate. I'm not kidding. I'm serious."

"See, that's what I mean!" she said. "That's why I like you. You do exactly what you want. You're not afraid."

The thought was laughable. And yet ten minutes later, they were pulling out of the driveway. Her face was scrubbed clean now, her skirt replaced (thank God) by loose jeans. She had brought a fluffy blanket and a stuffed backpack; Poland Spring water bottles (absconded from the yoga maniac roommate, no doubt) were crammed all over the place. He'd drunk one of the waters right away, hoping to flush some of the blurriness from his brain, and it worked, at least partway. The headache had started when the wine and pot began to wear off, though that wasn't so bad either; he'd felt worse things before.

But now, after hours of the pounding, he was ready to be done with it. Eric closed the gas tank cover, then went into the mini-mart and took the piss of his life. He splashed his face, though stopped short of rinsing his mouth at that sink. In the store, he bought two cartons of Tropicana, two bagels, a ham and cheese sandwich, a box of Fig Newtons, a large coffee, a bottle of Tylenol, a bottle of liquid tears, and a pair of cheap shades. He paid for the whole mess, then returned to the car. Dria was still sound asleep. He squeezed a stream of eyedrops into each eye, then popped three Tylenol and drank half of one Tropicana. Ate the sandwich, gulped down half the coffee. *Much better. Feeling human again.*

The clock said 10:03, which probably meant it was just before ten—something that suddenly bugged him. Eve knew it was fast, so why not just keep it accurate, so he didn't have to guess? He thought of her waking up, rolling over in bed, and finding him gone. But he didn't think she'd really worry—not yet, anyway. She'd probably assume he went to his studio at some point, and she'd just get up and on with her day. Anyway, he would call her soon. He just didn't know yet what he'd say.

Back on the road, Dria was still dead to the world; amazing how you could sleep at that age—though hadn't she said she had insomnia? Well. Perhaps knowing she was going to see her mother had cured her. Or having him take care of her until they got there. He smiled at the thought, then reached down to scratch his leg. His psoriasis itched—his right shin, the back of his head—but there was nothing to be done about that, with his cortisone cream home next to his bed. He could use a shower too. At some point he'd have to stop, clean up, sleep a bit. But he'd figure that one out later too, just as he'd figure out what to say to Eve, to Dria, his daughter—all the women. *All the women men were always accountable to.* He couldn't tell Eve the full truth ("Lying and its evil twin, absolute honesty," as Emerson aptly said), but neither did he want to lie. He had never lied to her before, probably because he'd had no reason to. He'd never betrayed her.

But she had betrayed him. Once, at least. He could still get worked up thinking about it.

The day was bright, too bright, though the sun was behind him. He popped on the shades—they made everything bright green and weird; oh well, what did he expect for $6.98—and thought about a sculpture he'd tried a few years ago, a large, ominous, eagle-like bird with a face that was almost human (it, too, was hiding in the back of his studio somewhere now, unfinished), and then about a girl he dated a year or two before Eve. Jesibel, a brilliant narcoleptic. She'd fall asleep within thirty seconds after certain situations: a fight, or sometimes even after they'd laughed together over something. It was weird, though he hadn't really minded; it made him feel protective of her—something new for him back then. But she was nuts otherwise, breaking up with him in a rage and then begging him to take her back, disappearing for weeks and then accusing him of not calling. The opposite of Eve in just about every way. In the end, with Jesibel, it was her instability, not her narcolepsy, that drove him over the edge.

He wondered where she was now—still in Brooklyn, likely—and how she was doing. He thought about the circle of friends he'd had back then: Jacob the bipolar painter, Gigi the banjo player, Ratman the black albino singer, his voice so childlike and full of yearning Eric was often moved to tears, in some smoke-filled, flesh-filled bar late at night, hearing him belt out something. Maybe they were all still there, doing their thing. Or maybe, like him, they'd left and married and had kids, and those days for them, too, were only memories now, colorful hard candy preserved in the mind's candy dish.

He flipped on the radio, turning the volume way down so he didn't wake Dria. They were almost out of Pennsylvania, he guessed. And wasn't there a town called Paradise in this state? Just as well that they'd missed it; how could a town called Paradise not disappoint? He wondered how long it would take to get to Arizona—sixty-some hours, he estimated—then let the thought pass. They'd get there when they got there. No need to rush or stress out or plan; he would not worry away this time with logistics. Nor would he think about his work, or about any art at all. *The madness of art.* My God, it had pulled him under for so long. It was time to surface and gasp a little fresh air.

He glanced at Dria again. Maybe she'd sleep the whole way. All the better if she did. He was happy to focus on the road and the things it displayed before him. A crippled tree, damaged in its journey upward (lightning? a kid with an ax?), now growing sideways; dappled sunlight on a pond; a cross-eyed cow chewing its cud; an owl catching his glance from a tree, sharing a moment with him. A wood fence that ended abruptly, keeping nothing in or out. A sharp metal fence that kept out everything. Or kept it in.

Ah, the road. He had always loved a road trip. And he loved that he was *doing* something finally—something besides going off to his studio each morning and coming home at day's end with not a thing to show for it. Avoiding his wife's downturned eyes, the questions he knew wouldn't come from his kids because they'd been told not to ask: *What did you do at work today, Dad?* He did nothing. Absolutely nothing, day after day.

But now he was doing something. He was driving west, taking a girl to see her sick mother, getting them both out of there. The road was calling, after so many years. And damn if he wasn't answering it.

4

"I'M SORRY," EVE said into the phone. "Would you mind repeating that?" It was Friday afternoon, and she was upstairs doing a local live radio show that was supposed to take thirty minutes but was going on forty-five. And Danny had just walked in from school. "Mom?" he yelled as he slammed the front door.

"I was asking," said the radio host in the phone, "about the single mother in North Carolina whose son will be taken from her custody if he doesn't make progress with his weight loss. I'm sure you know the story; the boy already weighs 255 pounds at just seven years old. He's been put on diets by doctors, but apparently he doesn't stick to them. I wondered what you thought about that, Eve. By the way, folks, we're talking to Eve Adams, author of *Feast on This: How to Eat Right, Feel Good, and Look Great in a Time of Nutritional Chaos.*"

"Hello?" Danny yelled upstairs. "Mom?"

"You know, I'm actually not familiar with all the details of that case," Eve said, unbuttoning her sweater and fanning herself. (In fact, she was not familiar with any of them.) "But in general, I don't support taking children away from their mothers, and in a case involving weight—I mean, there are so many reasons a child could be overweight. It could be at least partly genetic. And then there's—"

"Mom? MOM!"

"Um, there's the fact that kids today are constantly surrounded by calorie-dense, highly tempting, and extremely unhealthy food—

at school, in shopping malls and arcades, even on the street. Humans aren't programmed for that sort of environment. We're programmed for an environment where food is scarce." She covered her open ear to try to block out Danny's voice. "And some children eat compulsively," she said. "It's very very hard for a parent to control that, especially if she's a single mother who—"

"MOM!" Danny screamed at the top of his lungs. "ARE YOU HOME OR ARE YOU NOT HOME?!!"

"I'm sorry," Eve said to the host, along with however many people were out there listening. "Could you hold on a minute, please?"

She put down the phone, rushed out of her office, and half-yelled, half-whispered downstairs, "Danny, Jesus! I'm here, but I'm doing a phone interview! Can you wait a minute?"

"Well, what can I have for a snack?" he yelled back. "I'm starving!"

"Danny, I don't know! Take whatever you want!"

"Okay, but can I play with Star's PSP? She left it here."

"No!" Eve yelled, and then reconsidered; it would keep him quiet at least. "Fine!" she yelled. "Just—do whatever, I'll be down as soon as I can."

Back in her office, she yanked off her sweater, then picked up the phone again. "I'm sorry," she said. "Um. Oh. Yes. I think it's very hard these days to fault a mother for a child's weight problem, especially a mother who works. Good food can be hard to find, expensive, and time-consuming to prepare. And mothers who work sometimes spend the entire day away from their kids, with little or no control over what they eat. Then, poor neighborhoods don't always have safe places for kids to go out and play or exercise, so they're inside all day, often sitting in front of a screen. So, um, I would say, not knowing all the details of that case, that I would advocate, um, trying to educate the mother about feeding her child and then helping her get that food. And, if necessary, getting him into a program to help with compulsive overeating." She took a deep breath.

"Well put. Eve Adams, thank you so much. The book, folks, is

Feast on This: How to Eat Right, Feel Good, and Look Great in a Time of Nutritional Chaos. You can write to Eve at her Web site, at—" The line went dead. Eve waited a few seconds, then hung up. Immediately, it rang again. "How did it go?" asked her publicist, a curly blonde who seemed about fourteen. She was chewing something. Probably cherry Bubble Yum.

"Fine," Eve said. "I mean, they started late and kept me on for forty-five minutes, but—"

"Really? Great! That means you were interesting! Either that, or their next guest cancelled." She laughed. "J.K., I'm sure you were brilliant. I'll tell the team. And I just e-mailed you the interviews I scheduled for next week."

"Thanks," Eve said. "But I've gotta go now, because—"

"No need, I get it. I'll text you." She hung up.

Eve threw the phone on the bed and went downstairs. Magnolia had come in too and was already sitting at the kitchen table in front of her laptop, a family-size bag of blue corn chips open in front of her. *Eight servings,* Eve thought, wishing she didn't know such things. Last time she'd mentioned to her daughter that she might not want to eat the whole bag at once, Maggie had yelled, "Don't tell me what to eat! I am not two years old!"

"Hi, Mags," Eve said now.

"Hi," Maggie said, without looking up.

"How was your day? Did they find your phone yet?" Magnolia's cell phone had been missing all week. Lost or stolen—she wasn't sure which.

Maggie shook her head. "The assistant principal called me down about the form I filled out. He said there's little chance at this point, even if someone at school does have it slash stole it."

"Oh shoot, Mags. That stinks." Eve sighed. A new phone would cost a fortune. But it's not like you could go back once you'd given a kid a cell phone, especially since there were no pay phones anymore. Plus, it was how she kept tabs on her daughter.

"I know," Maggie said, still staring at her screen. "Thank God Emily has two, so I can use one of hers during school."

"Wait. Emily has *two* cell phones?" Emily was Magnolia's best friend, a tiny slip of a girl, lovely as a fairy-tale princess.

"One's her mom's," Maggie explained. "But her mom works at home, so she's online 24/7 anyway. She doesn't even notice when Emily takes hers."

Eve blinked. "But—why do you need one at school? And why does Emily need *two*?"

"Um, *hello*? Like, for *me*?" Magnolia actually removed her eyes from the screen to glare at Eve. "Since you're not letting me take Dad's, even though it's sitting right here doing nothing."

"It's out of charge," Eve said weakly, though of course the real reason was that she wanted Eric's phone here to see if anyone called it—ideally, someone who knew where he was. "Do you want some milk with those chips?" she added, watching her daughter shovel them in.

"Mom, no! If I wanted milk, I'd *take* milk!" Magnolia had already returned to her screen.

Eve sighed. "Okay, Mags. I just asked."

Maggie shook her head. "Ew. Nate's latest girlfriend is so sketchy, Mom. She's this totally random girl, and I honestly do not even think she's that pretty. Look, here's a photo of her on his Facebook, slutting all over him. Plus she's legit the biggest bitch I've ever met. If you say hi to her, she just glares you down."

Eve was tempted to rush over and see the slutty bitch who possessed the thing, the *person,* her daughter most wanted in life. But no; better to rise above the level of an insecure fourteen-year-old and say something wise and mature about how the girl was probably very nice, just socially awkward, or shy; or, if she truly was so unkind and yet Nate was with her, well, what did that say about Nate? Did Magnolia really want to be with someone who would choose a girl like that, a Mean Girl, as his girlfriend?

But Magnolia *did*, of course, if that person was Nate. That was the thing. And who was Eve to say a word when her own husband had fled with the babysitter? "Watch your mouth, please," was what she finally, pathetically, managed. She stood a moment, slightly dazed, then wandered into the living room. "Hi, Danny," she said.

Danny was lying on the rug, tapping furiously at a small hand-held video game. "Hi, Mom," he said after a moment.

"How was your day?"

Danny punched a key. An explosion sound came from the screen. "Ughhhh!" he yelled, happily.

"Danny?" Eve said.

Danny looked at her. "What?"

"We should return that to Star." Star was the fourth and young-est child of the next-door neighbors, Priscilla and Veronica (aka Ronnie). Right after Stream.

Danny began pushing keys again. "What?" he said, not bother-ing to look up this time.

Eve sighed. "Okay, tell you what. You take your screen time now, on that thing, and Maggie can have hers on Facebook. I'll finish my work. And at the end, we'll convene and have an actual conversa-tion." She went back to the kitchen and set the timer for thirty min-utes, then sat down at her computer, adjacent to Maggie's.

She answered most of her e-mail (none from Loretta, alas), then clicked back to the screen she'd been looking at before her radio inter-view. It was a long article about the Roux-en-Y—one of the three types of bariatric surgery and the one probably best suited to Michael—that a doctor, with whom she'd finally, if briefly, consulted, had sent her this morning. The timer rang. She turned it off and kept reading.

It was a tricky procedure, this surgery, with a patient's stomach reduced from approximately the size of a football to the size of a wal-nut or a small egg, and the small intestines divided and refastened to lessen the amount of time and space for food digestion and ab-sorption of calories. Afterward, the patient couldn't eat bread, most sweets, or too much fiber (a potato skin, for example) ever again. Nor could he eat more than a very small amount of food at a time without major complications—everything from severe nausea and vomiting to racing heartbeat to something called "dumping" (simul-taneous dizziness, sweating, nausea, severe pain, and diarrhea) to gallstones, infections, hernia, and intestinal obstruction. That said, the procedure had become far less dangerous as more of them were performed, with a mortality rate now of half of 1 percent—which, when you compared that to the dangers of obesity like Michael's, looked pretty good. What's more, up to 96 percent of patients saw their diabetes cured or improved, up to 90 percent had their high blood pressure drop, and up to 80 percent got relief from their sleep apnea. Patients who complied with the eating restriction—now easier, or at least more likely, because of their physical limitations—lost huge amounts of weight and kept much or most of it off, unlike most patients were able to do with only diet and exercise.

Eve was getting excited as she read. The procedure sounded very right for Michael—or as right as anything else out there, anyway. She needed to call him, tell him all this, and see if she could convince him and Diane to at least see a doctor to talk about it.

But she couldn't call him now; it was already dark out, she realized with shock. How long had she and the kids been plugged into their screens? She turned to her daughter, who was still glued to her laptop. "Hi, Mags," she said.

"Hi, Mom." Maggie rubbed at her eyes. "I can't figure out where Emily is. For some reason, she's not online. We were supposed to have plans."

"Mags, can you close your computer now?" The bag of corn chips was empty too, Eve noticed with a pang of anxiety. God, what a shitty mother she was. "Danny, come in!" she called.

Amazingly, they both complied, no doubt knowing they'd already gotten away with something. But at the table, they looked at her gloomily. "Mom, I'm starved," Danny said. "Can I make bruschetta?" He had made this once recently after finding a recipe online. It had turned out delicious, Eve had to admit. But they didn't have any tomatoes now. Or bread. In fact, she realized, she hadn't food-shopped in days, between her clients, the radio interviews, the research for Michael, and the kids. Today she hadn't even stepped outside the house.

"Danny, is food all you ever think about?" Magnolia said, and then, "Mom, did you hear from Dad yet?"

Eve shook her head. She had stopped making excuses for Eric. Really, why should she?

But Maggie stared at her, and then Danny did too, as if they suddenly suspected she had, say, hid him behind the duck sauce in the fridge or locked him in the basement in a large cage.

Magnolia frowned. "I don't get it. I really don't. No one's even, like, *worried*? I mean, he just frickin' disappears—"

"I know he's okay because he's charging gas and groceries," Eve said. (She didn't mention the motel rooms or the girl.) "I think he just needed a break, sweetie."

"From his own *family*? And he doesn't even call and *tell* you?"

Good point, Eve thought. "He doesn't have his phone," she said. "Remember?"

"Hello? Borrow someone's?"

"Magnolia. The snottiness doesn't help."

Danny was flipping through a *National Geographic Kids* now, a magazine Eric recently had ordered for him. "Hey, Mom," he said, looking up. "You know what's a great whiteboard eraser?"

"What, sweetheart?"

"Bread."

"Bread?" Eve smiled. "No way."

"Way! Mr. Kennedy used it at school today when he found a piece on the floor. I think it fell off of Zach's sandwich."

Eve laughed. "Well, that's too bad."

"Not really. Zach hates sandwiches. He probably dropped it on purpose."

"Mom." Magnolia stood up, tapped her foot. "If you don't need me here, I'm just gonna, like, get on with things."

"Wait a minute! We can have a discussion for five seconds without you running back to a screen."

Maggie sighed and made a face, but she sat.

Eve looked at them. "Hey!" she said finally. "Let's go out for dinner. It'll cheer us up. We can get sushi at Yo Mama, then browse in the stores nearby afterward."

"I'm not hungry," Magnolia said, but then, after thinking for a minute, added, "Could we go to the phone store?"

Eve hesitated. "We have to wait till the plan renews to get the phone, though. I can't afford another phone until then."

But in the Verizon store after dinner (hungry or not, Magnolia had managed to choke down two egg rolls, Eve realized as she signed the Visa receipt, plus the entire bowl of free crispy noodles Eve specifically asked them not to bring), a small miracle occurred: the manager gave them a recycled loaner phone to use until the new plan started. All Magnolia had to do was fully charge it, he said, as he transferred her number to the new phone. *Thank you, Naveen Gupta,* Eve said silently, reading his name tag.

Leaving the store, Magnolia was ecstatic, but Danny was quiet again. All week, he'd been sinking into these spells—no doubt, Eve thought, more worried and sad about his father than he would articulate. "Cheer him up?" Eve mouthed to Magnolia, and seconds later, they were in Dave's Pet City, squealing at the tarantulas, ogling the blue and silver fish, begging to take home a baby bunny. "Absolutely not," Eve said. "You know what happened to my bunny, Fluff-Ball aka Stink-Bomb." They laughed, because they did know. The one pet Eve's parents had ever agreed to, the rabbit had quickly grown to the size of a football and then lain immobile in its cage for four years, shitting nonstop and biting anyone who tried to pat him.

So instead they left the store with Batman, a parakeet for Danny, complete with the $89.99 deluxe cage and bird accessories kit. If Eric had been here, Eve knew, she would not have spent the money. *But he's not,* she thought. *Knock yourself out.*

At home, Maggie plugged in the phone to charge it, and Danny ran up to install the bird in his cage. And then the land line rang, and Loretta was on the other end. "Loretta!" Eve yelled, instantly forgiving her for the long response time.

"Eve, I'm *so* sorry. I was in New Mexico for a week—Howie took us, this Canyon Ranch clone outfit but for new mothers. You take your baby and they help you with all the stuff and bring you mildly alcoholic drinks constantly in between. Anyway. I just got back and got your e-mail about Eric. My God! Have you heard from him yet?"

With great relief—Loretta was the only person she'd told—Eve filled her in on the details of the past six days, pacing the floor as her best friend inhaled sharply and said "My God!" and "Are you serious?" at all the right times. "I honestly don't know what he's doing, Loretta," Eve concluded, falling into a chair. "I mean, he's charging gas and some other stuff, plus cheap motels, which is a dead giveaway where he is. Heading west. Possibly toward his mother in Tucson."

"Can you call her?" Loretta said. "Maybe she knows something."

"I don't want to worry her in case he's not going there. Not yet, anyway. Though I guess I'll have to call her soon if I don't hear from him." Eve shook her head, dreading the thought even as much as she liked Penelope. "Anyway," she said, "he took out money on the cash card, but just a couple of hundred. So it's not like—I mean, he's not fleeing forever, I don't think." She paused a moment, wondering if she was right about that. "But he hasn't called," she said. "And he's got to be with this girl. Either that, or it's an enormous coincidence that she hasn't been home since that night either *and* I can't reach her by cell." She exhaled with disgust. "That girl is twenty-one years old, Loretta. Can he actually be—" She'd been about to say "fucking a twenty-one-year-old" but couldn't bring herself to.

"Of course he's not," Loretta said, reading Eve's mind. "Whatever's going on, I'm sure there's a valid explanation."

"I'm ready to hear it." Eve sniffed hard. *That bastard,* she thought. "That bastard," she said.

"He's not a bastard," Loretta soothed. "He's going through a rough phase. He loves you madly, Eve. You know that. But you also know Eric, right? He's an artist. Didn't he do something like this once before? And it turned out to be nothing?"

"I can't believe you remember!" Eve jumped up. "Right before we got engaged. No one knew where he was, including me." She began pacing again. "Turned out he'd gone to his best friend's place, in Pasadena. Drove all the way there and turned around a day later, then asked me to marry him the night he got back. I was so mad. Though, of course, I said yes anyway."

Loretta laughed.

"Well, what was I gonna say? *No?* I was in love with him."

"You were," Loretta agreed. "You loved him from the first time you—"

"Can we change the subject? I'm so sick of thinking about him, I could puke. How are *you*, anyway? How's the baby, and Howard, and the boys?"

"They're all fine, they're fantastic, they all drive me nuts. God, I wish you could come down. I feel like we haven't talked for five years."

"I *want* to!" Eve practically yelled. "I'd *love* to!"

Loretta paused. "Okay, I'm just throwing this out there—oh, wait, she fell off, I have to latch her back on." Eve heard the baby fussing. "There. Okay, listen. Howie is going away tomorrow—a work thing, overnight—and I have all three kids all weekend. Why don't you and Mags and Danny come visit? Danny can play with the boys, and my mother can take a break from helping me, not that she'll back off easily, but there are ways around that. *Come,* Eve! Maggie can bring a friend if she wants." She laughed. "As long as they promise to hold the baby."

And so, the next morning, after Danny fussed some over the bird (he had colored tiny nameplates for his water and food dishes, which Magnolia glued on), and Maggie realized that the new phone had not charged properly and packed the phone and the charger to begin the process anew at Loretta's house, they hit the highway going south, Eve thinking, with a surge of Thelma and Louise–flavored anger, *Who needs a husband?* Three hours later, they pulled into Livingston, New Jersey, and five minutes after that, up the enormous round driveway to the home of Howard Silverstein, attorney at law, and his new wife, Loretta Rossi, PhD, as well as of Ben and Josh, nine and seven, during the 50 percent of the time they lived there, and the baby, Edie.

Inside, after hugs and baby gushing and exclamations of how tall everyone was, the three boys were released to the game wing, the two yappy terriers, each sporting a tiny pink sweater, leaping and barking after them. (The dogs were part of the custody deal, Loretta had told Eve. When the boys were at their father's, the dogs were too.) The girls proceeded to the living room, where Eve settled into half of Loretta's charcoal-gray couch and Magnolia flopped onto the other half, her stocking feet sinking into her mother's lap. Eve reached for one of the triangular sandwiches from the platter Loretta had ordered in. "Oh my God," she said, taking a bite. "What is this?"

"Sloppy joes, the New Jersey version." Loretta reached for one around the nursing baby. "Ham, turkey, roast beef, cheese, egg salad, tuna, cole slaw, and Russian dressing. On white. Sometimes all in one sandwich."

Eve laughed. "Heart attack on a plate." She wiped her mouth and took another bite, suddenly starved. "I hope you don't eat this stuff too often," she said, her mouth full.

"Only about four times a week. The boys call and order them in without asking me now. They know Howie's Amex number by heart. And really, who am I to—oops. Shit." A glob of orange dressing had fallen out of her sandwich and onto Edie's head.

Magnolia laughed loudly.

Loretta grinned, accepting the napkin Eve handed her. "Listen, you try feeding one of these suckers, no pun intended, 24/7 and you won't be laughing," she said to Magnolia. She wiped the baby's head, then turned back to Maggie. "So—tell me about *you*. How's violin?"

"I quit. Last year."

"Right! Sorry, I completely knew that. Why'd you stop?"

Maggie shrugged, then (having rejected the sandwiches straightaway) popped another chocolate from a large silver dish of them into her mouth. "I realized how bad I sucked," she said, swallowing and taking another. "Plus, I wanted more time with my friends."

"Bad*ly*, Magnolia, and you did *not* suck," Eve said, annoyed she had to use the word *suck,* which her daughter knew she hated. But she had to protest the sentiment, and not just for maternal reasons. Magnolia had played daily, and often passionately, for five years, mastering some impressive classical pieces by the end. Eve had thought the violin would see her through high school at least and had been stunned when Maggie quit with no warning last year; simply closed her case one afternoon and never looked back.

Maggie rolled her eyes. "Whatever, Mom. That's your opinion."

"Mine too, Miss Magnolia, I've heard you play too, don't forget." Loretta smiled. "So do you miss it?"

"No." Magnolia pointed at the baby nursing. "Does that hurt?"

"Not really, once you get used to it. At the beginning, don't even ask." Loretta shuddered. "So what else? Are you in love? Any weddings in the works?"

Maggie shook her head and made a disgusted face.

"Good," said Loretta. "Because I'd really rather get in shape before I have to buy a bridesmaid gown, and as you can see, I'm not doing too well with that just yet." She laughed and took another bite of sandwich.

She did look tired, of course, Eve thought—blue eyelids, deepening creases in her compact, classically beautiful face—but otherwise, not bad for a forty-two-year-old new mother. Her cheeks were flushed against her straight, slightly messy chopped black hair, and though she wore sweatpants and a button-down flannel shirt, she seemed, other than the anomaly of her newly large breasts, to already have mostly regained her tiny body. It was a body that ran in her family, Eve knew: Loretta looked exactly like a younger version of her mother, though the similarities ended there. Jeanette Rossi was a gently jovial Sicilian Italian who cooked a mean marinara, could sew a wedding dress in a day from a pile of tulle and silk, and made pizzelle like no one's business, but probably wasn't educated past sixth grade. In fact, all four of the other Rossis (Loretta's father and two brothers owned a landscaping business) had been baffled and amazed first by Loretta's continued education, then by her professorship, then by the publication of her book of poetry, not to mention the fact that she'd made it to her fortieth birthday with no sign of a husband or children—or apparent regret. When she'd married Howard Silverstein and acquired two insta-sons, a house in the suburbs, and access to however many millions her new husband possessed, her mother had been openly ecstatic.

Now, with baby Edie, it was all Loretta could do to keep her mother from moving in, especially as she lived less than a half hour away. "It took me forty years to get the hell out of *Sopranos* country and one wedding to slide right back in," Loretta had told Eve, laughing, but Eve knew it was more complicated than that—though not, she'd thought at the time, by too much. One day, Loretta woke up and realized she was forty and single and childless (or "child free," depending on her mood) and would probably stay that way for the rest of her life—which was *fine,* she said, she loved her job and considered her poetry book her firstborn child. . . but what was the harm of going on a few dating Web sites just to see what was out there? One week later, she'd met Howard Silverstein, forty-six-year-old recent divorcé and half-time father of two "active" boys, on JDate.com. She'd married him nine months after that, and given birth to Edie by C-section less than ten months after the wedding. Eve was trying to get used to it all; she still pictured Loretta in her tiny book-filled Manhattan apartment reading *The New Yorker* and *The Nation,* living on homemade espresso and takeout from Perfecto Pizzeria and reading poems about sexy policemen and blow jobs (poet or not, she had never lost her Jersey Girl touch) to her coterie of college girls with pierced chins and teardrops tattooed on their cheeks.

"So, are you writing any books these days?" Magnolia asked Loretta.

Eve looked at her old friend and laughed. "Yeah, Ret, come on! You're on maternity leave, aren't you?"

Loretta smiled wearily, then shook her head at Magnolia. "Not too many right now, though I did write a poem the other day about a woman who turns into a cow. You know that story *The Metamorphosis*? This is the female version."

Maggie grinned, and Eve smiled too. This trip had been a good idea—getting the hell away from their house and their lives for a bit. And Loretta had always brought out the best in Magnolia. Edie made a loud suckling noise, and they all looked at her. There was soft music in the room, something familiar. Eve looked around for a CD cover to identify it but saw no stereo or speakers. "Where's that music coming from?" she asked.

"What?" Loretta said, and then, "Oh—that? It runs through the whole house. Howie controls it with a remote—I don't have a clue how to work it, so I guess we'll get our fill of Peter Frampton, since he's not due back till tomorrow." She laughed, rubbing her eyes. "Unless he can control it from New York, which I wouldn't put past him. Is it bugging you? I'm sorry. I've gotten so I barely notice."

"No, no. It's fine. I like Frampton. A blast from the past." It was true. But it was funny, too: Loretta had always been incredibly sensitive to sound—anything from someone clomping upstairs to someone chewing in an audible way. Now, between the boys, the dogs, the baby, and the music, she was constantly surrounded by about a million decibels, and she seemed fine, more or less. *Must be the nursing hormones*, Eve thought, remembering how they'd relaxed her too.

Edie popped off Loretta's breast and let out a cry. Loretta put down her sandwich and buttoned her shirt, then sat the baby up and began burping her. But Edie wailed anyway.

"What's wrong with her?" Magnolia asked.

"She has gas. She wants me to walk her." Loretta suddenly looked exhausted. "She kept me up all night last night. I thought we were mostly over the colic, but apparently not."

Eve jumped up. "I'll walk her!"

Loretta looked relieved. "I thought you'd never ask."

"Are you kidding? I thought *you'd* never." Eve took the baby and the burp cloth (clean, white, with a cute little duck and three ducklings on it) and began pacing with her, relishing the powdery smell—slightly tinged with ketchup, she noticed—and the soft, downy little head. The baby cried, stopped, started again.

Loretta closed her eyes, leaned back, grinned. "Guess you're losing your touch, Mom."

"Shut up. I'm a little rusty, that's all. It has been a few years."

"Can I try?" Magnolia asked.

Eve glanced at Loretta, who said, without opening her eyes, "Hell, yes. Go for it."

Eve transferred Edie up to her taller daughter, coaching Maggie about supporting her head (even though the baby, now eight weeks old, could support it herself). Maggie began to walk. Instantly, the baby stopped crying and let out a big burp.

"Oh my God," Maggie said, looking horrified.

Both women laughed. "Nice work," said Loretta. "She didn't even spit up."

"Spit up?" Maggie looked suddenly nervous. "What's she doing now?" She turned stiffly so they could see the baby's head over her shoulder.

"That's the happiest I've seen her all day," Loretta said, opening one eye, and then, "Maybe her whole life. Want a job? You could be my au pair. Though you'd have to fight my mother, I guess. But I think you could take her. You're taller."

"I wouldn't mind," Magnolia said, after a minute. "I'll probably do something with babies at some point anyway, since I'm not having any of my own."

"You're *not*?" Eve stared at her.

"Well, *I* almost didn't," Loretta said thoughtfully. "And I'd have been fine if I hadn't. Not that I'm not thrilled to have my gorgeous Edie girl—*Of course I am, you fruit fly!*" she said in a higher voice, and then, in her normal voice again, "But it definitely changes your life in a big, big, *big* way. It took me forty years to be ready for that. And some women never are. And, of course, I still haven't tried to work since I had her, so we'll have to see how that flies."

"Do you ever think about quitting?" Eve hated herself for the teensy stab of jealousy she felt. Loretta could do whatever she wanted now, thanks to Howard Silverstein. She probably didn't have to work another day in her life. Not that Eve had had to either when her kids were that age. But things had changed since then. *As things tend to,* she thought, and then, admonishing herself, *You spoiled brat! You like your job, you're good at it, you're even making half a living now, give or take. Exactly what is the problem?*

Loretta was staring at her. "Are you kidding?" she said. "What the hell would I do all day? Plus, I love my work, Eve! The students, the books . . . really, it's who I was, every single day, for more than two decades." She sighed. "It's just that I've come to realize you don't just pop out a baby and get back to work in a week. That's all." She exhaled slowly, puffing out her lips. "What a fool. It's been eight weeks, and I still can't even take a proper crap."

"Why not?" Maggie asked.

Loretta shrugged. "The C-section incision, the fact that I still don't eat regularly, that I hardly ever get a second alone in the bathroom."

"Every woman I know thought she'd be able to go right back," Eve said, extra soothingly to make up for her apparent gaffe before. "You can't begin to know what it is to have a baby until you actually have one, is what it comes down to."

Loretta nodded, then turned to Maggie and fake grinned. "But don't let us dissuade you. If you do decide to have one, as long as you wait till thirty-five or forty, we promise it's worth it."

"Or twenty-seven, at least," Eve said.

Maggie nodded, looking doubtful. "Well, maybe I'd have one if I could have it with Nate. But otherwise, no way."

Loretta glanced at Eve, then at Maggie. "Is Nate the boyfriend?"

Maggie made a face. "As if. He hates me."

"He doesn't *hate* you, Maggie," said Eve. "He's just reached that age where he's having a good time playing the field."

Maggie shrugged. "Whatever, it all bores me to death. I'm gonna bounce." She held out the baby, like a doll, for Eve to retrieve, then departed stage left.

"My God, fourteen," said Loretta, as Eve began pacing with Edie again. "I don't envy her."

Eve nodded, patting the baby gently. "This Nate thing—I swear, it's tragic. And then there's her longtime best friend, Emily. Remember her? Tiny, shy, mouthful of metal? Well, the metal is gone, and she's suddenly a complete hottie, with her enormous push-up padded bra—they all wear those now. You can stick a pin all the way into their chest and never touch human skin."

Loretta laughed, and Eve sighed. "Anyway. Someone wrote in Emily's Facebook Honesty Box—that means the sender is anonymous, *honesty* being the new word for 'backstabbing'—they wrote, or I should say, *she* wrote, because it does identify the gender: 'Why do you still hang with Magnolia Knight when you can do so much better for a BFF?' Maggie found it when she was scrolling through Emily's Facebook. Emily was sitting right there when it happened." This, it had later come out, was what Magnolia had been upset about at Burritoville the night after Eric left.

Loretta's mouth fell open. "My God," she said. "What did Maggie do?"

Eve sighed. "She held it together, I think. Until she got home. Then she went ballistic on *me*."

They both smiled weakly.

"Emily was as good as she could be," Eve added. "She swore she'd told the person to fuck off, though, you know. Who knows. Wouldn't want to commit social suicide or anything."

Loretta shook her head. "The heart breaks and breaks and lives by breaking."

Eve looked at her.

"It's from a poem by Stanley Kunitz," Loretta explained. "The most beautiful lines: 'The heart breaks and breaks/and lives by breaking./It is necessary to go/through dark and deeper dark/and not to turn.'"

Eve let the words sink in. "That's intense," she said, but then, after a moment, "Anyway. It is what it is."

"It's appalling, is what it is! My poor godchild." Loretta shook her head again. "I wish you'd thought to tell me these things before I'd gone ahead and had a daughter."

"Sorry. And I guess I didn't do so well on the husband front either. Though hopefully yours won't go Lolita on you like mine did. Not to be a big downer today."

"Are you kidding? Seriously, Eve, this is big stuff. Obviously I couldn't ask in front of the kids, but what's the update?"

Eve headed for a chair to sit down. But as soon as she did, Edie started to cry. Eve stood again quickly, but Loretta motioned for her to give the baby back, then unbuttoned once more and suctioned the baby onto the opposite breast from before. Edie gulped hungrily.

Eve watched them a moment, half wistful, half relieved to be done with all that. Then she sat again. "No update," she said. "Never heard from him. No more Visa charges. Nothing." She shrugged as if it were all no big deal.

"Unbelievable." Loretta looked at Eve, her face firm. "I know there's a reason, Eve. I just know it. Eric is too good a guy to do this."

Eve shrugged. Loretta had loved Eric since the day they met, when she'd tried to pick a fight by goading him with some feminist political issue and he'd won her over by listening attentively and then agreeing with her completely. He wasn't a fighter in that way; was happy to defer on those sorts of things. He had older sisters, after all. Plus, he'd liked Loretta—her ballsiness, her cool, her dedication to what she believed. Eve wondered what he'd make of her now, sitting here in sweatpants nursing a mewling infant.

"What do you think it is?" Loretta asked after a moment. "I mean, was he acting weird at home? Did something seem wrong?"

"You know, I honestly haven't had time to notice." For the first time, Eve realized this was true. "But his work is—I mean, it's just not happening. He hasn't done anything in ages, Loretta. He's not making money. It's dire." She thought for a moment. "And maybe that's what this is, in the end. That's what I told the kids, anyway. That he needed to go off and figure things out. And if that's the case—I mean, I get that he needs space, you know I give him as much as I can, but the fact that he didn't tell me he was going, and that he hasn't called, and then there's this girl in the picture . . ."

Loretta was shaking her head, looking alternately sympathetic and baffled. "There's an explanation," she said finally, one more time. "You just have to wait until it surfaces."

"Well, I'm *not* waiting, anymore. I'm done with waiting." Sitting here right now, with Loretta, this felt true. "And you know what, Ret?" she added, and she glanced toward the hallway to make sure no one was coming. "To tell you the truth, having him gone—I mean, it's one less person to worry about. One less wounded ego to deal with." She sat up straighter, feeling herself gathering steam. "Because *fuck* him, Loretta! He left *me*! Why should I sit around for ten years, or even ten minutes, crying for him?"

"You shouldn't!" Loretta practically yelled, so loudly she startled the baby, who popped off her breast and began to scream. "Shit," Loretta said. "She just pooped. I actually felt it fly out of her. Oh, God, I'm so sorry! Where are my manners? That was disgusting."

Eve laughed, wiping her eyes. "It's not like I haven't been there myself with a baby." She took a deep breath. "Anyway, I know how she feels."

Loretta laughed too. "I *wish* I did." She sighed. "I guess I'm gonna have to go change her," she said, but she didn't make a move to rise. Edie continued to scream, her face bright red now.

Eve knew she should gather the baby and go change her for her friend. But she couldn't bear to stop talking. Not yet. It felt so good to vent, she almost couldn't believe it. She grabbed a cocktail napkin and blew her nose into it, waiting to see if Loretta would get up, but her friend continued to sit there while Edie bawled her face off. "So, you know," Eve said finally, yelling over the baby, "I'm just trying to pull us through. And it's okay. I mean, I bought Danny a parakeet yesterday, I got Mags a new phone, I'm making money—more than I have since before the kids, anyway. Not that it's enough. But we're here! With you! Which I probably wouldn't be if Eric were home. So, I'm not gonna lie down and die over this."

"Of course you're not," Loretta yelled. "You're a survivor and a pragmatist. Not to mention my new hero, now that I see what you've been up to all these years raising two of these." She gestured at the screaming baby with her chin.

Eve smiled a little, happy to change the subject, then stood up and took the infant from her friend, who handed her up gratefully. "It gets easier, I promise," she said. "Are you sleeping yet?" She began to walk, jiggling Edie, who now reeked. But she still didn't want to go off to change her.

Loretta ran a hand through her hair. "Not really. I mean, she still nurses every three or four hours, and sometimes she barely sleeps in between. But everyone says it gets better soon, so . . ." She shrugged. "I'm lucky," she said, looking anything but. "Howard is—I mean, he's not around much, but when he is, he's attentive, he's thrilled." She sighed. "And my mother's a saint, when she's not driving me nuts, and you know, no money worries, unlike if I'd done this on my own, not that I ever would have. And I admit it's sort of nice to have the approval of society after being single for so long. The awful ladies who once glared at my ringless hand and case of cheap chablis in the shopping cart are now the nice ladies who coo at me and Edie." She blew out a breath. "It's just . . ."

"What?" Eve said, patting Edie's back. The baby seemed to be quieting a bit, maybe realizing she wasn't getting her diaper changed so why bother. "Tell me!" Eve said. "*I* told *you*."

Loretta sighed. "I'm sure I'm just postpartum, or whatever, but sometimes I look at her and think, What the hell am I supposed to *do* with her all day? I mean, she relies on me completely for every-thing. Not just food and shelter, but her entire link to the world." She shook her head. "Sometimes that just freaks me out."

Eve nodded. That hadn't been her own experience—she'd al-ways had more than enough fun things to do with her babies, it seemed—but she knew other women who'd relate. "You're doing great," she said, glad it was her turn now to reassure. "You're doing it exactly right."

Loretta looked doubtful. "I mean, when I think that women used to do this eleven and thirteen times in their lives, I honestly just don't know how."

"For one, most of them didn't start at forty-two," Eve said. "In fact, most of them were dead by forty-two." They both laughed. "For another thing," Eve said, "they had a lot more help than we did. Whole villages full of help, supposedly."

"Yeah, but they never got any time to themselves, either."

"True. No 'Me Time.'"

They both guffawed.

"I swear, women's lives," Loretta said, and now she was the one wiping her eyes. "If it's not one thing, it's—"

She was interrupted by a stampede of barefoot boys: two wild redheads (who reminded Eve of Thing One and Thing Two), one beet-faced towhead, and two barking dogs. "*Mom!*" Danny shrieked. "Ben and Josh have a *Simpsons pinball machine*!! And an *Xbox 360* with an *Xbox LIVE Gold membership*! And they have a *whole roll* of bubble wrap, like those giant ones Dad used to have, but it's *all theirs* and they can unroll *however much they want and stomp all over it*!" He was panting, as if he'd just run several miles in the heat.

Eve stood up and handed the baby, who was almost asleep now, back to Loretta. "That's fantastic, sweetie pie," she said. "But listen, you have to calm down and have lunch. Look at these: they're called sloppy joes. Want one? They're delicious."

"Okay," Danny said, and immediately the two Silverstein boys plunked down at the glass coffee table, Danny doing the same. Eve looked at Loretta for approval (Eve herself would never let kids eat in this clean living room), and, receiving it with a nonchalant flap of her friend's hand, got the boys settled with sandwiches, napkins, and drinks. Then she let the dogs out in back and went to check on Magnolia, who she found watching *Mean Girls* on one of the TVs. When she returned, the boys were already finished, chomping at the bit to go back to their games. Edie was asleep on Loretta, who looked catatonic herself. "Danny needs to relax a second after he eats," Eve instructed the boys, and she pulled him onto the couch next to her while the other two galloped out of the room.

But she felt his impatience, and after a minute she sighed and let go. Immediately he jumped up and ran out to join them.

In high school, in a grueling English class, Eve had had to memorize parts of *The Odyssey*. Looking at her best friend, she smiled weakly. " 'But come now, stay with me,'" she recited, " 'eager though you are for your journey.'"

" 'So that you may first bathe and take your ease'!" Loretta yelled, looking suddenly thrilled. "That's Homer! That's Homer! Oh my God, thank you, Eve! My brain *is* still in there somewhere."

"Anytime," Eve said, and then, because the baby had woken again (when Loretta yelled again) and was just beginning to squawk, "Here, give her here. I'll go change her."

"Oh, would you?" Loretta looked at her with absolute love.

"Of course," Eve said, smiling. "Use me, baby. That's what I'm here for."

5

LATER, AFTER A walk to a park, and more games for the boys, and a shopping bag full of sushi that Loretta ordered in for all of them, and Magnolia's return to the TV room to watch *Clueless,* the women opened a bottle of wine and drank it slowly, talking about life and art and motherhood and marriage and sex, Edie alternately nursing and screaming at the top of her lungs, "Do You Feel Like We Do?" playing for at least the eightieth time on the full-home music system. In the morning, they all slept in (Loretta after getting up at two, four, and six to nurse Edie). Then they showered and dressed and, finally, went out with the dogs, grabbing slices at a crowded pizza place. When they arrived back home, Howard was there.

"Daddy!" the boys screamed, hurling themselves up into his arms while the dogs flung themselves at his legs. One by one, Howard tossed his boys, and then Danny, and then even his dogs, up into the air, dumping each one down gently on the rug before deflecting the boys' requests ("Play baseball with us?" "Take us bowling?") quickly and guiltlessly in that way only fathers can. ("Later, kiddo." "Another time." "Let me see my girls first, please, gentlemen!") He hugged Eve warmly, kissed Loretta on the lips, and swooped up the baby, covering her face and head with squeaky kisses. He was a big, loud man, well over six feet tall, and his presence filled the room.

"How'd you do, hon?" he asked Loretta, who blew out air through her lips and said, "We made it, thanks to Eve helping me. Howie, how the hell do you turn off that music? If I have to hear 'I'm in You' one more time, my head is going right in that oven."

Howard laughed, then glanced at the kids. "*Shh!*" he whispered. "They tell their mother when you say stuff like that!" Then, in a regular voice, "I *showed* you how, babe, remember? That little box by the bedroom door? You press those arrows up or down for volume, the one with the dot for on or off. Come on, I'll show you again."

"Show me later. 'Cause right now, you know what? Edie's soaked. If you could change her, I could see Eve out and collect myself before I have to open up the milk shop again."

Howard spread his arms for the baby, then turned to Eve. "You won't stay awhile? But I just got here!"

Eve muttered an excuse, not wanting to intrude on what suddenly seemed an intimate family scene. Twelve minutes later, she merged back onto the turnpike, heading north.

Danny fell asleep promptly, while Maggie, whose new phone had finally charged, scrolled through her texts from the past seven days. Moving into the middle lane and settling in, Eve thought about Howard Silverstein. He seemed nice enough (she tried not to judge him for divorcing his wife, fighting bitterly for half custody of his kids, and then, when he remarried less than a year later, leaving those kids mostly with his new wife), but frankly he wasn't at all who she'd pictured her best friend ending up with, if anyone—not him, not that house, not that life. *It just goes to show you,* she thought, although what it went to show you, she wasn't exactly sure.

"Mom," Maggie said suddenly. "Oh my God!"

"What?" Eve said, a bit reluctantly. She was vaguely hung over from last night and not really up for more drama. Really, she just wanted the drive to be peaceful, fast, and—

"There's a text here from Daddy!"

Eve felt her breathing cease. "What?"

"From Daddy! It's from—holy crap, Mom, it's from *last Monday*! See? I *told* you, this is *exactly* why I need a cell phone. Daddy! I can't believe he texted me!" She sounded thrilled.

Eve veered—calmly, calmly—into a slower lane. "What does he say?" she asked, and then, unable to resist, "What number did he send it from?"

Maggie clicked a few keys. "Some number I don't know. He says, 'Hi, Mags, wanted to tell you all I'm fine. Please tell Mom and D. Heading to Tucson. Will call from there. Tell Mom sorry I left so suddenly. Will explain. Love and miss you all lots. Love, Dad. P.S. You better not be reading this at school.'" She laughed. "Daddy!" she yelled.

Eve was silent. She wasn't sure whether the text made her angrier or less so. He had written, at least—last Monday, in fact. And she hadn't been wrong about where he was going. "I wonder why he didn't call *me*?" she said out loud, against her better judgment.

"He hates the phone," Maggie said matter-of-factly. "He totally prefers texting, probs. Like *everyone* now, Mom! And he probably knows you don't know how to pick up your texts, so he texted me instead. And then he was probably waiting to hear back from us, like all week. He probably thinks we're mad or something."

"We *are*!" Eve muttered.

"What?" Magnolia was clicking her tiny keyboard.

"Nothing. What are you writing?"

She clicked a moment longer, then snapped the phone shut. "I said my phone's lost, that's why I didn't write sooner, and we miss him, and we went to Loretta's."

Eve blinked. "That's all you said?"

"Well, what else did you want me to say?"

How about 'Fuck you, you selfish bastard!' she thought. *How about 'How's your new preschool girlfriend?' How about 'When the hell are you planning to come back home and help a little around here?'*

But she held up her chin. The truth was, they were doing fine without him—just as she'd told Loretta. "Nothing, I guess," she said.

"I'm gonna put on my iPod now," Magnolia said, and she tuned out, eyes closed, earbuds in. Eve sighed. There was only one reason she could think of for him to have texted Maggie rather than called her: he was with the girl and couldn't talk in front of her. Furious again, she flicked on the radio. Immediately, Maggie said, "Mom, can you lower that?" Eve rolled her eyes but snapped it off. "Fine—I'll just hang here on the cross," she mumbled.

Hours later, tired and bleary-eyed (the drive was tedious, she realized; normally, Eric drove wherever they went while she read or slept), Eve hauled Danny, half asleep, upstairs, stuck him in front of the toilet to pee, then pulled off his clothes and tucked him in bed (taking the opportunity to smooch him six times on his thin, milk-white neck). She checked the parakeet—alive and perky, phew—then filled his food and water dishes and headed down to the kitchen.

But halfway down she paused. Then she went back and got the bird cage and carried it downstairs with her. Maggie already had escaped to her room (with her cell phone, so Eve couldn't check the number Eric had texted from—*And just as well*, she thought; *I don't want to know right now anyway*), and Eve could use the company, so to speak. In the kitchen, she put the cage on the counter. "Hi, birdie," she said, peering at him. He was looking in his plastic mirror. "Are you lonely? Well, don't worry. We're back now, and we'll never leave you again. Ha. Believe that and I'll tell you another." She laughed. "Maybe I'll teach you to talk," she said, bending to unzip their weekend suitcase, which lay on the floor. "Maybe I'll teach you to say, 'Mommy, Daddy ran away with the babysitter! But you're gorgeous and perfect and *I* still love you at least.'" She laughed again, rubbing one eye, then dumped a handful of clothes from the suitcase into the washer and turned it on. Then she made a mug of tea and sat down at her desk, kicking off her shoes.

She clicked to her e-mail and scanned the long list. Her editor, a couple of doctors, her old boss . . . all mail she should probably return tonight. She dialed her voice mail. A message from her publicist: radio interview at seven the next morning (just when she needed to be rushing the kids up and out for school). One from another doctor she'd called about Michael, asking her to call back tomorrow at three (just as the kids got back home). The final beep sounded, and there was a pause, and then heavy breath, and then a deep, slightly muffled girl's voice and a baby crying in the background. "Hello. Mrs. Adams? This is Keisha."

Eve's mouth fell open. She couldn't believe the girl had even glanced at the card Eve left, let alone kept it and called her.

"I hope it's okay I'm callin' you," the girl said. "It's 'cause, uh, the baby, she's not doing so good. I think she have a fever. My mama's not here, so—I don't know. Well. I gotta go now." The phone clicked.

Eve stood up. The message was from 11:03 this morning. She pushed the caller ID button until the number came up, then glanced at the clock: 8:55. She debated a moment, then made the call, pressing the receiver to her ear.

It rang four times, and then Keisha picked up. "Yeah?" She sounded as if she'd been asleep.

"Keisha? This is Eve Adams. I hope I'm not calling too late. I just got your message."

A deep breath, and then, "That's all right."

"How is the baby? Is she okay?"

"She cry a lot today. I took her to the emergency room."

Eve sat down. *From the ER to me, of all people, with no one in between*, she thought. "Okay," she said. "What did they say?"

"They tell me nurse her a lot. And give her a bottle of water. But she won't take it."

"The water or the breast?"

"Water."

"But she's nursing okay?"

No answer.

"Keisha? Is the baby nursing okay?" Eve said, gently.

"Yeah, I think." The girl sighed. "I don't know if I have enough."

"Milk?"

A pause, and then: "Yeah."

Eve thought a second. "Well, if you're nursing her a lot more than usual, it might take your body a little while to catch up. Are you eating okay?"

"I eat what you say."

"Really? That's great! Do you feel hungry?"

"I don't know. Not really."

"Good," Eve said. "Okay. Then don't worry about the milk, sweetie. As long as the baby's suckling and her diapers are wet. And she doesn't have a fever." There was a sound from upstairs, a blunt slam over Eve's head. She listened a moment but didn't hear anything more. "Um," she continued to Keisha, "if the diapers stop being wet, she could be dehydrated, and you have to get to a doctor right away."

No answer.

"Keisha? What's she doing now? Is she asleep?"

"She just go down, about ten minutes ago. She cry all day."

"Okay. Well. Maybe now you can get some sleep too."

"Yeah. I jus' have my homework."

My God, Eve thought. There was another loud sound from upstairs. What the hell was Magnolia doing? "Listen, Keisha? I'll come see you tomorrow. Okay?"

"Okay. But I have school."

"I know. I'll come when you get home, just like last time. Around 2:15. Okay?"

"Uh-huh."

"Will you be there?"

"Yeah. I have work at four."

"I'll just stay for a little bit." There was one more loud sound from upstairs, and then a door opened. "I have to go now," Eve said. "See you tomorrow." She hung up and went to the bottom of the stairs. "Maggie?" she called.

A door slammed. And then Magnolia barreled downstairs, tears streaming down her face. "I *hate* her!" she screamed. "I *hate* her!"

"Who?" Eve moved out of the way to avoid being crashed into. "Magnolia! Who? What's going on?" She tried to touch her daughter's arm, but the girl squirmed away.

"Emily!" Magnolia sobbed. "Oh my *God,* Mom! She hooked up with *Nate*! That's why she's been avoiding me. They're trying to hide it from me!"

Eve took a deep breath. Emily had come over as recently as a week or two ago, and even then, as she and Maggie stood in the kitchen (in a cloud of cheap perfume, alternately opening their phones to type manically before snapping them shut again—they communicated, it seemed to Eve, with everyone but each other), Eve remembered sensing something wasn't right between them: some former connection or affection—*something*—seemed to have disappeared. And while Maggie had always been the more self-assured one, now it seemed to have reversed: Emily glided around, petite and self-possessed, her teeth a perfect row of white Chiclets, her golden hair newly silky and straight, while Maggie cowered and glowered and tried to disappear. Flipping through a *Teen Vogue*, Emily's dainty fingers had reminded Eve of small honeybees. So, *yes.* She could see why a boy would go for her. But please, not Nate.

"What do you mean?" she asked, stalling. "How do you know that, Mags?"

"*Everyone* knows," Maggie yelled. "Every single person except me. Ugh! I feel like the biggest loser that ever lived." Black mascara formed blotches and smears on her face. "Just—*never mind*!" Maggie sobbed. "You don't understand."

"Magnolia," Eve said, gently but firmly, "calm down. Let's go sit in the kitchen. I'll make us some chamomile tea—"

"Oh my *God,* Mom, you and your fucking tea! I'm out of here."

"Magnolia! You are *not* to go out that door."

Maggie barreled to the door and stormed out. The screen door slammed.

"Magnolia!" Eve ran to the door and opened it. "Maggie!" she yelled after her.

Her daughter was down the steps now and past their front lawn, running awkwardly on her newly long legs. Eve ran back inside, looked around, and threw open the hall closet. Boots, muddy sneakers, and a pair of ancient red clogs she sometimes wore as slippers. She shoved them on. "Mom!" Danny yelled from upstairs. "What are you doing?"

Shit. "Nothing, Dan," she called up, trying and failing not to sound frantic. "Go back to sleep, sweetie. Everything's fine." She rushed out the door, clomping down the steps.

In the street, she looked both ways. To the right, far away, she could just make out a human form. She turned and ran—or as close to running as she could in the dark in the stupid shoes.

At the corner, Maggie turned right, and Eve, when she arrived there, did the same. It took her two more blocks to get within yelling distance of her daughter (who by now had begun to slow down). "Magnolia!" Eve called, from about a half block away. Her feet were killing her, and she was panting hard. "Maggie!" she called again. *"Stop."*

Maggie stopped. She stood there, facing away from her mother, looking down.

Eve walked until she reached her daughter. She stood for a moment, breathing hard. "Come on," she said finally, opting for cool firmness over sympathy or anger, if only because Magnolia had always reacted better to that than to anything else. "We're going back. Danny's there alone."

Without a word, Magnolia turned and, still sniffling, began to walk back with Eve. *Thank you,* Eve said silently.

They walked all the way without talking, Eve keeping them at a clip despite her throbbing feet. It was cool and damp and dark, no moon in sight. She smelled an earthy wood fire, and then a skunk, a smell she'd have appreciated if she hadn't been so tense; it reminded her of pot, which reminded her of the early days with Eric in Brooklyn, when they'd get high in his studio (one or two hits did it for her) and lie on his futon for hours, breathing in hot wax and cold bronze, kissing or sleeping or doing nothing. *And look at us now.* She glanced at Maggie, who had stopped crying, at least. Eve started to say something, then decided against it. *Just get home*, she thought, and for a second she wondered if Maggie would have kept going if Eve hadn't come after her.

As they approached the front porch, she caught sight of Danny, standing outside in his underpants, clutching his skinny body. In the dark (no one ever turned on the porch light except Eric), he looked like a panicked white ghost.

"Danny!" Eve called, rushing up the steps. "Why are you out here like that? I told you to go to sleep!" Maggie brushed past them and into the house.

"You're the one who took off my clothes and didn't even put me in pajamas!" Danny said. "And then you guys wake me up screaming! God!" He started to cry. "Was Magnolia running away from home too?"

"No! No, no." Eve softened her voice, ushering him inside. His skin was ice cold, and though he'd put on some weight since his illness, she could still feel his shoulder blades, sharp and vulnerable beneath his thin skin. "Maggie is fine," she said, forcing calmness into her voice. "And I'm so sorry about the pajamas, sweetheart. It's because you were asleep in the car and I didn't want to wake you even more. Here, let me bundle you up." She grabbed a blanket from the floor (where it always was, no matter how many times she picked it up and folded it) and wrapped it around him. "Sssh," she whispered. "Let's put you right on the couch."

He allowed her to lay him down, and when she sat down next to him, he immediately closed his eyes. She rubbed his back through the blanket. "Go to sleep," she said. "Everything's fine." Upstairs, Maggie's door closed. Not a slam, at least. Eve took a deep breath and let it out. Danny was already almost asleep. She smoothed his hair away from his face, relishing his lovely pink eyelids, his half-sweet, half-sour little boy smell. *Poor baby,* she thought, though she wasn't sure why. But she worried about him. Magnolia, at least, had her rage.

She longed to lie down and snuggle with her son, to feel his silky limbs against hers as they drifted to sleep. But she forced herself up, and then up the steps. Just before she reached Magnolia's room, she remembered the bird and went back and got him. Upstairs again, carrying the cage this time, she knocked on her daughter's door.

"What?" Maggie mumbled.

"It's me. Can I come in?"

No answer. Eve opened the door. Maggie was sitting on her bed, leaning against the wall, holding the stuffed hippopotamus—once pink, now gray—that she'd had since the week of her birth. Her eyes were red and her cheeks were still black with makeup, but at least she'd stopped crying. "How are you doing?" Eve asked.

Maggie shrugged. "Why do you have *that?*" She pointed with her chin at the cage.

"He's lonely," Eve said. "I think he needs company."

Maggie looked at the cage. "He is?" Her voice softened a bit.

"Well, he *has* been alone all weekend," Eve said. "And that after being pulled out of a whole cage full of birds last week and stuck into a strange cage all by himself."

"Oh, that's so sad! Poor little birdie." Maggie sniffed, wiping at her cheeks with her hands. Then she got off her bed and came over to peer into the cage. "Hi, Batman," she said, and then, "I can't believe we named him that." She laughed a little, shaking her head.

Eve smiled. "I think it's a great name."

Maggie shrugged. "He's so pretty," she said after a moment. "Can I pet him?"

"Sure. Give it a shot."

Maggie opened the cage and stuck her hand in gingerly. The bird fluttered around a bit, then settled down, letting her smooth his wing. "He's soft," she said, stroking his back. "Like a little leather glove." She sniffed once more. "Danny's barely gotten to play with him yet."

"He can this week," Eve said. "Tomorrow."

"Doesn't he have kung fu on Mondays?"

"Maybe I'll let him skip it." Eve liked him to go. It was the only athletic thing he did, plus she loved the practice itself: how it taught both confidence and humility, both power and restraint. But Danny hadn't wanted to go last week, and she couldn't imagine how she'd have time to take him tomorrow anyway, with the visit to Keisha and the doctor she was supposed to call. She had to call Michael, too. "I'm so tired," Maggie said, stroking the bird.

Eve nodded. "I bet."

"Mom?" Magnolia looked at her. "Can I sleep in your bed?"

"Sure," Eve said after a brief hesitation. "We'll have a sleepover."

She wondered if she should've said that—Maggie might not like it put that way anymore—but the girl just said, "Let's get Danny too."

"Oh, Mags, I don't know. He'll probably sleep better alone."

"No! He won't, Mom, he never wakes up! Please? Just us three. And Batman. We'll put him near us, so he's not lonely."

Danny needed to be moved from the couch anyway. And the truth was, though she could use a good night's sleep, Eve also loved the idea of all three of them in the bed—like when they were little and Eric went away and the bed was one big stink of diapers and powder and breast milk and sweet baby's breath. The first time, she'd worried that Eric might not love them all being in their bed, but he'd come home and smiled and climbed right in with them.

Not much later (the hell with the work; she'd do it in the morning), crammed between her girl and her boy in her bed, Eve heard Magnolia sobbing again, though this time gently. She reached over and put her arm around her daughter. "You okay?"

Magnolia nodded, her curls bobbing. After a moment, she said, "It's just—my God, Mom. I mean, how could Emily miss the memo that you don't date your best friend's ex-boyfriend who she's still in love with?"

"I don't know, Mags. That was a bad one to miss."

Maggie took a deep breath. "I *love* him, Mom. I loved him and I still do." She turned over to face Eve. "He knows *everything* about me. I told him *everything*. And he's so not like this, the way he acts now. This isn't the real him." She was crying again. "He was mine, for so long, Mom. He was mine! We had each other. And now I can't have him. And I didn't even do anything wrong, except get big and fat and ugly. And that wasn't even my fault."

Eve wiped her daughter's tears even as she felt her own burn. "Don't say that about yourself," she said when she felt she could talk. "You know it's not true."

"It *is* true! And it's not fair. I *love* him! And Emily—she doesn't even *know* him."

"You're right, baby," Eve said. "It's *isn't* fair she gets him right now and you don't. But it'll be okay. I promise." *Oh, the lies parents tell,* she thought. "Shh," she said. "Try to sleep."

Later, after Magnolia had finally conked out and both kids breathed deeply next to her, Eve remembered a conversation she'd once had with Eric about what they would do when their children's hearts broke in love—how, as the parents, they themselves would survive that heartbreak. Now it was happening, and if it was as bad as she'd imagined—worse, even, given the events of tonight—here they were, getting through.

Here *she* was, anyway.

Sometime later, after Eve had fallen asleep too, the phone rang. Eve startled awake, untangling herself from her children as it rang a second time, then a third. Panting, disoriented, she raised herself on her elbows and leaned over Danny to see the caller ID. 520! That was Arizona's area code. Maybe Penelope's number. But Penelope wouldn't call this late. Eric would, though. So he had gone to his mother's after all.

It blared again, and she reached to grab it, then stopped. *No,* she thought. She would not talk to him now. It was after ten, she had a big day tomorrow, and though the ringing hadn't woken the kids, a conversation surely would. *No.* He had made her wait six days to talk to him. She would call him tomorrow.

Or not.

Eve let the phone ring one last time (it would go to voice mail now, finally), then reached for her children. One safely under each arm—her big, dark, fragile, sad girl and her pale, thin, birdlike baby boy—she closed her eyes and, as if the phone call had never happened, was asleep once again.

Part Two

6

ERIC HAD EXPECTED his mother to be home—as if (he realized now, reclining on her porch swing sipping the icy red drink he'd made using vodka from her freezer and a pitcher of berry juice he'd found in her fridge) she had nothing better to do than wait around for him to pop in, no notice at all, from his home 2,500 miles away. Instead, when he pulled up—tired, thirsty, excited to see her, it had been, what? Jesus, almost a year—her small dirt driveway was empty, the old CJ-7 Jeep she'd bought, well-used, fifteen years ago, nowhere in sight. He'd parked and gone inside (door still unlocked, he noted; she'd never been very good about that), and, after greeting Frank and Cherry, her dachshunds; using the bathroom; plugging in his new cell phone, of all things; and glancing around—the place was still the same, sparse in an admirable, minimalist manner, and dusky and dead still in that way of all Tucson places in the afternoon, blinds slammed tight against blinding sun—he'd concocted his drink, downed half and topped it off, then ambled on out here. The dogs were home, so . . . she couldn't have gone very far.

Not that he minded waiting. He loved so much about Tucson: the eerie calm, brought on by the intensity of the heat; the sometimes soothing, sometimes jarring, but always piercingly beautiful desert landscape; the velvety feel of the air—especially now, in the early spring gloaming, so dry and perfectly temperate he couldn't feel where his body ended and the ether began. He liked the town itself too, once you got away from campus and the dumb-blonde-coed element. Of course, like everywhere good anymore, the place had its ultrawealthy newcomers who were snapping up overpriced houses and land (and then immediately squawking for better food, entertainment, education, transportation . . .), as well as its retirement resorts—golf, football-field-sized pools, whatever else well-off aging East Coasters craved. But there were still enough of the Mexicans, Indians, and Anglos who'd spent their lives here—cooks and mechanics, builders and truckers and artists, as parched and worn down as the streets and driveways and benches—to give it the gritty reality he hoped would never disappear.

He took a pull of his drink, gently moving the swing with his foot, noting first the three black widow spiders ensconced in a ceramic pot near the door—all females; you could tell by their trio of red dots—and then the psoriasis patch on his shin, which had finally calmed down, no small thanks to the prescription cortisone Dria just happened to have brought along in her purse. She had eczema, it turned out—similar Rx—so they'd shared the cream for a few days, just as they'd shared conversation and meals and hotel rooms. But not beds. In fact, after that first night, she had behaved like a perfect young woman, while he himself (he'd been extremely relieved to realize), no longer drunk and stoned with her tongue in his mouth and her half-exposed crotch pressed up against his, felt nothing whatsoever toward her except vaguely fatherly. She was an easy, funny girl, curious and quirky—not unlike the way he hoped Magnolia would be once she got past her teenage years.

One of the dogs—Frank, it looked like—appeared at the screen and gave a yap, and Eric rousted himself to let the dog out and pull him up onto his lap. Then he sat back again, enjoying the blood-red Tucson sunset and his mother's scattered cacti (the cartoonish prickly pear, the squat, stubby barrel, and the spiny ocotillos, reaching up their arms as if in some sort of crazy sun dance) and hoping it wasn't a mistake to have brought Dria so far from where she lived. *There are no mistakes,* he had taken to obsessively reciting to himself a year or two ago, no matter how hard he tried to stop.

There is only what you do and what you do not do. The quote came from a movie—some big Diane Lane flick—and was spouted by the hot young French guy who was sleeping with Lane, just before her husband stopped by and bashed in the dude's pretty head with a snow globe. Eric had always wondered if the filmmakers meant that line ironically—given the bleak outcome of its speaker—or if they hadn't really connected the two.

Still, having witnessed this evening's reunion between Dria and her mother, he found it hard to believe he'd done anything wrong. The hugs and tears and squeals of surprise on the tiny cement porch of the cheap, run-down house made his heart, or some inside part of him anyway, feel better than it had in a long time. Even from the car, he could see that the woman was sick—her eyes hollowed, her hair thinning and preternaturally gray. And where the daughter was lean and lanky, the mother was bony and emaciated. After the two women spoke, the mother shuffled out to his car, holding a sweater tight around her chest in the heat, and tearfully thanked him for bringing back her girl. *And will you come in for a meal?* she asked, though not confidently—he figured the asshole husband lurked inside. "Thanks, but no," he'd said, anxious to move on anyway, find a phone and call Eve (he had no excuse now) and get on to his own mother's house. Dria hugged him good-bye through the window and made him promise to keep in touch. And then he was back on the road with a sigh of relief—not that he'd minded having her with him. Not at all. But being alone was its own luxury now that work was out of the question.

Eric shifted the dog so he could massage his lower back. The road had been good for him, as always. He'd seen things—not all pleasant, of course, but still, the things that were out there, the greater world he so rarely saw anymore. A car slamming into a skunk, the creature flying up and then falling, bloody, to the side of the highway, spraying as it fell; he could smell the spray, immediate and pungent, as he drove on. A storm, green and oddly pink clouds, rolling in like fast-moving lava, and then parting—an egg cracked in half—to release a wall of shimmery rain. And night falling and day rising, the sun migrating across the sky, not just once or twice but again and again. *"Again?"* a friend once told him he and his wife said to each other every morning on waking, like *Are you kidding?* But the world wasn't kidding. You got up and did it, day after day. That was the point, wasn't it?

And when you stopped wanting to—well, that's when you got in trouble. When the game you picked or fell into—whether it was creating beautiful things, or teaching people, or having babies, or doing good, or simply getting rich—when the game held no joy between the moments of pressure and sadness, that's when you'd better watch out.

Eric downed the rest of his drink, not wanting to go back to that dark place he'd spent so long in at home, wishing he could just chill here for a while before he caught up to himself. He would start by refreshing his drink. He put the dog down and stood up. But he heard a car, and behind the grapefruit tree (from which, he knew, you could pluck a yellow-white ball and suck the warm, sweet juice right out of the skin), his mother's midnight blue Jeep rolled in.

The dog waddled down the steps and raced toward her. "Frank!" Penelope said, stepping out of the car and practically onto him. "Why are you—" She glanced toward the house, caught sight of Eric, blinked, squinted, and then her mouth opened. "David? David!" She laughed, loudly and gaily. "My heavens, what are you doing here?"

He laughed too. "Just passing through town," he joked as he came toward her, and they embraced like long-lost friends. In her khaki shorts and hiking boots, skin gently tanned and aglow, silver hair pulled loosely back with stray pieces about her face, she looked healthy, happy—fantastic, really. She was just back from a hike with her friend Dorothy, it turned out. "It's her birthday, seventy-four," she warbled, "and I was going to cook her a dinner to celebrate, but she was so pooped by the end I just took her home. And how perfect: now you're here and I have someone to eat all this food with!" An hour later—she'd showered, fed the dogs, set the table, and made the meal, all without letting him lift a finger—they were seated at her old wood table. The steaming dish was chickpeas, spinach, and tofu sausage. (Since a breast cancer scare in her fifties, she'd avoided meat.) There was crusty bread and a block of Parmesan and lit candles and newly full glasses of red wine. His mouth watered at the sight, after the days of fast food and junk food and too much caffeine, and for the first time in ages, he felt hungry.

She clinked his glass and served him a hefty portion, and he dug in. "You know you have black widow spiders in that urn on your porch, Mom," he said, and he put the food in his mouth. Delicious. Smoky, salty—familiar, too, somehow.

"Oh, yes, aren't they perfect?" Her gray-green eyes sparkled.

"They're poisonous, Mom," he said, slightly amused. As if she didn't know that.

She waved her hand. "Only if they bite you. And why would they bite me? I like them."

"What if they bite Frank or Cherry, then? Or the mailman?"

"Well, if he's sticking his hand in their home, they have every right to." She laughed—it was one of the things people loved about her, that hearty, genuine laugh—then cocked her head at him. "Now, you're not about to start hounding me too, are you? Beth was down last week, and she nagged me for two straight days: My car is too old, my house doors should be locked, I need more vitamin D." She shook her head, then grinned. "Oh, David, I'm so happy to see you! Though it *is* too bad you missed Bethy. She'd have been thrilled." Beth was his middle sister, who lived outside Phoenix and did marketing for a natural dog food company. His oldest sister, Frannie, was a freelance copy editor in LA. "What brings you out here?" Penelope asked. She took a bite of food, chewed thoughtfully, then nodded her approval at the dish.

Eric shrugged. "Needed to get away, I guess. Got on the road, and next thing I knew, I was here."

"Huh. So Eve and the kids aren't coming, then." She looked at him, and he saw a questioning look cross her eyes. But she wouldn't push it, he knew. Even at her job, she was the kind of therapist who sat patiently waiting for you to be ready to tell your deepest secrets, not the kind who got all proactive and nudgy. "How's Magnolia?"

she asked, grating Parmesan onto her plate. "And Danny? And Eve! We haven't spoken in ages."

"Danny's great."

"Thank goodness."

He nodded. "Magnolia is . . . she gives Eve a run for her money."

Penelope laughed. "I bet, at fourteen. But Eve handles it beautifully, I'm sure."

He nodded again, broke off a piece of bread. "Her book is in its second printing. Not big printings, but the publisher seems happy. And she's having fun. She's doing radio interviews. A good number, actually." He took a deep breath. "She thinks it might even make some money."

"Oh, that's wonderful!"

"Yeah. We can use it." It was the first time he'd said that out loud, and though he had to work not to cringe, he was surprised afterward to feel some relief.

"And your work?" she asked. "What are you making these days?"

He shrugged. "Nothing." He took a large sip of wine.

"You're between projects, then," she said after a moment. "Are you teaching?"

He shook his head. "Took the semester off. Trying to jump-start myself."

His mother nodded. "It'll happen," she said, and he knew she believed that. His mother was so unlike him, with her confidence, her optimism, her ability to pick up and change things when they didn't please her. Maybe that's why they'd always gotten on so well.

So he must be more like his father, then. Dark and broody, Jewish, intense—at least from what he'd heard. "This food is so good," he said suddenly. "I feel like I've had it before."

"Well, you have, I'm sure, because Eve gave me the recipe. Or maybe I gave it to her. Who knows, it was ages ago." She laughed, like a song. "But she probably uses real chorizo, not the fake stuff, like I do. I'm sure it's much better that way."

Ah, yes. It was at home that he'd had it. Though not for a long time. Years, even. Maggie hadn't liked it, probably, so Eve had stopped making it. "So how are you?" he asked his mother, hoping to stay off the topic of himself.

"Oh, I'm good. I really am." She pushed her plate away, pulling her wineglass toward her. "Working only about a third of the time these days. Not for a lack of clients—everyone still needs a therapist, it seems, despite yoga and life coaches and everything else they've got going on now." She laughed. "But this is just right. Gives me time to sing in my chorus, do my book clubs . . . you know, all my silly things. I even still go on a date now and then."

He raised his eyebrows.

"They always disappoint me, of course." She laughed again. "No, I'm just kidding. I actually like almost all of them quite a bit."

"So it's not true that there are no good men left out there?" He smiled.

"Absolutely not! You just have to be willing to get out of your comfort zone." She sipped her wine. "For example, the last man I went out with was, let's see. Fifty-four? No. Fifty-three."

Jesus! Practically his age. "Robbed the cradle, hey?" he managed.

She laughed. "More like he robbed the coffin." She sipped her wine. "If you must know, he pursued me so vigorously I finally had to say yes to get him off my back."

Eric nodded. He didn't doubt it. "So how was it?" he asked after a beat.

"Oh, it was fine." Her voice almost trilled. "Perfectly lovely, really. Just—not enough to give up any more of my solitude than I already do. Honestly, sometimes I have more on my calendar now than when you kids were young." She waved dismissively. "Well, you know, one has to be social; otherwise all manner of terrible things might happen." She laughed, then sighed. "Still, I suppose it *is* nice to be able to pick and choose when to see people and when not to. Better than the alternative, I suppose."

He worried about her now and then, out here alone, but he had to admit she seemed absolutely radiant. How the hell did she do it? *So much for marriage making you healthier*, he couldn't help thinking. Some eight years ago, when she was around sixty-two,

Penelope had divorced for the third time—her choice, as with husband two, not to mention with several serious interim boyfriends. (She'd always laughed at the term. "My word, calling someone in his sixties a boy!") She couldn't stand his narcissism, she said of Three—"He has full-blown narcissistic personality disorder. To think I married him without diagnosing that!"—though they were still friends, as she was with the husband before him. Eric's father, in contrast—Husband One—was long out of the picture and not in touch with any of them.

"So how long did it take you to drive out?" his mother was asking. "You stopped along the way, I hope."

"A few times. I drove with someone, actually. A girl who babysits the kids. She has a sick mother in Hatback, so . . . I took her there."

"That was nice of you, David." She sat back a second and looked at him. "You don't mind that I still call you David, do you? I know I, of all people, should be able to switch." She was referring, he knew, to her lifelong attitude about change. (*Change is good*! she'd always told them. *Change is healthy*!) "But I don't know," she said. "When you have a baby and call him David all his life, well—it just feels too odd and self-conscious to call you something else now. Though if it bothers you, I really will try."

"No. I like it." It made him feel cozy. Connected to his past. And anyway, he saw her point. When Danny hit his teens and changed his name to Demetrius, or Dragon, Eric would still call him Danny. He thought of his son, sitting thoughtfully over a half-built Lego—pursed lips, milky face—and he missed him, suddenly and intensely.

"Well, I'm glad you don't mind, then." His mother smiled, then stood to clear plates, and he rose to help her. When they'd finished loading her tiny dishwasher, she turned on the kettle and brought out a small, square homemade cake. "Carrot," she said, setting it on the table. "Buttercream icing. It was supposed to be for Dot, but oh well." She laughed. "Shall I make coffee or tea?"

"Whichever you prefer."

She brought them each a mug of peppermint tea, then cut hunks of cake—his large, hers none too shabby either—and placed them on two lovely faded china plates. Healthy or not, his mother was no puritan. Like Eve. It was one of the things he loved about both of them.

For a second, he wished Eve were there. She would have enjoyed this. He took a bite of the cake. "Tell me about my father," he said, though he hadn't planned to.

His mother stopped pushing her tea bag around and looked up, first surprised, then thoughtful. "You haven't asked me that in so long," she said, and then, "Do you remember the year you made me talk about him every day for a month straight?"

Eric nodded. "I was what, like, fourteen?"

"Probably. Yes."

"And then I didn't ask about him again for a decade."

His mother smiled. "And barely then either."

"Because I wasn't interested by that point. I knew he'd never be a part of my life. And I didn't really mind, I don't think." He took a cautious sip of tea; his mother drank it very hot, despite the heat in the air. "Anyway, I still remember almost everything you said that month," he said. "But maybe I'll get something different from it this time."

"Well, okay, then. What would you like to know?"

"Why did he leave us?"

Penelope looked at him. "Actually, I left him."

"You did?" He stared at her, astonished.

"If you want to get technical."

"But you never told me that. Did you?"

"Probably not that bluntly. Not at that age, anyway. You were too young. And, of course, I didn't want you to hate me." She looked at him defensively. "But honestly, David, it's not like he didn't have one foot out the door already anyway. I mean, I cut him free, but he took off like the wind. I saw him exactly twice after that. You kids were there for one of the times."

"In Colorado. Right?"

She nodded. "Remember? He popped in, took one look at you all, and did an about-face. I think it just confirmed for him that he'd done the right thing to leave. Or, sorry . . . to let *me* leave. *Us.* To never come after us in any way." She glanced into her tea, then looked up at Eric. "Your father loved me, but he had no idea how to be a husband. And he was a lousy father to you kids. He had zero interest. Of course, some of that was the times: fathers weren't involved with their children the way they are now. But to let your wife and three children walk out of your life and never even protest or send a dime . . ." She shrugged, then smiled a little. "It proved everything I'd thought about him."

Eric poured some more wine, digesting her words. "So you never loved him, then." He was surprised to feel disappointed.

She looked up. "Oh, but I did! He was handsome, and charming, and *so* smart—well, at least when he was in a good phase." She thought a moment, then said, "He just wasn't meant to be a father. And I *was* meant to be a mother. So I pushed him, and he gave in, and then I pushed him again, and—" She smiled. "And then one last time, because everyone had three kids back then, and I wanted my boy. And I got him. And here he is, right at my table." She grinned, both victorious and adoring, and then took a deep breath. "But after that, it was time to go, because your father didn't want to share me with kids."

Eric was listening intently. She had told him things, yes, but never like this.

"I wanted a man who was either there for the kids and for me, or not there at all," Penelope said. "Because for what you give up for marriage—autonomy and sexual freedom, to name two pretty huge things—you'd better get something good in return. You'd better get a *lot.* Financial support, great friendship, a good parenting partner . . . one of them at the very least."

"But you did get one of them," Eric said. "He made money. Didn't he?"

"Sometimes. Again, it depended on the year, on what he had going on. He'd get involved with his friends, real estate, or they'd invest in something. He usually could eke out a decent living when he was around. Though once he was gone, I was on my own in all ways."

She smoothed a piece of hair off her forehead. "But that was okay. Because at that point, I realized I'd rather have none of it than just the money. I wanted more. Or less." She took a sip of tea. "So after he left, we weren't wealthy. In fact, we were poor." She laughed. "But so what? We made do. We did just fine, in fact. Don't you think?"

"We did," he said after a moment, but he remembered what Dria had said: *Maybe it was the loss of your father that made you an artist—the need to channel that sadness, that loss.* He thought about that briefly, then dismissed the thought. *So what if it was? There are no mistakes.* He pushed away his cake. "Was he like me?" he asked.

"Your father?" She looked at him a moment. "Well, I don't know, actually. I mean, certainly your looks—he was tall and thin and dark like you. I'm sorry I don't have more photos." She smiled. "Your complexion is his. Your expressions, too, I think." It was true. His mother was all light: open eyes, sunny demeanor, optimism. *Like Eve,* he realized, *but without the impatience and anger.* Though maybe his mother had had that too back then.

"But I mean," he persisted, "do I act like him, are my—my mannerisms—"

She waited for him to finish. When he didn't, she said, "He was a businessman. You're an artist. It's hard to compare." She thought a second. "You're much more involved with your kids."

"I *am*?"

She looked at him. "Of course."

He was silent. But he thought, with a level of emotion that took him aback, *I wish I were even more involved!* It was true. But for so many years he had been working. Working and working. Just like his father, maybe. And when he'd finally looked up—more by default than for any other reason—Eve was already doing everything, and beautifully at that. He shook his head. "It's too late," he said, as much to himself as to his mother.

"It's never too late," she said, and her eyes flashed with something—possibly anger. For a second he wondered if, had his father come back at some point, his mother would have welcomed him in spite of herself.

But no. Somehow he didn't really think so. "Women have so much power," he said suddenly. "They get to decide, *and* they get the kids."

"I suppose that's true," she conceded after a moment. "The smart, brave ones, anyway. The ones who aren't afraid."

He didn't answer.

His mother was looking at him. "David, are you okay?" she asked. "You seem a little—" She shook her head suddenly. "Never mind. I should stay out of your affairs."

He almost wished she wouldn't. He could use the help.

But she stood up briskly and began clearing the table. "Well, I for one am bushed," she said. "Dot and I hiked ten miles today! If you're staying awhile, I'll take you on that hike if you want. It's wonderful. We saw a roadrunner and two horned toads, and Dot almost stepped on a fat rattler. Luckily, she's a tough old bird, like me, so we kept right on going." She laughed, then waved her hand. "Oh, leave those dishes. I'll do them tomorrow. The bed is all made up in the guest room. Towels in the closet, as always. Do you need anything else?"

He shook his head. For a moment, he just looked at her. She was so beautiful—strong and self-possessed, all silver and gold and warm energy. He remembered a quote she used to recite to them, by the poet Mary Oliver: "Tell me, what is it you plan to do/with your one wild and precious life?" Clearly, she was doing what she wanted with hers. And was that a state of mind, or what you actually did? *Surely both,* he answered himself. "Dinner was perfect," he said to her. "Thank you."

She came over and hugged him. "Thank *you.* For coming thousands of miles to see your old mother."

"You're not old. And you're worth it. Plus, I like to drive."

She laughed. "Maybe next year I'll move to California, then. Sleep well." She scuttled off, calling back, "And do sleep in tomorrow. I'm taking the phone off the hook. My friends never hesitate to phone at 5:30 AM to check in."

The room felt empty without her; immediately, he felt his spirits start to sag. He finished clearing the table, then washed the bowls and pans despite her instructions not to. He turned off all the lights but one lamp, then glanced at the charging cell phone. Too late to try Eve again.

But not too late to text Magnolia! If she wasn't awake—and she'd better not be, at this hour—she'd simply get the text in the morning.

He sat down, opened the phone, found his contacts list (Dria had put in Magnolia, shown him how to use it—amazingly, the girl had his own daughter's cell number in her phone, while Eric didn't even know it, and began to type. *Hey mags.* Jesus, those keys were small! And typing words took forever. *just had dinner with grandma,* he pecked out. *youd have liked it. well xcept 4 the food.* He smiled. *anyway how are you doing. hows school.* He thought for a moment, then wrote, *i know we havent talked 4 awhile. but im listening if you want to.* He reread what he'd written (now he understood why kids used all that gibberish—it took hours to type this stuff), then added: *tell Danny to write me 2 if he wants. will you show him how.* He didn't know how to do a question mark. He paused, sitting back. A clock ticked somewhere.

please give mom my number, he finished. *ill try her again 2. i love you."* He pressed Send, wondered briefly if he should have waited for her to write back first (what if his messages only annoyed her?), then closed the phone and replaced it on the counter. So, okay. He could get used to this cell phone thing if this was how everyone did it now.

He sat back, thinking, scratching his leg. The thing was, the one time he'd called the cell phone company, it had left him feeling despondent for days—and after that, he'd just wanted to swear off the whole mess forever. He still recalled the conversation, so many times had he played it back in his head, wondering, honestly, if he really and truly just didn't fit into the world anymore. He had called to up the minutes on their family cell phone plan; Magnolia had gone $92 over talking to her friends, and Eve had freaked out, because, among other things, the bill arrived the same week her book appeared, on a day she had interviews with two local papers (he'd been as thrilled for her as he was shocked; who'd have thought?), plus her regular clients, plus Danny home with a fever and sore throat. She was squawking like a chicken at all of them, but when he offered to help (he had said he'd stay home with Danny that morning if she needed him to; he'd have welcomed the reprieve, actually), she'd glanced up from her computer and, almost as if annoyed he'd offered, said, "What? Oh. No. Just go, it's fine." He'd caught the subtext, or thought he had: *Go make money. You do your job, and I'll do mine.*

But that night, after doing his so-called job all day (he had sat in his office, smoked a cigarette he didn't want, surfed the Internet looking for inspiration he didn't find, eaten the lunch Eve had packed him, thought about pulling a long-ago-started sculpture from its drop cloth in the back but couldn't face it, etc. etc.), he'd come home and, finding her going ballistic about the phone bill, volunteered to deal with it. It was usually her turf; she liked the phone, she could banter, she knew what to say. But they only needed to find out what the next plan up was. How hard could it be?

She said yes, gratefully, handing him the phone. But when he called, every time he asked the question, or tried to, the person on the other end (if it even was a person; he had his doubts, though she had introduced herself with a name, Brandi, or Candi, or maybe Désirée) seemed to respond with a cheerfully phony answer to a completely different question. He had already given her his name and address and Eve's Social Security number and mother's maiden name, and he'd punched in her cell phone number (she was the account holder, not he) no fewer than four times just to get to Désirée. And even though this person referred to him as Mr. Adams numerous times (why, oh why, did they ask for your name if they didn't use it anyway?), he thought this at least was a sign that she had some information about his actual account in front of her. But when he said, "We're on the 700-minute plan, and we've gone over this month. What is the next level up, and how much does it cost?" she replied, in a pitch so high he wondered if she'd just inhaled helium, "Uh-huh, yes, if you bear with me a moment, Mr. Adams,

I'll do my best to assist you with this situation. Let me access your file. Can you run your soshe by me once more? Thank you for your patience! No worries! I'm showing that you have three lines and one has gone over by eight minutes and line two by no minutes while line three has gone over by 465 minutes."

He blinked. "We get 700 minutes total, right?" he said. "For all three phones?"

"Uh-huh. Bear with me a moment, Mr. Adams, so I can help you with that inquiry. You had the America's Choice 700 plan, and that plan was phased out. We can upgrade you to the Nationwide Calling Plan, which provides free service nights and weekends and unlimited text messaging."

"But don't we already have all that?" Even an idiot like him knew that nights and weekends were free.

"Correct. Exactly. Like I said, you already had all those benefits, but you had the old plan, the America's Choice plan, which no longer exists. You were grandfathered in."

Eric was in the living room, trying not to bother Eve, who was on her computer in the kitchen. Magnolia was MIA, and Danny was coming in and out of the room, tossing a rubber-band ball and singing, in his pure, sweet, high voice, a Nine Inch Nails song he no doubt learned from his sister about needles and drugs and hurting yourself. Eric massaged his temple. "So, uh. How, I mean, what does the new plan have that the old one didn't?"

"Well, bear with me a moment as I do my best to access that information, Mr. Adams, our systems are a bit slow this morning. Okay, here it is, *no problem*! With the new plan, Mr. Adams, you could upgrade to 3,600 minutes spread out over all three phones, for $365 a month, and you'd get the benefits of—"

He laughed. "$365 a month? We pay $70 now. We don't need 3,600 minutes. We have 700 now, and this is the first time we've ever gone over. What is the *next* level up?"

He heard shuffling, the voices of other reps talking. ("What have I become," sang Danny. "My sweetest friend,/Everyone I know,/ Goes away in the end . . .") "Right," said his rep. "Of course. I completely understand. Bear with me, Mr. Adams." (Was she in labor? Did machines even *go* into labor?) "Like I said, the next level up, which is the Nationwide Calling plan—because, like I said, we no longer offer the America's Choice package . . ."

It had gone on and on and on like this. He persevered—what choice did he have?—and, no less than 45 minutes later, he *seemed* to have succeeded in changing their plan from 700 to 1,400 minutes for an additional $35 a month, though he had no confidence that that's what he'd actually done, as he couldn't get the rep/machine to confirm his new plan. "You can log on to our Web site to access that data, Mr. Adams," she/it had recited, but when he tried, the system was down, and when it came back up, he couldn't get his password to work, and when he tried to have it sent to his e-mail address to confirm, it never arrived. And when the bill did come, it showed that they'd become the proud owners of three or four new paid features he'd never heard of, one of them allowing Magnolia to access the Internet from her cell phone. Eve had rolled her eyes, sighed, and reached for the phone. Within five minutes, she had gotten them to remove all the new features plus take off Maggie's overcharges from last month, all if they agreed to go up to the next-level-up plan—which, of course, was what Eric had been trying to do in the first place.

Eric stood up, walked through his mother's kitchen, and wandered out the back door.

In the desert at night, the scorpions came out in droves; if you shined a UV light on the ground in the foothills, he'd been told, you would see the iridescent bodies shining all over, throngs of moving desert jewels. He walked around to the front of the house, stopping at his car to retrieve the pack of cigarettes he kept hidden in the glove compartment. He carried it back to the swing and sat again, looking now not at the sunset but at the moon, a shiny half-quarter—maybe waxing, maybe waning, who the hell ever knew? (He remembered Danny once asking, at dinner, "Dad, doesn't Neil Armstrong own the moon?" and Magnolia answering, as usual before he could, "No, stupid, America owns the moon!" And all four of them laughed.)

Eric shook out a cigarette and the matches he'd stashed with the box. He had asked Eve, not long ago, if she thought it was arrogant to be an artist. "*Arrogant?*" she'd said (rather arrogantly, he noticed), and then she stopped for a second to think. "No! The arrogance comes only in assuming you're any good at it. I mean, it's okay to *think* you're good, I would think you would *have* to, just to keep doing it." She looked at him briefly but didn't wait for a comment. "But no, it's not arrogant to *do* it. It's your job to do it. How is it any more arrogant than running a company or, I don't know, teaching children? You're just trying to make sense of the world for people. Or to re-create the beauty or the pain of something. Or to take what's out there—" she waved her hand, as if it were that easy "—and put it into something, I don't know. Tangible. Real. That people can *see*." She sniffed. "Now, to *not* do it just because you might not do it perfectly, *that* to me is arrogance."

He could not help taking it as a reprimand.

Eric put the cigarette between his lips. If only she knew the desperation of being unable to create when people were counting on you to produce.

He lit the cigarette and took a long drag. *And for what?* He blew out the smoke, enjoying, after days of hiatus (he hadn't smoked since leaving the East, hadn't even thought to), the familiar mint-cherry smell, the vague burn of tobacco penetrating his lungs and whatever else inside him. So much of modern life, it seemed to him, was about producing. Starting from the minute we were old enough to want to sleep in or relax, we were taught to resist those urges and rush rush rush: out of bed, shove down breakfast, off to school, speed to work, where the people with "real jobs"—the few he knew, anyway—spent half the day e-mailing friends, surfing the Web, and talking to coworkers, if not fucking them in the wheelchair-accessible bathroom. The artists, in contrast, rushed to studios so they could sit there and ponder and stew and obsess. Eventually, of course, they all had to produce, create, innovate: make things, advance things, put something out there. You had to build things, or change things, "improve" things somehow, even if you actually made them worse. "Thneeds," as the brilliant Dr. Seuss called it in *The Lorax*. You had to make Thneeds: something "everyone, EVERYONE, *EVERYONE* needs!"

Eric leaned back, put his feet up, took another long drag. And in the end, when the villages were razed and species of creatures destroyed, all for the vital cause of making the Thneeds, what had you created? Technology so advanced that no one even knew how to use it, even as it usurped the only slightly older methods everyone had finally learned. Microwaves that caused cancer, Teflon pans that caused cancer, cell phones that not only caused cancer but cut you off midsentence and made it impossible to hear the person you were talking to, because in the race to have service in so many places—ever more than the competitors!—the service was so half-assed and shoddy that an actual conversation was out of the question. But no matter, because soon enough cell phones would be obsolete anyway, replaced by chips inserted in our brains that allowed us to communicate just by thinking—if thinking still existed by then.

And for what? The question, for him, came up again and again. *Speed + stress + stuff + innovation* added up to . . . what, exactly? Were things actually better than they used to be? Sometimes he thought he was the only one asking.

Eric stared out into the night. It wasn't that he hadn't loved making his sculptures. It wasn't that he didn't think they were beautiful or that they didn't have a place. But why did he have to keep making them when there didn't seem to be any that needed making at the moment? When whatever he made now would feel wrong, unworthy, even as the process of making them was no longer fun or inspired or exciting, but at best monotonous, at worst pure torture?

He shook his head suddenly, as if shaking a fly off his face, then stubbed out his cigarette. He had officially caught up to himself. Even here. *Wherever you go, there you are,* he thought—even here, in this still, dark Tucson night, the sweet smell of citrus blossoms on the breeze, the air a perfect velvet dome around him.

He stood up, went back inside, passed through the kitchen once more and into the bathroom this time, and then into his room. After slipping off his clothes and putting on only clean white socks (from the pack he'd bought, along with a toothbrush and T-shirts and underwear, along the way), he slid into his neat little bed. It had cool, clean sheets, a beautiful quilt his mother had probably made. He pulled them over him, surprised by the lightness. At home, Eve slept year-round under pounds of blankets; she liked the weight on her. Early in their marriage, he had tried to get her to shed some of them—really, it was like sleeping in a goddamn sarcophagus!— but she had flat-out refused, and eventually, for lack of alternative other than sleeping away from her, he'd gotten used to it: waking up drenched, his sweaty, disheveled wife next to him snoring pleasantly, wrapped in her flannel pajamas at least ten months a year.

Well. Tonight he would not have to sweat.

He rolled over, facing the ceiling. So it had been his mother, not his father, who left. But his father hadn't chased them. He hadn't wanted them back, or not enough to fight for them, anyway. He almost wondered if his mother had left purely to put him to the test.

He wondered if Eve missed him now. Or was she relieved to have him gone?

And then he stopped wondering, and his son's pure sweet voice came to him again, finishing the song he'd started during the awful cell phone company call:

You could have it all,
My empire of dirt.
I will let you down.
I will make you hurt.

Eric had read somewhere that this was the last song Johnny Cash recorded before he died. He fell asleep hoping it wasn't true. He had loved that crazy old man.

7

EVE SAT AT the packed food court in the Bloom-field Mall, drinking cheap, crappy coffee and playing a depressing game she sometimes couldn't help playing in places like this: find twenty people—just twenty out of the hundred or more in her view—who weren't overweight. She looked around. Three tables to her right, a couple of thinnish thirtysomething white women (dark blue suits, name tags) sat together, eating sandwiches from brown bags. And a few chairs to her left, a petite, raw-faced mother uncapped milk containers from Happy Meal boxes for her three yellow-haired, anemic-looking kids. Six, already! She found one hottish black guy on the Burger King line; a slim Asian couple contemplating (while dodging two manic sample offerers) the "Japanese" place; and a trio of teenage boys, one normal weight, two still rail thin, emerging from Friendly's. Other than that, though—oh wait, there was a skinny "redhead" (dark brown roots) at Sbarro, though she was *too* skinny, Eve saw, and dressed oddly, in short shorts and high heels, with bruises on her legs. Probably a heroin addict. Eve decided to count her anyway.

But other than that, she couldn't see much of anyone who wasn't carrying at least twenty extra pounds, and most of them considerably more. To her immediate right, a corpulent mother and her three portly children sat eating plates of watery pasta, a fluorescent-blue drink at each child's place. To her left, a middle-aged man alternately chomped onion rings and a multilayered sandwich and guzzled sips of Coke from a can, chin bulging atop his collar and tie, gut exploding over his pants. Directly in front of her sat four women—two Latina, it looked like, two white—three of them short and large-chested, their stretchy black pants and spike heels evident under the table, eating from plastic plates of orange meat and bright yellow rice and limp, oil-soaked vegetables. The fourth—a human beach ball with pillowy lips, a pretty face, and an enormous head of plastered-down ginger curls—picked at a salad and sipped demurely from a lidded cup the size of a small bucket. *Diet something, no doubt,* Eve thought. The serious dieters were almost always the heaviest.

Eve knew the stats well: more than two-thirds of the country was now overweight; a third of those were obese, with a body mass index of more than 30. Many of these were children—kids who would never know what it was like to sprint toward an end zone or round the bases, who often, in fact, could barely heave themselves up a staircase or out of a car. They couldn't touch their toes or ride a bike or see their own feet in the shower. And what difference, Eve sometimes thought, did it make if we'd cured polio and TB and smallpox if what we'd come to was a time and place of raising children so fat their legs grew in bowed from carrying so much weight; an era in which, for the first time in more than two centuries, our life expectancy—purely because of obesity and its resultant health effects—was shorter than that of our parents?

It was tragic, not least because, as Eve knew, most of these people, if not all of them, desperately wanted to lose weight. She watched an extremely large family walk by, the father a potbellied stump in gargantuan shorts and a Red Sox T-shirt, the mother's eyes buried in her swollen, bloated face, the boys—both well under twelve—two soda-toting blimps, feet flat as notebooks, legs widely spread. Around them—all over, it seemed to Eve—bloblike people waddled or limped by. Why, she wondered yet again, had the nutrition establishment failed to teach people how to stay reasonably thin—from how much to eat to how to stay away from the toxic sludge that so often passed for food these days? Yes, today's life-styles forced us all to sit on our spreading asses for hours on end, barely moving anything but our eyes and our hands. But *still,* it seemed that nutritionists, dieticians, and institutions like Beardsley somehow ought to do better than this.

On the filthy white plastic-mesh table, Eve's cell phone beeped. "New Text Message" flashed in the miniature window, and for a second she allowed herself to imagine it was Eric. But he never texted her, only Magnolia. He never called her either, for that matter, though that was her doing as much as his, if not more. In the beginning—almost a month ago now—after the initial days of no contact, he had called every day for a week, and she had neither picked up the phone nor returned his calls. *That's what you get,* she'd thought, again and again, as it rang, the caller ID flashing some Arizona number (it wasn't Penelope's, and Magnolia later confirmed it was his). But then he'd stopped calling. It had thrown her a little. She hadn't really expected that.

And it pissed her off, frankly. So, now he was actually *abandoning* them? When she let herself really think about it, which was as little as possible, she found it alternately enraging, terrifying, and absurd.

The most Eve could get from Magnolia was that he was in Arizona at his mother's, "taking a break"—a scenario that seemed even more likely to Eve because, uncharacteristically, Penelope hadn't called or e-mailed since he left. (Admittedly, Eve hadn't called or written her either, though she knew it was for different reasons: Penelope was likely respecting Eric's privacy and not getting involved, while Eve couldn't bear to tell Eric's mother he'd run away with the babysitter, or even that he'd run away—especially if she already knew.) The good news about him being at his mother's was that he probably wasn't with the bimbo. Even with Penelope's unusual liberalness about that sort of thing, Eve couldn't imagine she'd encourage Eric to bring his virtually underage mistress to her house—not that he'd have the balls to do that anyway. And he was still texting Maggie, a few times a day, from what Eve gathered. At least there was that. Still: *Screw* him. She was doing just fine without him. She hoped he was enjoying himself.

She opened the text, something Magnolia had taught her how to do just a few days ago. *Were at Abercrombie come now pleez*, it said.

Eve sighed. The other half of the *we* in *were* was Magnolia's new friend, Alexis, who had appeared at their house a couple of weeks ago wearing a tight white wifebeater T-shirt with a visible red bra (over an ample, ample chest), dark red eye shadow, glove-tight black jeans that descended into high-heeled fake snakeskin boots, and a silver stud in her tongue that made her lisp half her words. She had appeared once more the next day (same outfit save a gray wifebeater this time), the girls grabbing the package of Fig Newmans and the entire large container of organic strawberries Eve had just splurged on and closing themselves into Maggie's room (and devouring all of both before they emerged). After that, Magnolia had taken to leaving the house on nice nights after dinner to "take a walk with Alexis" for an hour or two. "You're always telling me to exercise," she had said to Eve the first night, and what could Eve say? It was true.

Eve knew little about Alexis beyond her appearance, except that she was older than Magnolia (Eve had tried and failed to get an exact age) and seemed to have taken an instant liking to Maggie, who admittedly, since her new friend's appearance, seemed to have come out of her depression over the Nate and Emily mess. That was something, Eve knew. And better that her daughter had a new friend than no friends at all. But, go ahead and shoot her, Eve didn't trust this girl. Worse, Magnolia had suddenly stopped confiding in Eve or even really talking to her much since Alexis had appeared. "So, where'd you go?" Eve would ask casually when Magnolia returned at 8:30 or 9:00—always having done her homework before she left, always returning by curfew. "Oh, nowhere," Maggie would say. "Just around." "With anyone else besides Alexis?" Eve would persist, and again the answer would come back sweet and elusive: "Couple of her friends." "Guys or girls?" Eve knew that now she was crossing the line, but her daughter just laughed. "*God*, Mom! Nosy much?"

And Eve again would back off, for better or worse. Maggie was a good kid, doing well in school. . . . She deserved a little space.

Still, Eve had offered her daughter this trip to the mall mainly to spend time with her—though she also allowed that Magnolia needed clothes, having outgrown almost everything she owned. She'd asked Priscilla and Ronnie if they'd have Danny for the few hours, offering to reciprocate with Star and Stream this weekend. And much as she disliked the Bloomfield Mall, she'd looked forward to the excursion with Maggie. But at the last minute, Alexis had appeared, and Magnolia had invited her along. So much for their cozy mother-daughter outing.

Now the two girls traversed the mall while Eve waited in the food court for texts from her daughter telling her where to show up and present her credit card. (She'd already charged Maggie underwear and pajamas before being shooed off again.) Eve sighed once more, dumped her phone in her purse, and tossed her cup on top of the pile overflowing the trash can. Weaving through the crowds (big, sticky strollers, young women and their own young mothers yelling at whining toddlers, walls of trashy-looking twelve-year-olds), she got on the escalator behind a heavy middle-aged couple who stood side by side, blocking her from proceeding until the moving stairway delivered them to the floor of their destination without their having to climb a single stair.

"Hello-how-are-you," sneered the skimpily dressed salesgirl at Abercrombie in a nasal monotone, giving Eve a blunt once-over before openly frowning. Eve ignored her, coughing in the thickly perfumed air (she imagined the smell, which seemed to be pumped in through the vents, to be a combination of semen, some man-made chemical designed to make you buy more stuff, and something chosen specifically to make anyone over twenty-one gag), and headed toward the dressing rooms, her gaze unwittingly drawn to the half-naked girls and boys having poster-sex on any wall not covered with shelves of clothing. In spite of herself, she glanced at the price tag on a sexy little pleated miniskirt as she passed a rack of them: $165. Jesus. Were they insane?

"Magnolia?" she called into the alcove of closed doors, and immediately her daughter piped up sweetly, "Hi, Mom!" *She must want something expensive,* Eve thought, and sure enough, out came Magnolia decked head to toe in Abercrombie, her personal dresser, Alexis, right behind her. "Isn't it cute?" Alexis asked (though it came out "*Ithn't ith cuthe*" with the stud), before Eve could say a word. "She looks way older," Alexis added. "Doesn't she?"

Eve never thought she'd long for the days when her daughter hid self-consciously behind cheap oversized sweaters. But now, in contrast, Maggie looked like a fourteen-year-old prostitute. Her legs appeared shrink-wrapped in her jeans. Eve wondered how she'd even gotten in them. Had Alexis held them upright so she could leap in from the dressing room shelf? The flouncy cotton top she sported had a neckline so low that Magnolia's entire cleavage showed—which was interesting, Eve thought, given Magnolia didn't actually *have* cleavage. Or hadn't as of earlier today, anyway. Now, though, her breasts—which were pushed up and together, tender as fresh peaches above the plunging V—seemed to have grown exponentially. "Alexis lent me money for a push-up bra at Victoria's Secret," Magnolia explained. "That's where everyone gets them. You need to pay her back, Mom. It's thirty-six."

Alexis smiled. "She needed it, Eve. It gives her something to work with."

Eve stared at her.

"It *does,* Mom!" Maggie yelled. "Don't you see how good this stuff looks now? I feel *so* much better—God, I *love* these clothes! Do you like the shirt? I brought it in other colors too."

"How much is it?" Eve asked, stalling. It was nice to see her daughter happy at least. And though she hated herself for her wimpiness, she didn't want to appear the uncool mom, the big, old, dorky naysayer.

"Fifty-seven," Alexis answered. "But those tops last forever. So do the jeans."

"Not if you outgrow them in a week," Eve muttered. "How much are the jeans?"

Maggie bent to look at the price tag. "Sixty-nine ninety-nine."

Eve laughed. Or rather, "HA!" she barked, because really, it was hardly funny.

"Mom!" Maggie moaned. "I need clothes so desperately!"

"I know, but seventy bucks for a pair of jeans, Mags? And they're so tight! They'll be too small the first time we wash them."

"They're preshrunk," Alexis offered.

"Alexis is gonna own a famous clothing chain someday," Maggie explained, and then, "Can I get them, Mom? *Please?*"

Eve felt a moment of desperation. "Have you tried anywhere less expensive?" she said. "What about the Gap or—"

"The Gap is for six-year-olds, Eve," Alexis said patiently.

"Well, what about H&M, then? Or Delia's?"

Alexis snorted. "Perfect if you like bright green spandex."

"How about if you pay for some and I pay for some?" Maggie suggested.

"With what money?" Eve said, but she felt herself weakening.

"I don't know! My birthday money from Grandma? Or I'll get a babysitting job! You can make a list of whatever you want me to owe, and I'll pay you back. Mom, these clothes make me feel *good*! I don't even feel that fat in them."

"You'll show that cocksucker Nate!" Alexis yelled. "Excuse my language."

Eve shook her head, wishing she could call Loretta, or even Eric, for advice. But she knew what he'd say. *Too expensive. Don't give in.* Well, huh. Easy for him to say, off who knew where.

"I'll buy the pants and one shirt," Eve said finally. "But you won't be able to get anything else, because that kills our budget. And I'll reimburse Alexis for the bra, only because I don't seem to have a choice, but I want you to pay me back for half of that, because you should have asked me first, and because $36 is absurd to spend on a bra. I get mine at Target for $12.99." *Yes, Alexis, I'm old and dowdy,* she almost added. *And believe it or not, someday you will be too, you little creep.*

Magnolia squealed with joy. "Thank you!" She hugged Eve, her hair smelling even more like the store than the store already did, and Eve realized, as she tried not to gag, that her daughter must have used the sample perfume liberally. "Mom, can we go to the food court after this?" Maggie asked. "I'm *starving*! I seriously might pass out if I don't eat, like, *immediately*."

Forty-five minutes, four slices of pizza (two for Magnolia), and a couple hundred dollars lighter than she'd been just a few hours before, Eve unlocked the car and the girls tumbled, laughing loudly, into the backseat—Magnolia reaching forward, as Eve pulled out of the lot, to blast the radio. Eve closed her eyes briefly before lowering the sound. She thought about all the work she hadn't done today.

But then she thought about Keisha and instantly felt better. She turned onto the highway, accelerating. For several weeks now, she had visited the girl every Monday to take her grocery shopping, sometimes also bringing fresh vegetables or a whole wheat bread from the Bramington farmers' market that she knew they wouldn't find anywhere near Keisha's house. She'd also brought an old car seat she'd found, left over from Danny, and a good baby stroller she'd seen on the street with a "Free" sign over it. Keisha wasn't demonstrative, but Eve thought she seemed grateful. And Eve loved seeing the baby grow more wide-eyed and active, loved that Keisha was warming up to her a bit. The girl told her a little about school and her job, talked some (not much) about her mother and an older brother who'd disappeared last year. Eve shook her head at the story. But Keisha had lost twelve pounds already, seemingly without even trying. Her progress was thrilling.

Eve had taken on a new client recently, too, a twenty-three-year-old woman one town over named Marcia, who'd lost eighty-five pounds on a liquid diet but was steadily (and predictably) putting it back on, leaving her panicked and depressed. She lived at home with her parents, working at an online job that never involved having to go anywhere. Six weeks ago, when she was walking with her mother in the grocery store parking lot, some boys had yelled at her out their car window—something so awful Marcia wouldn't even tell Eve what they said, though she choked up talking about it. Then they'd tossed a cup of soda, which hit her in the head and burst all over her. Since then, she had not left the house; she told Eve she was humiliated to be seen.

Together, after a sympathetic but firm pep talk in which Eve stressed the absolute necessity of both exercise and eating the right foods (real foods, not liquid shakes) if she wanted to keep off the weight, Eve had helped Marcia work out a short walk, almost all on side streets, that she could do twice a day to get physical activity and sunlight and get herself on the right track again. She would start with a halfway point of the mailbox three blocks away, mailing Eve a postcard when she got there. (Eve left her a stack, stamped and addressed.) Then each week she'd walk to a mailbox a little bit farther. If she felt really inspired, Eve told her, she could do it three or even four times a day. Eve urged her to wear an iPod if that helped, and together they made a playlist of inspirational songs: "Eye of the Tiger," "I Will Survive," "We Are the Champions." It was corny, but for some clients it worked. Then they picked out an outfit she could bear to wear for the walks, and Eve hugged her and left.

Eve had gotten her eighth postcard yesterday, and each time she got one, she felt a rush of happiness for herself as well as her client. On the latest one, Marcia had written, "Made it to the third mailbox already. Lost six pounds. Woo-hoo! Back in the saddle."

So all was well there, more or less.

Michael, on the other hand . . .

Eve veered off the highway and onto her exit, flushed with guilt just thinking about him. She still hadn't spoken to him since their visit—weeks ago, now—when she'd (half-assedly, as she recalled) suggested bariatric surgery. First, it had taken her a while to research it properly: the doctor she was trying to reach always seemed to call back in the late afternoon, when the kids were around and she was trying to make dinner, or in the evening, when she was paying bills, helping with homework, bagging up trash or recycling, and washing the dinner dishes—many, if not all, things Eric used to do. Then, when she finally got all the information she needed, she'd called Michael but gotten his voice mail. She'd left a message, and he'd called her back a day later—a few days ago now. She still hadn't had a chance to return that call yet.

She made a note to herself that tonight, no matter what else happened, she would call him—tell him what she'd found out, and set up another appointment, with Diane in attendance, to discuss the surgery in more depth. In the backseat, the girls were still laughing, texting on Maggie's phone (amazingly, Alexis didn't seem to have a phone; nor had she bought a single thing for herself at the mall, Eve realized) and talking quietly so she couldn't hear. But as they headed into Bramington's downtown, Alexis said loudly, "Oh, Mags, look! There's Skeeter and Jimbo!" and Maggie yelled, "Mom! *MOM!* Pull over here!"

With a quick glance in the rearview mirror, Eve swung into the right lane and veered to the curb. "Magnolia, I can't just stop like that!" she snapped, even though she just had.

"Sorry, Mom. Alexis, wait!" Magnolia called. Alexis had stepped out of the car and whistled loudly through her teeth, making heads turn all over the place. "Skeeter!" she yelled, and she turned back to Maggie. "Let's go see them!" She paused for a moment, seeming to reconsider. "Or should I just come to your house?"

Magnolia turned to Eve. "Mom, can I stay in town for a little while?"

Eve tried to see what boys Alexis was whistling to, but all she saw was a couple of men—one a paunchy, rough-looking guy wearing jeans and cowboy boots, the other a skinny guy in a T-shirt with a bandanna on his head. Eve sighed loudly. "Mags, where?" she said, and she hated the whine in her voice. "Doing what?"

"I don't know, Mom! Just *hanging*!" She laughed. "Mom, I'm *fourteen*! *All* the kids my age do this! And all we do is sit around and talk. It's fine. I promise."

Eve tried to think quickly. *Did* all the kids Maggie's age hang out in town? She had no idea. What had she herself been allowed to do at fourteen? But the question seemed irrelevant; the world was a whole different ballgame from when she'd grown up, back in a middle-class Ohio suburb, eating TV dinners, playing solitaire, babysitting for neighbors in her spare time.

She'd have to ask Gretchen or Renée, mothers of two of Magnolia's friends whom Eve liked and consulted on matters like this. But she couldn't exactly tell Maggie to hold on a sec while she quickly called them. She bit her lip. Bramington *was* a fairly tame, friendly place, especially at this time of day. (Glancing around, the most "threatening" thing she could find was two pretty girls making out.) And the last thing she needed was Alexis in her house. Maybe Danny would even stay at Star's long enough for her to get some work done. "Okay," she said finally. "But listen. Turn on your ringer, and *answer* if I call. And be home at 8:30."

"Thanks, Mom, bye! I love you!" Magnolia kissed Eve, then shot out of the car.

Eve drove the rest of the way home in silence. *You have to give your kids roots and wings*, she reminded herself, but she hadn't realized the wings would be so rude and slutty. And who the hell were Rambo and Scooter, or whatever their names were? She pulled into the driveway, parked, gathered Maggie's bags from the backseat, and went in, grabbing the mail on the way: another postcard from Marcia ("Seven pounds and counting!"); a Victoria's Secret catalog for Maggie (had they actually gotten her on the mailing list and delivered something since her purchase two hours ago?); solicitations from CancerCare and the Leukemia & Lymphoma Society, among others; several new bills (electric, Visa—Christ, it never ended). She tore open an envelope from their accountant, addressed to Eric: a reminder that their quarterly estimated taxes were due soon—another thing Eric had always taken care of.

"Eve?" came a female voice from the living room, and she jumped about three feet, dropped the mail, and clutched at her chest.

It was Priscilla, Ronnie's partner and Star and Stream's biological mother. "Oh my God, I'm so sorry," she said. "I *knew* I should have called to tell you I was here, but—"

"It's okay." Eve's heart was pounding. "What's wrong?"

"Nothing." Priscilla put her hand on Eve's shoulder. "Danny wanted to come home, and of course I wasn't about to leave him here alone. So I've been hanging here with him. Star and Stream are at our place, watching videos. Which, believe me, they're not minding one bit." She laughed loudly, as if this were a complete anomaly. "Ronnie's at work," she added. Ronnie ran the emergency room at a good-sized hospital nearby.

Eve, who wished it were Ronnie here and Priscilla at work, was trying to step from under the latter's hand without seeming rude. Priscilla was small with long curly hair and a buffed-out body—the sort that could be acquired in one's forties, Eve was pretty sure, only through hours and hours at the gym—that was always prominently displayed. (Today she wore tight, low-rise jeans and a tiny, midriff-baring T-shirt that said, "There is no 'choice' in being yourself.") She worked "in energy," she had once told Eve, and from what Eve could see, that seemed to mean that, along with attending the gym, she spent a lot of time at the mall shopping for new T-shirts and bumper stickers; the latest one she'd stuck on her car—just below the one that said "I ♥ my rescue mutt"—read, "I believe in dragons, good men, and other fantasy creatures." (Eric had once confessed to Eve that despite being eleven inches taller than Priscilla and a black belt in kung fu, he was seriously afraid of her.)

As far as Eve could tell, Priscilla was the uterus and the diva in their marriage, while Ronnie was the provider, the caretaker when-ever she was home, and the rock. But Eve also knew that Ronnie—a calm, blue-eyed, silver-haired lesbian with the subtle, masculine good looks of an aging Irish boy—thrived in the role; she liked being the go-to mom (not, Eve had to admit, unlike herself). Eve could easily see what Priscilla saw in Ronnie. The other side of the equation wasn't as obvious—but then, with most couples it wasn't.

With relief, she made it out from under Priscilla's grip. "Why did he want to come home?" she asked.

"He said he didn't feel well, and he just wanted to play with his bird." Priscilla smiled benevolently. "I understand. I think he just wanted to, like, be in his moment."

Eve sighed. "Priscilla, I'm so sorry you had to—"

"Hey, no stress! It's the least I can do for an awesome neighbor!" She shook out her hair, then pushed it back deliberately with both palms, as if to get it exactly right on her back. "Besides," she added, when she was done with the hair, "it gave me an excuse to get away for a bit and read. I'm a voracious reader, I'm sure you know. And this book is brilliant." She held it up so Eve could see the title: *Dear John, I Love Jane: Women Write about Leaving Men for Women.*

Eve smiled weakly. "Thanks. I appreciate that."

Priscilla looked pointedly at Eve, slowly letting her smile fade to earnestness. "So, like, how are you doing, anyway?" she asked.

Eve blinked. "Sorry?"

"I mean, with your husband gone and all that."

"Oh." Eve hadn't realized the neighbors knew. Maybe Danny had told them. How many other people in town knew too? "I'm fine," she said, perhaps a little too cheerfully. "We're all fine." She wondered if that were true. What the hell was up with Danny?

"Hey, that's excellent," Priscilla said. "Good for you. You go, girl. My ex pulled that shit a few times too. Taking off to go *find himself,* or whatever." She rolled her eyes. "I'm not too bummed out to be done with that racket, let me tell you."

"I don't think Eric's exactly *finding* himself," Eve said, though the truth was, she had no idea. "It's more complicated than that."

"Oh, I know. It always is." Priscilla looked at her pityingly. "Anyway, if there's anything we can do—seriously, day or night, three in the morning—give a holler. Nothing's more important than community in my book. Neighbors have to be homies, as the kids would say. We have to look out for each other."

"Thanks," Eve managed, and she closed the door a little too quickly. It was one thing for *her* to be angry at Eric, but another altogether for Priscilla to be; like the way you could call your own kid a brat, but if anyone else did, forget it. And though she'd do anything for Ronnie (who'd probably never ask anyway), she didn't much like the idea of having to be around-the-clock "homies" with Priscilla, or, for that matter, with anyone but her family and her close friends. She and Eric had always been private people, friendly with the neighbors but also keeping their distance. Good fences make good neighbors, she believed.

What's your problem? she reprimanded herself. After all, Priscilla had just taken care of Danny for hours. But she couldn't shake her annoyance. The woman had made her feel not only pathetic but also sad for Eric somehow. She thought of an article she'd read recently about heterosexual marriage becoming obsolete—about how men, beyond their sperm for procreation, were "no longer necessary." That was true, she supposed, if you were a lesbian, or if you didn't mind the whole communal thing. So where did that leave her? She liked her little nuclear family, flaws and all. She liked having an actual husband.

Or *had* liked. Her brief sadness for Eric snapped right back into anger. She turned and slapped the door, hard, with her palm. "Ow!" she yelled, stunned at her idiocy. (*Are you serious?* she could almost hear Magnolia saying.) There was a sound from upstairs, the first since she'd come in. With a sigh, she dumped the mail on the growing pile and went up, rubbing her hand.

Danny was sitting on a chair he'd put in front of his dresser, staring at the bird in his cage. "Dan?" Eve said, coming into the room. "Hi, sweetie."

"Hi, Mom," he said, without turning to look at her.

"Danny, what happened today? You had a stomachache?"

"A little. It's better now."

She waited a moment. "You didn't want to play with Star and Stream?"

He shrugged. He had still not turned toward her. "I didn't really care," he said, and then, "All they were doing was playing Wii cooking. It was boring." Coincidentally or not, she had never heard him use that word until Eric left. "Plus, I wanted to see Batman," he added.

Eve walked over and knelt down next to him. He was still refusing to go to kung fu—something he'd also never done until recently, except when he was sick. When she asked why, he'd told her,

"It's boring." Now a thread of alarm went through her. Quickly she dispelled it. He was allowed to outgrow something, for God's sake; one door closed, another opened. "Danny, the problem is, when you came back here, you made Priscilla come here too," she said.

"She didn't have to. I told her that."

"Well, it's nice you said that, but of course she wouldn't leave you here alone."

He didn't answer.

"Danny, look at me."

Obediently he turned toward her.

She smiled at the sight of his striking, odd little face. "You needed to stay there until I got home," she said, trying to sound firm. "That was the plan. Okay?"

"Okay." Danny nodded, then looked back at the cage and frowned. "I'm worried about Batman. I think he's depressed."

"Depressed?" Eve laughed, then immediately wished she hadn't. "Why?"

"I think he feels trapped. In his cage."

Eve took a deep breath. Her hand was still throbbing where she'd smacked the door. "Honey, he's used to a cage," she said. "He's been in one his whole life."

"I know, but that doesn't mean he *likes* it in there. He probably wants to get out." He looked at her. "Don't you think?"

She thought a moment. "I don't know," she said honestly. "Maybe sometimes. But, I mean, he has you, right? You're with him a lot."

"But I'm just his family. He's probably sick of his family."

Eve felt the by now familiar cringe of her heart.

"He's lonely," Danny continued. "In the store, he had a whole cageful of friends."

It was hard to contest that one. Eve sighed. "I don't know, sweetheart. Maybe we can find him a friend."

He looked at her. "Really?"

His face was so hopeful she wanted to cry. She pictured another parakeet, this one a female, and then the feather-flying, heart-attack-inducing attempt to mate them, then to nurture the laying and protection of the eggs. (Did parakeets even lay eggs? They must. She pictured them splatting to the bottom of the cage—oops!—as Danny attempted to change the water dish.) And then the screaming parakeet babies, and parakeets all over the house, shitting and squawking and flying into people's faces. "Maybe," she said weakly, and then, "Listen, if you're okay, I'm gonna go scrape up some dinner. Are you?" He nodded. "Are you *sure?*" she pushed.

"Yes, Mom!" He sounded exasperated suddenly. Another fairly new thing for him.

"Well, okay," she said, and then, "Anything in particular you want to eat?"

"No thanks." His eyes moved back to the cage, then suddenly lit up. "Mom, can I take Batman out? I want to teach him to sit on my shoulder and say hi to whoever comes up to us."

Good luck with that, Eve thought. "I don't know, Dan." She shook her head. "How will you get him back in the cage afterward?"

"Because he listens to me! He always responds to my voice. I'll be able to get him back in, Mom. I promise!"

It was a ridiculous promise from a kid his age, Eve knew. But she didn't want to say no to him at the moment. "Okay," she relented, against her better judgment. "Just—I don't know. Make sure your door is closed at least."

Downstairs, she stood in the kitchen trying to collect her thoughts. She needed to call Michael. But he'd probably be in the middle of dinner or putting the kids to bed, and anyway, she couldn't face that right now. She didn't want to work; she wanted to talk to someone who knew her, someone she could spill *her* woes to for a change. But who? Loretta would never answer. Eve picked up the phone and dialed her friend's cell, just in case.

"Eve?" Loretta said after one ring.

"Oh my God, you're *there*?" Inside, Eve sang out with joy.

"Where else would I be?" Loretta said. "Someone has to be here to babysit Freja."

The Danish au pair had started last week, Eve remembered now.

Loretta's maternity leave ended in a few weeks, and though she had one more month of summer after that, she had to prepare for next semester, which started in August. "Tell me," Eve said happily, sinking into a chair.

"Where to start?" Loretta sighed. "First off, she shows up from Denmark with strapless velvet minidresses, five pairs of pumps and slingbacks, and a suitcase full of hair products. No shorts, no jeans, no sneakers."

Eve grinned. "Oy."

"I know, right? So the first thing I had to do was take her shopping for some normal clothes. She didn't get the hint, though. She still wears full makeup at all times, and it takes her an hour to dry her hair, which she washes every day. Sometimes twice. It's long and blond, not that you needed to ask. To match her long blond legs."

Welcome to my world, Eve thought, thinking of Dria. "Any pluses?" she asked.

"Well—contrary to appearance, which is basically grade B runway model, she's actually great with the boys. Lets them climb all over her, paw through her stuff . . . they love her. And she's pretty good with the baby, when she's actually caring for her, though I worry about all that eye makeup flaking off into Edie's mouth or something. And it's nice to have time to take a shower again. And a nap! Oh, God, a nap." She sighed again. "But, you know. She's definitely not the sharpest pin in the cushion. I mean, if there's an emergency or something, I can see her literally running with Edie to the nearest hospital instead of thinking to call 911. In five-inch heels."

Eve nodded happily. She secretly cherished bad-babysitter stories, since they helped confirm her decision to have stayed home full-time with her own kids as infants.

"But it gets worse," Loretta said. "Last week, she asked to borrow the car."

"No."

"Yes. Apparently they all do."

"And she was going . . ."

"'Out.' To meet another au pair she'd met online. Guess if she cracked up the car."

Eve's mouth dropped. "You're kidding."

"I'm not. Just a fender bender, but still—$1,200 worth of damage. Hours filling out forms, more hours on hold with the insurance company. Now we have to get the car fixed. Of course, it all falls on me. Howard doesn't have time." Eve could almost see her shaking her head, stunned—*And aren't we all,* she thought—with the responsibilities of new motherhood. "Yes, he's busy making the money to pay for all this," Loretta said. "And he's very generous. I'll give him that. But his M.O. is, 'Baby, charge it, hire it out, whatever you need,' without realizing that what you hire you have to manage. Especially when it goes into your bedroom and finds the pearl earrings you inherited from Grandma Victoria and asks if it can borrow them."

Eve was too astonished to even laugh. "Get out!" she said, using an expression she'd gotten from Loretta herself, in earlier days. Eve loved Jersey-speak.

Loretta sniffed. "She's eighteen. She doesn't know better. Or so I tell myself, though, of course, when I was eighteen . . . oh, whatever. I'm trying to give her the benefit of the doubt."

"Of course you are," Eve said soothingly. "I'm sure she'll settle in."

"She'd better. Because I'm stuck with her for ten months unless I trade her in for another one, and then I just have to start this all over again."

Eve shook her head. "Do you ever think about taking a year off from teaching?"

"No," Loretta said. There was an awkward silence, and then she said, "I mean, I love the baby. She's amazing and perfect. You should see her, Eve. She smiles when she sees me. Her little eyes light up like—like—oh, whatever, I can't even come up with a decent simile anymore." She sighed. "The point is, I have to work or I'll go insane. You know?"

"Of course," Eve said, though she didn't, really. She couldn't imagine leaving a three-month-old baby with some crazy teenager from another country. Then again, look where staying home with her babies had gotten her. One off in the wilderness with Rambo and Scooter and Alexis, the other obsessed with his depressed bird.

Plus Loretta still had a husband.

But you have a book now, she reminded herself. *And a good business, with good people who need you. And your babies, of course. Screw the husband.*

"Anyway," Loretta said. "How are *you*? Oh, Eve, I can't believe I forgot to ask! What's happening with Eric?"

"Well, he stopped calling," she said. "I guess he got sick of me not picking up. He texts with Maggie, though. He's at his mother's, as predicted. Oh yeah, I told you that. Not doing much, from what Maggie tells me. Well. When I can get her to talk to me."

She paused, but Loretta didn't take the bait.

"Maggie's a bit of a challenge right now," Eve persisted. "Not to compare my stress level to your—"

"Oh crap, Eve, I'm sorry. Can you hold on a sec?"

"Sure." She heard the phone click down, and then voices talking. "But I just nursed her," Loretta said, and then, "Oh whatever, give her here, I'll try again." There was crying, then silence, then more crying, more silence. Loretta came back on. "Sorry, Eve, baby on the boob now, but I hope she'll stay quiet for a while. So continue."

"Um, let's see. Oh yeah. Magnolia." It felt so trivial suddenly. "Oh, it's nothing, really," she said. "Just the usual teenage stuff."

"It's *not* nothing, Eve! Tell me. Is she giving you a hard time?"

Eve nodded to the phone. "She's got this new friend. Alexis. She looks about twenty-two, and possibly actually *is*. And she's completely—"

The baby let out a wail. "Okayokayokay," Loretta said tensely. "Shhh! Okay, Edie. It's all right. Go on, Eve."

Eve sighed. "Listen, you need to go. It's nothing. I'll tell you another time."

"No no! I want to know!" Eve knew she did (or at least hoped so). But the baby was screaming now. "Shit," Loretta said. "Fuck me."

Eve laughed in spite of herself. Motherhood had definitely brought the Jersey girl back to Loretta. Or maybe it was just living back in New Jersey. "I'll e-mail you," Eve said.

"Oh, God, would you?" Loretta yelled over the noise. "Edie's so fussy today, I don't really know why. Freja says she's teething, but really, the girl is barely past teething herself, how the hell would she know? I think she might be sick, actually. I think I might have to take her to the doctor. Edie, I mean. Not Freja. Not that she's not sick too, in her own sick way."

Eve wanted to laugh again, but for some reason, she suddenly felt too sad to. "Well, let me know what happens," she said, and then, "I hope she's not sick."

"What?" Loretta yelled.

Eve started to repeat herself. But there were voices now over the crying, and then the phone was dropped, then picked up, then dropped again. "Listen, I've gotta go," Loretta said when she finally got the phone near her mouth. "I'll call you."

And a dial tone replaced her.

8

EVE STARED AT the receiver. Deep inside her, a cell of despondency formed and began to multiply. She leaped up, hung up the phone, grabbed the towering pile of mail, and got out the checkbook, then began tearing open envelopes. She paid the water, gas, and Visa card bills, sealing and stamping the envelopes. She paid for Danny's kung fu (even though he never went anymore); paid the monthly installment for the violin they'd splurged on for Magnolia last year (even though she never played now); paid the dentist's bill for Magnolia's two fillings last month. She paid their quarterly health insurance bill, a small fortune that, naturally, didn't cover the fillings, or any other dentistry—or really much of anything at all, it seemed. She threw out the charity solicitation letters except for MASSPIRG and the local food bank, to which she wrote checks for $5 each. (Better than nothing.) She paid the mortgage, and the rent on Eric's studio. (Oh, the irony.) At the end, there was $2,675 left in the checking account. She looked again at what they were supposed to pay in estimated taxes: $3,100.

Her stomach contracted. Eric, perhaps because he had long made most of their income, had also always handled their bills and accounts. She'd never thought much about what they paid in estimated taxes; the accountant's envelope arrived, she put it at his place at the table, and a few days later he mailed off checks to the city and the IRS. Now, though, she stared at what they owed with something like horror. The figure, she knew, was generally based on what they'd brought in last year—which now seemed not all that bad, if a hefty step down from years before. Eric had sold a couple of older pieces, taught a couple of classes at the Arts Center, and been paid for a commission he'd finished from the year before. Eve, along with seeing clients, had gotten the second of her three book payments, received on delivery of the final manuscript. This year they'd made much less so far, and while she thought that might mean they could pay less right now, she wasn't sure if Eric and the accountant had already adjusted the numbers down—and she didn't want to risk it, now that she was essentially a single parent. (She briefly imagined a policeman hauling her off in handcuffs, the kids wailing as another cop physically restrained them from lunging after her.) So how was she supposed to pay this?

She considered their savings. They had two $10,000 CDs, purchased eight and ten years ago, that were supposed to be for something special someday—fixing up the house, or taking a trip (though, actually, she realized with mild shock, college wasn't so far away). They had three little stocks they'd bought before they had kids, currently worth considerably less than they'd been even a few years ago—maybe a couple thousand each now. She could sell one of those, she supposed, though she didn't want to, especially in a down market like this. Plus she didn't have a clue about how to do that. Eric had handled all that with someone from Merrill Lynch. The kids each had a college fund with about $2,000 in it. ("A whole day of college!" Eve often remarked to Eric, only half kidding.) And she and Eric each had an IRA, with, she thought, considerable amounts in them—maybe $35,000 or $40,000 each. Maybe more. She honestly didn't know. But it didn't matter anyway, because you couldn't really take money out of those.

She'd gotten her third and final book payment—just over $6,000 after her agent's commission—on publication of the book a few months ago, and it had gone straight into their checking account. All gone now. With her clients and the BBBs—Mrs. Kalish and her friends—Eve usually made between $400 and $600 a week, though at the moment it was on the lower end of that. As for credit, they already had a couple of thousand in charges on the Visa bill and were now paying the minimum each month, with high interest charges. It was a stupid way to do it, and she would not borrow more. Both she and Eric feared debt, given their fluctuating earnings.

Eve sat down at the computer, opened her e-mail, and typed in her agent's address. She composed a quick note asking how the book was doing and whether she could expect royalties—and, if so, how much and when—and then hit Send.

She got up and rubbed her eyes. It was almost seven o'clock. There was little in the fridge. In the freezer, she found a family-size lasagna and stuck it in the microwave. It would take a while, but Danny wasn't exactly begging for dinner. She found a frosty bag of peas, slammed it on the counter to break it up, dumped some into a saucepan. Her e-mail binged.

It was from her agent. Single, twenty-eight, and wildly ambitious, Sophie worked day and night and always responded within minutes, though generally without much in the way of full sentences or punctuation. Now she wrote:

> *The book did well but not fantastic u may have some royalties coming but probably not a lot if any we wont know for awhile. Roylty payments are 2ce a year april and oct so u wont see anything til at least oct if then. how are u doing r u still doing radio*

Eve was doing little publicity now—the interviews had mostly stopped a few weeks ago, after a similar book came out with a competing publisher. But she couldn't bear to tell Sophie that, so instead she wrote, "I'm okay. Thanks for the info. I need money but I'll survive." She hit Send, then rolled away from her desk, ignoring all her other e-mail, and sat for a moment, digesting. So okay, the party was over with the book. Fun, but alas, she would not be the next J.K. Rowling.

She looked around the kitchen, as if the answer to her financial problems would appear (Rowling style) in the reflection on the sink faucet, or scrawled on one of the slowly rotting bananas in the ceramic bowl on the counter. Her eyes lifted to *The Contradiction*, and she stared at it a moment, trying to muster some of the passion she'd once felt for this piece. She had been speechless when Eric first showed it to her, awestruck and astonished. And she had gazed at it nonstop for weeks, amazed she was married to a man who not only could create something this lovely, this passionate and graceful and dazzling, but who seemed to have intuited and then expressed, even *glorified*, some aspect—some real truth—about her that she herself hadn't realized was there. And yet it *was* there. She knew this the second she saw the piece. He had captured something and presented it back to her in bronze, wrapped up with a big red ribbon.

But now? It was hard to remember what that truth was; she wondered if she even still possessed it. As for the sculpture, it no longer moved her—at least, right now it didn't. *Just a dusty old statue*, she thought, and she felt a wave of sadness as she realized the truth: she was no longer that girl, that innocent, curious, sweet young thing. And he was no longer the man who could create something like that, seemingly effortlessly. Those days were past.

She looked away, back at her desk, and once more, like ink soaking into a cloth, the sadness was replaced by disgust. *So there it is*, she thought bitterly. *Me here, him there, the bills not going away, no money to pay them.* Her eyes fell on her Rolodex, which she'd kept religiously for years. "No way," she said out loud. *Yes way*, her thoughts replied. She began to flip through the addresses.

And there it was, under "Sculpture, Eric." Below that, at a time that now seemed so long ago it felt more like a movie than her actual past, she had scrawled, "Interested in buying: Sam Rabinowitz. 369–2422." Sam was the father of someone who had played with Magnolia once when she was in preschool. He had come inside to get his daughter, seen *The Contradiction*, and stopped short. "Wow," he'd said. "If you ever decide to sell that, call me." Eve had laughed and told him it wasn't for sale, but maybe there was another piece of Eric's he'd be interested in? "Maybe, though I really like that one," he'd said, and he'd scribbled his name and number on the back of a gum wrapper from his pocket and handed it to Eve. She'd put it in the Rolodex, just in case, and that was the end of it.

Now, she picked up the phone and dialed the number—*Just for fun,* she told herself, *because it's not like he'll remember me if he's even still at this number.* The voice mail came on. Eve started to hang up, but then a woman's voice interrupted the recording. "Hello?" it yelled.

"Oh—I'm sorry, I'm sure I have the wrong number," Eve said.

The woman laughed. "I always love a good pessimist. Do you want to ask for someone, just in case?"

Eve laughed in spite of herself. "Sam Rabinowitz?"

"Moved years ago," the woman said.

"I knew it!" Eve said, relieved. "I knew it before I even called, actually, but—"

"Want his new number?" She rattled it off.

Eve sat still for a moment. Then she dialed the number the woman gave her.

A man answered on the second ring. "You're the sculptor," he said without saying hello. "Are you ready to sell the piece?"

Eve blinked. Even with caller ID, that was fairly amazing. "Um— actually, it's his wife," she said. "Eve."

"Hello, Eve. I remember you well. How's Magnolia?"

"She's—okay, thanks. How's, um, your daughter?"

"Fine. Away at boarding school, actually. Coming home in a few weeks."

"Oh, that must be hard!" Eve sat down. "Do you miss her?"

"Sure I miss her. But she's doing well, the time flies, everyone's happy. Plus I see her plenty. The school years get shorter and shorter." He laughed. "You know the saying: the more you pay, the less school you get."

Eve laughed. "I wouldn't know, actually. My kids go to public."

"Lucky you. So have you decided to sell that bronze beauty in your kitchen?"

Eve's heart began to thump. "I'm, um, I'm not sure yet. But I wondered if you might still be interested. If, you know. I do decide. To sell."

"Yes," he said.

"What?"

"Yes. I am interested."

Eve took a breath. "And how much—I mean, I'm not usually the one who does this, but—if you did want to buy, how much would you be interested in paying?" She shook her head. What an idiot, asking him what he wanted to pay!

"How about ten thousand? I know his sculptures usually go for more like eight these days. But that one's special. I knew it the moment I saw it."

Eve wiped her palms on her pants.

"You still there?" Rabinowitz said.

She nodded into the phone.

"Why don't you think about it a little," he said. "I'm not going anywhere. If you decide to sell for that, call me. Or e-mail me. Sam Rabinowitz, one word, at comcast."

"Okay," Eve said finally. "Thank you."

"Thank *you*." He clicked off.

She hung up. The room was dark; the sun had set at some point. She got up slowly, turned on the flame under the peas, added some water from the teakettle.

"Mom?" Danny said from a few feet away. Eve jumped.

"Who was that?" he said. "Was it Daddy?"

"What? Oh! No, it wasn't Daddy." She forced a smile. "You scared me!"

"Sorry, Mom."

"It's okay." Again, her poor heart. "Come here," she said, "and give me forty-three smooches, or at least one big hug."

He came over and embraced her, and she breathed in his smell, sweet and familiar, though also tinged, she'd noticed lately, with something new: a touch of pungency, a lessening of the sweetness. The slightest hint of preadolescence? She couldn't bear to think about it.

"Mom, don't kill me," he said into her chest, "but Batman won't come off the top of my curtains. He flew straight up there, and when I stood on my bed to get him, he flew over to my clock, and when I went over there, he flew back to my curtains." He spewed all this very quickly, no doubt to keep her from reacting, but now he was forced to take a breath.

"Oh, Danny," she said, stepping out of his arms, but she knew the blame was all hers. "Now what? Daddy's not here to get him back in his cage, and it's not like I—" She paused, trying to figure out what exactly she was trying to say. *It's not like I can do it?* But if Eric could, why couldn't she?

"I have an idea," Danny said. "How about if we just let him stay loose? He's not hurting anyone, and he'll have to go back eventually for food and to look in his mirror and stuff."

Eve thought about this for a second. "But you'll have bird poop all over your room. No, I don't think—"

"I won't, Mom! I'll clean it up."

She actually laughed. "Danny, do you seriously expect me to buy that? Have you ever in your life cleaned up bird poop? Even once?"

"That's because I never had a *bird*, Mom. I never had the *chance* to." His eyes were wide and earnest and also, she realized, slightly patronizing. "How about this?" he said. "The first time you see even one bird poop in my room, we'll put him right back in."

Eve shook her head, amazed she was even considering this. If Eric had been home, there was no way in hell she'd allow a loose bird in the house. When Eric was here, she had run a tight ship: clean house, punctual meals, laundry washed and folded at least twice a week. But if he wasn't holding up his end of the bargain, why should she hold up hers? The kids didn't care if the house was spotless or she did laundry all the time as long as they had something to wear. Not that Eric had cared either; nor had he cared about having three perfect meals a day, though certainly he'd appreciated it. But the pressure, she realized, had come from herself. As a wife, she'd had them all on a strict regimen and taken pride in it.

And look where it had gotten her. *Screw virtue!* she thought. *Screw righteousness and responsibility and respectability. And screw catching the bird.* So what if he pooped? Things could be cleaned. Or replaced. Or, hell, left dirty. At this point, who really cared?

She had to get down off her pedestal, is what it came down to. "And if you do find a poop," Danny was saying, "which you *won't*, Magnolia will help me get him back in the cage. Or I can ask Priscilla or Ronnie. They could do it, I'm sure."

Eve adjusted her thoughts back to the present, then frowned. "Ronnie, maybe. But Priscilla?" Without intending to, she snorted.

"Priscilla's nice!" Danny said, sounding surprised. "And she's really strong. She can bench-press, like, 85 pounds or something."

Eve looked at him. What did he know about bench-pressing?

The front door opened, then closed again hard. "Hi, Mom," Magnolia called, heading straight upstairs. Eve heard her bedroom door slam.

"Thank you, Mom!" Danny yelled, and he turned and made a beeline upstairs.

"Wait!" Eve started to say, because she hadn't said yes yet. Had she? But she heard his door, too, open and close again, and she decided to just let it be.

Back in the kitchen, she turned off the peas and dumped them into a colander. Then she opened the fridge and poured herself a glass of wine so full she had to take a large gulp before she could carry it anywhere. She walked it to the steps, taking several more gulps as she went. "Magnolia?" she called up when she'd drunk about half the glass.

"Yeah," came the voice after a second.

"Come down for dinner, sweetheart. I made lasagna and peas." *The hell with virtue, yes, but that didn't mean a whole lasagna should go to waste.* "Danny!" she called. "Come down, please."

"I'm not hungry," Magnolia called.

"Well, come down and sit with us for a few minutes anyway. Danny!" she said again.

"Be right there," Danny yelled.

"Mom, why?" Magnolia yelled. "I have a ton of homework! Plus I have to take a shower."

Eve took another large gulp of wine. "Because. I want to see you."

"Mom, no! You can see me later."

Another gulp. "Magnolia, please come down here," she said, and though she regretted the words even as they came out (now she'd have to get the girl down here), she was also a tiny bit relieved that she hadn't fallen off her pedestal completely.

In the kitchen again, she took out the lasagna to cool, dumped the peas in a bowl, adding a small chunk of butter, and poured Danny milk, finishing and refilling her wine (only three-quarters, this time). "Magnolia!" she called up again. "Danny! Come down."

No answer. Eve sighed, then put down her glass and went upstairs.

Magnolia was in the bathroom, shower running. Eve knocked on the door, then tried to open it. Locked. "Magnolia!" she yelled, banging now.

"What?! Mom, I'm *taking a shower*!"

Eve shook her head. "Why are you taking a shower when I just told you to come to dinner?"

"I know, but, Mom, I felt gross! My face was greasy from trying on clothes. I can't eat till I get clean. Oh, and Mom? Thank you *so* much for those clothes! They're *so* cool! I can't wait to wear them."

Eve felt herself soften, helped by the nice little chardonnay lift she had going now. Maybe that was her problem: she didn't drink enough. "Well, good," she said. "You're welcome." She paused. "Try to hurry, okay?" she said finally. "We'll start without you."

Danny had run past her and downstairs. Eve joined him at the table, where, in less than five minutes, having failed to either drink his milk or eat more than two bites of lasagna, he proclaimed himself done. He was full, he said. He wanted to play with Batman.

Eve sighed as he cleared his plate and ran upstairs, watching his skinny body retreat. But he seemed a little happier at least; maybe it was a good thing she'd told him he could have the bird outside its cage. Maybe he'd get some physical activity chasing it. *Or cleaning up the poop,* she thought, and she shook her head, then began to silently clean up the kitchen, pouring and sipping a third glass of wine along the way. She turned on the dishwasher (without Eric home it never seemed full enough, but it was day three and the dishes were starting to reek), then went upstairs herself. Danny was talking up to the bird, who was perched on the train shelf now. "Hi, Batman! Hi, Batman! Hi, Batman!" he said. Eve watched him a moment, swaying a little as she stood, then said, "Danny, time to get ready for bed. Go brush your teeth, please."

She waited to make sure he got started, then went to Magnolia's room and knocked. "Mags?" she called. She cracked the door, then opened it. The lights were out. Magnolia was asleep in her bed, the back of her head turned toward Eve. The bags of clothes sat next to the bed, the tags from the pajamas torn off and deposited on the floor.

Eve went over and peeled back the covers just a little. Magnolia was wearing the new pajamas.

She felt a rush of warmth. Poor thing. It was hard enough being fourteen, without your boyfriend dumping you for your best friend, your own father walking out to do who knows what. *Find himself,* Priscilla had said, and it sounded so *un*Eric that she didn't know whether to laugh, cry, or cringe. She wondered if Eric had texted Magnolia lately, if they'd maybe even connected tonight. Maggie's phone was next to her bed. Eve was tempted to look. What exactly did they text about?

But no. She knew parents who read all their kids' e-mails, checked their kids' texts every night, but she believed that even children needed a certain amount of privacy as long as they were safe. *As long as he's being good to Maggie,* she thought, and she knew he was. She remembered the weeks just after Danny was born, when she was nursing all day and Eric had taken over five-year-old Magnolia with a vengeance that, except for during his and Eve's first few weeks as a couple, Eve hadn't seen directed at anything but his art. They went off together for hours on end, came home with little projects they'd made, things she'd conceived and he'd created with her. And then again, when Danny was sick and Eve was tending to him nonstop and endlessly researching his symptoms online, Eric had reappeared to rescue Maggie once more—taking her all over town, playing basketball with her, making the sculpture of the little girl with the violin that Maggie still kept next to her bed. Eve had been thrilled. Maggie was a hard one to reach, and Eve was deeply grateful when Eric made the effort. But then, as before, it ended as fast as it started: Danny's illness became part of their routine, Magnolia hit adolescence, and Eric returned to his office, Eve to her post in the house whenever the kids were around.

She closed Magnolia's door.

In Danny's room, while the bird watched from the curtains, she read him *The Lorax* for the forty-third time (they kept a tally at the front of their favorite books) and a chapter from *The Adventures of Huckleberry Finn*, trying not to slur her words. Just around the part where Huck and Jim catch a 200-pound catfish, Batman swooped down and landed on Danny's bedpost, which made Danny squeal with delight and Eve shriek. "My God!" she yelled, laughing a little. "Are you sure you want him loose in here tonight?" He confirmed that he did, and she left, closing his door. By 9:08, she was back downstairs with both kids asleep.

And no husband to worry about. She could do naked aerobics while watching *The Bachelorette,* she could dump chocolate chips straight into the jar of peanut butter and eat it with a spoon or even with her hands. She could have an affair right here, in her very own house, without worrying about anyone walking in.

And then you could lose the house for not paying the mortgage, she thought, and frankly, that seemed the most likely possibility of the four. With a sigh, she sat down at her desk. She did her best to answer only the crucial e-mail, which took about twenty minutes, then remembered she had to call Michael tonight.

She just needed to eat first. She'd never had dinner—plus, that would help clear her head before she called him. She got out the lasagna and put some on a plate. As the microwave whirred, she heard footsteps, and then Magnolia was there, in her new pajamas, one hand held—oddly—in front of her face. "Mom?" she said.

Eve wondered if other mothers felt this too: relieved—excited, even—to get away from their kids, and equally excited the second they saw them again. "You're up!" she said, smiling, and then she realized Maggie was crying. "What's wrong?" she said.

The girl moved past her and sat down at the table, facing the other way. "I'm afraid to tell you," she said. "You're gonna kill me."

Oh no, Eve thought, and the list went through her head: *Pregnant, AIDS, crabs, new Abercrombie jeans already too tight . . .* "What?" she said, almost wearily.

Magnolia shook her head; her curls sprung back and forth and then settled again.

"Magnolia!" Eve said. "*What* is going on?" She walked around the table to look at her daughter, but Maggie put her head down, her hand still in front of her face. Eve reached out and lifted her hand, without resistance.

She drew in her breath. Magnolia's nose was a bright red ball, swollen and shiny. "My God," she practically whispered. "What happened to you?"

"I got it pierced!" Maggie yelled. She began to sob. "I'm sorry! It was stupid, I know. I just didn't think—"

"You got your *nose* pierced? Are you kidding?"

"Alexis's friend did it," Maggie said, coming clean now the way she always did with Eve. "It *killed,* Mom! She did it with a *needle!* And then she stuck the ring in, and then she had to shove the *back* on, up my *nose!* It was *horrible!* And I think she made it too tight, because it's been killing ever since."

Eve examined the damage, though when she tried to touch it, Maggie shrieked and jerked away. "It's too swollen for me to even try to get the ring out," Eve said. "It looks infected." She shook her head. "I can't fucking believe you did this."

Magnolia laughed once, still crying. "Sorry, but—I don't think I've ever heard you say *fuck.*"

Eve made a sound of disgust. She would have to take her to the emergency room, of all ludicrous things. The girl probably needed an antibiotic, maybe even a tetanus shot. Eve pictured hours in the beamingly lit room full of sick people—Danny restless on her lap, Magnolia whining in pain—followed by a bill for hundreds, even thousands, the health insurance covering none of it. Missing work and school tomorrow. "God*damn* it, Maggie," she yelled. "You know what? That's it for Alexis. I don't want to see her face in this house ever again. And forget going out with her either. In fact, you can just stay home for a few weeks now. Forget going anywhere at all. School and home. That's your new life." *Have fun enforcing that one,* she thought, drunkenly.

Maggie didn't even protest. She was in real pain, Eve could see. Her nose was hot and tight to the touch. "Go get dressed," she said, sighing. "I'll wake Danny." But as she climbed the stairs, she thought of something, and she turned around. Back in the kitchen, she dialed the number for Bramington Pediatrics. Maybe the answering service could get her to someone who could somehow walk her through this.

"Hello?" said a male voice, picking up right away.

"Dr. Hamilton?" Eve said. "My gosh, *you're* there?"

"I'm in catching up on some things. Is this Eve?"

"Yes!" Eve slurred, flattered. Though they'd had a lot of contact the year Danny was sick, it had been a while since then. "I can't believe you remembered my voice!" she added.

"The caller ID helped." He laughed pleasantly. "What's up? Danny okay?"

"He's great," she said, feeling like an imbecile now. "It's Magnolia, actually. She—well, she had a friend pierce her nose earlier today. Completely, completely stupid, she sees now, but meanwhile, I think it's infected, and I can't get the stud out." She was talking way too fast, she realized, as if he might disappear before she got the words out.

"Why don't you bring her over now," he said, as always completely unfazed. "I'm here anyway. I'll take a look."

Eve raised her eyes in gratitude. Twelve minutes later, Danny asleep on a couch in the empty waiting room, Dr. Hamilton escorted Eve and Maggie into an examining room.

It was the first time Eve had seen him without a tie and a doctor's coat (he wore jeans and loafers, a dark blue collared short-sleeved shirt), the first time she had been in a room with him without at least one other adult: a nurse, an assistant, someone typing the info while he assessed the patient. During the whole thing with Danny, she had often wished she could have a real conversation with him. He had been wonderful, working with her on whatever research she found, e-mailing back whenever she sent thoughts or questions. At one point, he'd invited her to call him by his first name, Rick. She hadn't, though. She liked keeping him on a pedestal, she'd realized. Eve revered the people who helped raise her children: doctors, teachers, coaches. With few exceptions, she had crushes on them all: male and female, old and young, straight and gay.

Dr. Hamilton was on the older side—well into his fifties, she guessed—and weathered in exactly the ways you'd want a pediatrician to be, his no doubt once bold energy (which showed in both his bright green eyes and in the way he occasionally got excited about a diagnosis, say, or a new vaccine) having mellowed into a perfect combination of patience, knowledge, and overall cheer. He was a solid man, medium tall with a head he shaved bald and, Eve had noticed more than once, very large, gentle hands. As he asked Maggie questions, felt her forehead (a nurse would have used a thermometer, Eve knew, but he didn't need one), touched her nose—the girl winced but let him do it; even Magnolia liked Dr. Hamilton—Eve thanked him silently, grateful almost to tears to have her crazy daughter in someone else's capable care.

He was asking Maggie questions now: Did this hurt, did that (yes and yes), one Eve missed—maybe about the kind of needle the girl used. "Let's let your mom leave the room for this part if she wants," Dr. Hamilton said finally. "It won't be fun, but we've got to get that thing out of your nose. If it's in there too tightly, it lowers your resistance to whatever bacteria might be in there too, which, in a nose, can be considerable. Probably once we remove it and clean it up, you'll be fine." He turned to Eve. "But I'll give you a prescription for an antibiotic, just to be safe."

Eve nodded and went out. She collapsed next to Danny, leaned back, and thought of Dr. Hamilton's big hands touching Danny's sore little stomach, Magnolia's poor, ravaged face. Amazing that hands so large could be so tender and precise. She remembered her own pediatrician, a creepy, hawkish dude, despised by children townwide, who had always examined her with a little too much interest. Dr. Hamilton, in contrast—sensitive, brilliant, humane—was beloved by patients and parents alike.

She closed her eyes, imagining those big hands on her own face now, then on the back of her neck, the bones of her shoulders, the curve of her waist. *How could you!* she thought, as her mind worked his hands down, but she savored the wave of desire that washed over her. So rare that she got to feel that chemical rush now. She and Eric had a decent sex life (or *had* had, anyway), at least compared to some married couples she knew—as in, they still had sex (less often than he wanted, probably slightly more often than she did), they both got off, he tried to make her happy and usually succeeded . . . they weren't one of the dreaded "sexless" couples who did it less than ten or twelve times a year. But still. Married sex was married sex. Like comparing a Stop & Shop panfried burger to— what? Caviar, white truffle mushrooms, Densuke watermelon from Japan. Not that she liked any of those, or would, if she ever got to taste them, which she probably wouldn't. But still.

Marriage sucks! she thought, suddenly vehement. *I hate marriage!* She reminded herself that in a way, she wasn't even really married anymore, and she waited for the thrill of this realization to sink in. But for whatever reason, the idea instead filled her with dread, so she went back to thinking about Dr. Hamilton's hands, moving, touching, awakening every one of her nerves from the peaceful, boring, married slumber they'd been in for years and years.

And then the doctor was returning, his arm around Magnolia's shoulder as he led her into the waiting room. Eve jumped up, blushing as if they could read her thoughts (as if it were about *her* right now anyway!), and there was her big, tearful, overgrown baby girl, nose beet red but stud-free, praise the Lord. Maggie flopped next to Danny and lay down half on top of him, closing her eyes. Dr. Hamilton motioned to Eve to come with him.

Interestingly, she had not been in his office before. They had always had their discussions in the general examining room, in front of the kids. *He must reserve it for after-hours guests*, she thought, sitting down in one of the two chairs in front of his desk. She looked around. Awards and honors certificates on the walls, a thank-you for helping children in another country, another for aiding underprivileged children here. "Well," he said, settling on the chair next to hers—rather than his own across the desk, she noticed—and turning it toward hers. "Mission accomplished. She was very good. I know that wasn't fun for her."

"Or for you, I'm sure."

"Easier than the fish hook I took out of a kid's cheek earlier today." He smiled, triumphant, and in an instant Eve saw both what he got out of all this and what he had looked like as a boy: adorable, round-faced and smiley.

"At least the boy didn't put it there on purpose," she said.

He laughed. "That's true." His green eyes gleamed, and she saw both the spark, the devilish fun, that had always been there, and the wisdom and age that had mellowed it—shielded it from emerging and wreaking havoc, as it no doubt had in his early days. It made her insides flutter. She wished briefly that she had put on lipstick before she left, then chastised herself for the wish—*He's the kids' doctor, you lush!*—and then thought, *Well, at least you wore the pale green sweater.* It was one of Eric's favorites.

Dr. Hamilton leaned toward Eve, resting his arms on his long legs. "So," he said, looking into her eyes. "That seems like fairly unusual behavior for Magnolia. Any guesses what's up?"

Eve tensed. Did he know about Eric? "Well, for one thing, her boyfriend dumped her," she said after a moment.

He clicked his tongue in sympathy.

"And took up with her best friend."

He made a wincing face.

"I know." Eve was silent for a moment. "And Eric left me," she said suddenly, and once she started, the words spilled forth in a rush. "Almost a month ago. No warning whatsoever. He just disappeared one night. We didn't hear from him for days. Then he started texting Maggie. As far as I know, they text each other a few times a day now." She paused. Her eyes were tearing a little. And she was mortified that she'd told him all that. She sniffed hard and held her breath.

But he was listening and nodding, all warmth and compassion. "And you?" he said softly. He handed her a box of tissues. "Does he text you too?"

"He calls," she said, taking a tissue, "or did. I didn't pick up. I have nothing to say to him." She wiped her eyes, but, not wanting to blow her nose in front of him, just sniffed again.

He nodded once more. He seemed to be searching her face. "Okay," he said after a moment. "I guess that might explain her acting out."

"That and her age, I guess."

"Yes. Her age doesn't help." He looked thoughtful a moment. "I could give you the name of a therapist who's very good with teenagers. She's right in town."

Eve felt like climbing into his big, warm lap, curling up and going to sleep there while he raised her children, paid her bills, fixed her broken ice maker, mowed her overgrown, weed-filled grass. "Yes, please," she said.

He stood and walked around the desk, typed something on his keyboard, then scribbled on a piece of paper. He came back around the desk and handed the paper to her.

"Thank you," she said, standing—reluctantly, but there seemed to be no choice—and taking the note. "Thank you for all of this." She sniffed once more. "If you hadn't picked up that phone, we'd probably be sitting in the ER right now behind twenty people with contagious diseases."

He laughed. "You're welcome. I'll call in that prescription to CVS, so it'll be waiting when you get there."

She nodded. "Oh!" she said suddenly. "How should I—I mean, should I pay you right now, or do you want to bill me?"

He shook his head. "This one's on me. We won't tell the authorities."

"Are you serious?" She blushed once more (*Really, Mom?* she heard Magnolia's sarcastic voice ask), then looked down to hide it.

"I still feel awful about not diagnosing Danny more quickly," he said. "Stomach things can be so tricky, as you saw, especially in kids. You never know how much might be stress related or even psychosomatic. You can do all kinds of tests—and you know we did them all—" Eve was nodding "—but if they come back negative, it's sometimes better to wait, if he's functioning okay with the proton pump inhibitors, than to try a treatment that might have other negative consequences when you can't find anything real to treat. As you saw with the antidepressants."

"Oh, those were the worst," Eve remembered. They had made him lethargic and anxious, besides not doing a thing for the stomach pain. "But listen," she said, "we don't blame you at all! We realize doctors aren't magicians. We were just grateful for all the time you put in." She wished she hadn't said *we*. It was just her now, wasn't it.

The doctor nodded, though he still seemed troubled. "Anyway," he said. "If you ever want to talk more about any of this, or if you have more trouble with Magnolia, I hope you'll give me a call. Or an e-mail—whichever you prefer. You have my address.

"I do. And I will. Thank you, Dr. Hamilton."

"You can call me Rick, you know." He smiled again, and she thought she saw a gleam in his eye, an invisible wink. Was he flirting? Or was she just deep in fantasy by now?

"I actually don't think I can," she admitted.

He laughed once more. He seemed to find her completely amusing. "Well, I obviously can't force you," he said, and he stood now, too, and extended his hand, and when she took it, her hand disappeared inside his. Again, something seemed to pass between them, though again she wasn't completely sure. *Maybe this is part of the whole package,* she thought. *He probably does this to all the patients.* But she hoped not.

Later, in the car with prescription in hand (Magnolia had already taken the first dose in the store—her nose already looked less swollen by then, a small miracle—and now both kids slept in the backseat as she drove), she replayed the handshake with Dr. Hamilton, the conversation as they'd sat in the chairs, and she wondered again if there'd been anything to any of it. She knew he was married. But so what? She was too.

For some reason, she wished she'd told him about her book. He'd probably be surprised to hear she was a published author. No doubt he thought she was just one more goofy mother, dragging her messed-up offspring in for him to fix.

At home, the kids once again in bed, Eve found herself wide awake. And there, on the counter, was her wineglass from before, still half full. She drank it down. Then she sat again at her computer, that source of the entire outside world for all stuck-at-home mommies, and opened a new e-mail screen. She typed in Dr. Hamilton's address (she still knew it by heart) and, in the subject line, "THANK YOU." "*Dear Rick,*" she wrote, then erased "Rick" and wrote, "Dr. Hamilton," then erased that and wrote, "Dear Dr. Hamilton/Rick." She frowned—still not right—but she seemed to have run out of options, and anyway the wine had nicely reignited her cavalier state of mind, so who really cared? "Thank you again for seeing us tonight, and for curing Magnolia so fast. (Her nose already looked better by the time we hit CVS.) And thanks for not charging us, which was so nice of you." She added a smiley emoticon, then erased it, then erased the whole line and wrote, "I was wondering if I might take you out to lunch sometime to thank you properly, for that and also for your wonderful care of Danny over the years." She thought a moment, then wrote, "If you're too busy, I completely understand. Warmly, Eve." She read it, took out "Warmly" and wrote "Sincerely," then deleted "Sincerely" and wrote "Yours," and added "Adams" to the "Eve," even though he'd see that from her e-mail address. Then she closed her eyes and hit Send.

She took a big, loud yoga breath. Okay, then! She got up, found the almost empty bottle of wine in the fridge, and poured the rest into her glass. She dropped the bottle sloppily in the sink, then opened another blank e-mail page and typed in "SamRabinowitz@comcast.net." In the subject line, she wrote: "Eric Knight sculpture." In the message box: "I've thought about it, and I'm ready to sell at the price you suggested. Let's talk about where and when." Once more, she hit Send.

Then she finished her wine, left the glass on the desk, and went up to bed.

9

FOR MUCH OF his life, along with practicing kung fu, Eric had run regularly. Only in the past two or three years had he slacked off with both, always feeling he should be in his studio (having accomplished so little that day/week/year). By the time he'd come to Tucson, it had been months since he'd so much as taken a jog, and he couldn't remember the last time he'd gone in to a kung fu school even to run some forms or kick the heavy bag. But here, he'd been going every day to Desert Kung Fu, a place he'd come upon, shortly after arriving, while wandering in a not-yet-gentrified neighborhood south of downtown. He'd made himself walk in and, finding the place decent-looking, sign up for a class, which ended up being exceptionally well taught. At the end, the teacher, who also happened to be the studio owner, approached him to compliment his skills and ask where he'd trained, how he'd come to be here. Eric told him the bare minimum—he was in town for a while, not sure how long—but did mention that he had a son who did kung fu. The owner, Diego, instantly warmed; his own son, Christian, studied there.

Two days later, when an instructor bailed on him, Diego asked Eric if he wanted to teach the guy's classes that afternoon. Within a week, Eric was teaching one or two classes every day. The money was a relief, even with his expenses being nominal (the occasional tank of gas, the carne seca chimichanga he made himself choke down every noon at Mi Nidito; he wasn't hungry, but needed the energy). And the job, which at first simply gave him something to get up for in the morning, had quickly progressed into what kept him going day after day. He liked his students, the little boys especially, in their tiny cropped pants and tight belts and sashes, feigning toughness but really shy and adoring, calling him Sifu, Sifu. And he liked the adults too—both the ones in his adult beginner class and the parents of his students. One-third white and two-thirds Mexican/Hispanic or otherwise, give or take, they were polite and deferential; some of the mothers, especially, smiled at him shyly, and one hugged him after he told her how well her son was doing.

There was one mother, though—Natasha—who was anything but obsequious. She had stormed in the first day, tiny and gorgeous—enormous black eyes, shiny dark hair down her back—stomping on three-inch platform sandals as if she were killing a trail of roaches in her path. Her son, Johnny, was new here, she told Eric in a heavy accent (Russian? Spanish? He was embarrassed he had no idea). This was only his second class, and she wasn't sure why there was a new teacher already, but okay, let's see what happens . . . but just know that the boy has had a lot of change at home lately, and she'd appreciate some consistency here. And in fact, if he acted up, that was why. "His life is not easy right now," she said, calming down a little as she realized Eric was listening. "This is supposed to be a—what you call it? Relief? No—*release*. Right, okay. But if he doesn't behave right in your class, I want to know about it. Natasha. That's me."

Eric nodded. Absolutely.

She stomped off, Johnny's hand clamped into hers. Hair swinging, body (Eric couldn't help noticing) like a teenage gymnast's.

After that, he had found himself watching the boy—who was fine in class, if a bit subdued and humorless—with interest, wondering what all the change at home had been. He'd even given Johnny a little extra attention, keeping him after class to practice a form or just to talk to him, trying to draw him out a bit. His mother tended to be late for pickup anyway (Natasha had a job, Eric knew; an older woman who spoke no English delivered him to the studio and then left), and Eric worked with the boy long enough for her to see Johnny getting time with him well after the class. He didn't mind at all; he had nothing to rush to, and he liked eliciting a rare smile from Johnny—really, it was the highlight of his day. And he loved watching Natasha warm to him, her raging exterior slowly melting as he gave her rundowns of her boy's progress, had him demonstrate forms and stances to her.

It wasn't that he had a crush on her exactly. No matter how far he was from Eve at the moment, he was hardly looking to have an affair—and anyway, his sex drive, like his hunger, had pretty much disappeared. But Natasha was easy on the eyes, and he missed being close to a woman: her smell (mint, leather, something a little bit floral, in Natasha's case), her emotion and intensity, her abundant, smooth hair. He could feel, like an infusion, his relief at having something to offer this one. The evening she told him she preferred him to the first-day teacher—"he was a leetle too young for my taste"—Eric had smiled with pride in spite of knowing better.

But today, alas, was a different story. From the moment he arrived, Johnny had seemed out of sorts, and as the class progressed, he got ornery, first refusing to warm up properly, then mangling his stances, and finally purposely kicking another boy in the shin. He was small but strong—like his mother, no doubt—and the other kid, though brave about it, ended up crying. Eric made Johnny get an ice pack for the boy and apologize in front of the class, and then he made him meditate on the side until he felt ready to participate again. After a while Eric invited him back, but Johnny wouldn't come; he sat with his arms crossed and head pressed to his chest, refusing to look up or move.

After class, when most mothers had left (Natasha hadn't yet arrived), Eric went over to Johnny. He knew he had handled the situation well, but he still felt bad about it, disappointed in both the boy and himself. He hated the idea of telling Natasha they'd had a setback, but he didn't see a way around it; she had asked him to keep her informed. He sat down next to the boy on the wood floor. Johnny pretended not to notice.

The place was almost empty; there was no class from 5:30 to 6:30, and then everything revved up again. He watched a couple of lingering mothers chatting in Spanish while one of their toddlers attempted a somersault on the mat—her big white diaper emerging like a soccer ball every time she stuck her butt in the air—and the other pulled up on a pile of chairs, the mother rushing over just in time to stop the chairs from toppling. They all left after that. Eric sat quietly, trying to breathe out his tension. Whenever he stopped moving, the details of his life flooded back, and he was aware of the fact that in the end, coming to Tucson had not only not made him feel better—had not taken away his overall lethargy or cleared his foggy brain—but had also only multiplied his problems, which now expanded like a blob in a closet in his mind, oozing from cracks on the top and bottom and sides, pushing against the thin, flimsy door. He turned to Johnny. "So," he said. "Want to tell me what happened today?"

The boy didn't respond.

"Johnny?"

"What?" the kid mumbled.

"You seem a little angry today, pal. Want to talk about it?"

"No."

Eric couldn't blame him. *I know how you feel, dude,* he wanted to say. Instead, he said, "Do you know, I have a son just a little older than you? His name is Danny. He does kung fu too."

No response for a minute, and then Johnny said, "Is he a black belt?"

Eric laughed. "Not quite yet." He scratched his leg. "It takes a lot of years for a black belt. Danny might not ever get it. And that's okay if he doesn't. It's up to him, really. Depends how hard he wants to work at it."

Johnny lifted his head and looked at him. "Does he work at it here?"

"What?" Eric said.

"Does he go to kung fu here?"

A slow, dull pain started up somewhere inside him. Eric forced a smile. "Not right now."

"Well, where does he go, then?" Johnny's eyes were intense, black like his mother's; already, at age seven, he had a worry line between his eyebrows.

"He lives in Massachusetts," Eric said after a moment. "He goes to a school there. Hey, listen, do you want to work on your—"

"Why?" Johnny said.

"Why what, bud?" Eric regarded him warily.

"Why does he live in Massachusetts and you live here?"

Why the hell couldn't he have kept his mouth shut? Every time he opened it, he dug himself into a corner. "He lives with his mom at the moment," Eric said. "And I live here, so that's the story with that. Hey, did your mom tell you what time she was coming today?" He sneaked a peek at the clock. Where the hell was Natasha, anyway?

"Are you divorced?" Johnny asked.

"No," Eric said, and then, gratefully, "Speaking of moms, here comes yours. Come on. Let's go see her." He stood and gave the boy a hand up.

He put his arm around Johnny's shoulder as Natasha approached, lifting her big sunglasses to the top of her head. She wore a tight dark tank top with a rainfall of silver necklaces. "Sorry I'm late," she said. "My boss kept me over. *Asshole.*" She muttered the last word, shaking her head. Then she looked at Johnny, and Eric saw her readjust her face, her emotion. "Hey, baby," she said, smiling. "How you doing? Did you have a great day?"

Johnny shrugged.

"He didn't have his best class today," Eric said. He dreaded the words; hated to disappoint her, plus he didn't want to set her off or make the kid feel bad. "But that's okay," he said quickly. "We're working on it. Right, Johnny?"

The boy didn't respond.

"What happened?" Natasha said to her son. "Tell me."

Again, no response.

Natasha gave him a warning look, but Eric said, "It's okay. He had a time-out, and he's good to go now. Right, Johnny? I don't think it will happen again."

His mother was frowning. "Go use the bathroom," she said to the boy.

"I don't have to."

"Do it anyway. Now!"

Eric cringed. The boy glared at her, then shuffled away.

When he was out of earshot, Natasha looked at Eric. "What happened?"

"Really, it was nothing. I wouldn't even have mentioned it except that you told me to tell you if he seemed out of sorts. He did today a little. But no big deal. Mostly he just didn't want to participate." He took a step back—she was so small that, even with her heels, she was looking way up at him and he down at her. Even little Eve was a giant compared to the women around here. "My son's like that too sometimes," he added, to be helpful. "He gets in moods where he doesn't want to do anything."

"You have a son?" Her eyebrows rose. "I didn't know. How old?"

"Eight. Almost nine. I told Johnny that too."

She smiled a little. "I can tell you're a father. The way you are with the kids."

"Thank you," he said, and he felt a burst of hope that their friendship, or whatever you called what they had, might stay intact after today.

But she was frowning again. "Johnny was a perfect boy before," she said. "He made A's in school, his teachers loved him, not one problem. Now he's so angry."

"What happened?" Immediately, Eric wished he hadn't asked; he didn't want to intrude.

"His father," Natasha said. "*That* happened. Cheating on me. I'm not embarrassed to say it. He denies and denies, and then where is he now? Living with *her*." She shook her head, her black eyes suddenly glittering with fury. "I don't care for myself, because what do

I want with a man who does that anyway? I'm over him, for *me*. But what kind of man leaves his son?" She did something then that shocked him: she turned and spit into the corner of the room. Not a lot—it was more about the gesture than anything—but still. "I hate his guts," she said, glaring back at Eric. "If he wasn't the father of my son, I would wish him dead."

"I'm sorry," Eric stammered after a moment.

She looked at him. "Why? You didn't do anything. It's my fault. I picked a bad man. I fell in love with a loser." Her words were a stab in Eric's side. "My mother warned me not to marry him," she said. "I didn't listen. Stupid girl." She made a sound of disgust through her teeth.

"I just meant I'm sorry for the situation."

"The situation." She shook her head. "But? It's all over now. For me, anyway. I'm done with him forever. Johnny, though, he's stuck with him. A rotten, selfish father." She narrowed her eyes. "Disgusting."

Johnny had come out of the bathroom and was walking back now, though slowly, chin still pressed to his chest. As he approached, Eric saw with a pang of emotion that he was crying. "He's upset," he mumbled to Natasha. "Can I talk to him? I don't want him to feel bad about this."

But Natasha shook her head. "We need to get home." She turned to her son. "Johnny, let's go! Time for dinner. Come on, baby." Back to Eric now. "See you later."

He felt unusually crushed. "Natasha?" he called after her. "If there's anything I can do . . ."

She was walking, but she turned, almost as if to humor him.

". . . let me know," he finished.

She smiled then, the first time today other than the fake smile she'd flashed her son. "You're already doing it," she said, and then, "I wish all men were like you."

He couldn't even answer. His mouth opened and shut, like a fish.

When she was gone, he felt utterly deflated; he could keel over and crumple, a Mylar balloon emptied of air. Instead, he went to the supply closet and took out a bucket, the mop, detergent. He filled the bucket with soapy water, then pulled it out into the room. Then he began to mop, starting where Natasha had spit.

He mopped the mats quickly, not missing a spot. Then he hauled them to the side and mopped the floor under them. Sweat covered his face, pooled at his neck, ran down his rib cage and hips. (The place had a swamp cooler—a fan that blows air through a cold-water-soaked mat, he had learned—that was better than nothing, though hardly an air conditioner.) When he finished, he got a towel and dried the floor. The 6:30 class would arrive soon; he had to hurry. At 6:25—people already milling around, warming up, tying their belts and sashes—he dumped the bucket in the utility sink, rinsed his hands, grabbed his shoes and wallet, and got out of there.

Outside, the sun was still a high-beam spotlight, the air like an oven; already it was in the 90s every day. Eric took off his T-shirt and tossed it into his car. His sneakers were shot—no good for running—but he put them on anyway, though he had no socks. Then he took off for Santa Rita Park, almost at a sprint.

The park was crowded: baseball games in full swing, brown-skinned families—babies, mothers, toothless old men—grilling food or resting in lawn chairs or dancing to loud, festive Spanish music. For some reason, the music made him feel worse; perhaps it was the contrast with his own lack of merriment. But the running helped in its way. He ran hard on the rough, yellow grass until he was covered in a different kind of sweat from before. A homeless man lay on a bench, feet bare, pants filthy and wet. Eric ran past him, past a couple kissing under a tree, past blooming bushes and overflowing trash cans. He ran until his head pounded and his heels burned, until he literally couldn't run another step. Then he walked—limped, really—back to his car and drove to his mother's house.

He should shower, he knew. He should eat, and he should talk to his mother. Maybe she'd have some suggestions for how to handle Johnny. Instead, he walked in, dropped his shoes at the door, and headed for his room.

"David?" his mother called. "Is that you?"

It was all he could do to get the words out: "It is, Mom, but I'm pretty wiped out. I think I'll just go to bed."

She came toward him, drying something—a zucchini, a squash—with a dish towel. "Are you sure? Are you okay?

He was in his doorway now, half closed in. "I'm fine. Just really tired." He forced a smile. "Sorry. Hope you didn't prepare anything."

"I was making ratatouille, but it's just as good cold. You can have it when you feel better."

How he loved her. "Thanks. I will." He smiled—genuinely this time. And though he thought he would likely never eat the ratatouille, he said, "Tomorrow. I'll have it then."

10

THE MUSIC DRIFTED downstairs and into the kitchen like cool silver rain, like a long-awaited gift wrapped in rich, flowing ribbon that was meant directly for her. Eve stopped typing, closed her eyes, and sucked in her breath. It had been months since Magnolia had picked up her violin; ever since she'd "quit" (right after, Eve recalled all too often, they'd splurged on her new violin). And now here came Mendelssohn's Concerto in E Minor, strong and steady and as if she'd never even stopped for a day. Eve felt her mind and her muscles relax into it, and for a second she allowed herself to think, *It will all be okay.*

But Maggie struck a sour note. Played through it, struck another one, and stopped. After five or ten seconds she started back up, and Eve sighed with relief. But she flubbed again, stopped again. Tried a third time. Eve held her breath. *Please, let her get through it, even just once.* And the playing resumed, several seconds, several more, and then she flubbed again, and that was the end. There was a smack on the floor, and Eve's eyes popped open. "Magnolia!" she yelled up, because, she swore to God, it had better not be the violin.

Her daughter's door opened, and Magnolia barreled downstairs and into the kitchen, her face dark and ominous. "What?" she snapped, and then, "I thought we weren't allowed to yell up or down to another floor anymore."

Though it was a rule she had made recently, Eve ignored the comment. "What the hell was that noise?" she said.

Magnolia cocked her head. "I stamped my foot. Am I not allowed to stamp on my own floor anymore either?"

"I'd prefer you didn't," Eve said, a little less tensely. "Not that loudly, at least. But as long as it wasn't the violin . . ."

"*God*, Mom! Do you really think I'm retarded enough to throw a violin like that to the floor?" Maggie glared at her. "Give me a little credit, please."

Eve sat back down in her chair. "I'm sorry."

Maggie shrugged.

"And the playing was so beautiful," Eve said—pushing it, she knew, but it was the truth, and she wanted to say it.

"It was not," Magnolia said. "Don't lie. I suck at violin. After five years of lessons. I never should have taken it in the first place."

Just be quiet, Eve told herself. *Don't say a word.* "Magnolia, that's an absurd thing to say," she blurted. "You play gorgeously. When I hear those notes drifting down, I actually feel transported. It's like the most beautiful—"

"Mom, stop."

"—the most—"

"*Stop!*" the girl repeated. "Okay? Please. Sorry, but I can't listen to that anymore. You don't know what's good and bad. No offense, but you have no idea. So it's really just easier for me if you don't talk about it."

Eve's mouth snapped shut.

Magnolia went to the fridge, opened it, and started pawing around. "We have nothing good in here," she said. "We never have anything decent to eat." She took out a mozzarella cheese stick and began unwrapping it.

"What exactly would you want?" Eve said coldly—again, against her better judgment.

"I don't know." Maggie sighed, looking around the kitchen as if for inspiration. "Chocolate pudding? Cheesecake?" She took a bite of the cheese, chewed, made a face. "*One* fun thing. *One* thing that isn't totally healthy. One thing that—" She stopped mid-chew. "Where's Dad's sculpture?" she said, staring at the empty spot over the sink.

Eve glanced at the spot, and then back at her daughter. "It's gone," she said calmly, though her heart fluttered just once. "I sold it."

"You *what*?"

"I sold it."

"To *who*?" Magnolia said. "What *for*?"

"To *whom*," Eve said loudly. "A local man. He just picked it up this morning, actually. You and Danny were still asleep." *And now we have ten thousand dollars in the checking account,* she thought. *Enough to pay the bills this month and next with some left over for a rainy day. So put that in your pipe and smoke it, both you and your dad.*

Magnolia was staring at her with a combination of hatred and disbelief. "You *sold* the sculpture of *you*?" she said. "That Daddy *made* you?" Tears sprang to her eyes. "How could you?"

"There are bills to pay, and I can't pay them on my income." Eve would not cave to Maggie's emotions right now. "I'm sorry if you miss it, but, well, you'd miss food too if we didn't have any. Or clothes, or a roof over your head." Once more, she knew she should stuff a sock in her yapper. But why should she? If Magnolia could dish it out, she could learn to take it. Besides, it needed to be said.

"That is so unfair," Magnolia said. "It's just so unfair you did that."

"Unfair?" Eve laughed rudely. "What exactly is unfair about it?"

"How would you feel if *you* went away for a little while and Dad sold, like—like—I don't know. Something you really love."

"If I went away, I guess I wouldn't have much say in the matter, would I." Eve began to fly around the kitchen, shoving dirty glasses and dishes into the sink, clean ones into cabinets. Power and energy buzzed through her. "Besides, how do I know it's just for a little while?" she yelled. "Dad hasn't told me when he's coming back, if at all. Has he told you? Has he texted you *that*?"

Magnolia blinked, and the tears crossed the edges of her eyes and started down her face. "*God*, Mom! What are you *talking* about?"

"What's going on?" Danny had drifted into the kitchen, Batman perched on his shoulder.

"Nothing," Eve said loudly. "Don't you worry about—"

"Mom sold Dad's statue," Magnolia said. "We needed the money. Otherwise we wouldn't have any food."

"Maggie!" Eve said, and the horror of what she'd just done, the things she'd said to her daughter, began to seep through her. "Danny, that's not true," she said to her son. "Of course we'd have food. Your sister is just upset."

"I am *not* upset! *GOD!*"

Danny looked at Magnolia and then at Eve, and she saw that his eyes had that look they'd taken on lately, like someone had pulled a not-quite-sheer curtain over them. "I got Batman to say 'Hello,'" he said. "Want to hear?"

"Yes!" Eve yelled. "That's so cool! I'd love to hear that, honey!"

Magnolia was shaking her head. "I'm going out."

"You most certainly are not," Eve said. "For one thing, you're still punished. For another, I need you to watch Danny. I have an appointment today."

"Oh, what. To sell more of Dad's artwork?" She shook her head. "No wonder Dad left you. You don't appreciate *one thing* he does. I swear, you are such a—"

She stopped. Eve stared at her, enraged. "That's *enough!*" she screamed. "Go to your room!"

Magnolia turned, stalked upstairs, and slammed her door.

"Mom?" Danny said.

Eve turned to Danny. She was shaking, she was so angry. "What?" she tried to say, but nothing came out.

Danny walked over to her, bird and all, put his arms around her waist, and squeezed.

Tears spilled from her own eyes now, and she stood there and let him hug her, the best little boy who'd ever lived. "Thank you," she said when she could talk again, and she tried to wipe her eyes before he could see them. "That was exactly what I needed." She hugged him a moment longer, then backed up and forced a smile. "Can I hear Batman talk now? Is he ready?"

"Yes. Okay, wait, I have to get him down to my hand." He

reached up and offered his finger to the bird, who walked onto it with curved little claws. Danny lowered his hand to his face. "Hello," he said into the bird's face. "Hello. Hello. Hello."

The bird glanced around with jerky little motions.

"Batman," Danny said. "Say hello. Hello? Hello?"

"Squawk," said the bird.

Eve laughed.

Danny smiled. "Mom, I swear he can do it. He did it upstairs. Batman! Hello? Hello?"

The bird began to clean under its wing with its beak.

Danny shook his head. "I guess he feels shy right now."

"I guess so."

"But he'll probably do it later."

"I'm sure he will. And I'll be right here to see it."

"But you're going out today. Right?" He looked nervous suddenly.

Eve took a step closer and bent down so she was right next to him. "Yes, but then I'll be back," she said. She reached to pat the bird, but it twisted away from her hand. "I'll never leave you," she said. "Or your sister. I know you know that," she added. "I was just reminding you."

Danny nodded. "I know. Because you'd be too bored if you did, right?"

"I'd be so bored, I don't even know what I'd do. And lonely too."

"You'd probably work or whatever. And then you wouldn't be lonely."

"Yeah, but—then I'd want my family around me the second I was done. I'd miss them too much."

He nodded, looking at the bird. "Do you miss Daddy?"

Her heart stirred. "Sometimes," she said. "Do you?"

He nodded. "When do you think he'll be done replenishing?"

She smiled sadly. "Honestly? I don't know, because he hasn't told me. But when he does, you'll be the first to know."

"And Magnolia too," he said.

"Of course. You and Magnolia."

He nodded, the dreamy look returning to his eyes, then reached up to pat the bird.

Eve needed to shower and get ready. She was going to see Keisha, who'd had to cancel her appointment this week because she'd had to make up a math test she'd missed one day when the baby was sick and couldn't go to work with Keisha's mother. And she had finally done all the research about gastric bypass. She had everything organized to explain it to Michael now, the way she should've when she first mentioned it, and then again days ago, when she'd been all set to call but then something came up . . . oh, yes: Magnolia's nose piercing. Anyway, she hadn't found a time to call again since then, nor had he called her, but she absolutely, positively would do it today, when she knew Diane would be home with the kids. Last but not least—and most amazing—she was meeting Dr. Hamilton for a late lunch. He'd responded to her e-mail a day or two after she'd sent it: "Sure, love to have lunch. Name time and place." And after a quick glass or two of wine late one night, she had done just that. So. Today was the day.

Eve straightened up again, suddenly anxious to get going. "You keep working on Batman," she told Danny. "When I come home, I want to hear him say not just 'Hello,' but 'Hello, Mommy, you are so cool.'"

Danny laughed.

"And make Magnolia play with you," she said. "Don't let her sit on her iPod all day."

"She will. I mean, she *won't*. She always plays with me."

"I know. Who wouldn't?" She kissed his cheek. "And you can have one hour of Wii."

"Thanks." He scratched his head, then rubbed at his nose with the back of his hand, and Eve watched him a moment, the joy of her life, making her smile in spite of everything. "Hey, Danny?" she said, and when he looked at her, she said, "Thanks for being my dreamboat."

He laughed again, a glimpse—rare, these days—of the old, familiar Danny. "Thanks for being mine," he said.

*   *   *

Fifty-five minutes later, Eve pulled into a parking lot downtown, parked, spread Michael's file and her notes about bariatric surgery as neatly as possible on the passenger seat, and, at long last—and not without some nervousness—dialed his home.

Diane answered, sounding breathless, as if she'd run in from outside.

"Diane!" Eve said. "It's Eve Adams."

"Oh. Hi, Eve."

She didn't sound angry exactly, but neither, Eve decided, was her voice warm and fuzzy. "How are you?" Eve asked.

"I'm—okay, I guess. You?"

"Good! I'm good." Eve took a breath. "How's Michael?"

There was a pause. "I don't know," Diane said finally. "I just really don't know. I mean, he's the same. He doesn't seem to me to get any better. But maybe he'd tell you differently. He's really stopped talking to me about all of that."

Eve nodded, waiting for her to go on.

"He's out with the kids right now, pushing them on the swings," Diane said. "First time he's been out in two days. But Bella asked, and he can never say no to her. Thankfully, in this case." Another pause. Eve heard the shouts and laughter of children, maybe out a window. "Anyway, I'm glad you called," Diane said. "He will be, too, though he might not act it at first. I think he expected you to call sooner."

"I know," Eve said, blushing with shame. "I'm so sorry. I just—I haven't had a chance to do the research until now." Diane was silent. "I did call a couple of times," Eve couldn't resist adding, "but I got the voice mail, and then—"

"I know. It's not your fault," Diane offered, and Eve knew she was being generous. "He feels bad to call back since he's not paying for sessions right now, which"—she sighed—"to be honest, we just can't afford. But I know he misses talking to you."

"Well, I've got an idea for him," Eve said, relieved to jump in.

"Last time I saw him, I mentioned bariatric surgery—gastric by-pass—and he immediately said no. And he's got good reasons. It's definitely a last resort, not at all easy or fun." She switched the phone to her other ear and looked out the car window without seeing, talking excitedly now. "But I've been researching it a lot, something called the Roux-en-Y procedure, and I really think he should at least consider it at this point. It used to be a very dangerous operation, but the complication rate is much lower now, and it has the highest success rate of any weight-loss method in terms of both losing the weight and keeping it off." She took a breath. "But he has to want to do it. It's not something I could talk him into, nor would I. He'd have to be completely on board."

"Really?" Diane's voice had taken on a slight note of hope. "Tell me more about it—or, wait, let me get him on the phone. I'll bring it out. Is it okay if I pick up an extension?"

"Yes!" Eve wished she were there, talking to them both in person. "That would be great," she said. "Because this is definitely not a decision he'd make alone. It would be really hard on you, too, for a long time afterward. But in the end—"

"Okay, wait," Diane said. "Let me get him."

There was shuffling, kids' voices, the sounds of outside, and then Michael picked up, and then Eve heard another extension click on. "How are you!" she said to Michael (perhaps a little too gushily, she realized).

"I'm fine, thanks. How are you?" He sounded distant, even cold, for him.

"Listen," Eve said. "I know I said I'd call you back weeks ago, and I'm *so* sorry."

"It's fine," he said, on cue, but she knew he took it personally, and she wanted to yell, *It's not about you, it's about me! My husband left me! I have no husband!*

"I didn't want to call until I'd done the research," she said, "and it took me a little while, but now I've done it. And I have tons to tell you."

"Do you want to come down?" he asked, a little less coldly. "I'm around this afternoon."

Eve's heart sank. "I do," she said. "I'd absolutely love to, because I think this should be done in person, and I'd love to see you anyway. But I can't come today. I have another client, and then an appointment." She paused. "How about tomorrow?" she said, though she didn't relish leaving the kids again, especially with Magnolia in such a foul mood.

"I can't tomorrow." Michael's voice was cold again. "We're going to church, and then to Diane's mother's. Not that I can fit in the pews anymore. Or in the car. I'm not sure how I'll do it, actually."

"How about Monday, then?" Eve said quickly. "Or I have openings next week."

"That's okay," Michael said. "Let's just talk now, on the phone. I can pay you for the time."

"Of course not," Eve said. "This is material I should have had for our last session. You've already paid me for this. So don't you dare try to moral upper-hand me."

To her great relief, he laughed (she was using his expression, after all), though the laughter led to a coughing fit, which lasted several seconds. "Thank you," he said when he stopped.

"Don't thank me. Just listen." She proceeded to tell him everything she knew about the Roux-en-Y surgery, without sugar-coating any of it: how it worked, what would be expected of him, what the odds were of success and failure. She told him where he could have it done and the names of two doctors she knew of who did it. She told him that insurance eventually would pay for it, but they would have to build their case about why it was "medically necessary." She told him it was a last resort, not a miracle, and that the weight didn't come off easily or painlessly. It took perseverance and discipline, and no small amount of suffering. But, she said, for people like him, it could be a lifesaver. (She didn't mention the vomiting, though that was pretty much a given, especially at first, when patients were learning how much food they could handle.) She wrapped up by recommending a couple of books he could read about it.

"Honey, I think it sounds really promising," Diane said. "I think we should call the doctor Eve said and ask about it."

"I don't know," Michael said. But he sounded less adamant than when Eve first suggested it, and, to her great relief, his voice was soft and husky again.

"Think about it," she said, glancing at the clock and realizing she now had only twenty minutes to get to Keisha's. "And call me anytime to talk more about it or if you have questions. In the meantime, both of those doctors know me, and they both know you might call. So I hope you do. They also both have their own teams of nurses and dietitians who specialize in all this. So you'd have someone much better than me to help you." *Someone who wouldn't take a month to call you back,* she didn't add.

"Well, I'd rather have you," he said, and it was the nicest thing she'd heard all day.

"Thank you, Michael," she said, touched, and then, "And you will, if you decide to do this. I'd be with you from day one. Believe me," she added, "I am not going anywhere."

"Well, good."

"So. Will you think about it?"

"I will."

"Will you read the books?"

"Maybe."

She laughed. The clock ticked ahead, and she realized she was sweating. She turned the key partway in the ignition so she could open the windows. "That's good enough for now," she said. "I'll call you soon and see what you're thinking."

"Okay," he said, and then, "Thank you."

A refreshing breeze blew in as the windows slid down, and relief, both physical and otherwise, dulled her guilt, assuaged her fear, made the errors of her past and even the hell of this morning recede like the tide. "Thank *you,*" she said.

*   *   *

Was it just Eve's perception, warped as it surely was by the absolute regression that constituted her own daughter's passage these days, or was Keisha's baby, Amani, simply miraculous in the advances she made week to week (advances, Eve realized, that she herself seemed almost more excited about than the baby's own mother)? At nine or ten weeks old—only a few weeks after Eve first laid eyes on her as a tiny, bleating, lace-clad conehead—Amani, still impeccably dressed, though her lacey duds were bigger now, was paddling, kicking, moving in her pink infant seat on the table as if she were running a race with the air. Not that she didn't lie quietly when ignored, staring at the wall or her own tiny white shoes, but if anyone ventured near and engaged her, she immediately snapped to— as with Eve right now. "Hello, little beauty!" Eve gushed, grinning down at the baby, and immediately Amani grinned back. "Look at this!" Eve said, turning to Keisha. "Look at this!" She shook a black and white rattle—one of the toys she'd brought here from the box in her attic marked "for when babies come over"—near the baby's hand, and Amani reached out and gripped it. "Did you see that?" Eve said proudly, as if she herself were the mother. "She took it!"

"Yeah, she do that." Keisha was at the stove learning to cook a bag of Swiss chard Eve had brought. (She'd also brought a loaf of warm eight-grain bread and three huge, lovely, fragrant tomatoes, all of which she'd picked up at her local farmers' market on the way.) Eve was going back and forth between Keisha and the baby, alternately coaching and gushing.

"So what I do next?" Keisha asked. "I already put the oil."

"Now you sauté the garlic." Eve had brought a little jar of minced garlic last time.

"What you mean, *sawtay*?"

"Um, just like fry it a little. In the oil. Just a pinch. Hi, Amani! Hi, gorgeous girl!"

Keisha shook some garlic into the pan.

"Good," Eve said. "Now in a minute, just dump in the chard— there you go—and stir it around so it doesn't burn. It's okay if it's still a little wet. The water helps it cook." They had washed it together when she got here, dried it as best they could without a salad spinner. "You could also add chicken broth at this point, or a touch of soy sauce or lemon. But you don't have to. I like just adding salt. Just garlic, oil, and salt. But not too much, because too much salt isn't good for you, and oil is pure fat. It's good fat, though, from olives. Vegetable fat, as opposed to from animals. And we all need some fat. Just not too much. I think the baby wants to be held. Can I hold her?"

Keisha, concentrating on the chard, didn't answer, but Eve, knowing she wouldn't mind—it was part of their routine, after all—unstrapped Amani from her seat and picked her up happily. "Look what Mama's making!" she said, walking the baby toward the stove so she could see. "Mm, that's so yummy! That's Swiss chard. Rainbow chard. See how pretty? All that yellow and red. But you can't have it yet, not for another few months. I'm sorry. That was so rude of me, to bring something you couldn't have. Next time, I'll bring, I don't know, Swiss formula, or something."

Keisha smiled, and Eve did too. "It's probably ready to come off the stove now," she said. "You don't want to overcook it, or you'll take away some of the nutrients. Give it one more good stir, then dump it into a bowl. Do you believe how little all those leaves made? That's because it's mostly water. But what you have left is so good for you."

Keisha had found a white plastic bowl to dump the chard in. Holding the baby with one hand, Eve retrieved two small plates from the cabinet and two forks from the drawer, then sat down at the table and perched the baby carefully on her lap. Keisha brought the bowl to the table, and portioned out some for each of them. She sat down, then stared at it doubtfully.

Eve laughed. "It's *good*," she said. "Taste it."

Obediently Keisha took a bite. She chewed and swallowed.

Eve watched. "What do you think?"

Keisha shrugged. "It okay. Taste like collards."

"That's true! I guess it does, sort of. Do you have collards a lot?"

Keisha shrugged again. "Sometimes."

"Well, either one works," she said. "They're both good for you. Just whichever you can get. Or any leafy green, really. Spinach, or kale, or bok choy, or beet greens. . . ." She didn't mention what to do if you couldn't get any of those, being sixteen with no car or license and living in a city, or a part of the city, that barely has even frozen vegetables in the grocery stores, let alone fresh.

But she didn't want to focus on that. It was too much fun to focus on the good stuff. Like the fact that Keisha was losing weight like a dog shedding fur in spring; she'd lost fifteen pounds in a month just by following Eve's advice. Or that she was like a different person with Eve now: warm, forthcoming, even laughing occasionally. "So," Eve said, using the code they'd developed. "Scale of one to ten. School?"

"Five. Well, six, I guess. I got a A on my algebra test."

"That's *fantastic*! Good for you."

Keisha laughed. Eve knew the girl probably considered her a big dork, but at least she didn't tell her so—unlike, say, Eve's own daughter. "Work?" she asked.

Keisha frowned. "Four, I guess. But the boss giving me a raise next month."

"Seriously? That's amazing." Eve wanted to hug her. "And how's my little girlfriend here?" she said, looking at the baby. "What's she up to that I haven't seen yet?"

"She smile a lot. Poo in her diaper a lot too."

They both laughed. "Welcome to motherhood," Eve said, and then, "Are you still nursing her at all?"

Keisha shook her head. "She won't take it no more. She just want the bottle now."

"Well, that's okay. You gave her a lot of good breast milk in those first couple of months. You should feel proud of yourself."

Keisha looked down at the chard, took another small bite. "You not having any?"

"I actually have a lunch date right after this. I can't show up reeking of garlic." Eve smiled, then pushed her plate to Keisha. "You have it. Or save it for tomorrow. You can refrigerate it and put it in an omelette, or just eat it cold. I love it for breakfast."

Keisha made a face.

"I know, I'm weird," Eve said. "Believe me, my daughter tells me." She pushed her chair a bit away from the table, bounced the baby on her leg.

"You got a daughter?" Keisha looked at Eve with interest.

"Daughter and a son," Eve said. "Fourteen and eight." *Just not a husband,* she thought, and then, *So what? Neither does she. Neither does her mother. Who needs men?*

"What they names?" Keisha asked, and again, Eve was flattered she cared to ask. But before she could answer, she heard the front door open.

"Who making collards?" came a voice, and then a woman who could only be Keisha's mother walked in, a full-figured, pretty but stern-looking black woman, probably a few years younger than Eve. She was dressed in jeans, a bright blue sweatshirt, and clean jogging shoes, her hair pulled back into a neat, ironed-straight ponytail, and she carried several plastic bags—one containing diapers and toilet paper, Eve could see. She surveyed the scene quickly. "Who is this?" she said, looking at Eve but talking to Keisha, and then she walked over and took the baby from Eve, who stood up quickly.

Keisha stood too. "This Eve," she said. "She the lady from the school who been helping me with my weight."

Eve put out her hand. "Good to meet you, Mrs. Williams. You have an excellent daughter. And an excellent granddaughter, I should add."

The woman nodded once at Eve, ignoring her hand, then looked at Keisha. "Why she holding your baby?"

"I'm sorry," Eve said, blushing. "Keisha was cooking, and Amani seemed to want to be held, so I—"

"You cooking?" The mother slit her eyes at Keisha. "Why? What you making?"

"Swiss chard," Keisha said. "Eve brought it."

"Swiss *what*?" The woman looked at Eve, then back at Keisha. "Who pay for that?"

"The school," Eve said, though she had no idea if they would. "Don't worry."

"Eve show me how to cook, Mama," Keisha said. She didn't seem too worried about her mother. "She bring me groceries sometime. She bring some rattles for Amani, and—"

"You don't need to know how to cook yet," the mother said. "I thought she was supposed to tell you how to lose weight." She was frowning. "You get food at school and you get food at work. And I bring you food. Where you think I was now? Food shopping. Don't I feed you?"

"Yes, ma'am."

"So why you need people coming in the house bringing you different food? And why you need to be cooking when you got homework to do?"

Keisha sighed—not unlike, Eve noticed, Magnolia sometimes did. Though in general, she had to admit, Keisha was much more respectful to her mother (who, she thought, was much harder on her daughter than Eve was on Magnolia). "She showing me some *healthy* stuff, Ma," Keisha said while Eve cringed. "She helping me lose weight. That food I eat at work make me fat as a house. How you think I gained so much?"

"You gained weight because you *pregnant*," her mother said. "Who say you're suppose to be skinny when you pregnant? How you think your baby get nice and round? Huh? From you eating. That's how." She still hadn't said a word to Eve.

Keisha sighed again, shaking her head.

"And when you last change this baby, huh? She stink."

"I changed her," Keisha said, though she hadn't while Eve was there. "She have gas."

The woman picked up the baby and stuck her nose in its butt. "She have a poop. She need to be changed. Why don't you take care of your own baby instead of cooking white-people food you won't never get to eat anyway?"

Eve stood up. "Listen, I should get going. Nice to meet you, Mrs. Williams, and I'm sorry if I surprised you by being here. I thought you and Ms. Feldman conferred about our visits."

"She tell me you coming. She just didn't tell me you be cooking and holding her baby."

"I'm sorry." Eve blushed again. "I was trying to help, but I'll get out of your way now. Keisha, I'll speak to you before next Thursday" *to see if we're still on,* she added silently.

Keisha nodded. But the mother turned and addressed Eve head-on. "What happening next Thursday?"

Eve froze, unsure of how to answer. She turned to Keisha.

"Next Thursday when we talk," the girl said (being purposely vague, Eve thought, silently approving that decision). "She call me and see how I'm doing."

Mrs. Williams was looking at Eve. "If you from the school," she said, "why you here on Saturday? Don't you work weekdays?"

"She normally come Thursday, Ma. She only here today 'cause I had a test on Thursday."

Mrs. Williams pursed her lips, thinking. Finally, she said, "Thank you for what you done for my daughter. I do appreciate it. But she just fine now. She losing her weight, and the baby fine too, as you can see. So you don't need to come here no more."

Eve looked at her. *But I want to come here!* she thought, and she had to stop herself from saying it. She looked at Keisha for help, but the girl was looking down at the table.

"Do I make myself clear?" said the woman. "She no longer be needing your services."

Eve glanced once more at Keisha, who looked at her now, finally, her face either apologetic or noncommittal, Eve couldn't tell which. But it hardly mattered, did it, because what could she do? This was her mother. And she was sixteen.

Eve collected her purse and walked to the door. "You are clear," she said. "Very clear." She opened the door, walked out, and closed it again behind her.

* * *

It was all she could do not to peel her car out of there. But she pulled out slowly, despite shaking with rage and sadness, and drove the speed limit all the way to the crappy grocery store where she sometimes took Keisha—the closest place she could think of with a parking lot. She parked, turned off the car, and cried the river that had been building all day, all week, and all year, held back by the dam of maturity or stubbornness or whatever it was that was now officially depleted. *How dare she!* she thought, as she wiped at her face, but she got it, of course; she understood exactly where Keisha's mother came from, and she couldn't really blame her.

But still: "Fuck you," she said out loud. "Fuck you, then." (After all, she had started out this day acting fourteen; why stop now?) On she cried, not only at the injustice of every single thing, not only because she wasn't sure she'd ever get to see Keisha and Amani again, but because, when all was said and done, there was no one to call and tell about it. Not Eric—the old Eric, the one who sat in his office waiting for her to dial up and tell him about her day. That Eric was gone. And not Loretta, because hard as she tried, she simply didn't have time, with all her new obligations, for Eve and her little problems. Not Magnolia, who hated her (the old one of her was gone too, the little girl who'd idolized Eve, who wanted only to be home with her family), and not Danny, who was no longer her baby, content to lie in her arms and be cuddled all day. Not even Penelope, who used to be Eve's friend before she gave safe harbor to Eve's MIA husband. Eve understood that, too—she would do it herself, if it were Danny—but still. Now she couldn't call Penelope and Penelope couldn't call her, and Eve couldn't help feeling a tiny bit betrayed. Plus, she missed the intrepid old girl.

She cried for twenty-five minutes, until her nose was a beet and her eyes tiny staples, her sweater blotched and wet. And then she looked at the clock and said, "Shit." In forty minutes she was meeting Dr. Hamilton.

She started the car and sped up the highway and into Bram-ington, where she parked at Starbucks (the one chain store in her town, and thus the only one with a bathroom), secured the key, and locked herself in. Then she went to work. First, she took off her sweater and bra and laid them carefully over the bar for people with disabilities. Then she drenched her face with cold water, splashing it again and again. She dried it (awkwardly) under the blower, long-ing for the days of messy, lovely, carbon-producing, trash-forming paper towels. Then she soaped up her hands and washed her arm-pits, careful not to get her skirt wet. She rinsed and dried those too, playing Twister under the dryer until she accomplished it.

She blow-dried the sweater next, smoothing out the wrinkles and tears, then put her clothes back on. Someone knocked, and she jumped, then yelled, "I'm in here!" She got out her makeup bag. Thank God she carried foundation, which she nor-mally didn't wear, but the blotchiness from the bawlfest was still evident. She spackled some on, then rubbed on blush, then mascara, then lipstick. Then, realizing she looked like an aging streetwalker, she wiped most of it off with a napkin she found in her bag (thank God they still had napkins at least), then re-applied the makeup in much smaller amounts in much more strategic places.

Someone knocked again, and she ignored it this time, turning on the blower once more, this time to fluff up her hair (which, thanks to the low humidity, didn't look too wild today). She straightened her skirt and blouse, took off her shoes and blow-dried each foot, one at a time, then stuck the shoes back on again.

Another knock. "Just a minute," she called, pleasantly now. She thought for a second, then dug in her purse and found a tiny tube of grapefruit-scented perfume that had been a free sample at the mall the day she'd taken Magnolia there. She applied the scent to one wrist and sniffed—whatever, could be worse—then rubbed that wrist to her other wrist, and then both wrists on her neck. She glanced in the mirror. Not bad. She stuffed everything back in her purse and opened the door. Four people were lined up, all glaring at her. "Sorry," she said breezily, and she sashayed past them, hoping they all got a whiff of her lovely, citrusy scent. She felt, if not beautiful, as least passable, which—at age forty-two, after sobbing in a car over her nonexistent husband and then washing in the Starbucks's bathroom—was as good as it got. Maybe it was as good as it got anyway.

11

SHE HAD CHOSEN Le Jardin—the same place Eric took her on their last night together, their last night as a normal married couple—though now, for the life of her, she couldn't imagine why. For one, despite a scaled-down menu at lunchtime, it was way too fancy. For another, sitting here waiting for the doctor (she'd arrived three or four minutes early, and he was already a full two minutes late), she found that all she could think about was what she said to Eric that night, in this very restaurant, to have made him walk out of her life. But anyway, the doctor clearly wasn't coming, so it didn't matter how fancy the place was. She'd sat here for—she glanced at her watch—seven full minutes now and no sign of him, so she might as well just—

"Eve!" he said, and there he stood, looking as flustered as she'd ever seen him, which wasn't very. "I'm sorry I'm late. I have a young woman in labor who was my patient until not long ago, and her OB had some questions for me. She's diabetic—juvenile, not type 2—so I figured I'd better call him back, even though I'm not on call today. But I'm sorry to make you wait."

"I wasn't waiting," Eve said, and then, "You're not late"—two obvious lies that made it immediately evident she'd been sure he was standing her up.

He smiled. "Well, good. I'm glad you don't mind." He sat down and put his napkin in his lap, and she quickly did the same, trying not to stare. She had hoped he'd be a little less stunning when he wasn't in his office saving one of her kids' lives, but alas, he was as appealing as ever, with his big hands and cleanly shaved head, his eyes both kind and intensely bright. He had a tiny hint of beard, as if he'd shaved last night instead of this morning, and she saw that his hair, back when he'd had it, was strawberry blond. A redhead! She almost laughed. She should have known, with those green eyes, that confidence and energy. . . . And then she felt a flash of panic. What the hell was she supposed to do with him, now that she had him here?

A waitress arrived for drink orders, and Eve busied herself ordering a glass of Shiraz, remembering that she and Eric had split a bottle that night and it had been fantastic. She thought about suggesting they do that now, actually—she could easily have two glasses, possibly three—but then the doctor said, "I'll just have water, please," and immediately she thought, *Great, Eve, way to drink when he's not. Next time just order a whole case, you lush.*

He excused himself to wash up, and the waitress returned with their drinks, and he came back and sat down again. Eve took what she hoped was a dainty sip of her wine, then offered him one, which (happily, for her) he accepted. Specials were presented, orders taken: hers for a sea scallop dish (loaded with garlic, she realized afterward, plus she was too nervous to eat—but she'd been trying for something easy to fork up), his for a chicken sandwich. Menus collected, waitress having departed, they were on their own. "So," he said, smiling at her. (*Warmth* and *amusement*, the eyes seemed to say this time.)

Eve smiled back brightly. "So! Thank you for coming."

"My pleasure. Thanks for asking."

"Well, I wanted to thank you for all your, you know—great service over the years."

He laughed, and she realized how absurd that sounded. *Service?* What was he, a doorman?

"You're welcome," he said. "Again, it's been a pleasure." He took a sip of water. "How's Magnolia?"

"You mean her nose? All better." Eve sighed. "Now if I could just fix her attitude."

He nodded. "She's fourteen, right?"

"Very much."

"Well. Give it another year, and it'll probably start to fix itself." Eve nodded back, and he said, "And Danny?"

"He's good, I think. He got a parakeet." Oh my God. She was boring even herself. "How about you?" she said quickly. "Do you have any kids?" She thought he did but knew nothing about them, she realized. Or about him, really. Except that he had a wife. Who probably hadn't run away.

"I do," he said. "Two sons and a daughter. All grown up now. One's in law school, the other just finished his oncology residency. Those are the sons. Both in D.C. My daughter's in Seattle, though, so I don't see her much." He paused, and though he looked wistful, Eve couldn't help thinking that that arrangement—your daughter clear across the country—sounded rather nice right about now. "She's a photographer," the doctor was saying. "But she's about to have a baby, so I'd imagine that will keep her from her work for a while."

"Oh!" Eve said. "So you'll be a grandfather!"

He smiled. "I will."

She shook her head, trying to fathom how anyone so old—a grandfather!—could be so youthful and beautiful. How old was he, anyway? With a son who'd already finished his residency, he must be at least fifty-five, and probably closer to sixty, or even . . . "Does she know what she's having?" Eve asked, snapping to.

"Yup. A boy.

Eve smiled, remembering Danny as an infant, all chicken legs and enormous oval-shaped eyes. "That's wonderful," she said, then added quickly, "Not that a girl's not wonderful too. I mean, I feel so lucky, you know, because I got one of each." She cringed inside. *I'm not this boring!* she wanted to scream. "Well. As, I mean, as you know," she added. *Oh my God,* she thought.

He nodded. "Indeed I do." His eyes flashed.

She took a deep breath. This was hard, she remembered now, sitting across the table from a guy you didn't know, trying to figure out not only what to say, but what he thought of you. Was he interested or just being friendly? Attracted to you or thinking about the Celtics game tonight? There because he wanted to be or because he felt somehow obliged? She remembered how, after falling in love with Eric, she'd been so relieved all that was over—that she'd never have to guess or put herself out there again.

And yet, here she was, talking to his man and wondering: Were they flirting or just having a conversation? Was there chemistry between them? Or did he look at all women this way?

She took another sip of wine, determined to find out, to take this conversation to the next level. "So," she said, "what made you want to be a doctor?"

He laughed. He seemed to find her quite amusing, for better or worse. "Well, for one thing, I was good in science," he said. "And obviously I like to work with people."

My Lord, she thought, *could he be more unlike Eric?*

The waitress appeared with their plates, and there was the obligatory rigmarole, her offering him a scallop and him accepting (good, now he'd have garlic breath too), him offering a bite of sandwich and her politely declining. "Anyway," she said. "You were saying why you wanted to be a pediatrician."

"Actually, I think you said *doctor* before. But pediatrician is the easier question. I like kids, of course. Specifically little ones. Which might seem counterproductive, since half the time I'm making them cry, but I like working with them. They charm and entertain me." He took a bite, chewing thoughtfully. "For example," he said, "last week, this little guy comes in, seven years old, extremely precocious. And he says to me, 'I have severe, stabbing pain in my abdomen, and a slight fever. I think I have appendicitis. Either that or gallstones.'"

He laughed, and Eve laughed too. "Turned out he'd gone on the Internet and typed in his symptoms," he said. "And that's what he came up with. Appendicitis or gallstones."

Another sip of wine. Her glass was half empty already, and no

way could she order more. But at least her body had finally un-
clenched. "So what did he end up having?" she asked.

"Gas."

She laughed, and he joined in again, his eyes sparkling. "So, tell me
about *you*," he said, and he looked into her eyes, that warm, deeply
interested glance that *seemed* to border on flirting, but who knew?

"Well, what do you want to know?" She took another sip of
wine. Might as well drink it all and be done with it.

"What do you like to do—I mean, besides raise your children?"

"Well, I'm a registered dietitian, for one thing."

"No kidding! I didn't know that."

"Yeah. And I published a book recently, so that's been kind of
a trip."

He put down his sandwich. "You published a book?"

"Just a nutrition book," she said. "Not, like, a *book* book, or—"

He motioned for the waitress, his eyes staying on Eve's. "Can I
get a beer, please? Whatever's on tap. And bring her another glass
of wine, would you?" Off she went, and he said, "A book! I've always wanted to write a book. This calls for a celebration."

Eve felt a rush of both pride and relief. (She also thanked him
silently for the extra wine, which would not go untended.) "Well,
what do you want to write about?" she asked.

"Oh no no. This is about you, not me. Tell me all about your
book! Please."

So she told him, trying to keep it brief. Then she told him about
her little business, and then about Michael, and Keisha (leaving out
the events of this morning), and even Nancy Kalish and the BBBs.
At the end, she took a deep breath. "Whoa," she said. "I've talked
too much."

"Not at all. I've enjoyed hearing it." He took a swig of beer,
without breaking eye contact, and sat back. "So what's your favorite
thing to cook?"

Oysters on the half shell, she thought, reaching for her new glass
of wine. *Lobster chunks dripping with butter. Whatever you want,
I'll cook it.* She put down the wine and shrugged. "At the moment,

I don't have time to cook anything. It's all I can do to drag in Chinese for the kids."

He laughed.

"Well, it's partly that Eric is gone," she admitted. "No one left at home who really cares about dinner. Magnolia would just as soon eat a bag of corn chips, and Danny would just as soon play a video game."

"That's right," he said after a moment. "You mentioned that about Eric last time." He raised his eyebrows. "Where is he?"

"Arizona. With his mother." She shrugged. "As far as I know, anyway."

He nodded. She could tell he wanted to ask more, but probably wouldn't out of politeness. "I haven't spoken to him since he left," she said, helping him out. "Over a month ago now." Amazing that it had been that long. She took another sip of wine.

"Huh," he said. "Must be hard on the kids. Not to mention you."

She shrugged, hoping for nonchalance. "We're getting by. Maggie texts with him, so that helps. Danny—I don't know. It's always hard to know with him."

The doctor drank more beer. "And you?" His voice had softened, and he looked directly at her, his gaze solicitous and inviting, until she felt that same thing she'd felt in his office, that palpable thing coming from him, and a wave of desire and emotion swept through her.

"I'm fine," she said. "I mean, I have my moments. You know. But" —she laughed softly—"this isn't one of them."

He exhaled through his nose, a half laugh without sound. "Well, that's good. I'm glad."

It occurred to Eve that he hadn't once mentioned his wife, though he did wear a wedding ring—a simple gold band, like hers. Still, maybe she'd died. Or, no. Divorced him or something (and he just hadn't gotten around to taking off the ring yet). Maybe he too had some energy to burn, hell to raise. The waitress appeared, and he handed her a credit card before Eve realized it. "Hey!" she said as the girl departed. "I'm supposed to get that! I invited you."

He shook his head. "Never mind. I'm glad you did."

"Well then." She smiled. "Thank you."

"My pleasure."

She felt like a teenager suddenly, coy and giddy. She took her last sip of wine, trying to remember where they were before the check came. Ah yes. Why Eric left. "So, I don't know," she said, picking it back up. "Maybe he needed to do this. He's been in a bad place for a long time with his work." *And with me too, I guess,* she thought, and she kicked away the sudden wash of sadness, not wanting to be brought down.

"That's generous of you," the doctor offered.

"It is!" she said after a moment, and she laughed. "And I admit, that's the first time I've said that. Most of the time I'm just calling him a bastard."

He smiled. "Must be the wine. It's making you generous."

"Must be," she said, and she thought, *And the company.* She was looking right at him now, boldly meeting his gaze. Surely there *was* something between them, fighting to get up from below the surface. But verboten. Or was it? *I want to kiss you,* she thought. *I want to fuck you. So here I am. What do you want from me?*

The waitress returned, and he took the check and signed it, closed the leather pouch, and pushed it away. He returned the credit card to his wallet, then the wallet to his pocket. He looked at her. "Well," he said. "I would love to stay here all day. But unfortunately, I have an appointment at five that I need to get to."

"An appointment?" *No!* she thought, and then, recovering, said, "Of course. I should get home too. I left the kids by themselves. Well. Obviously."

He stood up. "I'll walk you to your car. Unless you'd rather just—"

"No! No. Please. Walk me. It's behind Starbuck's."

Outside, the sky was majestically blue, the weather cool and dry with the perfect hint of fragrant, summery breeze. They passed a Japanese maple, new leaves as red as fresh blood, and then a garden of peonies and irises, purple bursts atop swaying stalks of deep green, balls of candy-pink puffs in between. She felt dizzy with joy, all the stress of the morning and early afternoon gone, replaced by happiness and honeybees. "All the world is a stage at this time of year," he said, and she nodded and thought that though he actually was a bit shorter than Eric, he seemed to tower over her in a way Eric didn't: It was his overall bigness, she realized, the solid mass of him. She felt herself skittering to keep up, her heels clacking, and hoped she wouldn't trip and tumble to the ground, legs splayed, head humming with wine and idiocy. "Am I walking too fast?" he said, as if reading her mind.

"No no," she said, pushing hair out of her face.

He slowed down anyway. "I'm sorry. All those emergencies, I guess. My kids always complained I walked too fast. I did better for a while, but when they left, I regressed."

She laughed. "That's okay. Here, I'm right here." They had arrived at her car. Sadly (she didn't want this to end), she dug for her keys, found them, promptly dropped them on the ground, and giggled. He picked them up and handed them to her.

"Thanks." She sighed, then unlocked the door. "And thanks for lunch. It was perfect."

"It was," he agreed. "I don't get to do that too often."

"We should do it again!" This from her, though somehow she knew they wouldn't. This was a one-time deal, was what it was.

"We should," he said, looking at her.

She opened the door, stepped a little toward it. "Well," she said. He was smiling at her—almost, she thought, as if waiting to see what she'd do next. *Okay,* she thought, and she reached up to hug him, rising to her tiptoes. He opened his arms and hugged her back, and she closed her eyes, her heart thumping against him. "Good luck," he said, releasing her, but when she stepped (ever so slightly) away, instead of averting her eyes, she looked right at him. And then she leaned up once more, this time to kiss him, because she swore he was waiting for her.

But he turned his head, ever so slightly, so their kisses landed on the side of each other's mouth, not the center. And though he touched her waist lightly as he did, she got the hint, loud and clear. They were friends. Two friends kissing good-bye. Nothing more.

She pulled away and looked down, mortified, praying she'd shrink to the size of an ant and someone would have the mercy to step on her. But she thought, *You don't get to do that, you know. You don't get to look at a woman like that and not expect her to—*

"I just have to say this," he said suddenly. "You remind me so much of my daughter."

She blushed to the core. She got it now, or she thought she did. In the end, attracted or not, tempted or not, they were two married people who would not transgress. Or he wouldn't, anyway. Instead, then, he would admire and regard her in a fatherly way, and that would excuse all of both of their behavior; that would let her off the hook, and everything would be warm and cozy again.

Or maybe she had just misread him all along. Maybe he was just being his warm, enthusiastic, affectionate self and wasn't remotely attracted to her in that way. Maybe, as usual, she was just a big stupid ass.

But he reached for her hand, and she let him take it. "Listen," he said. "I'm glad everything happened just as it did. And I want to tell you this. You're a beautiful woman. Beautiful and smart and fascinating, just really a lovely person. Your husband is a silly man to leave you. And I bet he regrets it, wherever he is."

She shook her head a little, feeling a tiny bit better. So, okay. She could move on from here, she supposed; bury her acute humiliation and proceed in a grown-up manner. He probably had some hideous flaw anyway. Maybe he was a closet pedophile. Yeah, that was probably it. Or at least he was a slob who left his underwear on the floor. *Please*, she thought. *Let him be a terrible slob.* "I'll tell him you said that," she said, "if I ever see him again."

He smiled. "I have a feeling you will."

She took a deep breath. Then she got in her car, closed the door, turned on the motor, and pulled out of her parking space. Out of the side of her eyes, she could see him watching her, arms crossed, mouth raised in a half smile. *Best face forward,* she thought, remembering what her mother used to say, and she rolled down the window, forced a smile, and gave him a wave, one final *Good-bye* and *Oh well* and *It was nice while it lasted.* And then she turned back to the road, put the car in drive, and headed home to her children.

Danny and Magnolia were sitting on the porch playing Yahtzee when she pulled up. Eve blinked, and for the tiniest second, the present flitted away and life was just like old times: kids who played at home together, husband off working hard, mother pulling in from wherever. "Hi, Mom!" Maggie called as Eve slogged up the front stairs.

"Hey, guys. How did it go?"

"Good," they said in unison.

"That's good. Did you have a good time?"

"Yeah," they both said, and Eve laughed. "What is this, the Adams-Knight choir?"

They both laughed.

But then Maggie got up. "Be right back," she said, and she went inside. Eve heard the bathroom door close. "Well, *she's* in a good mood," she said to Danny, "compared to this morning. Complete one eighty."

"I know. She was really nice to me." Danny flicked at the dice. "I texted with Daddy."

"You did?" Eve felt herself snap to attention. "What did you say?"

He shrugged. "I don't know. Nothing, really. Maggie helped me, but—I don't really like texting. I like seeing the person in person."

Eve nodded. "Me too."

"But Maggie texted him a lot. Then that man came ov—" He clapped his hand to his mouth.

"What?" Eve said.

Danny glanced nervously inside.

"Danny," Eve said, "what *man* came over?"

"Shh!" He glanced inside. "No one, Mom! God, chillax! I was just kidding!"

The toilet flushed, and the bathroom door opened, and then Magnolia was back. She sat down, crossing her legs Indian style.

Eve scrutinized her. She didn't seem drunk or high (though frankly it was a little hard to tell, when Eve could hardly pass a Breathalyzer herself). She actually looked good, Eve thought. She was smiling, for one—an anomaly these days—and though she had on some makeup, it was not only not the usual garish mess, but actually looked attractive: her skin was even, and her eyes looked pretty. And though she wore the Abercrombie hooker outfit, it somehow wasn't as tight and trashy as usual. *Maybe she's starting to grow into her body,* Eve thought, almost happily.

But then, what about this *man*? "Thanks for babysitting each other," she said, trying to figure out how to play her cards here.

"You're welcome," they both said, and they started to laugh yet again, but then Magnolia's phone rang and she jumped up and walked away to take it. Danny watched her go. "I'm going in to get Batman," he said after a few seconds.

"Is that him?" Eve said, trying to listen.

"Who?"

"The man who came over?"

"Mom, a man *didn't* come over! I *told* you!"

"Was he driving a car?"

"I'm not telling!" Danny said. "And anyway, there *was* no man!"

Magnolia laughed into the phone, then said something, then threw her hair back. Eve felt a growing alarm. "Is that why she's in such a good mood?" she asked.

"I don't *know,* Mom! God! I'm going in now." The door closed behind him.

"I'll call you later," Eve heard Magnolia say, and then she closed her phone and came back, attempting to walk past Eve and on into the house.

"Wait!" Eve said, trying to sound light and low-key. "Sit down with me a sec, Mags. I haven't seen you all day. Who were you talking to just then?"

"What?" Magnolia said, and then, "No one."

"Magnolia. Who was it?"

Maggie frowned. "Mom, none of your business. A friend."

"Then why'd you have to walk away from me to talk?"

Maggie glared at her now. *So much for the good mood.* "Um— because I wanted some privacy?" she said, and then, "You're giving me the third degree because of a *phone* call? After I babysat Danny, like, *all day*?"

Eve put up her palms, because this was going nowhere. "I'm sorry," she said. "You're right. You're allowed to have privacy on the phone, as long as—"

"As long as *what*?"

"As long as I know you're safe."

"Why wouldn't I be *safe*? I've been sitting here *all frickin' day.*"

Because your brother just told me . . . Eve wanted to say, but betraying Danny wouldn't help any of them. "Okay," she said, and then, after a moment, "I just want to remind you, Mags, that when I'm not home, no one is to be here without my permission."

"Who said anyone was?" Maggie's eyes narrowed.

"No one said anyone was," Eve said, and then, because she knew Magnolia couldn't lie to her, "But *was* someone?"

Magnolia sighed. "My friend Theo stopped by for, like, five seconds. He didn't even come into the house."

"Theo who? Do I know him?"

"Believe it or not, no," Maggie said, and then muttered, "Imagine that."

"Magnolia, lose the attitude."

"Okay! But, God, Mom! I'm allowed to say hi to someone passing by. I'm fourteen, not two. You act like I'm quarantined or something!"

Eve let that one sink in. Maybe she *was* being too hard. How the heck were you supposed to know? "Did Danny talk to him too?" she asked.

"Why would *Danny* talk to him?" she spewed.

"I don't know! I'm just asking." Eve sniffed. "So, what, he was walking? Or riding his bike?"

"If you must know, he was driving. Okay? He has his license. And guess what? I will too in two years."

Eve stared at her.

"You get your permit at sixteen," Magnolia said. "Remember?"

Eve fell onto a porch chair. How could Magnolia drive so soon? And who would teach her if Eric wasn't here? Not that she couldn't drive herself, but. . . . She lowered her forehead to her fingertips and pushed, hoping to ward off the approaching headache. "So your friend Theo is sixteen?" she heard herself ask.

Maggie laughed. "I am not answering one more question. You told me to babysit, I babysat. You said not to have people over, I didn't. You told me to play with Danny, I did. Seriously. What else do you want from me?"

Eve shook her head.

"Good! Then I'm going in now. Because I—" Her phone beeped, the signal for a text, and Maggie pounced on the phone and opened it. She read the text, laughed, and typed something back. Then she closed the phone and walked into the house.

Danny came out. "Hi, Mom," he said.

Eve sighed. "Hi, baby."

"What's wrong. Do you have a headache?"

She lifted her head and smiled at him. "No no," she said. "I'm just a little tired." She looked at him. "What's in your hands?"

His hands were cupped together, one atop the other. "Batman," he said.

"Batman?" Eve sat up. "Danny, I don't think you should have him out here unless he's in his cage. He could get loose."

Danny peered into a little space at the top of his hands, then looked up at Eve. "Do you think he wants to?" he asked.

Eve stared at him, vaguely recalling a similar conversation they'd had. "Not really," she said, hoping she was being consistent. "I mean, he loves you. And you take such good care of him. Right? So why would he leave?"

"Daddy left."

Eve blinked. She thought of all the things she could say—*But Daddy will be back,* or *But Daddy didn't know what he was doing,* or *But Daddy was fucking the babysitter*—but none of them seemed quite right, and, try as she might, she couldn't come up with anything else.

"That's true," she said finally. "But, I mean, if Batman flew away, he might get hurt, or he might—I mean—"

"Daddy might get hurt too."

"He won't. You just texted with him, right? Did he say he was hurt?"

"No," Danny admitted.

"Well, all right then." She forced a smile. "Daddy is a big boy. He'll be fine." They sat for a moment, and then she said, "I think Daddy just needed a break."

"From who? All of us?"

"No," Eve said firmly. "Not from you and your sister."

"From you then?" Danny looked up at her, wide-eyed.

Eve sighed. She motioned for him to come onto her lap, but he shook his head—just as well, since he still had the bird in his hands. "I don't know," she said honestly. "Maybe from me. I guess I'll find out when I talk to him."

"When will that be?" Danny asked. "When *will* you talk to him? You never answered when he called. And now he never calls you anymore."

How did he know all this? "You don't worry about that," she said. "I'll figure that out. Hey, are you hungry? Should we make some chicken strips and broccoli, or—"

"No thank you."

"Well then, let's see. Do you want to play cards? Or another game of Yahtzee?"

He shook his head no without looking at her.

"Okay. But we should go in, Dan. You should put Batman back."

Danny shook his head once more. "I don't want to," he said. And then he lifted and opened his hands, and before Eve could do a thing except watch in complete disbelief, off went the bird, a flapping, fluttering, rising blue blur of confusion and ecstasy.

*   *   *

Hours later—the middle of the night, it felt like, after she'd fallen into a troubled half-sleep, her mind filled with the distressing events of the day (the awkward encounter with Keisha's mother, her virtual rape of the family pediatrician, poor little Batman getting smaller and smaller as he rose up and away)—Eve awoke to the sound of a car pulling up to their house. She opened her eyes: 12:28. Hardly the middle of the night. And it was probably just a neighbor. The car motor turned off, and she relaxed a bit before remembering that Eric had called her tonight. First time in weeks. The phone had rung around eleven while she was washing her face, and she'd let it go to voice mail. When she checked the caller list, it was that same Arizona number: not Penelope's, but the other one she now knew was his. He hadn't left a message.

She had wondered why he was calling her at this point. *Maybe to tell me he's coming home*, she thought, and for a second—before she had time to think too much about it—she'd felt a warm flash of joy. But just as quickly, she grew furious. How dare he waltz in and out of their lives, thinking of no one but himself? What made him think she would even take him back? *You can just stay there,* she'd thought, and she'd climbed angrily into bed and fallen restlessly asleep, glad to end this humiliating, unfortunate day.

The steps creaked, and Eve opened her eyes again, this time wide and fast. And then she heard the front door open, slowly but surely. She shot up in bed, dove for the window, and stuck her head underneath the shade. It was black outside, almost impossible to see, but she could just make out the car. And then the passenger door opened, and Magnolia slid in and closed it again.

Eve tore out of bed and pounded down the stairs and outside, barefoot in her nightgown. "Magnolia!" she screamed. She ran toward the car, kicking up dirt and grass.

Magnolia opened the door and jumped out, Eve straining to see who was in there before her daughter slammed the door again. "Mom!" she said, looking horrified. "What are you doing out here like that? Go back to sleep!"

The car motor went on. "Who *is* that?" Eve yelled. She stepped toward the car, but it pulled out and away. She turned to her daughter, panting. "Who was that, Maggie?"

Magnolia hugged her arms. She wore a white T-shirt, no bra (her breasts had grown, Eve saw; she almost no longer needed that padded bra), and jeans, with bare feet. "My friend," Maggie said. "He stopped by to pick up a CD."

Eve stared at her. "A *CD*? At one o'clock in the morning?"

"He's going on a road trip," Maggie said. "He texted to see if I was up and I was, so I said I'd run it out to him. Anyway, it's not one o'clock," she added.

Eve was vaguely aware that something hurt her somewhere, but she was too enraged to try to figure out where. "Get in the house," she hissed.

Magnolia slunk in, and Eve followed her into the dark entryway. "First of all," she yelled, "what are you doing up and dressed at this hour? I thought you went to bed a long time ago."

Maggie shrugged. "I don't know. It's Saturday night. I wasn't tired."

"And second, how old was that guy, Magnolia?" Eve was so angry she was practically spitting. "He looked *my* age!" She wasn't sure that was true; she'd only gotten a quick glimpse. But he had definitely not looked like a kid.

"Well, he's not," Maggie said. "I don't know how old he is, but he's definitely not your age."

Eve took a deep breath, trying to calm down. She knew she had to say something, do something, but she didn't know what. Magnolia glared at her. She looked at Eve's nightgown, and Eve saw revulsion all over her face. But then, just as quickly, her face transformed, eyes wide, eyebrows raised. "Oh my God, Mom, you're bleeding!" she said. "Look at your foot!"

Eve looked down, and there was the source of her pain: her two left baby toes were covered in blood. "Oh, *shit*," she said, because really, did she need one more thing?

"Did the toenail come off?" Magnolia said. "Wait—did you do that just now?"

"Yes, I did that just now. Running out to rescue you from some creep who was about to take you away." She shook her head. She must have stubbed it on that root she'd been meaning to do something about.

Maggie looked at her. "He wasn't gonna *take me away*, Mom. You're paranoid! He actually wanted to meet you, but I told him to leave because I knew you'd yell at him. So if you want to blame someone, blame me. Come on, I'll fill a bowl so you can soak your foot."

"I don't need help," Eve snapped. She wondered if that were true, that the guy had been willing to meet her. She doubted it—though, again, her daughter had never been much of a liar.

Magnolia was getting a bowl and a clean washcloth, running warm water over it. She rung it out and handed it all to Eve. "Here," she ordered. "Soak it and clean it."

Eve took the cloth and dabbed at her toe, wincing.

"Does it hurt?" Magnolia asked.

"Yes. It hurts."

"Sorry, Mommy."

Eve looked at her.

"I really was just giving him his CD," Maggie said. "I wasn't running away."

"I certainly hope not." They were silent for a moment, and then Eve sighed. "Are you gonna tell me who he is?"

"His name is Theo. Like I said. He's a nice guy. That's it."

"How old is he?"

"I don't know! I already told you that. But it doesn't matter, anyway. We're just friends."

"It still matters, Magnolia."

"Why?" Magnolia shot back. "If he's nice, who cares how old he is?"

Eve stared at her. "Where did you meet him?"

"In town. He lives around here. He plays music."

"What does he play?"

Maggie laughed. "Acoustic guitar. Is that bad? If it is, tell me and I'll say 'violin.'"

Eve shook her head. "You can't see him, Magnolia."

Magnolia frowned. "Why not?"

"Because. Even if he's nice, being friends with an older man at your age is—it's—"

"It's *what*?"

Eve looked up at the ceiling. "It's hard to explain. The fact that this guy, however old he is, wants to hang out with a fourteen-year-old girl makes me suspicious. I'm not saying you're not a great kid, or even that he's not a nice guy, but why isn't he with people his own age? And driving over here at 12:30 at night . . ."

"I already told you why he did that."

"Well, that's not a good reason. It would be one thing if you were seventeen, but fourteen? You're too young for that, Magnolia. I know you don't feel that way, but you *are*. And that's exactly why someone his age can't be good friends with you. Either he doesn't realize how young you are, or he *does* realize, which is even worse. He should know better." There. It wasn't brilliance, but at least it was something.

Still, Magnolia narrowed her eyes. "You know," she said, "you don't know how it feels, Mom. You're little and pretty. You were probably pretty all your life. Right? Well, I'm not. I'm big and ugly, and my hair is frizzy. Nate dumped me, and Emily dumped me, and other guys my age don't want me either. But Theo is nice to me. He *wants* to be around me. He even thinks I'm pretty. He told me that! He said I'm beautiful, inside and out. And not in a sketchy way, either. He really thinks it! I can tell. He told me in two years I'll be gorgeous, and interesting too. And he never touches me. Not once. We just talk. Sometimes he plays me music. So why would you want to take that away from me? Why would you not let me see the one guy who wants to be with me and makes me feel good about myself? *Why?* We're not even doing anything!"

Eve stared at her, openmouthed. She honestly didn't know what to say. Was it possible the girl had a point? *This is why you need a husband,* she thought, without wanting to. *So you can ask him: What the hell do we do now?*

"So if you want to tell me I can't see him, go ahead," Maggie said. "But I can't promise I'm gonna listen." She shrugged. "So, that's that. Do you want me to wet your washcloth again?"

Eve shook her head. "No. I'm going to bed."

"Me too, then."

Eve looked at her. "Listen, Magnolia," she said, and it took all her strength to get out the words. "If someone comes here for you, especially if they're over fifteen, I want to see them and meet them, at very least. Do you understand? I don't want you running out in the middle of—"

"*Okay*, Mom! I get it."

Eve hurled the washcloth at the sink. Then she hobbled upstairs, Magnolia behind her.

At the door to her bedroom, Magnolia turned around. "Sorry to wake you, Mom," she said, and she sounded completely sweet now. "And sorry about your foot. I really am."

Eve put her hand on her doorknob. "That's okay," she managed. Though it wasn't, of course. Nothing was, these days.

She started to open her door. But she felt her daughter behind her, and then Maggie's arms came around her. "I love you," she said.

Eve closed her eyes, letting herself be hugged. "I love you too," she said.

12

SITTING IN THE examining room of Dr. Jennie Koenig's office (he found the gown a bit much, but they'd told him to put it on and he wasn't one to protest), Eric stared at his foot with something like awe. Amazing that it could swell to this size and color; it honestly looked more like an eggplant with toes than a foot. Even so, he wouldn't be here if his mother hadn't called her longtime doctor and set up the appointment. He'd twisted the foot late last night, running around and around Himmel Park in the dark. And though when he awoke—at 6:52, after his usual few hours of restless half-sleep—it had looked and felt mangled, like someone smashed a brick down on it, he'd limped off to teach his classes, his motto, as always, *If it doesn't kill you, ignore it.* But Penelope had flagged him when he'd limped back in this afternoon, and when she saw his foot, she'd gasped and picked up the phone (at one point stepping into the living room, where Eric couldn't quite hear what she said). Next thing he knew he'd been squeezed into Dr. Koenig's day. And now here she was, walking in.

"David?" She held out her hand and smiled. She was younger than he'd expected—his age, maybe slightly older—and had that enviable air of authority and competence so many women seemed to have now, as if nothing intimidated them. Eve had it too—though she hadn't when they'd first met. In fact, her vulnerability back then had been one of the things he'd first loved about her. "Well, I have to say, you don't look like your mother," the doctor said.

He smiled a little. "Guess not."

"Though it looks like you did inherit her gene for stoicism. Let's see that foot."

He braced himself as she examined it, gently poking and twisting. "Does this hurt?" she asked.

He couldn't help laughing as pain shot through him. "Yes."

"And this?"

He winced, nodded. He smelled rubbing alcohol, suddenly.

She cocked her head and sighed. "Hate to say it, but you've got either a fracture or a serious sprain. I'm gonna send you over to an orthopedist. He's just a few blocks away. I'll call him and let him know you're on the way. It might take a while, but he'll get you in today." She smiled sympathetically. "Hope you didn't have any big plans."

Eric felt a wave of panic. *A fracture?* He held his breath, waiting for it to pass.

Dr. Koenig stepped back, crossed her arms, looked at him. "Your mother said you did this last night."

He tried to formulate an answer. He had thought she was finished with him.

"How?" she asked after a moment.

"Running," he said, but it came out too softly. He was still trying to slow his racing heart. "It was dark," he said, louder. "I tripped and twisted it, I guess."

"And how was it this morning?"

"Uh—swollen."

"Painful?" He nodded, and she said, "So did you stay off it today?"

He saw what she was getting at now. "I had to go to work," he said. "I teach kung fu."

She gave him a look. "I'll be honest. Your mother is a little worried about you. She thinks you're pushing yourself too hard right now. Not taking care of yourself."

He raised his eyebrows. His mother was usually asleep when he went for his late-night run; he hadn't thought she'd known how long he stayed out (pretty long, as he was up to eight or ten miles by now). And when he wasn't out running or at kung fu, he generally slept. It was true he wasn't eating much, but—

"Do you think it's true?" the doctor asked gently.

"No," he said, but then he thought for a moment. "Physically I've been pushing myself, I guess. But it's all I'm doing right now." He didn't add that the teaching was the only time he believed he deserved to be alive, the running the only thing that made him stop asking himself if he did.

"What do you normally do?" she said.

"I'm a sculptor. Taking a break."

She nodded. "Sounds interesting. Where do you live? You're visiting, right?"

They hadn't ever really discussed his leaving here, he and Penelope. When or if. "Massachusetts," he said.

"Wow. Long way from home. When's the last time you had a full physical?"

"Uh. Six years?"

"Mind if I listen to your lungs?"

He nodded, and she put the cold stethoscope on his back, had him breathe, did the same on his chest but without the breath. "Heart and lungs sound good," she said, "though your heart is racing a bit. Do you smoke?"

"One or two a day, give or take. Cigarette, not pack," he added.

"Okay. None a day would be even better."

He didn't feel she was nagging. Happily, Eve had never nagged him about that either. Still, it was nice to have someone care, or at least fake it. "Maybe I'll quit," he said.

She laughed. "Doubtful, though, right?"

He smiled a little. He could see why his mother liked her.

She took his pulse and blood pressure, looked in his eyes, ears, and throat, asked if anything hurt other than his foot. She massaged his neck glands, tested his reflexes, palpated his abdomen. Then she told him he could get dressed and left the room.

When she returned, she sat in the chair and looked up at him. "Physically, you're good, other than the foot," she said. "Your blood pressure is perfect. Your weight is low, though. How much do you normally weigh?"

"Around 172. Maybe 175."

"You're down to 161."

He stared at her. "I am?"

"Any idea why you've lost all that weight?" she asked, watching him.

He felt the panic again, a wave of nausea, cold sweat just beneath the surface of his skin. He wondered if she'd let him just lie here and rest for a bit.

"How long were you planning to stay in Tucson?" She said it gently, as if the question might upset him.

"Hadn't thought about it, really," he managed, though the truth was, he thought about it all the time, every day. He missed Magnolia and Danny. He missed certain things about Eve: the way she'd suddenly laugh when he didn't even realize he was saying something funny (which made him laugh too); the way she always knew exactly what she wanted to do next, so that he could tag along without having to think or plan anything. He missed the routines: the dinners, the evenings, her presence in his bed both before she fell asleep (her piles of books, her cheap, enormous reading glasses) and after (her warm, smooth limbs next to his, the way she'd let him drape himself all over her in the morning during the one snooze she allowed herself before rushing up to fill the house with the smell of butter and French toast or eggs). But he didn't miss the way he'd felt around her in recent years. And when he thought about going back to his studio, he felt physically ill. He couldn't do it. *Anyway, you can't go back if your wife won't even talk to you,* he thought, and though he knew it was a cop-out, he felt better. He might be the one who'd left, but it wasn't all his doing, was it? Like when his mother "left" his father; he'd had one foot out the door already, she'd said.

"You have kids," Dr. Koenig said, looking at his chart. "Fourteen and eight?"

He nodded. "Daughter and a son."

"And they're back home with your wife?" She looked up at him.

He wondered if she was part shrink or something. "Yes," he said. She waited, and he said, "I text with my daughter, though. Every day. Sometimes more."

"That's nice." She smiled. "I text with my daughter too. She's twelve."

He nodded, for some reason glad she had a child.

"I actually find there's a certain intimacy to it," she said thoughtfully.

It was true, he realized. He loved when Magnolia texted him. In a way, it made him feel closer to her than they'd ever been—or at least than they'd been for a long time. She told him things, just a line here or there, but still: what she was doing that minute, what kind of mood she was in. She told him she missed him and loved him, things she rarely said at home. If anything, back there he was merely something she had to get around to get to Eve. At one point, a few weeks ago, she'd told him she had a new friend, Alexis, but that seemed to be over now. "Mom h8s her," she had texted. "She said I dont want 2 c her face in this house again." He had cringed when he read that. What was Eve thinking? But he'd been careful in his response, knowing better than to take Magnolia's side against Eve. And besides, he trusted Eve as a mother. Whatever else she did wrong—not answering the phone when he called, to name one, not giving him a chance to explain himself (not that he could, but she hadn't even let him try!)—she was a good mother. Too good sometimes. No room for him.

"And your son?" the doctor asked.

Danny didn't text yet, of course. Once, Magnolia had actually dialed Eric's number and handed him the phone to talk, but after saying "Hi, Dad," he'd sat silently and made Eric ask endless questions, to which he'd either given one-word answers or said, "What?" ("Do you have wax in your ears?" Eric had asked at one point, only half kidding, and Danny, of course, responded, "What?") It was almost like he was purposely not listening.

"He doesn't like the phone," Eric answered, and thought, *Like his father.*

"He might feel a little betrayed," the doctor said, not unkindly. "You're not there. He might not understand that as well as his sister or his mother."

Eric sighed. "I'm not sure his mother exactly 'understands.'" He thought a moment. "Though she should. I'm giving her a break."

Dr. Koenig looked at him oddly. "Why would you think she wanted a 'break' from you?"

Eric shrugged. "One more person to take care of, maybe."

The doctor frowned. "Is that how you think she sees you?"

He wished now he'd kept his mouth shut. "I don't know," he said.

"If I can be presumptuous," she said, "because it is my job, to some extent: Do you think maybe that's how *you* see *yourself*?"

She was looking at him, warm, brown-eyed, composed. "I haven't had the best year workwise," he offered, because he had to say something.

She let that sink in. "And last year?"

He couldn't answer. The panic was creeping back now, as always when he thought about work: that heavy-limbed, low-grade buzz, as if he were being slowly electrocuted.

"David?" she said.

He nodded.

"Are you okay?"

"I'm fine," he managed, but he wondered if she could actually hear his heart, fast and loud and frantic.

"Is it that your work isn't selling or that you're not producing it?" she asked—again, gently probing.

He swallowed. "The latter."

She sat back, assessing him. "Do you know why?"

"Not really." Torturous as it was to talk about this, he also felt, from deep down somewhere, that faint, distant lightness of relief.

Maybe, somehow, she could actually help? "I think—I'm not sure I have anything left to say," he said. "In my work. And if I did—"

She waited.

"If I did, I'm not sure I could sell it anyway." The words made him want to cry. For more than half of his life, he had woken up thinking about what he'd make that day, gone to bed thinking about what he'd done. His work was his guide, his religion, the thing that kept him upright. If he couldn't work, who was he?

"Why?" she asked after a moment. "What makes you think that?" She sounded as curious as she did shrinky now, like she wanted to know for herself as much as to help him.

He took a deep breath. "People like beautiful art," he said, practically quoting Liza, his gallery owner. "They don't want to buy ugly, depressing things. And that's what I think my art would be now." He sniffed hard, swallowed, sniffed again. "And I need to sell my art," he added. "That's how I support my family." *Or did*, he thought, and he again felt like crying.

"Do you *know* people wouldn't want to buy it?" she asked, and now he wished she'd be quiet, because he did know. He knew from *The Runner*. "Have you made anything like that?"

"My dealer told me," he said, choosing her first question.

"Maybe you need a new dealer."

Or a new career, he thought, but he didn't say anything.

"You know, not everyone wants happy art," she said, after a considerable pause. "Nor does 'depressing' have to mean ugly. I mean, look at, I don't know—Frida Kahlo. Or Picasso."

He almost rolled his eyes. Like he hadn't thought about this ad nauseum for the past three decades? She should stick to her field, and he'd stick to his. "Those were different eras," he offered—generously, he thought.

But she wasn't listening now, he could tell; her mind was going in a different direction. And then she said, "Have you considered that *you* might be depressed?"

He stared at her. He felt punched and hollow, empty and disgusted. "No," he said, and he turned away, finished talking now. Enough already.

"I'd like to give you some material about anxiety and depression," she said, and the casual, professional tone was back. She'd gone back to doctor from shrink or art critic or whatever she'd been trying to pull off. "Just to think about," she said. "That's all. You don't have to do a thing, of course. But there are drugs that might help you feel better."

And now the drugs, of course. He should have known. He wondered how much she was getting from the pharmaceutical companies to push this stuff, how many free trips and spa visits she'd had courtesy of the makers of Prozac and Zoloft and Paxil.

She stood up. "I'll have the nurse bring you some pamphlets. You might find something helpful in there. And I'd like to have her take blood, if that's okay. If you haven't had a blood count in six years, it's time." She smiled a little, then stood up, and he knew he should thank her, if only to show he had no hard feelings for her suggestion that he was a depressed, unproductive cipher of his former self, a fraction of a man who'd fled his family, moved in with his mommy, and now sprained his fucking ankle so he couldn't even do the one last thing he'd been doing to make money before he dropped dead.

But the words wouldn't come out, and after a moment, she picked up the ball. "Nice to meet you," she said. "I wish you much good luck." The door closed behind her.

Later, sitting in the car in the orthopedist's lot, he lit a cigarette just to be an asshole and looked at one of the pamphlets Dr. Koenig had given him. "Do you have an anxiety disorder?" it said on top, and he shook his head. Another *disorder*. He had read about all this, how the drug companies created disorders now to make you think you were sick and needed their medicines. Antisocial personality disorder (he surely had that one!), overactive bladder syndrome (hey, who wouldn't want to pee less, but did that really mean most of us had a *disorder*?), erectile "dysfunction," which, when medicated, allowed you to fuck like a teenager until you were eighty—not that he'd mind some of that either, in ten or twenty years, but still. It was creepy, taking a drug to have a twenty-year-old dick when you were ancient. Prescriptions for psychotropic drugs had gone up astronomically in the United States, he'd read. We were a nation of medicated freaks.

He tossed the pamphlet on the seat and flipped open another. *Symptoms of Depression*, the inside page was titled. *1. Excessive sadness or crying. 2. Loss of interest or pleasure in activities that used to be enjoyable. 3. Poor concentration or having difficulty making decisions. 4. Agitation or doing things more slowly.* Okay, so he had all of those. But who didn't? It was like the tarot card reader who started by telling you you'd recently met an important person, or something scary had happened to you not long ago. Just because life wasn't one big cakewalk didn't mean a person needed to medicate himself into a zombie. Look at Picasso, for God's sake—just as the doctor had said. Like he wasn't sad during the Blue Period? Or Van Gogh, admittedly not the most chipper dude on the planet, but the guy still got up every morning and painted his sunflowers, ear or no ear. *5. Feeling tired.* Well, who the hell wasn't, trying to live in this hyper, accelerated world? *6. Feeling worthless or guilty.* Please. Like every artist didn't feel worthless at times? It was part of the deal. Depression was an attitude, nothing more. You accepted it and worked through it, found your escape—booze, pot, meditation, serial fucking—and moved on the best you could.

He remembered telling the doctor that he hadn't done a thing in two years, and he wished now that he could take back those words too. *An artist's productivity waxes and wanes, comes and goes,* he would tell her now. *Mine waned, and with luck it will wax again.* But when he pictured his studio, his palms grew hot, his head buzzed. He could not go back there.

He flipped the pamphlet over. *Depression affects more than 14 million Americans today*, it said. *Some 30–35 million Americans will be depressed at some point in their lives.* He shook his head. So maybe the problem was America, not the 35 million people. Maybe we needed to alter our mind-sets—or our lives—not our brain chemistry. He tossed the stupid thing into the backseat, ground out his cigarette in the ashtray (at home he never did that, but here who really cared?), and limped, wincing, out of the car, slamming the door behind him. *Thank God it's your left foot, so you can drive,* he thought, as he headed into the orthopedist's office. *And thank God it's your foot, not your leg, so you can limp.* See? He could see the glass as half full if need be. Look at all the money and humiliation he just saved by not popping a vat of pills.

Three and a half hours later—tired, hungry to the point of nausea (he hadn't eaten since morning), his foot positively throbbing with pain inside the clean white cast he'd just been encased in—he tossed his new crutches into the backseat of the car and worked himself back into the driver's seat, wiping sweat from his forehead, trying to calm his yet again racing heart, which must have banged out twice as many beats as usual in the past twelve hours. *Jesus Christ,* he thought. *Let this day end.*

He wanted to go back to his mother's and climb into bed, not get up until things were different—somehow, some way. Instead, he drove to Desert Kung Fu. He gimped in, found Diego bent over his desk in concentration, door ajar. Eric knocked lightly on the frame.

"Eric—come in!" Diego said, his smile relaxing and transforming his wide brown face to its usual position. "What brings you around at this hour, man?" (It came out like "mang." Diego spoke excellent English, Eric had noticed, but he couldn't—or wouldn't—lose the last bit of Mexican.) But when he saw Eric's cast, the man stood up, his short, muscular frame filling up the little room. "Ay ay ay," he said. "What'd you do?"

Eric shook his head. "Sprained it. Last night running."

"They gave you a cast for a sprain?"

"It's a Grade 3 sprain, supposedly. Whatever that means." But he knew. *Frequently worse than a fracture,* the doctor had said. *More*

swelling, more pain, more chance of recurrence once you're healed.
Cast for ten days, then rehab. (Rehab. He had tried not to laugh.)

Diego frowned. "But you taught earlier today! Didn't you just say you hurt it last night?" He shook his head. "You should've told me, man. You might've made it worse."

Eric shrugged. "It didn't hurt that badly earlier," he lied. The truth was, he hadn't wanted to bail on Diego—or forfeit the money. Or not teach his classes.

Diego glanced down at the cast. "Looks like it hurts now."

"Like a motherfucker."

Diego laughed. "You want something for it? I'm sure Adriana's got some pain pills around." Adriana was his wife, a hot little tamale with an occasional bad back.

"Thanks," Eric said, "but I've got a prescription here. Just have to go fill it." But he couldn't face it—another stop, another wait, another foot-throbbing hour.

"That's crazy," Diego said, as if reading his mind. "Do that tomorrow when you feel better. Or get your wife to go, but in the meantime . . . wait." He got up. "Sit," he said, indicating the chair.

He returned with a handful of blue pills and a tall glass of water. "Brought you a few extras, just in case Mr. CVS is out at the theater tonight."

Eric wanted to kiss him. He swallowed two of the pills, slipping the rest into his pocket, and drank the whole glass of water without taking a breath. "Thanks a lot," he said afterward. "Wish I'd run into you twenty hours ago."

"Just be careful, man. Those things knock you out. But you'll feel good, trust me."

Eric nodded. He took a deep breath. "Anyway, I just wanted to come by and let you know about this. I'm really sorry, Diego. I'll help you hire someone else if I can. Just let me know what I can do." But he felt like kicking something as he said it.

Diego shook his head. "Don't worry about me. This isn't the first time this happened, believe me. You just take care of yourself and get better." He smiled a little. "I can't lie, though, I hate to lose you.

The truth is, I don't have anyone nearly your level teaching right now. Ricky's good; he's got potential. But he's young. Still more swagger than skill. He doesn't always get it *up here.*" He tapped his head. "And the kids love you. Christian tells me."

Diego's son was a beautiful little guy, both feisty and obedient, small as a beetle at age six, but already fearless. Not like Danny at all, really, but still brought him to mind.

"And my adult beginner class almost doubled." Diego grinned. "The ladies."

Eric allowed himself a small smile. There was one woman, Marietta—a ballsy redhead, one of his better beginners—who'd brought a bunch of friends with her the past few times. After the class, a couple of them had stayed around, joking and talking with him, asking him questions he mostly avoided: How come they hadn't seen him around before? What was he doing tonight? It was flattering, though it had gotten a little old by this point; still, it wasn't like he minded.

"Plus," Diego was saying, "how many guys scrub the floors and wipe down the mats?" He was talking about the night with Natasha, of course. The night she'd asked him, *What kind of man leaves his son?* The night he'd asked himself, *How is it that I've done to my family what that asshole did to his?* The night he'd started running.

And again, that wave of panic, that cold, brutal sweat. "I don't mind," Eric managed, and though Diego looked at him curiously—he knew the man wondered what his deal was—Eric didn't offer more.

"So? Then." Diego shrugged. "Go get healed, and then call me. I'll have work for you when you're ready."

Eric almost laughed with gratitude. "Thanks," he said, and he wiped his brow with the back of his hand.

Diego nodded, then snapped his fingers. "I need to pay you." He pulled a wad of cash from his pocket, peeled off three hundreds and held them out.

Eric shook his head. "That's too much." He was breathing fast and shallow, trying to quell the nausea.

Diego waved him off. "Consider the rest the disability you're not collecting off me right now."

Eric hesitated a second longer, then took the money and stuffed it in his pocket.

"Now go home," Diego said, "before you fall asleep on the road and break the other foot too. You need a ride?"

"No, thanks. I'm fine."

"Fine my ass." Diego smiled. "But when you get that thing off?" He wagged his chin at the cast. "You know where to find me."

The oddest thing: Eric's eyes clouded up. He averted his head, so Diego wouldn't see. "Thank you," he said.

Back in the car—once he'd gotten himself there, with the crutches— Eric waited for the nausea to pass. Then he popped two more pills for good measure, swallowing them dry, and took out the cash. He counted it quickly, then opened the glove compartment and dug through the stuff Eve kept in there until he found an envelope and, miraculously, a couple of stamps. A pen he found under the seat (God, the amount of crap Eve and the kids left in this car!), a piece of paper—an ancient memo about Parents Night from Danny's old school, which Eric found himself rereading several times—in the road atlas on the floor of the passenger side. He folded the memo inside out around the cash, then thought for a moment. "I'll send more when I can," he finally wrote on the paper, and then because it was true, "I miss you." He stuck it all in the envelope, sealed it, and addressed it to Eve; for the return, he wrote his name and his mother's address. The letters looked shaky and weird, but legible enough. He drove until he saw a mailbox, got out of the car, and dumped the envelope in. *There.* Hopping back on the crutches, relief, wonderful and unexpected, washed over him.

The pills, no doubt. They were doing a beautiful job on the pain—which felt distant now, as if it were someone else's—and he loved where they were taking him: a warm, dreamy haven, lemon and gold and aglow; a world where he hadn't run away from his family, where no one was angry at him. He put the car in drive and eked out another mile—was he heading away from his mother's house instead of toward it?—before slowing to a crawl on what appeared to be a remote road, the houses few and far between. Shadows of saguaros all over, like solemn old men. His eyes were closing. He inched to the curb, went too far, and felt the wheel bump over and fall gently back down. *Shoot.* He would have to pull over and rest a minute before figuring out where he was and getting the rest of the way home.

In the room the women come and go/Talking of Michelangelo. The line drifted into his brain, and he smiled dreamily. When he was a kid, eight or nine, Frannie used to read him *The Love Song of J. Alfred Prufrock* so often that both of them memorized it. He had recently read that no one really knew what that poem was about—that there were all sorts of interpretations. Maybe Eliot himself didn't know. Maybe he was just messing around, making something beautiful but meaningless, and the joke was on everyone for thinking it was profound.

With effort, he locked the doors, pulled the keys from the ignition. He tried to put them in his lap, but they fell to the floor, and, knowing he had no prayer of picking them up, he watched them go, like coins falling into a grate. Someday he'd get them, and then he'd go home. But right now, too tired to even adjust his seat to recline, he hugged his arms, closed his eyes at long last, and drifted into a deep, heavy sleep.

He awoke to a pounding on his window rivaled only by the one in his head, opened his eyes into staggering sunlight, and slammed them shut again. His mouth seemed filled with a dry, bitter powder; his legs were numb, and his body felt encased in concrete, as if he couldn't move any part of it. Except that he needed to throw up. He retched, pain searing through his back, neck, and head, then swallowed, praying he wouldn't puke—and his prayers were answered, though there was nothing to puke anyway. But now his heart was pounding too. God, he felt sick.

"Sir, are you okay?" came a male voice, and then the mind-blowing rapping again.

Eric tried to raise his hand, eyes still closed. "Yes," he croaked. "Just give me a second." But the words came out like a bunch of garbled mumbling. He managed to swallow—progress!—then slowly tried to move his rigid body: shoulders, hands, arms, head.

"Sir," came the voice. "I'm gonna need you to open your vehicle. I need to see some identification."

Eric forced his eyes open—they were pierced by the sun, but he held them this time. And then the car door was ajar and he seemed to have found his license and registration, because the cop was heading back to his car with them to do whatever it was cops did in their cars while you sat there and waited, like a naughty kid.

The officer returned way too soon. "Sir," he said, holding the papers back out to Eric, "did you know your mother called the police to report you missing?"

Eric blinked. Christ. How long had he slept? And where the hell was he, anyway? None of it looked familiar. But he must have gotten himself here.

"Apparently you've been gone for more than twenty-four hours," the cop said, helping him out.

"What time is it?"

"Four eighteen PM."

"Jesus. Are you kidding?"

"No, sir, I'm not. Would you care to explain yourself?"

The cop was impossibly young, Eric saw now: a teenager for sure, with cropped black hair, a sprinkling of zits on his forehead. He swallowed again. "I pulled over last night to rest," he said. "I took some medication for my foot"—he indicated the cast—"and I guess I fell asleep."

The cop looked in at the cast, then nodded, relaxing a little. "Okay," he said. "You need to get home now, though, until you're more stable. Do you know where you live?"

Eric smiled. "I do." He recited his mother's address. (*Good boy,* he heard a woman's voice saying—his grandma, or his preschool teacher, maybe.) He could see the cop trying to figure out what to do next: Cuff him? Depart with a smile and a wave? "Tell you what," the kid decided. "Why don't you step out and proceed to the squad car, and I'll transport you back to that address. Meanwhile, my partner, there"—he nodded at the police car—"will follow us in your vehicle."

Eric shook his head. "I don't think that's necessary." He said it clearly—he was sure of it—so was horrified to hear that his words still came out melded. "I'll be fine," he tried again, this time louder and more clearly.

The cop shifted, looking nervous again. "Nonetheless," he said, "that's how we're gonna do it. Unless you want me to call you an ambulance."

Eric almost laughed. "No, no. I'll come into your car, then. Thank you."

The boy nodded, clearly relieved. "Out you go, then," he said. "I'll just need your keys for my partner."

Eric thought a moment. *Oh yes. On the floor.* He reached down to grab them, but the angle was such that, especially with the cast, he couldn't quite reach, even though he could see them perfectly. They were right there.

The cop watched him a second, hands at his sides, then said, "That's okay, sir. I'll grab those. You just get out of the car, and I'll take it from there."

For some reason, the statement—or maybe just the tone of it, no longer firm, only gentle, even pitying—struck Eric as unbearably sad. He made his way out of his car. His foot was throbbing again, now that the pills had worn off.

"Would you like me to get out your crutches?" asked the cop. "I see them now, in the back. Or I can just help you to the squad car."

It was a good thirty feet away. But Eric didn't trust himself on the crutches at this point, and there was no way in hell he could hop there without them. The kid was short, but solid, nicely built. He could probably hold Eric easily—especially given Eric's newly low weight, according to Dr. Koenig. "Okay," he said finally, and he let the kid move in and support him. He put his arm around the kid's shoulder and let him help the gimpy old man with the kung fu black belt travel ten yards and sit down again.

The other cop—older, whiter, beefier—got out as they approached, nodding to both of them. The young one nodded back, then helped Eric into the rear of the squad car. "You okay?" he asked when Eric was settled.

Was he okay? Eric honestly didn't know. "I'm fine," he said. "Thank you, officer."

The kid smiled, and Eric saw that he had a beautiful smile, dimples and perfect, straight teeth. Like an angel. Or what an angel should look like, instead of wings and haloes and silliness.

"No problem, sir," the kid said.

13

EVE WALKED INTO Bramington Brew, ordered a coffee, and, glancing at her watch, sat down at a table near the door to wait. A half hour ago, out of nowhere, Michael had called her at home. "Eve!" he said when she picked up, and he sounded happier than she'd ever heard him. "Diane and I are in Bramington—without the kids, believe it or not—and I'm wondering, and please don't feel you have to say yes. . . ." He paused, and she heard him breathing in his labored, husky way. "We're wondering if you might have a few minutes to let us buy you a coffee. I have something to tell you, and it would be fun to do it in person, though if you can't, I completely understand."

"Of course I can! I'd love to come meet you." Eve was thrilled to hear him sounding so well, especially after the past few less-than-upbeat visits. And the timing was perfect: Danny had just gone next door for Stream's birthday party, and Magnolia was off babysitting. "Do you know the local coffee shop?" Eve had asked, and she'd arranged to meet them here, just about now.

It was a warm, sunny Saturday afternoon, and the place was hopping, though most people got their drinks and gluten-free cookies or muffins and took them outside to stroll. Eve had barely sat down when Diane and Michael walked in.

She stood and gave them each a warm hug. "How are you?" she

asked Michael, but before he could answer, someone said, "Excuse me." They were blocking the entryway.

"Sorry," Michael said.

"No problem," said the person, but as Michael shifted to the left, Eve saw that he'd need to move from this space and also that he wouldn't fit at the table she'd picked for them. She should have chosen a roomier restaurant, she realized—though few would accommodate someone his size. "I'll wait outside," Michael said to Diane, no doubt realizing the same thing, and as he made his way back out the door, people turned to stare. Eve looked away. At one of their first appointments, he had told her he didn't like to look people in the eye, both because he didn't want to subject them to his ugliness and because he didn't want to see their expression when the sight of him registered on their face. She'd found that so sad she'd been unable to respond for several seconds, and then only badly, something unhelpful and clichéd.

Diane procured their coffees, and they headed outside to join Michael, and then across the street to the park. Like the coffee shop, it was lively: dogs, kids, two bald tattooed adults of indeterminate gender, a guy in rainbow pants riding a unicycle. Eve scanned the area for somewhere to sit. Michael wouldn't fit on a bench, at least not comfortably. "How about here?" he said, pointing to a grassy hill beyond the main drag. "Good," she said, and in a minute they'd all settled on the lawn, Michael very awkwardly. But he still seemed excited—euphoric, even. Diane, in contrast, looked more tense than usual. She handed him his coffee, and he thanked her and put it down next to him.

"This is a great town," Michael said, watching someone in hemp with bells around both ankles lead a kitten on a leash. "Kooky, but great. You must love living here. I hate to sound like a newscaster reporting on a neighborhood murder, but everyone really does seem so nice."

Eve laughed. "It's a good place. We moved here from Brooklyn years ago. Eric found it." A friend of his had mentioned it, she remembered. They'd taken a day trip up to see it, and that was that; six months later, Eric was handing over the down payment for their house, money he'd earned selling sculptures in less than two years. She wondered briefly if Eric considered all that a mistake now— leaving New York, moving here. *Maybe he regrets his whole life,* she thought. *Maybe he wishes he could start all over: different place, different wife.* "Anyway," she said, a little too loudly, "how are you doing, Michael? And what's the big news?" She took a sip of coffee.

Michael smiled. "Well, for one, I've decided to do the surgery you recommended."

"Really!" Eve wedged her cup between her legs so it wouldn't spill, then clapped her hands. "Excellent. Have you talked to one of the doctors I suggested?"

"I have an appointment for an initial consultation with Dr. Shetland. It's a week from Thursday, though." He shrugged. "That's the soonest they could get me in."

"Good," Eve said. "I don't know him well, but he's supposed to be great."

Michael nodded quickly. "But here's the real news. Right after I talked to you last time, I started reading about gastric bypass, and I realized that with my history of binge eating, I'm gonna have to show them I can stick to a regimen. So I started a diet that day." He smiled happily. "And I've stuck to it, Eve! I haven't cheated once. And I've lost sixteen pounds already."

A red flag went up in Eve's mind. "Sixteen pounds?" she said, trying to sound casually excited. "That's great, Michael, but it's a lot. You don't want to lose it too fast." She glanced at Diane, who was nodding. "What are you eating?"

"Very little," Diane answered for him. "Almost nothing, honestly." She motioned with her chin at the drink. "That's black coffee. No sugar, no cream."

The red flag was waving now, flapping in the breeze. "Michael," Eve said, "I don't know if—"

"That's the amazing part!" he interrupted. "I'm not hungry! I don't know why. Maybe it's excitement, or maybe, I don't know,

I'm just so ready for this that my body is starting early. Anyway, whatever it is, I'm going with it."

Eve nodded uncomfortably. She had never seen him hyped up like this. "The thing is—" she started to say, but again he interrupted.

"And the best part is, I haven't felt this good in ages. I have energy! Sometimes I can't even sleep, I have so much to burn. I've even started walking a little. And the pounds are melting off. It's like a gift from God. It's fantastic." He felt around for his coffee, found it, and took a tiny sip. "Black coffee. That, a grapefruit, a piece or two of dry toast. And that's it. That's all I need in a day." He took a deep, raspy breath. "I already feel like a new person, and I haven't even had the surgery yet. I'm so excited, Eve. Forgive me for talking so much. But I'm optimistic for the first time in years."

He coughed once, and then again several times, his huge body convulsing. Nearby, a little boy turned to stare. "Jasper," called his mother. "Please come over here."

Diane put a hand on his back. "You okay, Mike?"

He nodded, holding up a finger. He coughed for several more seconds, then stopped. "After the surgery, I might never have to do that again," he choked.

"I know, hon," said Diane. "Shh. Calm down now."

She stole another look at Eve, and the two women's eyes met. Eve didn't blame her for being worried. She had seen this before— the euphoria that came with dramatic weight loss, especially at the beginning. The problem was, the loss didn't last. At some point, the hunger returned and the weight came back on, hard and fast. The mental fallout could be disastrous, especially for someone like Michael, who was fragile already.

But she didn't want to discourage him either. "Well, okay," she said. "It's great you decided to move ahead with the surgery counseling, Michael, especially if you've read about it and you know what you're getting into. But I definitely advise against losing weight too quickly now. Even if you're not hungry, you need to eat three meals, even small ones. Otherwise you might be tempted to binge at some point."

He shook his head. "That's the thing. I'm *not* tempted."

"I know. I just want to make sure we keep it that way. And you don't want to tax your body before major surgery."

He gave her a look, as if he knew she was treating him like a child but he didn't really mind. "Okay," he said finally. "You're the boss."

"Damn right," she said, and he laughed.

They were all quiet then, watching a guy in the distance play a ukulele, two teenage girls in cutoffs and bare feet hurl a Frisbee back and forth. Nearby, a little girl was trying to climb a tree. She'd shimmy easily up to one certain branch, but the next was just out of her grasp. After reaching for a while, she'd jump down and start over, but the same thing happened at the same branch. "Darn it!" she said loudly. Her mother, or maybe sitter, was ignoring her, reading a magazine.

"I remember that," Michael said. "Climbing trees."

"Me too," said Diane.

Eve sipped her coffee. "Me too. Though I was more the type to yell a cheer from the bottom while someone else did the climbing."

"Not me," said Diane. "I was the type to rush over and shove my big brother off to prove I could beat him."

Eve laughed. "I don't believe that."

"Believe it," Diane said, and for the first time, Eve saw a glimmer of toughness inside the fuzzy nurse exterior. *Good*, she thought. *They'll need it if he's doing gastric bypass.*

"I was the type to lift my little brother up first," Michael said. "Then I'd climb up." He smiled. "Not that I was so noble. I just didn't want to be all alone up there."

"Ah," said Eve. "The old selfishness disguised as chivalry."

"Exactly." Michael smiled a little. "Though if I knew how it would end up . . ."

"Let me guess," Eve said. "He's a Wall Street whiz kid now, with, let's see, three yachts and a Lexus."

"I wish," Michael said.

"He died," Diane explained. "He was hit by a car when he was ten. Michael was twelve."

"Oh—wow," Eve said. "I'm so sorry."

Michael shrugged. "It's okay."

"Do you have any other siblings?" Eve asked, trying to dig herself out.

"One sister. Much older, though. We were never close. Even less after James died."

"James. Is that . . . James. Is that who your son is named for?"

Michael nodded. After a second, he said, "That's when I got like this—after James died. I wasn't fat before that. I mean, chubby, of course. We were Italian, after all." He laughed a little. "And my father was a big guy. Which is a nice way of saying he was about eighty pounds overweight." He shifted on the lawn, trying to get comfortable. "But after James died, my mother just sort of shut down. She stopped cooking, for one. Which, of course, you would think would mean I ate less, but . . ."

Eve shook her head. "That's not how it works."

"You know." Michael nodded. "Thus began my entry into breakfasts of Entenmann's doughnuts, lunches of school cafeteria pasta and cookies, dinners of Fritos, Suzy Q's, Ring Dings—whatever was cheap at the 7-Eleven. I'd sit in my tiny bedroom, on James's bed, and eat my way through the evening. No one really noticed. My mother was in bed. My father was at work, and then in front of the TV, and then in bed too."

Eve took a sip of her coffee. He had never told her any of this.

"Anyway." Michael brightened. "Enough about my happy childhood. What about you, Eve? What was your childhood like?"

"Quiet," Eve said. "Solitary. I was an only child."

"Really?" Diane looked interested. "I figured you for a firstborn."

Eve shook her head. "I was one of those kids who was twenty-two when I was six. Never acted like a child—probably because it wouldn't have gone over well in my house anyway."

Michael raised his eyebrows. He was a good listener for a man, Eve had noticed—very tuned in. *Like Eric,* she thought, without wanting to. "And now?" he asked. "You have two kids, right?"

Eve nodded. "Girl fourteen, boy eight."

"Wow," said Diane. "Fourteen, huh?"

Eve shook her head. "Don't ask."

"Believe me, I won't. I don't want to know."

Michael laughed. "And she's married to a sculptor. Eric Knight, right?"

Eve looked at him. "How did you know that? You know of him?"

"You mentioned it to me at one of our early appointments, and I Googled him. Talented guy. I love his work."

"Thanks," Eve managed.

"That's so neat!" Diane said. "A sculptor? What kind of stuff does he make?"

"Brass sculpture. Mostly large, mostly people—athletes, dancers . . ."

"I'll show you," Michael told her. "He has a Web site."

"It's a little out-of-date now," Eve said quickly.

"That's okay," Diane said. "I'll get the gist, anyway."

They were quiet another second (to Eve's relief; enough about Eric), and then she realized that Michael was struggling to get up. After a second, Diane rose to help him. Eve watched uncomfortably, not wanting to jump in too—surely that would make him feel worse—but also feeling guilty not to be helping. What must it be like, she thought, to be trapped inside unmanageable bulk, dragged down by your own massive limbs? She wondered how he'd gotten into the car to get here. Maybe the newly lost pounds had been enough; a few weeks ago, she remembered, he hadn't been able to go anywhere.

"Where are you going?" Diane asked him when he got to his feet.

"Restroom," he said. "Be right back." He headed again toward the coffee shop, his giant back retreating. The bathroom in there was small, Eve knew. How would he be able to use it? *He must be used to things like this,* she told herself, trying not to think about it.

Diane was watching him. "I'm nervous," she said to Eve when he was gone. "He's losing weight very fast. Which I guess is good in a way, but he's manic, Eve. You saw some of it. Even the kids have noticed. James said to me, 'Why is Daddy acting like Barney?'" They shared a guilty smile. "It's not that I'm not excited for him," she added. "It's nice to see him happy, obviously. It's just—" She sighed. "I wish he'd take it a little slower. I don't want to have him disappointed."

Eve was nodding. "I know. He needs to get in to see the team before he gets too revved up. First, he has to be assessed to find out if he's even a candidate for the surgery. I think he will be, but I'm not an expert in this. Then, if he is, they'll get him on a plan; he'll be working with experts. When's his appointment again?"

"A week from Thursday. Still a ways away."

"Let me see if I can get it moved up," Eve said, sounding more cavalier than she felt.

"Oh, could you? That would be fantastic."

"I don't know," Eve admitted. "I'm not close to Dr. Shetland. I only know of him, but I'll see what I can do."

Michael was returning. Eve watched him approach. He wasn't smiling now. "I couldn't get in the bathroom there," he said when he arrived. "There was a line. It was too complicated to wait. Anyway, we should go, Diane. We've taken enough of Eve's time." He glanced at his wife, then at Eve, and then, as if remembering something, he seemed to shift back into a happier place. "Thank you, Eve," he said. "Thank you for everything. If it weren't for you, I wouldn't even have thought of this surgery. And now it's already changing my life for the better, and I haven't even had it yet."

Eve stood up. "I'm so glad you called. I was telling Diane, I'll call Dr. Shetland and see if I can get your appointment moved up. If I can, I'll let you know."

A Frisbee came at them suddenly, hard and fast. "Look out!" Eve said, but it was too late; the Frisbee whacked into Michael's left side, then bounced to the ground.

Eve inhaled quickly. "Are you all right?" she and Diane asked at once, just as the girl who'd thrown it jogged over.

"Oh, wow," she drawled, pushing back several messy blond braids that fell into her face. "I'm, like, totally sorry. Are you hurt?"

Michael was bending down, as if he were. But then Eve realized that he was simply trying to pick up the Frisbee for her. "I'm fine," he wheezed, and, with effort, he got his big hand around the disk and got himself up again. He was about to toss the Frisbee to her when he noticed her partner, heading over now too, but still a distance away. He turned toward her and gently lobbed the Frisbee perfectly in her range.

She caught it with one hand, then laughed. "Nice throw, dude!" she yelled.

The braided girl looked at him. "You play Ultimate?"

Michael grinned. "Not at the moment. But I'm thinking of taking it up again."

"Tuesday evening pickup, behind the Unitarian church," she said. "You should come sometime. There's, like, buttloads of people."

Michael's face was radiant. "I will," he said. "Definitely."

The girls pranced away, all filthy feet and neon rope ankle bracelets. "Later," one of them called back.

"Later," Michael said, raising and lowering his hand. He turned to Diane. "Did you hear that? She called me dude!"

Diane rolled her eyes. "I heard. Let's not let it go to our heads, shall we?"

"Are you kidding? It's already etched there in gold."

She laughed. "Should I be jealous?"

"Absolutely."

She laughed again. "Come on, lover boy. We need to go relieve my mother before the kids give her agita." She turned to Eve. "We'll talk to you soon?"

"Yes." Eve felt a sudden glimmer of hope, an unexpected flash of warm light on a horizon that otherwise had been cold and gray since Eric left. Michael was happy, he was living again, and it was at least partly because of her—he'd said as much. So she hadn't failed him after all, then.

And if that was the case, then maybe she wouldn't fail everyone else either; maybe she could do this on her own after all. Her job, her house, her kids . . . maybe it would all be okay in the end.

It was a heavenly feeling, a high she longed to hold on to. "I'll call as soon as I talk to Shetland's office," she promised the couple.

Diane smiled. "Great. Thanks again."

Eve tossed her empty cup; it slam-dunked into a trash can. "My pleasure," she said.

14

THERE WERE TIMES when Eric could convince himself he had some feminine qualities; he was a good listener, for example, and he never gave Eve advice unless she asked for it (hardly ever, the past few years) or tried blithely to solve her problems for her, as so many men apparently did. But when he sat around the table with his mother and sisters, he never felt so much like a guy. He had heard that a man averages 7,000 spoken words a day to a woman's 20,000; with his mother and sisters, that sometimes felt more like one or two hundred to five or ten million, minimum.

And tonight that ratio seemed even higher, given his inability to articulate much of anything right now combined with the fact that— so far, anyway—they all seemed to be tiptoeing around any discussion of him. Beth had driven down from Phoenix this afternoon, and Frannie had flown in last night from L.A. Penelope had summoned them here, "To help cheer you up," she'd told him. But since they'd arrived, after showering him with hugs and kisses and sympathy about his foot, they'd pretty much let him be. Which was just as well, since he felt only nominally better than he had days ago when the police car pulled up out front and hand-delivered him to his mother. She'd carted him in, practically force-fed him chicken broth and toast, and then put him to bed, where he'd slept for another seventeen hours. He'd woken up yesterday morning, to be told his sisters were on the way—a fact that had filled him half with dread (he couldn't bear to face anybody right now) and half with what would have been excitement had he been able to feel such a thing. He loved his sisters. And he hadn't seen them in much too long.

Now they had just finished dinner—lentil soup, a salad with goat cheese and tangerines and almonds, hot white bread and cold butter—food his mother had dished out and placed before him and of which he'd eaten as much as he could (not very much), sensing it was delicious but being, as usual, neither hungry nor much able to taste. She hadn't given him wine, he'd noticed—the girls were working their way through a second bottle of pinot noir—and, to his disappointment, he hadn't had the wherewithal to ask. But they had offered him a gourmet chocolate from the box Beth had brought, and he'd accepted, knowing, in theory at least, that it would be delicious. (*How did women always find chocolates like this? Eve did, too. She'd have loved this whole meal.*) But he hadn't mustered the enthusiasm to eat it. It sat like a small black stone next to his plate.

Not that there'd been enough of a lull in the conversation for him to focus much on any of that. At the moment, Frannie and Penelope were egging on Beth, who was telling a story they all knew would end up being about her dogs, two crazy hounds famous for devouring everything in sight. "My housecleaner kept saying, 'Beth, I promise, you forget to pay me this time,'" she said. "And I'm like, ''Suela, I *swear* I left the money on the table, where I always do.' I knew I had, because I'd had only one twenty that day so I'd had to dig up small bills. You know?"

"Yeah," Frannie said, nodding. "Yeah. Yeah."

Beth picked up her wineglass. "So, I told her I'd repay half of it, but not the whole thing. She accepted, but we both were pissed. We both thought each other was lying. *Were* lying?"

"'*Was*,'" Frannie said. "'We *each* thought *the* other *was* lying,' I would say." Frannie was their resident copy editor.

"Right. Anyway, so guess what happened?" Beth took a large gulp of wine, relishing the withholding of punch line.

Obediently, they all shook their heads.

"The dog shit a twenty?" Frannie said finally.

"No!" Beth put down her wine, grinning. "The dog shit a *one*. And then another, and then another, till she'd shit out fifty-four of the sixty dollars."

She shrieked, slapping her thigh, and the women all laughed for a good fifteen seconds. Eric tried to smile along, though he wasn't completely sure his face was complying. But it had been years since the four of them had sat down like this, and he knew, at least in theory, that the night had been a treat: lovely food and drink, lively conversation, candles burning all over the place. The room was bathed in deep orange now, with enormous, exaggerated shadows on the walls and floors; muted trumpet notes, from a CD Frannie had brought, floated in the background, and a warm breeze wafted in the open windows, flickering the light and, Eric noted, making their faces appear to surface and recede, surface and recede, like ocean waves.

"Anyway," Beth said. "Needless to say, I paid her back with a crisp $100 bill, keep the change, bla bla bla, apologizing profusely the whole time." She shook her head. "Jesus, though. For a while there, I thought I was forty-nine going on ninety-eight."

It was quiet a moment, finally, everyone thinking, drinking, taking deep, sated breaths.

"But enough about me," Beth said suddenly. "How are *you*, Davey? I haven't heard nearly enough about you, considering you're the honored guest at this fine event."

Eric did not want to be honored. He didn't even want to speak. He much preferred this old pattern, his sisters yapping, him observing and absorbing, his mother a little of each. Beth, as usual, had done most of the talking. She had always been a little different from the rest of them. Even their mother's abundant and contagious laughter was downright subtle compared to her middle child's often raucous humor, and, as a marketer for a small dog food company in Phoenix, Beth was also the only one of the siblings who wasn't an artist at heart. It worked well, Eric had often thought. Bethy lent a touch of mainstream lightness, not to mention directness, to what otherwise might have become an overly introspective, nonconfrontational group.

They were all looking at him, waiting for him to say something. He guessed his mother had filled them in on his status, though he wasn't sure how many details she'd supplied. He hoped not many. "I'm okay," he said. God, why did the words always come out so jumbled? "I'm fine," he said, louder and more clearly.

"That's good," Beth said, as if she didn't believe him. "And how are Eve and the kids?"

Eric gave her a look, just to let her know that, dummy or not, he wasn't completely stupid. "They're good," he said, and then, "Why don't you just tell me what Mom told you? Then we can cut to the chase." His words were slow but at least decipherable now. He was working on it.

Beth laughed; the other two smiled, but looked vaguely embarrassed. "Well, okay," Beth said. "First, we asked Mom what the deal was with you being out here—whether Eve kicked you out, or you were separated, or whatever."

"And I said I had no idea," Penelope said, "as it was your business and I hadn't asked."

Eric attempted a smile of gratitude.

"And then Mom told us that a cop brought you home the other night, because you fell asleep in your car," Beth said.

Here we go, Eric thought.

Beth took a chocolate from the box, examined it, put it back, took another. "So what *is* going on?" she said, looking at Eric and trying but failing to sound casual. "You okay, baby bro?"

"I'm fine," he said, because really, if he wanted a therapist, he'd hire one.

"Well, you don't seem fine to us, honey." Beth bit the chocolate. "Oh, man," she said. "This tastes like what sex would taste like if sex were food."

They all laughed, even Eric, a little. His sister was such a piece of work, even when she was interrogating him.

"I think what she means," Fran picked up, gently, when they'd all finished snorting, "is, are you and Eve okay? I mean, is she okay with you being gone for this long, for one thing? And what brought you out here in the first place?"

"I drove our babysitter to Hatback to see her dying mother," Eric said slowly. "I thought I'd take a little vacation. Visit Mom, stay awhile."

Frannie nodded. "And Eve was fine with all that?"

Eric shrugged. "I'm sure. Her book just came out. She was doing all kinds of radio interviews, so—"

"Really?" Fran said. "That's fantastic! Good for—"

"Wait," Beth interrupted. "You're 'sure' she's just fine? As in you're *not* sure? As in you haven't asked her?"

Eric suddenly wished for a cigarette. *If you have to know, Beth, then no, we haven't talked,* he thought, but he said, "I called a few times, and she didn't pick up or call back. So I stopped calling." He was speaking a little better now, at least. Faster, more clearly.

"Wait." This was Frannie now. "So you haven't talked to her for a *month*?"

He could lie, but what good would that do? Besides, they probably knew anyway. "Actually, five weeks," he said, but he felt the impact of the words the second they came out. *Five weeks!* Since they'd married, even gotten engaged, he and Eve had rarely gone more than twenty-four hours without communicating.

"Wow," Frannie said, echoing his thoughts. "That's a long time to not—not to—I mean, I'm not, I'd never—" She paused. Somewhere in the room a candle flickered out, and the room darkened the tiniest bit. All three of them were watching him. "You talk to the kids, though," Frannie concluded. "Right?"

"I text with Magnolia," he said, though it had been days since he'd heard even from her, despite his still writing to her daily (though sometimes as little as "Hi. I miss you"—whatever he could muster right then). He didn't know why she'd stopped texting him, but it made him feel bereft and slightly terrified, as if one of his lifelines had been whisked away. And when he thought about Danny, his funny little ghost of a boy, he felt a pang in his heart, like an actual stab.

"Well, that's good," Frannie said finally. But they all looked taken aback now. Even Penelope.

Eric sat up straighter. "Listen," he said. "Eve's a strong person. She's fine." But he knew the words sounded rote and clueless, and for the first time, he wondered if they were true. Panic played at the edges of his mind, filling him with nausea.

Beth was giving him a look somewhere between skepticism and sympathy, or maybe just pity. "Well, I think that's a lot to assume, hon," she said. "Especially if it was your idea to go."

Another breeze wafted in, and this time Eric smelled, vaguely, cars, gasoline. A cigarette might help—when had he even last had one?—but he didn't know where they were and couldn't face looking for them. Plus, the last thing he needed was a lecture from Beth about the dangers of smoking. He took a deep breath, hoping he wouldn't actually throw up.

"I think what she's saying, David," Fran said, "is that none of us wants to see you mess up this thing you've built. Your beautiful family." She reached out and squeezed his hand. "I mean, not if you don't want to. If you want to—well, that's another story. If it's time to move on, okay, but then you need to face that and realize what you—"

"Of course I don't want to *move on*," he interrupted, but then Beth interrupted him.

"That *is* what I'm saying." She sat back and looked at him, and it occurred to him that of the three of them, it must be hardest for her to forgive his being out here. Beth was the most traditional in the family, and, unlike Fran and his mother, she got her comfort from other people. She was the one who'd always longed for the husband and kids, the minivan in the driveway, the fluffy dog and white picket fence. For him, the equivalent had come along when he met Eve—and had been welcome by then—but Beth had been seeking it since childhood, with her Easy-Bake Oven, her bride costumes at Halloween (while Frannie was Margaret from *Are You*

There God? It's Me, Margaret and he was David Partridge or Edgar Degas or, one year, a soul, dressed all in white, floating like a wisp down the street). In her urge to get it quickly, she had married at twenty-three, a steely-eyed, fakely chivalrous golf pro named Greg who called gay men "fairies" and overweight people "pigs" and got off on telling you the end of movies he'd seen that you were going to that night. When she'd dumped him five long years later, they'd all sighed with relief.

But since then—almost three decades now—Beth, though she'd dated on and off, had never found another man she loved who also loved her, and she'd slowly replaced her dream of having children with the feisty dogs she adopted. She was not unhappy, he knew—she'd made peace with her life and enjoyed it—but she'd compromised big things along the way. And to her, it must have seemed he hadn't had to compromise; good things, dreamy things had presented themselves to him with little or no effort on his part. And now he was messing it up, breaking it apart, like taking a hammer to a gleaming sculpture.

Frannie was a different story. An artist through and through, she had never wanted children and had always had mixed feelings even about marrying. When she'd met R.J., a cabinetmaker, older, with two grown kids and a small, well-kept house of his own, she'd been satisfied and happy to hook up with him—and she still was, as far as Eric could tell. And then there was his mother, who'd wanted the kids but, it seemed, not the husband; after three marriages, all of them ended by her, you had to form some conclusions. She sometimes claimed she'd still like to find her life love. ("It would be nice to have someone to pull out the jumping cholla," she'd once told them glibly, after recounting how, as she'd hiked alone the previous week, a clump of the clinging cactus had embedded in her shin and she'd had to rip it out herself, using a comb, rather than close her eyes and let someone do it for her.) But Eric didn't think she really wanted a full-time partner.

He understood that choice. He really did. But it wasn't what he himself had chosen, and it wasn't what he would choose now. He wanted—still—exactly what he'd chosen back then: Eve, the kids, his house, his home life.

So then what the hell was he doing out here?

"The thing is," he said to Beth, very softly, "sometimes it's more complicated than what you want and what you don't want."

"What do you mean?" She looked at him blandly, and he knew she was working not to roll her eyes and dismiss him—one more inarticulate man.

"Sometimes you can't control what happens in a marriage," he said, almost angrily now. "Sometimes it just happens, even if you don't want it to. Something else triggers it." He thought of his work, of how it had gone down the crapper, no matter how hard he'd tried to rescue it as it swirled away. And how that had led to everything else (though he supposed one could also make the chicken-and-egg argument): his insecurity, and his need for something more from Eve—more attending, more coddling—and, eventually, of hers from him (more money, more income). When he hadn't been able to give it, she'd gone out and gotten it on her own. And with it came power and confidence and chutzpah—and, let's face it, impatience—hers increasing, it seemed to him, as his further faded. *And really,* he thought now, *more power to her for it.* But it made him feel like an aging pet, something that had to be fed and watered purely because you'd once acquired it, back when it was still cute and relevant.

"That's true, of course," Penelope said, looking thoughtful. "Sometimes you *can't* control what happens in a marriage."

Beth did roll her eyes now. "Please, guys, don't patronize me. I mean, look at my life. I'm not saying it's not great or even that I'd trade it at this point. Honestly, I wouldn't; I'm very content. But do you think I would have chosen to be single and childless in my fifties?" (Eric thought of Eve's friend Loretta, who *had* picked it, it seemed, until last year, when she'd gone on a sudden e-mail search for a mate.) "Or look at the dog I gave up last year," Beth said. "The one I couldn't train. I gave him back, and they probably euthanized him." Her lower lip quivered. "But at least I tried, David. I tried so hard with that dog. I took him out every hour, I let him shit and piss all over my house, I let him bite me till I bled. Because otherwise, what's the point? You know? I mean, you don't just give up."

"I didn't just—" Eric tried, but Beth was still talking.

"You don't just *run away*," she said. "You don't just *leave*! You have to *deal* with it!"

There was a long silence while her words made their way through Eric, each its own little blade. He felt like smashing something. He felt, actually, like smashing Beth—or all of them. Instead, he rose and, not without effort (and some humiliation), hopped to the bathroom, narrowly missing trouncing the dogs asleep on the rug. He slammed the door, steadied himself, and peed against the side of the toilet; his sisters had trained him early not to aim straight into the water and make too much noise, and though he couldn't care less what the hell they thought now, he couldn't quite break the habit. He flushed angrily. How dare she accuse him of giving up! Beth, who had never even been married, except for five minutes to some jerk before she divorced him. *She doesn't know a damn thing about marriage,* he thought, but as he watched the water disappear, he couldn't help thinking, *And you do?*

He leaned down to scratch (ineffectually) at his leg above the cast; the psoriasis, now frustratingly underneath it, had worsened the past few weeks without his cream. Giving up, he washed his hands and splashed cold water on his face, dried himself on his mother's towels, tan and rough and smelling like her: clean, natural, complemented by the scent of the dried lavender she'd placed in a soup can on the sink. He sniffed the buds, trying to calm down, then caught a glimpse of himself in the mirror without wanting to. He looked gray and ill and craggy.

He wanted to go straight to his room, but he knew he'd never get away with departing that way. *Ten more minutes and I'm out of here,* he thought as he hopped back, grabbing his cigarettes from the counter on the way, lighting up as he sat down again. If they didn't like it, they could leave. *Where are you going?* he would say. *You don't give up! You don't just run away!*

The thought almost made him laugh. He took a long drag, blowing the smoke away from the table even though he felt like aiming it straight in their faces. "Aren't you gonna give me shit about the smoking now, Beth?" he said. "Since you've already trashed me in every other way."

He knew he was being a baby, but it felt good anyway. But Beth looked at him, and her eyes began to tear. "Oh, Davey," she said. "I'm only saying it because I love you."

"So do I," Frannie said. "And we're worried about you."

"Well, don't be," Eric started to say, but Beth said, "Mom thinks you're depressed. And apparently her doctor does too."

Eric turned and stared at his mother.

"I'm sorry, David," Penelope said, looking slightly ashamed. "But it's true. And I know therapists aren't supposed to analyze their own children, and I've tried not to, but I think it's reached a point where you need help with this." She took a deep breath. "I wouldn't be taking care of you if I didn't tell you."

"I didn't ask you to take care of me," Eric started to say, but he could barely spit out the words. Here he was, after all, sitting at her table, sleeping in her house, practically asking her to wipe his sorry ass.

"Of course you didn't," his mother said. She smiled at him sadly. "And you're welcome to stay here forever if you want."

"But we hope you won't," mumbled Beth.

Frannie looked at her and then at Eric. "We're just saying you need to realize what you're doing here," Frannie said gently. "And then figure out how to deal with it."

Eric blinked. "Deal with *what*?"

"Your depression," Beth said, and then, also gently, "Don't you agree you're depressed?"

Eric closed his eyes, opened them again. "I don't know," he said wearily. "But I don't really see how it matters."

"It matters," said Fran, "because if you accept it, you can work on it, and maybe even fix it. And when you start to fix it, you'd be amazed at how suddenly the things in your life that have been messed up for so long start to fix themselves." She picked up her wineglass and swirled it thoughtfully. "When I'm depressed—and I don't mean just *unhappy*, or *down*, or whatever, because that's not really what depression is; it's more about inaction. Shutting down the factory, opting out of the whole stupid mess." She put down her glass and looked at him. "Anyway. When I'm depressed, I mean really, clinically depressed, I can't face any of it. I don't want to do anything, go anywhere, see even my friends or my family. I can barely drag myself to work, and sometimes I can't at all. I sleep away entire weekends."

Eric stared at her. "Since when are you clinically depressed?"

Frannie shrugged. "Since I was, what, Mom, like, eight?"

Penelope smiled. "More like eighteen," she said to Eric.

"Though you wouldn't know it when I'm on the right meds," Frannie said. "I've been on medication on and off for about three decades now. And when I'm on a good one, like now, I feel fine, except for a few side effects."

"My friend Delilah gains weight no matter which one she's on," Beth commented. "And she can't have an orgasm. Big check in the 'forgetaboutit' column if you ask me."

"Me too," Eric mumbled, though he couldn't remember the last time he'd had one himself, or even wanted to. Well. It didn't help that Eve was a million miles away.

"I don't have those problems, thankfully," Frannie said. "At least not on this drug. And honestly, they're worth it even with side effects when you look at what they take away."

Eric frowned. "Well, aren't there other, more natural ways to—"

"Oh, believe me," Fran said. "I'm no stranger to yoga, meditation, acupuncture . . . you name it, I'll give it a whirl. Not to mention diets. Dairy free, vegan . . . Last time I got off meds, besides cutting out gluten—and that's a task; do you know there's gluten in *soy sauce*? In *chicken broth*?" She shook her head. "Anyway, I also did a triathlon. It worked for a while. The endorphins, I guess. Plus, when I'm off my meds, I have so much energy. It's great for a while, and I'm always like, 'I don't need the drugs, I don't want to live a medicated life.'" She sighed. "But then I start to go down again, no matter what else I do. Last time it happened, I was absolutely riddled with anxiety. I'd leap out of bed in the morning chanting, 'Oh my God! Oh my God!' R.J. thought I was heading toward a heart attack. And eventually I can't even go to yoga anymore, because I'm too much of a mess." She twisted a strand of her long, wavy hair, which was pulled back into a loose ponytail. "It's not a way to live," she concluded. "I won't go off them again unless there's a real reason to."

Eric was still trying to digest this. "How come I never knew any of this?" he asked.

"You're her baby bro," Beth said. "You're not supposed to know this sort of thing." She smiled. "Not that you weren't a little clueless too, hon."

His sisters both laughed.

The room grew quiet again. For all of their talking, the Knight women knew how to embrace a productive pause. Though he still felt awful, Eric was less angry now, and he was glad; he hated being angry at his family. Hated being angry at all, really. He'd never known what to do with anger other than attempt to channel it into his work. He had no respect for people who yelled and ranted and stormed around like bulls. It was rude and juvenile and selfish.

He leaned back. Now the breeze floating in smelled both soothing and pungent, like freshly cut limes roasting over a wood fire. Creosote, maybe. He took a long, deep breath, trying to find solace in it, then looked around the table. "So, any other confessions?" he asked. "Beth, are you on antidepressants too? Mom?"

"Not me," Beth said. "Thank goodness. I'd be a tank."

Frannie laughed. "You would not." Beth was shorter and stockier than Frannie, though she was neither short nor stocky. She was fair, like their mother, with highlighted blond hair that she too wore long and wavy—hair that, Eric had noticed, had some silver streaks now. Frannie, for her part, was tall and dark and lanky. Like him.

"I'm not on them either," Penelope said. "I've never been depressed. At least nothing a little R and R and an adjustment in outlook couldn't cure. Very lucky in that way. Though I've certainly seen plenty of patients who are." She had made a pot of Earl Grey tea, and now she removed the bags, squeezed them dry, and put them on a saucer. "One thing I will say," she said, passing out mugs. "If you are depressive, this is a great time to be alive."

"Why?" Eric asked, because he felt the opposite: everything was so complicated now, ridiculous and accelerated and insanely reliant on technology. Even books were on their way out. Pretty soon you'd need a screen and an electrical outlet to read *Stuart Little* or *Goodnight Moon* to your kid. The other day, he'd seen someone in a T-shirt that said, *The Internet was down today, so I decided to go outside*. He'd laughed, and then wanted to cry.

"Well, the drugs now, for one," Penelope said. "They're fantastic. Not perfect, of course, as Frannie points out. And, yes, too many of us are on them who likely don't need to be, and too many of us who do need them aren't getting relief." She shrugged. "But they know so much more about all this than they ever did, and there are so many options now. Thirty or forty years ago, if you were depressed, you had to take a tricyclic—or an MAO inhibitor, which could kill you if you drank a glass of wine or ate the wrong piece of cheese. Before that, there was the psych ward, electroshock therapy . . . or just living with it, and whatever fun came with that." She leaned back and sighed. "Your father, for example."

Beth and Frannie both nodded. Eric looked from one of them to the other.

"Not that he'd ever have admitted it," Penelope went on. "But back then, few people did. Especially men. Not until they could no longer function, at least. And then people found out, whether you wanted them to or not."

Eric felt an odd urge to defend his father against these three women, all ganged up against him. "Maybe if he didn't think he was depressed, he wasn't," he said.

Penelope smiled. "Well, of course, there are various levels of depression, like everything else. There's always a spectrum." She shrugged. "But, you know. A diabetic can ignore the blurred vision, the thirst, the numbness in their feet, but they still have diabetes, and they're living an enormously stunted life until they treat it. If it doesn't kill them first."

Eric ashed his cigarette onto the edge of his plate, wondering what his father had done that was so terrible. Really, he knew so little about Benjamin Knight. He hadn't been in any of their lives since Eric was two—since, Eric now knew, Penelope had left him. In fact, the last Eric heard, his father had moved to Brazil and lived there with his third wife. *He probably did nothing terrible at all,* he thought, answering his own question. *Except in the eyes of three critical women.* But he'd never thought of his sisters or even his mother that way; he'd always trusted their judgment, their view of the world.

Once more, silence drifted over them, and now, despite his unhappiness, Eric felt their warmth and sympathy, the bath of love he'd always felt from his nutty, smart, loyal family of females. He looked at his mother, and she smiled, put down her mug, and said, "Tell us more, David. What part aren't we seeing? How can we help you?"

Eric took a last drag of cigarette, then extinguished it carefully in one of the spent tea bags. Where to even start. "I don't know my kids," he said, and he blinked, surprised that that's what came out, surprised again because he felt it was true. "Which might be okay," he added, "if I was never home because I was working to support them, like—" He thought for a moment. "Like fathers used to be. Like *I* used to be. But that's not the case anymore. I haven't worked well in years. I don't really know why. And I'm not home either, because there's no room for me there. So I'm not sure where I am. I feel like—like I'm using all my energy to stay afloat, day after day. And I'm sinking anyway."

It was a big speech for him, and when he finished, he felt newly exhausted.

Penelope got up and came over and put her arms around his shoulders from behind, and he closed his eyes and leaned against her. He was practically crying; it was such a relief to finally say all this. "Oh, honey," she said. "I'm so sorry."

"So whose fault is that?" Beth interrupted, and he opened his eyes. "Whose fault is it that you don't know your kids, David? Is it Eve's?"

Yes! he thought. *Yes!* But he couldn't say it, or he'd be no more wise than Magnolia at age two, when, on a regular basis, she'd trip or bump into something, turn to whoever was around, and yell, "*You did dat!*"

His sisters were both looking at him again, their eyes filled with love, or what he hoped was love, anyway. "Go home, David," Beth said, and she reached out, took his hand, and kissed it. "Go home and tell Eve you want a piece of those kids. Open your mouth for a change. Go back to your wife. Before there's nothing left to go to."

"What if she doesn't want me when I get there?" The words shot out. Embarrassed, he stared at the table.

"I don't think it's really about *want* at this stage," Beth said—a little snottily, he thought.

"I'm not sure I'd agree with that, actually," Penelope said, and Eric thought, not unkindly, *No, you wouldn't.* His mother had, like yet another of Priscilla's bumper stickers instructed, generally "followed her bliss." And it had worked for her, more or less. Nor did her children seem any the worse for wear, though really, who could tell? You couldn't go back and do it over differently. And even if you could—if Beth had, say, had the confidence or role modeling to have chosen a better husband, and gotten her babies—well, so what? Kids hardly guaranteed happiness. Maybe she'd be fleeing now too. Just like he was.

"Well, okay," Beth said impatiently. "Of course you have to want your life. I mean, you have to get some enjoyment, obviously. Nor am I against divorce, as you all know, if the sight of the person's face makes you want to stab yourself and then put a plastic bag over your head while you're bleeding, just in case." They all smiled, remembering Greg. "But at some point," she went on, "it becomes about something other than your, your—"

"Joie de vivre?" Frannie offered.

"Maybe," Beth half agreed. "At least not every second, if even every year. And I'm not just talking about responsibility, either, though, of course, that's part of it. I'm more just saying, if you leave a life like yours at this point, David, what would be left? What would you have?"

Relief, Eric thought, but again, it sounded pathetic now, even to himself. And what he'd found here in Arizona was hardly relief in the end.

Beth was smiling a little but not completely kindly, like a school teacher telling you that even if for the right reasons, you'd still broken the rules. And through the flickering light and the haze of wine and the cloak of the breeze wrapped in cigarette smoke and whatever else was in here and out there, he felt her transfer, in some small way, some portion of her hopes and dreams onto him. "Go home to your lucky wife," she said, "and your beautiful kids, and *make* them want you. But do me a favor, David. First, fix yourself. Do whatever it takes. Because you know what?" She picked up her wineglass, saw it was empty, and, with a sigh, put it down again. "This world's not about to fix you."

There was a long silence as everyone took in her words.

And then: "But we can help," Frannie prompted.

"Oh yeah." Beth laughed. "I forgot about that part."

Eric looked from one of them to the other.

"I've got the name of a therapist who can see you," his mother said, stepping in. "Jenny Koenig recommends her, and I've already called and made an appointment, though unfortunately, the soonest she can see you is late next week. In the meantime, Jenny called you in a prescription for Lexapro, and I filled it for you. Lexapro is one of the more common—"

"Mom," Eric said. "I know what Lexapro is."

"Oh!" Penelope laughed. "Anyway, Jenny thought it was a good place to start. Take half a pill, and if there are no bad side effects after a few days, go up to a whole and see how you feel. It can take a while to kick in, though. That's the hard part, especially because there might be some stomach stuff at first—nausea or diarrhea— and people get discouraged, because they're not feeling better yet and they're also feeling lousy in ways they didn't before. But most or all of that stops after a while."

Eric was staring at her. "I can't believe you filled me a prescription for Lexapro," he said.

"I did," his mother said. "It's up to you whether to take it, of course, but now it's here if you want it. And frankly, I don't see what harm it could do at this point."

"Neither do I," Frannie said.

"That makes three of us," said Beth.

Eric shook his head. He wanted to make a joke—something about being mown down by a bunch of batty, neurotic, crazy-assed women—but he couldn't think of one. He wanted to run out of the room and into the desert, wailing. But he couldn't even walk, let alone run.

"So?" said Beth, and she reached to touch his face. "Will you try the drug, hon? And go see the person Mom's doctor recommends?"

He shook his head. So, okay. What did he have to lose by trying? *Just your principles and your dignity*, he answered himself—but hell, maybe he'd get something for those. Certainly he wouldn't mind feeling better. Maybe the drug could do that. "I'll think about it," he said. He would take the pills if it would shut them all up. He'd pop one right now if they'd just get out of his face. And then, God willing, he'd go back to bed.

"I'll think about it," he repeated, and that was that. But on his way to his bedroom—all of five seconds later—he grabbed the bottle from the kitchen counter (where, he saw now, his mother had conveniently left it) and stuck it in his pocket. Safely in his room, he stared at it for a long time. And then he uncapped it, shook his head in disgust, and swallowed his first one. "Ta-da," he mumbled, low enough so that no one could hear. "Are you all happy now?"

In the morning, and then again the following morning, he woke up and felt exactly the same: pathetic, despondent, wiped out. *What a joke,* he thought (not sure whether he was describing the pills or his life), as he alternately wandered the house aimlessly, occasionally going out for a smoke before retreating back to his bed to elevate his foot for a bit. He had found a box of old Archie comics in the closet—his own as a kid, uncharacteristically saved by his mother— and he was making his way through them, amazed at how sexist and unfunny they were. He had texted Maggie twice, with no response. Twice more, he picked up the phone to call Eve (maybe, just maybe, Danny would answer), but hung up before he finished dialing. What could he possibly say at this point? She must despise him by now. He wouldn't blame her.

On the third day, the diarrhea kicked in. *Lovely,* he thought, and he tossed the pills in the bathroom trash can, then retrieved them again. His mother had spent money on them. He'd give them a week. After that . . . well. Cross that bridge when he came to it.

On the fifth day, he woke up, early, and felt—different. Not good, exactly; he was too tired and rundown, too nauseated and disgusted to approach anything that optimistic. But something was different. He sat up in bed, trying to figure it out.

His head was clearer. That was it. Just a tad—almost impercepti- bly, but still and definitely, clearer than it had been in months. No. *Years.* The white noise that had plagued him, that monotonous and overwhelming ticker tape—the one that alternated between broad- casting that he was a loser and a failure, that he would never make anything decent again . . . and asking him what was the point of his life, of life at all, of all of human existence—had faded and retreated just the tiniest bit. And in its place was whiteness. Not white noise. Whiteness. A blank palate.

He got up, found his crutches, and hopped outside to the porch, then sat down on the swing. His mother was gone; not unusual for the morning, as she often walked or hiked with her friends. She was busy most afternoons, too—sometimes working, sometimes shopping or gardening or browsing a local bookstore. Her life was full and active, he had noticed, and she seemed to thoroughly enjoy it. He lit a cigarette and smoked it, staring, through already hot sun, at the bold and beautiful Santa Catalina Mountains. *Okay,* he thought. *So what are you gonna do?*

His clothes stank. His body reeked. His hair had been dirty for days. He finished the cigarette, ground it out and held on to the filter to throw away inside, picked up his crutches again. He would go in and clean himself up. And then he'd change his sheets and straighten his room. He was embarrassed he had let himself come to this.

In the bathroom, he bathed, his cast wrapped in a plastic trash bag his mother had thoughtfully put in his bathroom the night he'd gotten hurt. He lay in the water in the tub, breathing deeply, sweating and thinking and staring at the clean, white, empty ceiling. After a while, he drained the tub and filled it again. *Warm water,* he thought. *What a thing.* He rinsed off and got out. Dried himself and hung his towel on the hook and then shaved. Then, bracing himself, he took a hard look in the mirror. Staring back was a gaunt old man, grizzled and ugly. But clean-shaven, at least. Clean-shaven and clean.

The next day, he felt the same. Not good, exactly, but clearer. More focused, less agitated. "Do you want me to go grocery shopping?" he asked his mother, because he wanted to pick up Pepto-Bismol, English muffins—which, for some reason, he craved.

She looked at him with interest, watching him for so long he had to turn away. "Why don't I come with you?" she suggested finally. So they went together, him on crutches, her pushing the cart, both of them deciding what should go into it.

On the seventh day, he woke up, took a bath, and went out to the table. It was 9:45. His mother was home, and she made him a poached egg and toast, then sat with him while he ate, glancing at the newspaper, sipping tea. It was Sunday, he realized.

"How are you feeling?" she asked, eyes still on the paper. "Is your stomach any better?"

He shrugged. He'd gotten used to it: the nausea, the churning. The Pepto was helping, as was the fact that he was eating regularly. There was nothing else to do, after all. If he didn't watch himself, he might even get fat.

"I'm gonna go home," he said.

"What?" His mother looked up. She put down the paper.

Once, across a crowded street in New York, he had seen a gentleman, dapper but elderly, trip and fall. The man had missed the curb, and then he was lying facedown on the pavement, his pressed trousers torn at the knee, his besweatered little wife wringing her hands as the traffic sped past. Just as Eric jogged over to help— heart pounding; eyes, atypically, stinging with tears—he saw three young men, two white, one black, lift the man (who must have told them he was fine) and, in one quick motion, set him back on his feet. They replaced his cane in his hand, stuck his fedora back on his head, and held him a moment—one with a palm on his back, the other two grasping his arms—until he got his bearings. Then they withdrew their hands, as you would from a toddler learning to walk, and the man and his wife resumed their slow, even shuffle to wherever they were off to: the newsstand, the diner, the bank.

For some reason, Eric thought of that now. At the time, the sight had undone him. He kept imagining how it must feel to smack to the pavement, to lie there with people and traffic around you, to lose not just your footing but your dignity—and to know that now that it had happened once, now that you were vulnerable in that way, it would likely happen again, more and more as you aged. Finally, unable to let it go, he'd told Eve what he'd seen. But when he finished, she said, "What a great New York story! Everyone stops to help and then goes along their merry way. Even the little old man!"

It hadn't remotely occurred to Eric to see the scene in that light. And it was one of those moments when he knew he'd married the right person: someone who could take in the same thing he did but interpret it a different way, and then, in sharing her version with him, pull him ever so slightly away from the dark place he tended toward. So that after that, when he thought of the incident, he remembered not only the man's fallen body in the street (fedora upside down in the gutter, skinny legs splayed), but also the determination on his face when he got up again; the decision, whether natural or obtained through great effort, that even if he had only two or three years—or months—left, he would keep moving forward.

Eric had known then, as he knew now—as he'd known almost immediately when he met her—that it was Eve he wanted. And happily for him, she'd wanted him, too. But part of what she'd fallen in love with, he knew, was his work, and with it—even if she didn't say it, even if she didn't even *know* it, in this crazy, post-feminist age—his ability and potential, even as an artist, to provide. And that had been fine with him. So she could build their nest and raise their babies and take care of all of them, including him, so that he could take care of *them*, in the best and only way he knew: by making sculptures, day after day. But what, he asked himself (because he had the wherewithal now; that's what the blank palate had provided), happens now? What is the role of the long-working husband when he can no longer provide? "*Make* her want you!" Beth had said, and as much as he wanted to drown out her voice, he knew she was right. But how was he supposed to do that?

"I'm going back," he said to his mother, again. "I've got to go back."

His mother removed her reading glasses and blinked rapidly several times, and Eric noticed, for the first time, the papery creases around her lips, the folds on her neck. She had aged, he realized. Beautifully, gracefully . . . but nonetheless.

"When, were you thinking?" she asked.

He loved her so much. Loved her for not telling him he was crazy, insane, idiotic. "Today?" he said. "I mean, unless, you know, you need me for something."

"You don't want to see the therapist first?" she asked. His appointment was in two days.

Eric shook his head. "I don't think so."

She nodded. "I'll come with you."

"Sorry. What?"

"I'll come with you! I'll ask Dorothy to watch the dogs. She loves to have them."

"Oh, Mom." Eric wanted to hug her. "That's okay. I can do this myself. Really. Otherwise, I wouldn't attempt it." He was lying, of course; he had no idea whether he could do it, only knew he had to try. And in fact, he loved the idea of Penelope going with him. She would share in the driving, maybe foot the bills for hotels. They'd eat together in the lonely old diners. A road trip with his mother! It was brilliant. But only if she was coming because she wanted to, not because she thought he couldn't do it. "Do you really want to?" he asked.

"Yes!" She clapped her hands. "It will be so much fun. I'll call Dot right now. And I'll cancel my patients for tomorrow and Wednesday—that's all I have this week, and I never cancel, so they'll understand. After that, I can be ready in—" She glanced at her watch. "Two hours. Okay?"

Excitement mounted inside him—real excitement now, further pushing out the fear and the dread that had overwhelmed him for so long. Forever, it seemed now. "Yes!" he said.

She smiled, a beautiful, warm smile, and he was thrilled to see that she no longer looked old now, only happy and radiant. As ever. "Well, all right, then," she said. "Let's do this thing."

"Ready when you are," he said.

15

EVE STOOD AT the kitchen counter flipping through the *Nutrition Awareness* newsletter she'd just brought in from the mail, amazed anew at how many different ways they came up with to make it sound like news that people eat too much crap and not enough fruit and vegetables. The cover story this month, "Food and Fractures," featured a questionnaire called a FRAX (Fracture Risk Assessment Tool), as well as a long list of foods and their measure of PRAL (Potential Renal Acid Load)—something that apparently, when too high, was linked to bone loss. The culprit this time was grains: rice, bread, cereal, and everyone's favorite whipping boy, doughnuts. The solutions (along with spinach, which, with kale, was always a given) were raisins, apricots, and kiwi. Kiwi! *Organic and raised locally, of course,* Eve thought, rolling her eyes. And how much would that set her back for something the kids would take one bite of (Magnolia would probably only *lick* it) before tossing it in the compost bin? Frankly, the whole thing made her want to go straight to Dunkin' Donuts, scarfing a Kit Kat Dark on the way.

She smiled at the thought. If she said that to Eric—which she would, if he were here—he would laugh.

Early last week, out of nowhere, she had received a letter from him containing $300 in cash—or, rather, she'd received $300 wrapped in the briefest of notes: "I'll send more when I can. I miss you." She'd been simultaneously thrilled (He was out there! He missed her!) and angry (Why didn't he write a real note? Why didn't he just tell her what the hell he was doing?). Nonetheless, she'd marched straight out, feeling as if she'd just won the lottery, and spent it on two new pairs of pants for Danny; toiletries for Magnolia, including the expensive razor cartridges she liked, the kind with the soap built right in; and a box of her own favorite muffins from Bramington Brew, which she never ate anymore (too expensive, no time to get there). After scarfing one on the spot standing at the counter, she had frozen the rest, taking out one every morning since to microwave for her breakfast. It felt like the biggest luxury she'd had in years.

She'd checked every day for more notes. But so far, a big fat goose egg.

Eve closed the newsletter, tossed it onto the unopened-mail pile, and went outside.

It was a gorgeous afternoon, flooded with dazzling spring sunshine. She stood a moment, breathing in the splendor and warmth before walking to the side of her house to behold the miracle that was her little flower garden—an endeavor she'd started when they'd first moved here, with a packet of lupine seeds Eric had given her before leaving New York, and then added to annually. By now, the garden was an explosion that never failed to amaze her when it emerged from the barely thawed ground every year. At the moment, some of the late-blooming tulips were (miraculously) still intact—purple and magenta folds framing velvety black stamens, their tips exploding with pollen—and had been joined by her peonies (the deepest dark red) and peach daylilies with cranberry centers that, thrillingly, had just bloomed today. The violets were so fragrant and sweet she wondered why anyone needed crack. Sniffing them, she felt downright tipsy.

She had come out here to escape thoughts of Eric, but now she couldn't help thinking how sad it was that he would miss this phase of the glory, which would end in another week or ten days, giving way to bleeding hearts and foxglove, portulaca and lupine and all the different coreopsis (sunfire and lance-leaved and moon-beam) . . . and then to bee balm and black-eyed Susans; fluffy, ball-like hydrangeas; and festive purple gomphrena, like pom-poms on a costume for the tiniest clown. Then finally there'd be the white mums and the towering morning glories, which would ascend the trellis Eric had put up before they burst into heavenly blue sideways lampshades that—

Her cell phone rang.

Eve reached into her pocket and, because she could no longer see the caller ID without reading glasses, answered blindly. "Hello?"

"Oh good, you're there. I realized something and I have to tell you. It's Loretta, by the way."

"I know. What did you realize?"

"That all we do now is talk about *me*. I've become one of those horrible women who can only talk about themselves, their baby, and their boobs. Meanwhile, you're the one whose husb—"

"I don't want to talk about him," Eve said, though she sort of did, a little.

"Point taken. But then can we talk about *you*? For five minutes? Since, let's face it, that's probably all I'll have before I have to get back to—say it with me—"

"Yourself, your baby, and your boobs?"

"Exactly."

Eve laughed. "Okay. Though, you know, I actually don't mind talking about any of those."

"Well I do. We're boring. And unkempt. All four of us. I feel like Ma Fucking Joad, pushing a stroller and all the baby crap around New Jersey. See? There I go again. Stop enabling me. Tell me something about *you*. What are you doing? What were you thinking when I called?"

"Um—I was thinking about my garden, actually."

"Really? What about it?"

"I was thinking that the reason old women become avid garden-ers is that their gardens—unlike, let's face it, themselves—actually grow *more* beautiful each year, not less. Of course, you do have to work at it. Trim this, add that, be relentless about keeping out the aphids and weeds and—"

"Or let them come, the little adulterers, but then be willing to overlook them," said Loretta.

"Exactly. Draw your lines, and then be forgiving, or not. But whatever else you do, if you want it to flourish, you have to observe it and think about it and tend it and change it if necessary. Either that, or don't complain when it all goes to shit."

"Again, not unlike marriage. Not to be overly metaphorical here."

"Not at all." Eve bent to smell a peony, carefully avoiding the ants that clustered on the lush, almost (she had to admit) *vaginal* blooms, where they'd suck at the resin, which some gardeners, Eve among them, believed helped open the dense double buds. "And then, of course, there's the mother-child metaphor," she said. "Like one's children, a garden is something you create and nurture, watching it grow and change every year. But unlike one's children, it does not get up one day and walk away. You don't have to 'give it roots and wings.' Only roots."

"That's fantastic!" Loretta yelled. "I love it! I see a course on the literary garden, you as guest speaker."

"I'm there. Especially if there's a stipend, now that I'm—oh wait, there's another call coming in, of all things. Can you hold on?"

"Just call me after," Loretta said. "Or later. Whenever. If I don't answer, you'll know why."

"Self, baby, boobs."

"You said it, not me. But at least you'll know I miss you."

"Thank you," Eve said, meaning it. "I miss you too."

She pressed buttons until, miraculously, another voice said, "Eve?"

Eve blinked. "Penelope?"

"Yes! Listen, I only have a minute, unfortunately. And I fear I'm doing something very bad right now, because Eric doesn't know I'm calling you. I've wanted to for weeks, just so you know, but I haven't because I didn't want to get in the way of—well, whatever is going on between you two. But I gave in now, because I feel you should know what's up."

Eve's heart had been thumping since she first heard the voice. "I'm listening," she said.

"Okay. Well, he's very depressed, first of all. Maybe you already knew that? Anyway, he was bad when he arrived, and he only got worse."

Eve felt her breath disappear. "Is he okay?"

Next door, the dog dashed out the front door, a snarling, drooling pit bull mix that Priscilla had rescued from a shelter and promptly dumped into Ronnie's care. He circled their yard twice at high speed, like a demented racehorse, then skulked into the corner to piss on a plant.

"He's okay now," Penelope said. "He's better, I think. He went on medication, and amazingly, it's already working. He's lucky. Even when it works, it usually takes a lot longer. But I can see the change in him the past couple of days. I'm hopeful. But I'm concerned about him, too. And I'm so sorry for all this. You must be beside yourself. Oh! I've got to go. He's coming. But listen: he loves you, Eve. You and the kids—he lives for you three. And he needs you right now. You're his love and his savior. I just wanted you to know. I'll try to call again, but I don't know if I'll be able to." She clicked off.

"Munchkin," Ronnie called, coming out after the dog. "Munchkin! Get back in the— Oh, hey, Eve. I didn't realize you were out here. Hope the psychopathic mutt there didn't scare you."

Eve looked at her. Then she looked at the phone. She folded it closed and put it in her pocket. "No," she said. "Not at all."

Ronnie caught the dog and began to calmly half walk, half drag it back in by the collar, the dog straining and dancing on its hind feet.

"I was talking to my mother-in-law," Eve said, as if Ronnie cared.

"You called her? That's impressive." Ronnie grinned.

"Actually, she called me."

Ronnie raised her eyebrows, as if she were doubly impressed now. "Nice. She have anything good to say?"

"I'm not sure," Eve said, slowly. "I'm still, um, processing it."

Ronnie laughed. "Well, good luck with that. Feel free to call if you decide you need a hand, and I'll do my best."

Wait—can't you just help me now? Eve thought, but Ronnie waved and moved inside with the dog, and then she was gone. And then a car pulled up, a little red beat-up thing, and Magnolia got out.

The car pulled away. Magnolia turned to wave to its taillights, then turned back, smiling. Then, seeing her mother, her smile vanished. "Oh—hi, Mom!" she said.

Eve took a breath. "Hi, Mags. Who was that?"

"Who?"

"The person who just dropped you off."

"That?" Magnolia shrugged. "Just some kid I know."

Eve wished she could fling herself into her garden and snort her peonies and violets until she was sloshed and inebriated, maybe even passed out completely. "Magnolia," she said instead (because after all, she was the parent), "why didn't you take the school bus?"

"I missed it."

"Why?"

"Uh, because I went in for extra help in math?!"

Score one for her, Eve thought, but she said, "I'm glad you went in for help, obviously, but Magnolia, you know the rules. I don't want you in people's cars I don't know. If you miss the school bus, call me and I'll come get you."

Magnolia cocked her head, stuck her hand on her hip, and smiled. "That was forty-five minutes ago. Were you home?"

Eve hadn't been. After seeing two clients this morning—one of them new—and then stopping to pick up eggs and milk, she had come in maybe a half hour ago.

"Obvs not," Magnolia went on, gathering steam, "because you told me this morning that you had to go to Springfield today and might not be back yet when I got here, so I should watch Danny. Remember? So I started walking home, because what else was I supposed to do? And then a kid I know drives by and offers me a ride, and what am I gonna say, like, 'No thanks, I have to wait for my mom to get home from work and come get me, because she thinks that if I get in someone's car, I'll instantly die?' Oh! Mommy! I got A's on two tests today! Pound it!" She held out her fist, which Eve was supposed to touch with her own fist, ghetto style, if she wanted to be as cool as her daughter, not to mention abandon the conversation they were having.

Eve shook her head. "Maggie," she warned. "If I find out you've been in a car—"

"Oh look, here comes Danny. Hi, freak!" Magnolia yelled.

Danny was shuffling toward them, with Star, his bus having deposited them at the end of the block. Star was chattering away— you could actually hear her—while Danny stared at the ground, occasionally nodding. When he heard his sister, he raised his hand, then let it fall again.

"Magnolia," Eve resumed, but Maggie interrupted, "Mom, can we drop it? I won't get in a car with anyone ever again, as long as I live. Okay?" She turned and went inside.

The moral centers of the brain do not develop until almost seventeen, Eve had read in the local paper recently, *even though the emotions and hormones have been churning. Teens have an adult body with all the capabilities, but they are still using a child's brain, and the teenage brain often cannot see the consequences of actions.*

"Hi, Mom," Danny said, approaching as the door slammed behind Maggie, and then, "Mom, can I go to Star and Stream's?"

Eve looked at him, then at Star, then back at him. "Don't you want to go to kung fu?" she said. "You haven't been there in weeks, Dan. It'd be good for you to get some exercise."

"I told you, I don't want to go anymore," he said. "It's boring."

Why had it never been "boring" when Eric was still here? "Well then, how about a bike ride?" Eve tried. "It's a beautiful day, and I really—"

"No thanks. I just want to go over to Star's."

With dismay bordering on alarm, Eve recalled the manic two-minute spew he'd fired at her the last time he'd come home from

Star and Stream's—after (Eve had eventually extracted) several hours of a video game about snipers and ammo and explosions and energy swords and pwning noobs (whatever that meant), knives soaring through windows to hit people in the eyeballs or windpipe and knock them bloody and butchered to the floor. Ever since he'd released Batman, Danny's interest in video games had mushroomed as his interest in everything else had diminished to almost zilch. "Star should ask her moms first," she said, stalling, and then, hopefully, "Maybe they have stuff they need to do, or they'll need Star to—"

"Oh, they won't," Star said. "Ronnie's working from home today, and Priscilla just lights candles and meditates in her sanctuary after she gets home from the gym. She won't care."

Eve stared at her. "Well, come in and have a snack first," she said finally to Danny, and then, to Star, "He'll be over in a little bit."

"Thanks, Eve," Star said. "I'll expect him."

Inside, Danny flipped through a magazine as Eve took out an apple, washed it, and began to cut it up. "How was your day?" she asked.

Danny shrugged one shoulder, not looking up.

"Scale of one to ten?" Eve opened peanut butter, began to spread it on the apples.

He shrugged again. "I don't know. Four, I guess."

"Four?" She forced a smile. "Why so lousy?"

He shrugged once more. "It was boring," he said. "Not one fun thing happened." He looked her directly in the eye. "That's why I want to go to Star's."

It was as if he were almost challenging her to ask him one more thing. *Then go,* she wanted to say, but instead she handed him the plate, which he took without thanking her. "Thank you," she reminded, like some hideous schoolmarm.

"Thank you," he echoed, sulkily.

"You're welcome." She turned and went upstairs. She had decided to drop the car ride thing with Maggie rather than continue the fight before enforcing some punishment that would be a nightmare for both of them. She had made her point, she reasoned. Besides, she had the BBB group tonight, and she needed Maggie to babysit. So not the best time for a blowout with her.

She approached the girl's door (closed, as usual), then stopped. Maggie was either talking on the phone or Skyping with someone, and she was laughing. Eve smiled suddenly, happy to hear her daughter happy, immediately telling herself that she really did seem better lately, despite Eric's absence—*more cheerful, less tortured*—but then, in the interest of honesty, admitting to herself that Magnolia had simultaneously gotten even more distant from Eve: more secretive, less confiding. The other night, she'd come in from a party—on time—and gone straight up to bed, not sharing any details or even stopping to hug Eve good night. Eve had gone in to see her, but even then, her daughter had little or nothing to say.

Magnolia laughed again, loudly, and Eve stepped up and knocked on the door. "I've gotta go," she heard Maggie whisper, and then, a second later, "Come in!"

Eve opened the door and stepped inside. The room looked like a tornado had swept through: bed unmade, clothes coating the floor, bottles of perfume and makeup and hair products lying all over the place. It smelled like nacho cheese, which came, Eve saw, from an open bag of Doritos on the desk (purchased at school, probably, as Eve didn't buy that brand). Maggie sat at her desk, her laptop opened to Facebook, her phone inches from her computer. "Hi, Mom," she said tensely. Immediately, the phone buzzed with a text. Maggie glanced at it, laughed, picked it up, and typed something back. Then she put it down again and looked at Eve.

"Who was that?" Eve asked, casually.

Maggie sighed. "Why are you always asking me that? It's a friend, Mom! If I told you the person's name, you wouldn't know it anyway."

"Try me."

"Schuyler."

"Schuyler who?"

Maggie laughed. "Like you know any Schuylers?"

Score another for her, Eve thought, but she said, "I just ask because I'm interested in your life, that's all. It seems like we haven't caught up in a while."

Maggie nodded, trying (but failing) not to seem impatient. "What do you want to know?"

Eve shrugged. "I don't know. How are you, you know, doing these days? How do you feel?"

Magnolia thought for a minute. "Good, actually."

"Really?" Eve raised her eyebrows.

"Yeah." Magnolia nodded. "I'd have to say I do."

"Well, that's good. I'm glad to hear it."

"Yeah, I—" The phone buzzed, and Maggie glanced at it. "Oh wait, I've gotta answer this, Mom. It's Bridget, and she had a homework question before. You don't know her either, by the way." She picked up the phone, typed for a few seconds, closed it again. "Sorry," she said, as if she weren't.

"That's okay." Eve thought about asking her to turn off her phone for a minute, but figured it wasn't worth the risk. She resisted reaching down to pick up the Tide pen, set the hair gel upright and put the cap back on it, gather the piles of dirty clothes and take them to the washer. Instead, she said, "I like your hair like that," because she did: Maggie had been wearing it loose and curly lately, but with the front pulled back. It flattered her.

Maggie smiled. "Thanks," she said. "So does—" She stopped short.

"Who?" Eve said.

"No one."

"Tell me!"

"*No*, Mom! *No* one! My God, you're *so* nosy!"

Eve took a deep breath.

She wanted to ask Maggie if she'd talked to Emily or Nate, but then thought better of it, in case the answer was no. She thought of asking about Alexis, but that seemed unwise, since Eve was the one who'd put the kibosh on that friendship. So what could she ask, besides the clichéd *How's school?* "Have you heard from Daddy?" she said before she could stop herself.

Magnolia shrugged. "Not really. I mean, I haven't really checked."

Obviously she had checked; the girl checked her texts obsessively. Eve felt a ping of alarm. "So you don't talk to him every day anymore?" she asked, casually picking at a nail.

Maggie shrugged again, which Eve took to mean no.

"How come?"

One more shrug. "You know what?" she said after a second. "You were right, what you said the other week. If he cared about my life, he'd be here. And he's not. And you are. So—you're the one I'm faithful to." She smiled.

My God, had Eve said that? *If he cared about your life, he'd be here?* The ping of alarm was now a clanging bell. As pissed off as she was at Eric, she didn't want him out of Magnolia's life. She needed him there. "You know, Dad and I aren't enemies," she started to say, but Maggie's phone buzzed again, just as she started to wonder, *Wait*—are *we enemies?*

Magnolia glanced at the phone. "Mom," she said, "I'm sorry, but I really need—"

"Okay! Okay. Give me one more second." Eve took a breath. "Tonight is the BBB group. I need you to watch Danny."

Maggie touched the phone, and it silenced. "As long as I can do my homework," she said, glancing at the phone.

"Of course." *One hour of homework, six hours of texting*, Eve thought, but she said, "He'll be next door for a while anyway. But I want him home for dinner. I'll make something before I go. I actually have to leave in"—she looked at her watch—"shoot, less than an hour."

"Well, don't make dinner now," Maggie said, taking a Dorito out of the bag. "I'm not hungry at all." She stuffed the chip into her mouth.

Eve sighed. "I guess you can heat a frozen pizza, then, whenever you're both ready. I'll steam some broccoli and leave it on the table."

Maggie shrugged. "Whatevs."

"Should I take the rest of those chips so you can get hungry for dinner?"

Maggie smiled. "No thanks," she said, and then, when Eve frowned, "Kidding!!! Here you go, Mommeroo." She held out the bag. "Close the door behind you."

Downstairs, after seeing Danny off to Star's ("Be home at 5:30," she'd told him) and eating a large handful of Maggie's Doritos before disgustedly hurling them into the trash, Eve quickly steamed some broccoli for the kids. Then she made a cup of instant coffee and took a nasty sip, remembering how Eric had ground dark beans every morning before he went to work, brewed a fragrant pot, and left half of it home for her to microwave throughout the day. *Cut the pity party,* she admonished herself. *If you care, learn how to make it yourself.* She took another slug from her mug, then, glancing at the clock, sat down to think.

This morning, she had seen a new client, a thirty-eight-year-old woman, Rita, who'd recently had the same gastric bypass surgery she was recommending to Michael. Though Rita already had counsel from a nutritionist on her gastric bypass team, she had hired Eve to help her with the rigid post-op food requirements, and Eve had read several helpful books and articles, a couple of which she was sending to Michael; they were packed up and ready to go on her counter. But to her annoyance, she couldn't find his mailing address. So she had called him this morning and left a message to please leave it on her voice mail. It was the second message she'd left him and Diane this week, the first to tell them, apologetically, that she'd had no luck trying to get them in sooner with Dr. Shetland. He was booked solid, the receptionist had told her; the demand for gastric bypass was increasing by the day. Eve had passed on the message a few days ago. They still hadn't returned her call.

Now she needed to check and see if they'd called back this time. The thing was, she hated picking up the phone anymore. A steady dial tone reminded her, with that reliable stab of anger and sadness, that—Penelope's phone call notwithstanding—Eric was still gone; sooner or later, she had to face that in a way she hadn't yet allowed herself to. A pulsing tone, on the other hand—a waiting message!—always made her hopes soar, and then the panic and anger were postponed until she called in, hands shaking, only to find a message from Star for Danny or from one of Maggie's friends who, for whatever reason, didn't have her cell number.

She picked up the phone. No pulse. No messages.

She hung up. Then she jabbed on their old answering machine, which was still attached to the land line. They'd never removed it, even though Verizon had put voice mail on their line—and started charging for it—without their ordering it. "Voice mail is so much cooler," Magnolia had said at the time, and so, taking their cues from a then twelve-year-old, they'd turned off the machine and gotten used to the new way. But now? *Screw cool,* Eve thought, and she set the pickup to three rings to supersede the voice mail's four. Then she picked up the phone and dialed Michael again.

She reached the voice mail once more, Diane's cheerful voice reciting that they'd get back "just as soon as we can." Eve didn't want to leave another message. She had hoped to mail the package to Michael on the way to the BBBs, but— Oh well. If he couldn't even call her back with his address, maybe he didn't want it.

She hung up and busied herself with what to say at the BBB meeting tonight.

Once a month, usually at Nancy's house but sometimes at Reenie's or Gracie's, she met with however many of the BBB women showed up, to talk about how they were doing and what they were eating, share recipes and health news and tips for diet and exercise. Eve was the moderator, but at this point they pretty much took it by themselves. In fact, she had offered several times to stop coming at all; it was during dinner hour at home, which she didn't like to miss. (The BBBs all stayed after she left and had dinner together.) But the women had sworn that without her, the group would fizzle away; they needed her encouragement, her presence and hand-holding, they told her, and then offered her a $25 raise. So once a month, off she went.

Last month, after they'd finished with the catch-ups and preliminaries (which usually took up most of the hour), she had talked a little about fish: how much tuna you could eat without getting too much mercury, what kind of salmon was okay to eat in what amounts (there was farmed and organic farmed, Atlantic and Pacific, wild-caught and Coho—the list seemed endless), and what other kinds of fish you could eat that were better for the environment and, when prepared well, were equally good and healthy. That had gone over well, and they'd all welcomed the recipes she'd brought for cod and tilapia and striped bass, swearing to make them and compare notes next time. Tonight she didn't have time to prepare that sort of thing, but perhaps she could talk about FRAX and PRAL (she'd bring the nutrition newsletter, finish reading the article at red lights along the way), reminding them, at the end, that local veggies would get better and better now that summer was coming: green beans, corn, chard, tomatoes, beets, baby lettuce. After months of absence, of living on canned or frozen or wilted, tasteless vegetables and fruits from afar, it was all coming back once again.

There. She had enough to fill up the time. She glanced again at the clock, then chugged the rest of her coffee, practically gagging. "Magnolia?" she yelled upstairs. "I'm going."

There was a pause, and then, "Okay—bye, Mom," came down.

Eve gathered her jacket, her purse, the newsletter, her keys. As she reached the door, her eyes fell on the package for Michael. *One last try*, she thought, and she stepped back in, grabbed the phone, and hit Redial. The Cardellos' phone rang three times, then four. Eve was about to hang up when she heard a voice. She pulled the receiver back. "Hello?" she said.

"Hello." It sounded like Diane, but Eve wasn't sure; something in her voice sounded off.

"Is this Diane?" Eve asked.

"Yes," Diane said after a moment.

"Oh—sorry, Diane! You sounded different somehow. Anyway, this is Eve, and I'm calling to get your address, because I have some information to send Michael about—"

"That won't be necessary," Diane said.

"What?"

"That won't be necessary."

There was a long pause, and Eve wondered if Diane was about to tell her off or at least fire her. "I'm sorry," Eve said finally. "What did you say?"

"That won't be necessary," Diane said one more time. "Michael is dead."

16

HE HAD DIED the night before, of a heart attack, presumably in his sleep. When the rest of the family woke up this morning, Diane had told her, he was dead on the living room floor, where he'd been sleeping lately on a pile of blankets. He had not yet gotten in to see the bariatric team; his appointment was days away. He had lost eight more pounds since they'd met her in Bramington.

Numb, devastated, stunned to the core, Eve turned left and then right, accelerated then braked, putting herself through the paces until she reached Nancy Kalish's house. The funeral would be Saturday. Around her, the impossibly green lawns felt exaggerated and garish, surreal in their manicured perfection. She parked her car, set her face into something she hoped passed for pleasant, and made her way to the door.

There were six of them tonight besides Eve: Nancy, Reenie, Bobbi, Winnie, Geri, and Grace. Hugs were exchanged, seltzer poured, and then everyone settled in, chatting furiously. Reenie's oldest son had had another baby; she produced photos, which everyone gushed over suitably. Someone asked after Winnie's husband Herb's prostate cancer, and the update took on a life of its own. Eve kept the mild expression on her face, making sure to nod here and there. Twenty-five minutes in, they seemed ready to cut to the chase. Last month's fish recipes were discussed at length: who'd made which ones (and which nights, and for whom), how they'd turned out, how they'd be altered next time. "I absolutely *despise* fennel," announced Reenie. "If I never have to see another piece of fennel as long as I live, I'll go to my grave a happy camper."

"Speaking of graves, can we talk about funerals?" This from Geri, who was jovial and stout with slightly bulging eyes, a helmet of butter-colored hair, and a toothy, oversized smile that perfectly matched her personality. She also, Eve had noticed, possessed some sort of thought or speaking disorder that made her not quite able to complete most sentences, though you could usually figure out what she meant. Now everyone turned to her. "This will probably sound disrespectful," she said, "but I promise it's—I mean, if anything, the person who died would be completely—" She flung her hands in circles around her face. "Anyway, they had the most incredible food there, right down to the desserts, which were, I mean, mini caramel cheesecakes, white chocolate dipped—it was unreal! I must have put on five pounds in the space of—" She took a breath. "But the thing is, at funerals, I have such a hard time with—I mean, it's so sad, and then there's all this food that's just, like, the highlight of the—"

"Yes!" yelled Nancy. "I *do* know! And I find that hard too, that whole thing where you want to feel better, plus the food is *right there*, plus you feel like it's almost *rude* not to eat. How can you not be tempted at an occasion like that?"

They all turned to Eve.

She tried to smile. *Say something,* she thought, but all she could think of was Michael's funeral. Would they find a casket big enough to hold him? Would Diane bring the kids?

"Eve?" Nancy said. "Is something wrong?

Eve shook her head. *Focus,* she thought, and she said, "Well, you could always—" She burst into tears.

"Eve!" Nancy said. She stood up. "What's the matter?"

Eve shook her head, as if to say, *Why, nothing at all! I'm just perimenopausal! You all know how it is.* But her tears spilled as fast as she could wipe them. *Speaking of funerals,* she wanted to tell them, *Michael Cardello is dead. And it's my fault. If I'd gotten him help sooner—if I'd done my job right when I went to see him last month, if I'd advised him responsibly—his wife would still have a husband. His children would have a father.* "Eric left me," she blurted.

She could almost hear the collective intake of breath. "What?" Nancy said.

Eve stood up too. "I'm so sorry," she said. "But I think I should go."

"Wait a minute." Nancy rushed over to Eve. "You can't go any-where like this." She put her arm around Eve's shoulders and ma-neuvered her back down. "Sit a minute until you feel better," she ordered, and she handed Eve a cocktail napkin from the table. "Blow," she said.

Eve took the tissue and blew her nose, feeling exactly four years old.

"Good," Nancy said. "Now tell us."

Eve took a deep breath. "My gosh," she said. "This is completely unprofessional, especially when you all have much more important things to discuss than my—"

"More important than someone's husband leaving? I don't think so, sweetie." This from Reenie, who had grown up in Brooklyn (and still had a fair amount of accent).

"How long has he—I mean—when did he actually—" Geri tried, and Winnie said, "Do you know why he left? Or where he went?"

Eve sighed. "He left five weeks ago, and he's at his mother's, in Arizona. As for why, I guess—I guess he just doesn't love me anymore." But even as the words came out (and a fresh batch of tears along with them), she didn't think they were right. Whatever else was wrong—with him, with her, with them—she had never sensed a lack of love on his end. Though at this age, "love" seemed to be closer to hatred than to fondness sometimes. But still, even if pushed, she didn't think he could say he didn't love her. He *did* love her. She knew it. "I mean," she said, posing the question in a way she hoped wasn't rhetorical, "why else do you leave someone, after sixteen years of marriage?"

"Tons of reasons," Reenie announced. "When my husband left, it was because—"

"Your husband left?" Eve stared at her. Reenie—the prettiest of the group, Eve had always thought, with her doelike eyes and lush lips, her dark, loosely curled, still beautiful hair—talked often about her husband, a plastic surgeon named Barry, who last year, at seventy-two, had bought a Harley for himself and an extra helmet for her. She'd brought it in to show the group. Silver with "R" engraved in diamonds on the side.

"He did." Reenie nodded. "I was thirty-two at the time. The boys were five, four, and—let's see—Charlie was still one, I think. Yeah. Like, eighteen months."

Eve blinked. "Do you know why?"

"In retrospect? Of course. I was bitchy and burned out. Well, who wouldn't be, with three little boys? And Barry was working like a dog, and he'd get home and the house was chaos, I wouldn't have made dinner, I didn't want to have sex, as in, I wasn't even willing to fake it—" They all laughed, and she said, "Please! I hadn't slept through the night in six years! You show me one wife who would want to have sex in that situation, and I'll show you a—"

"Speak for yourself," Winnie said.

They all looked at her.

"What?" Winnie blushed. "I *like* sex with Herb! Or *liked*, I should say."

A couple of them tsked sadly—Herb was in the later stages of cancer—but Winnie said, "It's okay. We had a lot of good years."

"You did," Nancy soothed. "Herb is a good man."

Winnie nodded. "I was lucky. He never had an affair, never left me. . . ."

"Barry's a good man too," Reenie said, a tad defensively. "But he had his lapses, and that affair was a big one. He was an absolute bastard, leaving me with those three little boys. All I'm saying is, when I look back now, it's not hard to see why it happened. You put two and two together, you line up the facts, you—"

"What did happen?" Eve said. She had mostly stopped crying, if only so she wouldn't miss a word of this.

"He started shtupping a patient. Original, right?" Reenie rolled her eyes.

There was silence, and then Nancy piped up, "And then he crawled right back! He couldn't stay away."

Reenie smiled at her—they were decades-long friends, Eve knew, with Reenie the queen bee and Nancy her loyal subject. "He was gone for two weeks and five days," Reenie said. "I still don't know where he went, nor do I care to. All I know is, when he came back, he told me he'd had an affair, it was over, and it wouldn't happen again. And I said, 'Okay. Let's move on.' Not that I wasn't pissed off. Believe me, I was pissed off. I was meshuga, if you have to know. I wanted to put his balls in a vise and tighten it till the two ends met." She laughed. "But? I wasn't so stupid as to let a little transgression ruin our marriage."

"She loved him," Nancy said, directing the comment to Eve.

Reenie shrugged. "What can I say? He's the love of my life. We're married forty-five years this July."

Eve sniffed hard. "Wow," she said. "That's a good story."

"Happy ending, at least." Reenie tossed her head, then smoothed down her curls. "I did tell him at the time that if he ever so much as looked at another girl again, I'd be out the door so fast he wouldn't know what hit him. And I'm glad he didn't test me. Or at least not that I ever found out about." Her eyes flickered for a second in a way that made Eve wonder if there might have been other incidents that Reenie chose not to "find out about." "Because the truth is," Reenie continued, "I needed him as much as I loved him. Divorcing, with the kids—well, I'm personally not cut out for that. For one thing, I might have had to get a job. And I was born to be a domestic goddess."

Nancy laughed, then looked at Eve. "It was different in our generation," she reminded her, a little guiltily.

"Yes." Reenie nodded. "And not that there's anything wrong with having a job."

"No—not at all!" This from Bobbi, the newest and quietest member of the BBBs and the one Eve knew least. She was average height, boxy but almost thin (she'd lost ten pounds since joining the group a few months ago), with chin-length dark brown hair, a deep crease between her eyebrows, and a smile she covered up with her hand. "I feel like I discovered who I was only after Norman—after my husband left me," she said. She looked pointedly at Reenie, then at Eve.

Eve was staring at her. Her husband had left too? And not come back, it sounded like. "What do you do?" she asked, adding, "I'm sorry, I should know that by now."

"No no. It's fine." Bobbi smiled, and Eve saw that her smile, when she let it be seen, was demurely pretty. "I teach special ed," she said. "Or *taught*, I should say. I retired last year."

"But she still volunteers a ton," Nancy chimed in. "Everyone loves her. Her school had a huge celebration for her when she retired, and all these people told how much she'd changed their lives. Students, parents—it was a total tearjerker. We were all there, bawling away."

The women nodded, throwing warm glances Bobbi's way.

Bobbi looked down at her skirt, and Eve could tell she both loved the praise and was made somewhat uncomfortable by it. She had a manner, Eve noticed, that oscillated between warm generosity; fluctuating (sometimes defensive) confidence; and blatant insecurity. "Anyway, the point is," Bobbi said, looking up again, "not that I'd have chosen for Norman to leave, but I'd never have accomplished any of that if he hadn't."

Eve wanted to ask a million questions: How old were you? What happened? Did he remarry? Did you have kids at the time? Are you still in touch? But, of course, she didn't dare.

"I feel so boring," Nancy said suddenly. "My husband never left *or* had an affair."

"Neither did mine," Geri said, almost sadly.

"You don't know that for sure now do you," said Grace. "All you know is if *you* did."

They all turned to her. In her black buttoned-up cardigan and neat trousers, her hair naturally gray and pragmatically short, Grace sat, legs primly folded, her two dabs of red lipstick—the only makeup she wore—forming a hint of a smile.

"Gracie Flynn!" Reenie said. "Are you trying to tell us something?"

Grace raised her eyebrows. "Make of it what you will."

"Don't be coy," Reenie admonished. "Did you or didn't you?"

"I did not."

"Bu-uut . . ." Reenie pushed.

"But—" Gracie smoothed her trousers. "I came very close."

A squeal arose in the room. "Spit it out, dollface," Reenie said.

Gracie sighed. "I've never told anyone this. Well, not like there's anything to tell anyway! Plus it happened so long ago."

They all looked at her expectantly, including Eve.

"Oh, okay. Fine. It was with my doctor, actually."

"It wasn't Barry, was it?" Reenie said, and they all laughed.

"It was not Barry," Gracie said. "It was my obstetrician, if you must know."

"Of course we must," said Reenie, looking relieved.

"Well, okay, then," said Grace. "It was during a bad phase in my marriage, I suppose. We'd been trying to get pregnant for a while, Duncan and I, and it wasn't taking. And Duncan was—I don't know, he was getting restless. He wasn't around much, and when he was, he just—well, he wasn't that nice to me, is what it came down to. He wasn't *mean*, mind you. But I was bored, and depressed, and I had nothing to do, and I felt, well, unnoticed. Uncared for. I don't know. I was probably just being a big baby."

"You feel how you feel," Reenie said, wagging her hand. "You can't change that."

Gracie nodded. "Anyway. The doctor was very attentive to me, very complimentary. And one night he asked me to meet him for a drink in the bar of this fancy hotel a town away. So I went. And unbeknownst to me, he'd rented a room, and he somehow got me up there, but in the end—well, in the end, I didn't do it. I didn't even kiss him, except good-bye, on the cheek. I just told him I couldn't, and lucky for me, he didn't push it. But that was after we'd sat on the bed and talked about it for almost an hour, which frankly—" She blushed. "Well, for me, it was almost better than the real thing. The thrill without the guilt, in some ways."

"In *some* ways," Winnie said, and they all laughed.

"Anyway," Gracie said. "In the end, I think I just didn't want to do that to Duncan. Inattentive or not, he wasn't violent or unkind, and he was faithful and he was providing for me and I didn't feel that he deserved it. And as soon as I made that decision, I knew it was the right thing. And it was, because afterward I was so glad I hadn't. I couldn't have stood the guilt."

"But you could just go to confession!" Nancy said. "I've always been so jealous of Catholics in that way."

They all laughed again, including Grace. "Confession doesn't remove guilt, unfortunately," she said. "Or maybe a little of it, but . . ."

"Though in your case, you had nothing to be guilty of," Reenie said.

"Well, that depends how you look at it," said Grace. "I mean, even the fact that I went out with him, that I went up to his room, that I thought about it, we talked about it . . . I mean, some would consider that an emotional affair."

"That's absurd," Eve said. She was thinking about her indiscretion with Kirk all those years ago, how thrilled she'd be if she'd only talked to him, not gone ahead and—

"Is it? I don't know." Grace shrugged. "It *is* betrayal, in a way. And I've also wondered, over the years—I can't believe I'm confessing this—if I might *not* have been able to resist if he'd been a little more attractive to me. He was a good-looking man, but I wasn't head over heels. So, much as I like to give myself all the credit and make it out to be a big moral victory . . ."

"It was really more about him than you," Reenie finished.

Gracie sighed. "Well. I never did know."

"Take the credit," Reenie advised. "What could be the problem?

You didn't do it, and that was probably harder than just doing it at that point, attraction aside."

"Yeah," said Geri. "Especially if he was telling you—I mean—that you were—you know—attractive, and—"

"Exactly," Reenie said. "A turn-on in and of itself." She fanned her neck, long red nails flying. "So then what happened?"

"Well, I used the whole thing as a wake-up call. I went home to Duncan, and I told him I wasn't happy, and if he didn't pay more attention to me, I wouldn't be responsible for what happened to us."

"Wow," Geri said. "And did—I mean—did he—"

"Rise to the challenge?" Grace frowned. "I don't know, actually, because I got pregnant right after that, and that changed everything. I had things to learn, places to go—and a community of women, other mothers and mothers-to-be. And then I had the babies, and you know how that goes. Here we are, forty-three years later."

"Tell me about it," Nancy said, and they all nodded and took sips of their seltzer almost simultaneously.

Reenie put down her glass and looked around. They all seemed to have forgotten this had started with Eve—which was fine with Eve, actually. The truth was, nice as it had been to have a few minutes of sympathy—and, let's face it, mothering—there was little anyone could say to make her feel better about Eric, except possibly Eric himself. She wondered what even he could say at this point. Maybe nothing. Maybe it was already too late.

"Well, I guess there are bumps in the road no matter what you do," Reenie pontificated. "Sometimes they derail you, and sometimes they don't. But a lot of the time, it's not about what happened so much as what you want to happen next. Do you want to break up, or don't you? Would you rather be with this person than with someone else or possibly with no one? If the answer is no, then the affair has done its job: begun the process of ending a marriage that needed to end anyway. But if the answer is yes on both ends—if he wants to come back, like Barry did, and you want to be with him, like I did, even though at the moment you'd be happy to bungee-cord him to the front of your car and speed down a dirt road going 100 miles an hour . . ." Someone snickered; probably Nancy. "Then?" Reenie shrugged. "You get over it. You forgive and forget, or at least pretend to, and get on with things. If you're lucky, you might even get a diamond biker helmet in the deal. Even if it takes the bastard thirty-five years." She laughed.

"But what if he doesn't want to come back?" Eve said. "What if he leaves, and—"

"Well, look at Bobbi!" Reenie said. "Did she sit around crying for the rest of her life? No! She took her new hand and played it, and look how far she—"

"I did sit around crying for at least two years, though," Bobbi said, and Eve wanted to kiss her for her honesty.

"Well, but then you moved on," Reenie urged. "Just as I would have if Barry hadn't come slithering back. No way I'd have sat around sobbing for the rest of my life."

Eve felt that Reenie was skating on thin ice now. Her husband had been gone for all of two weeks! What did she know about really being left?

"I read this great poem once," Nancy said, and Eve bet that even she was trying to shut Reenie up at this point, "that marriage is like holding up a ceiling. Sometimes you're holding it together, but sometimes one person takes down their arms, and the other one has to do all the work. And at those times, it's tempting to take your arms down, too, and just let the whole damn thing fall. But if you stick it out, at some point the other person will join back in. And then *you* get to rest."

"Exactly," Reenie said, apropos of nothing.

"Of course," Nancy added, "if they don't join back in, well, that's when you say forget it and go shopping for the cute little condo where the landlord holds up the ceiling, *and* you can decorate all in pink wicker if you so choose."

They all laughed again, and then they all glanced at Bobbi— some surreptitiously, others directly, smiling. *They're patronizing her,* Eve thought, feeling defensive on Bobbi's behalf, and she wondered why a woman whose husband had left—and who'd gone on to a noble and distinguished career—would subject herself to this group of conservative longtime wives. And then she remembered: this was a weight-loss and maintenance group, not a marriage therapy session!

She glanced at her watch and saw that they'd already talked for close to an hour and a half. The women were chatting among themselves now, and she heard various catchphrases—"Did you think," and "no idea," and "completely planned to have him make it up to me." Bobbi, she noticed, had gone off to the bathroom.

As soon as she returned, Eve clapped twice, loudly. "Women," she said (because she had never used the word *ladies* and never would, no matter how obnoxiously in vogue it was now). "We've gotten off track tonight, and it's my fault. I want to apologize, but I also think we should try to get something done before I have to go. So let me ask: Does anyone have questions or comments related to food or weight or health? Anything you want to discuss, or vent, or—"

"I do," Winnie said. "I have a confession." She took a deep breath. "My granddaughter was over yesterday, and we bought a big bag of marshmallows because we were making hot cocoa. She had a few, and then I put the bag in the fridge for next time she comes. But last night, after Herb went to bed, I got them out and I stood at the stove with a shish kebab skewer and roasted the entire bag, one by one, over the burner, eating each one hot off the flame." She laughed, though she clearly was none too happy about it. "Of course, I feel bloated and disgusting today. And I'm wondering if—well—what I can do."

Eve felt a flicker of panic. Winnie had always been prone to binge eating. She thought of Michael's last binge—the last one he'd told her about, anyway—and her heart began to beat harder. Who was she to be giving advice at this point?

She looked around. "Anyone want to answer that?" Secretly, she crossed her fingers.

At first, no one spoke. Then Nancy said, "Throw out the marshmallows next time?"

"Of course," Reenie piped up. "Because why tempt yourself? If you're a person who can stop after one or two, then no need to go to extremes. But if you're not? Get rid of them. Pour nail polish remover on them. And then if you're still craving something, go buy something small. A nice popsicle, or a few chocolate-covered nuts at the health food store, or—"

"Exactly," Eve said, happy she'd actually taught them something. "A food that feels like a treat without derailing you." She looked around. "So what else? What can she do today?"

A pause, and then Geri said, Oprah style, "Forget about it."

"Yes!" Bobbi said. "Forget it happened! Forgive yourself, and start over."

Eve nodded. "Though I hate to even use the phrase 'start over,' because it implies that she ended something, when in fact it's a continuum. Nothing ended. You had a bad day, you ate too much, so tomorrow you get up, have a healthy breakfast, take a walk, and get on with it."

"Well, that *is* what I did," Winnie said. "Today *is* tomorrow." She smiled, and Eve could see her lean back and relax. "Thanks, everyone. I feel better already."

How easy, Eve thought. *People just need reassurance. That's really all so many of us need.*

"Don't mention it, sweetie," Reenie said to Winnie. She smiled and tossed her hair. "It's the least we can do."

At the time, Eve had silently thanked them for at least partially rescuing the session for her. But later, driving home, she said a prayer for Winnie to stay in control, with Herb's illness and everything else. *Of course she will,* she told herself. *She's nothing like Michael.* And then, as much because she didn't want to think about Michael as anything else, she added, out loud, "And you're nothing like Bobbi."

She blinked, embarrassed even though no one had heard. How weird, when your mouth revealed a thought your mind hadn't even recognized yet. *And a silly one,* she thought, but for the first time since the week Eric left, her hands began to tremble again. He no longer called, no longer communicated with the kids. Other than sending the money that one time, he was completely out of all of their lives now. She was an abandoned wife, a single mother, and her children no longer had a participating father. It was time to face this, accept it and tell people and figure out what the hell to do next.

"Hire a lawyer," she said, again out loud, as if speaking the words in a pragmatic tone could make it all easily happen, but then she literally spluttered with emotion: fear and confusion and deep, almost stunning sadness. *A lawyer! Against Eric!* She couldn't begin to imagine.

Still trembling, she turned on a jazz station, focused on the orange lights on the highway. *Did I take him for granted?* she asked herself. *Is that what this is?* Because really, it was the little things she missed most about marriage: the way he'd lock the door and turn off the porch light at night, or happily eat the leftovers so she didn't have to throw them out, or bring in the mail and read it so she didn't have to. She missed having him to talk to about Michael's death, hearing his reassurance that it wasn't her fault. Eric would have done that without thinking twice. He'd have believed it, too, whether or not it was true.

And sex? It wasn't the act itself she missed—not often, anyway—so much as the things that went with it: Eric's weight, his warmth, his presence in the bed. She missed lying facedown and having him lie facedown on top of her—heavy, musky, a giant human blanket anchoring and shielding her. *So maybe I did take him for granted,* she decided. But what could she do about that now? Time marched on. Time didn't reverse.

She pulled into her driveway and turned off the motor. *Home,* she thought with a rush of gratitude. *My house. My children.*

Inside, it was oddly quiet for just after ten, the kitchen unusually clean. There was a note from Magnolia saying they'd had dinner, cleaned up, and gone to bed. *We luv u so much!* she'd written, with a line of hearts after it, like she used to do. (The thing about fourteen: you never knew if you'd get a smart eight-year-old or a naive twenty-two.) Eve put down the note and went up to check. Sure enough, they both were asleep. In Danny's room, she noted the empty bird cage and turned away.

She closed their doors and went back downstairs, half wishing Magnolia was up—even if only to fight with her—so she wouldn't have to be alone with herself. In the dining room, she poured a finger of scotch. She took a couple of fast gulps, then carried it back into the kitchen, where she turned off the lights and sat down in the dark.

Moonlight shone in the window. Glancing out through the blinds, Eve saw, past the hemlocks, the moon itself: swollen and round, gleaming and bright, taunting her with its ripeness and optimism. She finished her drink. Then she put her elbows on the table and dropped her head in her hands.

Eric is gone. Michael is dead. She closed her eyes, trying to escape into herself, but she felt the world close in around her and stay there, like a scent. And then something cracked and the questions flooded in. *How did this happen? What should I do? How does one get through this?* A light flashed against her eyelids, pulsing and insistent. Wearily, she opened her eyes again.

The old answering machine broadcast a red number 1, as if nothing could be more urgent. With a sigh, she got up and hit Play. Then she sat on the desk chair and listened to the ancient tape rewind, a sound she hadn't heard for ages.

The beep came. There was a pause, and then some feedback noise, and then—and then Eric. "Eve?" his voice said. "It's me."

Her head went blurry, and a rush of warmth washed over her, heat so intense she broke out in a sweat. *But surely it's an old message,* she cautioned herself, *playing from some random point in the tape.* Still, she stood up, straining to hear. "I know you won't pick up, because you never do when I call," his voice said. "But I'm coming home. And if you don't let me in, or you don't want to see me, well, I'll understand, but I'm just gonna keep try-ing. I want to come home. That's all I can say." A long pause, and then his voice again, and she could tell he'd been crying. "I love you," he said. "Eve? I love you. I'll see you soon." And the click.

Eve dropped the phone and melted to the floor. Eyes closed. Arms splayed. Heart open.

Part Three

17

FROM WHERE HE sits—on the porch of the empty house almost directly across the street from his own—Eric's view of his home is so clear, and his house itself so close, he could probably shoot an arrow through his living room window if he tried. Of course, he'd have to shoot around the overgrown yew bush that's camouflaging him, not to mention the FOR SALE sign on the lawn of this place. But he could do that. He's always had decent aim, decent vision.

Eric glances at his watch, pulling himself back from his little Robin Hood fantasy. He's been here for almost two hours now, watching and waiting, hoping to catch a glimpse of his family and figure out his next move. Now that he's finally back in town, the last step of coming home is proving harder than pulling into his driveway and walking through the front door. Eve did not return his call after he left the message that he was coming back—three days ago now. He hadn't expected her to, really . . . but still. What if she has a friend or, worse, a man in the house? He cannot face appearing at her door, bright-eyed and hopeful, only to walk into something like that. Not that he doesn't deserve it. But still.

A light goes on in his house, and Eric sits up, alert. Magnolia's room. He sees his daughter come to her big window and look out, and his heart clenches and releases, sending through him a cocktail of joy and wonder and hesitation. She looks different: sharper, older, more striking, her hair longer and calmer, her body more filled out on top, no longer so awkward in the middle. Face less odd, more refined. Is it possible that in the almost six weeks he's been gone she has changed from a gawky girl to a woman? Surely not, but the image could fool him; she is exotic and almost—yes— beautiful now. She stares out into the night, as if seeking or antici- pating something, and he wonders if some part of her senses he's here. Then, abruptly, she turns away from the window, and after a second the shade goes down, like a slap.

Eric takes a deep breath. He'd expected his mother to be here to do this with him; her cheerful, loving presence surely would have taken some emphasis off his lowly own. But two days ago, in a diner somewhere in Indiana, she'd announced that she would go see an old friend in Connecticut first. "You have some things you'll want to do before you need a visitor," she said, explaining where he should drop her off. "I'll come see you all when you're ready for me." He'd protested, of course, but she wouldn't budge.

She had given in on the driving, at least. Around New Mexico, he had insisted he was fine to be behind the wheel—even with the foot, the queasiness, and everything else—and, to his surprise, she'd said yes. He'd been thrilled. He was ready to be back in con- trol. And he'd relished feeling the car swallow back, under the soft swish of tires on highway, the same road he'd spit out six weeks ago. The same asphalt, stretching before him, but calling from a different direction now.

And did the pills do that? He's asked himself this again and again, and though he likes to think he would have come to this point without ingesting a little white chemical dot every day, he has his doubts. He had needed something. His crisis wasn't just psy- chological; it had been physical—physiological—too. He'd learned that the day he felt the curtain of muck and dread simply lift from his brain and float off somewhere: the bell jar, the heaviness, what- ever it was that had hidden him from the light for so long, that had zapped his confidence and kept him from feeling worthy or good, no matter what else happened. *So, okay*, he thought. *What if it* is *the drugs? What are you gonna do, stop taking them?*

But even the drugs aren't invincible; he's glad to know it. Because when he pulled into town, even as his excitement mounted, his confidence plummeted; the very air of the place, it seemed, shoved him hard back a step. *What if they don't want me?* He couldn't stop asking the question, drugs or no drugs. He'd reminded himself it was natural to feel doubt at this point. (Really, what would be terrifying was if he didn't.) And the drugs, he saw, simply gave him the strength and wherewithal to proceed with his journey; they didn't take the journey—or conclude it—for him.

So he proceeded. Drove to his studio first, trying to get back his mojo. Parked and went in, closed the door behind him, looked around. It smelled good, like wax and metal and cold air. He didn't let himself turn on the light, didn't want to see the place too brightly yet. But again, something inside him stirred with excitement, and he gave himself a warning: *Don't get ahead of yourself. Just because you aren't withering at the very thought of the work doesn't mean you don't have to* do *it.* So he left, closed and locked the door for now, but it was okay, still okay. A new beginning, maybe. Something, anyway.

He went to Mickey D's next, ate—in the car, not wanting to run into someone before he saw Eve—what he hoped was his last shitty cheeseburger in front of a steering wheel for the rest of his life. Chewing methodically (he still wasn't hungry, but he had to put back on some of the weight he'd lost the past few weeks, maybe months), he watched a willowy woman pump gas under the early evening light, her hair fluttering in the breeze, and though he's not sure why, that's where he'd gotten the idea to come here, to this empty house that, he remembered, had been for sale before he left. A purgatory before attempting his own home and family. He'd parked on the next block and sneaked here through the backyards, praying no one would see him. *What a fool,* he'd thought, as he gimped through the brush on his crutches, trying to scrunch down and make himself small, before dragging himself up the side of the porch (couldn't risk the front steps) and settling here, on the shiny painted wood: bad foot protruding before him, mind whirring, eyes fixed on his house.

He'd seen Danny first. Not ten minutes after Eric arrived, the boy emerged from the neighbors' and trod across their lawn and his own, stopping to look at the bees and the butterflies buzzing over Eve's garden, dipping for sips of nectar. Eric held his breath. Danny's hair was long—longer than Eric had seen it since before Eve had tearfully taken him to the barbershop, just after his second birthday, for his first haircut. Now as then, when he'd come back stunningly different—white curls gone, huge eyes, and mug-handle ears now making their angel baby into simply another male child—the difference felt stark: the boy seemed taller and even thinner, if that was even possible, his jeans riding up around his ankles, his body newly hunched over, as if he were trying to escape down into himself. Or was Eric projecting? Maybe Danny was fine. He seemed to be reciting something as he watched the insects, or just softly singing. After a moment, he drifted to the front steps and went up and in, and Eric heard him call, "Magnolia? Mom?" *Interesting,* Eric thought, *that he'd say his sister's name first.*

Then he'd waited again—slapping at mosquitos as the air darkened around him and the moon rose, a perfect circle but for its starkly severed right edge—for something to happen, though he wasn't sure what. But now, finally, there is a car: an old pine-green boat, pulling up slowly, quietly, but to the side of the house, where it sits idling. Eric squints at it. Why not the front? And who drives a car like that anymore, and why isn't she—or he—getting out?

The house door opens; Magnolia steps out onto the porch. She glances back behind her, then slowly closes the screen, and even from here, Eric can tell she's trying not to make a sound. He sits up straighter, still behind the bush, watching hard. *Where is Eve?* he thinks, as Maggie saunters across the lawn to the car. She wears cowboy boots, tight dark jeans, a loose white tank top that's sexy and bright in the night, and again, his heart dips and rises, a skier racing over moguls. *When did she get so feminine, so mature?* Her hair is a curly mass down her back, her carriage erect. He feels dizzy with wonder. His baby girl is a woman! And then, just as quickly, he's heavy with sadness; a chapter of her life, of *their* lives, closed forever, and he'd missed the final pages.

Magnolia glances back at the house and then approaches the car, and the passenger door opens from the inside to admit her. Eric squints again. The driver is a *man*! He has a visible mustache, not the scraggly ones that teenage boys have. Maggie pulls the door closed, quietly clicking it shut, and again it seems obvious to him that her intention is to not be heard. Eric's heart beats faster. Who the hell is this guy? And if she's sneaking out, he should stop her anyway. But how can he know for sure—and what would he say?

A cigarette flares in the vehicle—he sees the flame, then the tiny orange tip—and then, before he can agonize more, the car pulls off, in the direction opposite the house, but slowly, as if the driver is more concerned with being quiet than with actually getting somewhere. It crawls to the corner, then inches around. And it's gone.

Eric's heart stops.

Relax, he coaches himself, trying to unclench. *It's surely the father of one of her friends.*

But then, where was the friend? And why didn't he pull up in front? And why was the car moving so slowly, so quietly?

And then he's on his feet, like a horse at the gate. "Shit," he says. "Shit shit shit."

He grabs for his phone to call Eve. But he stops. What will he say? That he's sitting in the neighbor's bushes and just happened to see Magnolia sneak off with some man? Along with sounding ridiculous, it's presumptuous. Who is he to breeze back in town and assume he knows something Eve doesn't? Especially when it comes to the kids.

Still, he opens the phone, thinking. Seconds click by. Just as he starts to punch in their number, the car rolls slowly back from the other side of the street (they must just have circled the block, he's relieved to realize)—though, again, to the side of the house, where it's hidden from the view of most of the windows, not to mention the light of the porch. The dude cuts the motor this time. The orange tip in the car is still there. He sees it float, as if being passed back and forth, and then that too flickers and dies. And then nothing for a while; the car sits idle and dark, no one getting out or in.

Eric moves. He grabs the crutches and jumps off the porch and gimps as fast as he can toward his house. If he's seen, he's seen; he has to know what's going on in that car. But as he reaches the opposite end of his lawn from where the car sits, the passenger door starts to open once more, and he lunges behind the shadow of his house, dropping the crutches, breathing fast. Low music (something croony, a little sexy, and from *his* generation . . . Rod Stewart?) floats out of the car and into the night. "I can't," he hears Magnolia say, and there, in the voice, is his baby again; grown-up body or not, she's still a child inside, petulant and uncertain. "I've gotta go back in," she says to whoever's in the car. "My mom doesn't know I'm out here."

He hears the man say something—he can't make out what—and then his daughter again: "No. She was asleep when I left." She laughs. *Is she nervous?* But despite her protests, beyond opening the door, she still hasn't made a move to get out of the car.

The man's voice again, a low drawl, and Eric smells the pot now, clear as day. Anger rises inside him, and his palms itch to pound the fuck out of this jerk. *Wait!* he tells himself, because he needs to see what unfolds, find out who this guy is. Once the dude pulls away, it's only a matter of time before Maggie finds him again, if that's what she wants to do.

The guy stops talking, and now his daughter does step out of the car. "I've gotta go," she says again, though not wholly convincingly. "You should take off, Theo. Seriously. My mom will go ballistic slash psycho if she sees you." She laughs. "But thanks for coming. Thanks for, you know. The weed and all that. It was cool; you were right. Good times." She laughs again, giddily. "Well, bye," she says, and she closes the car door and takes a step or two toward the house.

The driver's door opens and the asshole steps out: longish hair, black rock-tour T-shirt, skinny legs clad in hanging-off-his-ass jeans. And that mustache. *Is he fucking kidding?* Eric has to stop himself from rushing out and pummeling the bastard to death. But along with knowing he needs to wait and see, his years of kung fu stop him too: learning over and over that "a virtuous warrior," as one martial arts master put it, "is one who defeats his opponent without engaging in battle." He preached as much to his own classes not two weeks ago.

"Wait up, Magnolia," the freak says, ambling toward her on the lawn, and he has long legs, Eric sees, though not as long as his own. "Can't you stay out a little longer?" he says. "We'll just sit here quietly. Enjoy the night together."

Magnolia is almost to the steps, but she stops. "I shouldn't," she says, but she giggles and tosses her head, and Eric wants to vomit. "Oh my God, we're gonna get *so* caught."

The man shrugs. "What are we doing that's so wrong, anyway?" She doesn't answer, and he says, "I'll be bored when you go. You're such a beautiful girl."

Magnolia stands still, clearly absorbing his words.

"I mean it," the guy says, seeing he's caught her attention. "Just looking at you makes me happy. I'm not shitting you. You're one of the most gorgeous girls I know. I think you could be a movie star. I really do."

Magnolia laughs. "As if."

"Yes, as if! I'm for real, man. You have the kind of beauty that's completely unique. And you're nice too. That's the thing. Not all full of yourself, like so many girls."

Maggie observes him. She looks at the house, and then back at him. "I guess I could sit for five more minutes."

He smiles. "That's great. That's awesome. Here, sit right here, with me."

He plants his skinny butt down on Eric's front steps, and Magnolia settles in next to him. Eric wants to scream, wants to howl like a rabid werewolf, but he stifles himself, still watching. The two are silent a moment, observing the luminous sky. And then the dude's arm snakes around her. He mumbles something, and Magnolia laughs. "No way," she says.

He nods, mumbles something again.

She shakes her head, then laughs once more. "No. I can't."

He mumbles a third time. And then he leans in and kisses her, his vile, putrid mouth on her beautiful, young, naive one.

Eric pounces. In three quick steps—pain ripping through his ankle as he steps on it hard, once, then again—he is there. He grabs the douche bag by the shoulders, throws him off Magnolia and down the steps, onto the walk. "What the fuck is your problem?" he yells, and he crouches over the guy, his fists balled, panting. "How dare you touch her? How dare you put your filthy, disgusting—" He's hyperventilating now. "Who the hell are you, anyway?" he yells. "How do you even know her?"

The guy gapes up from the ground, clearly terrified, palms up in surrender. "I'm—I—"

"This girl is *fourteen years old*, you sick fuck! I could have you arrested right now. I could drag your disgusting, pathetic ass right down to the—" He can't find the word. Hot lava flows through his ankle, his biceps, his brain.

The dude shakes his head, a cowering dog. "Don't hurt me, man," he says. "We're just friends. I've never touched her in my life before this. I didn't even—"

"Shut up," Eric says.

"Daddy?" Magnolia is watching them, eyes wide. "Daddy? When did you—"

"Can you tell him, please, Magnolia?" the guy pleads. "Tell him we're just—"

"Shut up!" Eric yells. He wonders if he'll pass out before he can finish this.

"It's true, Dad," Maggie says, breathing hard herself now. "He's my friend."

Eric wants to kick the shit out of every pansy-assed bone in this lowlife. "Get up," he spits.

The guy scrambles to his feet, then touches his head and looks at his hand. "Shit," he mutters, seeing the blood.

"What's your name, asshole?" Eric demands.

The guy shakes his head. "Theo, man. I'm a friend of hers."

"Friends my ass. How the fuck old are you, you fucking creep?"

"Daddy," Magnolia says.

Theo shakes his head. "Listen, I'm gonna go now. I'll just leave, okay? Take it easy, man."

"That's right," Eric sputters. "You leave. Get the fuck out of here, and don't let me ever see you again. And if I find out you've been anywhere near my daughter, I'll beat the shit out of you *and* have you arrested."

Theo is nodding. He is almost to his car now. "Okay," he says.

"Get in that car, and drive the fuck out of here."

Theo gets in. Two seconds later, his car pulls away.

Eric turns to Magnolia. "Are you okay?"

She nods.

"Are you sure?"

She nods again, then bursts into tears. "Daddy? Are you—did you come home? Are you staying with us?" She rushes over and embraces him, sobbing into his shirt.

He holds her for a long moment, not speaking. Then he says, "Come on. Let's go in."

She goes first. He yanks himself up the steps, by the railing, his heart banging away.

The smell of the house hits him like a drug. He had never realized their house had a smell, but now that he's been gone, he's overwhelmed by it. Later, he'll break it down: pinewood and shellac (from, he guesses, the living room shelves he'd built last year), Magnolia's perfume, Eve's meat sauce: tomatoes, thyme, rosemary. Lovely, all of it, distinct and inviting, though right now it's merely overwhelming.

And his foot is aflame.

He staggers to the living room and onto the couch, raises his cast and drops it heavily on the arm, then falls back into the cushions. "Jesus Christ," he says, wiping sweat from his upper lip. He closes his eyes, fighting waves of nausea. He probably reinjured the thing. Probably have to start again at square fucking one.

But what if he hadn't gotten here when he did? What if . . .

He shakes the thought away. He did get here.

He opens his eyes. Magnolia is kneeling at the couch at his side. "You broke your foot?" she asks, and she sniffs, wipes her tears.

He shakes his head. "Sprained it. Running one night. Like an idiot."

She laughs, still crying.

"Mags," he says. "Would you get me a glass of water?"

She nods and runs out.

When she's back, he takes a sip, waits to see if it stays down. "Thank you," he says, and he reaches to set the glass on the table, then leans back again. God, his foot hurts. And how sad that his first task with his daughter will be the pot and that creep, but it has to be done.

But maybe he can wait—just a minute, at least. He looks at Magnolia, and for a long time, neither of them talks or turns away. "You look different," she says finally.

He lets this sink in. "You do too," he says.

"I do? How?"

"Older. More sophisticated."

She blushes, then smiles. "Thanks. And guess what?" She waits a beat, then says, dreamily, "Nate said hi to me today."

"Nate?"

"You don't remember him?" Maggie stares at him, astonished, then says, "Never mind. I'll tell Mom. She'll get it."

Tell me! he wants to say, but he knows it's not the time. "Magnolia," he says instead, and he braces himself. "Who was that guy?"

She frowns, and her eyes tear again, just a little. "He really is my friend, Dad. He's not a bad person. He's actually really nice. He was just a little—well—not himself tonight."

"He was wasted."

She shrugs. No point in denying it when she knows he knows.

"Does Mom know you were out with him?" Eric asks, though he knows that answer too.

She looks nervous suddenly. "Not really. But—"

"Then what were you doing out there?"

"I went out to say hi."

"And that's what you were doing in that car? Saying hi?"

She shrugs once more. "It's not a big deal," she tries. "I was just—"

"It's a *huge* deal," he says. "Let's start right there. First off, leaving the house without your mother's permission. Second, getting into a *car* without your mother's permission. Third, getting into the car of an adult Mom and I don't know, a *man,* and not just that, but a man who then proceeds to get stoned and attempt to get *you* stoned. Magnolia, what are you thinking? That guy is old enough to be your father!" The reverse irony of that sinks in briefly—*so blatantly, appallingly obvious: her daddy disappears and she finds another one*—but he pushes it aside for now, not wanting to kill his momentum. "And fourth, *you* then proceeding to smoke whatever you were smoking in that car, which—"

"I *didn't* smoke!" she says. "I totally faked it to shut him up, because I felt bad he got it for me. I swear to God, that's the truth. I didn't inhale once. I don't even like pot. I almost gagged from the smell, to tell you the truth."

He has to stifle a laugh, it's so Bill Clinton. "That's not the point," he says, holding on to his frown, his harsh tone. "Pot is illegal. And because you don't know where it comes from, you don't really know what's in it, or what it will do to you. And then to be in a *car* with someone who's high, who's *driving* you around—and some *man,* Magnolia, who could easily—"

He stops, unable to say more.

"Okay, Dad," she says after a second. "I get it. I really do."

Eric takes a deep breath. "I meant what I said to that creep. If I see him anywhere near you again, you'll be grounded for a year, and I'll have him hauled off to jail. If I so much as see his name on your phone or e-mail list, I will call the police. And I'll be looking. Do you hear me?"

She nods, almost happily. "Yes, Daddy."

"You delete his filthy, pedophile information from everything you own. Is that clear?"

"I don't text him anyway," she says. "He doesn't have texting." She looks at Eric. "Anyway, can we talk about something different now?"

"We'll talk about something different when I'm ready to," he says, but he's happy enough to drop it.

They are quiet a moment. Then she says, smiling a little, "You sounded like Mom."

He'll take that as a compliment, whether she means it that way or not. But he has possibly never talked so much in his life. His brain feels fried from the effort. "Where *is* Mom, by the way?" he says. The house is mostly dark, he realizes; there's a faint sound coming from upstairs, a TV or radio, maybe.

"Sleeping," Magnolia answers. "She went to bed at, like, five o'clock."

He looks at her. "Why?"

"One of her clients died this week, and today was the funeral. She came home so sad she just went to bed."

He shakes his head. So unlike Eve. "Which client?"

"Um—the one with two little kids. A guy. Michael, I think. Yeah. Michael."

His heart flips a little. He remembers Eve talking about Michael. "Oh," he says. "That's terrible. How did he die?"

"In his sleep. A heart attack or something. Mom blames herself. She says if she'd done a better job of—"

"That's crazy."

"I know. I told her that too, but . . ." She shrugs. "She's been totally weird ever since."

He feels a rush of emotion: guilt and sadness that he hadn't been here to help her, or any of them; fear—and astonishment, really—at the thought of Eve operating at anything but full capacity. The fact is, the one thing he'd never worried about when he left was that she'd fall apart in any way. *And why not?* he thinks now, and for the first time, the enormity of what he's done—leaving without warning, not calling for days, staying away for so long—hits him full force, like a punch in the gut.

He sits up, or tries to. "Where's Danny?" he asks.

"Upstairs playing Wii. Oh my God, Dad, Batman flew away! That's his bird. I texted you he got a bird, right? He was so cute! But Danny let him go, it was so random, he was sitting outside with Mom, holding the bird, and then all of a sudden he just opened his hands, and the bird took off. Mom was totally freaking, probably because we got all this stuff, the cage and this little teeny mirror . . . Plus I think she thought Danny was gonna be depressed without the bird, because he was with him every second before that. But he just started playing even more video games. That's all he does now, he never even goes to kung fu anymore, he—"

"He doesn't go to kung fu?"

Magnolia shakes her head.

"Do me a favor," Eric says. "Go get him down here."

Magnolia rises and goes to the bottom of the steps. "Danny!" she yells up (surely waking Eve if she's actually been asleep). She begins to climb the stairs. "Danny," she calls. "Dan? Danny! Don't you hear me? What the hell are you doing?"

Her mouth. He'll have to work on that too. Eve has probably given up. Maybe on all of it.

He pictures her coming in from the funeral, walking slowly to her room, head down, clothes rumpled, eyes red from crying. Curling into a ball on their big bed, alone.

His poor wife. His poor little Eve.

Magnolia clomps back down, boots pounding the floor. "He's coming," she says, and she kneels again beside Eric. She looks at him and grins. "I'm so happy to see you!" she yells, and she reaches out and hugs his head to her chest, practically smothering him.

"I'm happy to see you too," he says when she finally lets him breathe. "I missed you."

"Well, why did you leave, then?" Her face is serious now. "What were you doing there?"

Before he can think about how to answer, Danny races down

the stairs. He skids into the living room, looks at Eric, and blinks. "Dad?" he says.

Eric is bursting inside. "Danny," he says, and he holds out his arms. But Danny stands still. "You broke your leg?" he says finally.

Eric shakes his head. "No no—just sprained my ankle."

"Oh," Danny says, and he doesn't move, just stares at Eric until Maggie says, "Danny! Give Daddy a hug, you retard!"

"It's okay," Eric says, but again he feels punched as Danny edges over and bends awkwardly to hug him. The boy has changed. *Did I do this?* he wonders as the smell of his son tingles through him, and he shakes his head. Of course he did this. Of course he did.

So okay, then. He'll have to fix it, that's all. But he wonders if that's possible at this point. Danny seems half gone—like his bird. Soaring in the clouds, navigating his own world somewhere. *Of course it's possible,* he tells himself. *Get started.*

He lets go of his son, and Danny backs up slowly. "Did you have fun on your trip?" the boy asks, uncertainly, and he glances at Magnolia, then at his dad.

Eric takes a breath. "Some parts of it. But I'm glad to be home. I missed you guys a ton."

Danny nods. He stands for a moment, clothes twisted, hair dirty and mussed, one hand holding the fingers of the other. Then he says, "Do you mind if I go finish my game?"

"Oh my God!" Magnolia says. "Danny, you are seriously freaking me out. You'd rather play a *video* game than see your *own father*? I'm sorry, but that's the sickest thing I've ever heard."

"It's okay." Eric raises his hand to quiet her. "Listen," he says, thinking fast. "I have an idea. If you go outside and get my crutches, Dan, which I dropped at the side of the house, maybe I can get upstairs and you can show me what you're doing up there. What do you think?"

"Yes!" Danny smiles, finally. Then he runs outside, leaving the door open.

"Dad," Magnolia whispers. "Do you see? He's an absolute addict."

Eric does see. And he is not unalarmed. "Listen," he tells her. "We'll figure it out."

She nods. "We have to. Because Mom is so worried, but she can't really do anything, because the minute she leaves to go see a client, or whatever, he runs upstairs—or over to Star's, because they have better games than we do. And even when Mom's here, she can't pay attention, because she has so much work now. She works *so* much since you—since—" She takes a deep breath. "But maybe now that you're back, she won't have to—you know—"

He sees the doubt rise into her eyes, and he wants to slap it away. She *won't* have to! he wants to say, but he can't, of course. He has no idea what his work life, his earnings, will be. "You know what?" he offers. "Maybe now that I'm back, *I* can spend more time with you guys."

She frowns, though he thinks he sees a tiny bit of pleasure somewhere in the disgust and dubiousness on her face. "Doing what?" she asks.

"I don't know. Clothes shopping? What are you into these days?"

She laughs. "Clothes shopping. But you'd totally hate it."

"For you? I'll put aside hatred if that's what it takes."

She laughs again. "Okay. This Saturday, eleven o'clock, the Bloomfield Mall."

"Deal," he says, trying to fathom it, and then, "As long as your mother's okay with it."

"Why wouldn't she be?" she says snottily.

He laughs. "I don't know, Mags. You tell me."

Danny bursts in, carrying the crutches. "I found them! They're so cool. Can I try them?"

Eric nods, and Danny, too short to use the things properly, sinks to his knees and begins to hop around, the handgrips under his arms. But he crashes to the floor, sending the crutches flying. Magnolia bursts into hysterics, laughing so hard that for a moment her face is frozen and no sound comes out. And then all of them are laughing, and for one small, sparkling instant, everything is okay. Eric registers the moment: *This is it. This is what you came back for.*

But he thinks of Eve, upstairs in their bed, and it brings him back to earth. "Okay," he says. "Danny, let's go. Fifteen minutes upstairs, and then it's time for bed. Mags, wanna come?"

"What, play video games?" She makes a face. "I think I'll pass."

In one of the hardest feats he's ever performed, Eric swings his throbbing foot down, pulls himself onto his crutches, and gets to the stairs, and then up—one flight, then another—to the third floor, to experience the wonder of Danny's world, cyberworld, of remotes and screens and video games.

Later, the kids finally in bed, Eric showers quickly (or as close to a shower as he can, with the cast), brushes his teeth, and hops on his crutches, wearing only a towel, to his and Eve's room. He opens the door and steps into a cave of slumber and darkness, the whir of the sound machine she uses. He can barely see her—the shades are down—but he can smell her sleeping breath, along with the wine in the glass on her night table, the lemon-scented lotion—or whatever it is—she's used for as long as he's known her. *Forever,* he thinks.

He leans his crutches against the wall, drops his towel to the floor, then lifts the covers gently and slides, naked and clean, into the cool silk of his bed. *His own bed.* He lets out a breath it seems he's been holding his whole life. There is nowhere on earth he would rather be right now. Absolutely nowhere. Next to him, her back: warm and inviting, soft as butter, sweet as cream. He is dying to reach out to her. But he doesn't dare. It's her bed now. She calls the shots, not that she didn't always. He lies still, trying not to breathe.

"Eric?" she says softly, and he knows in that word that she knows everything: what happened downstairs, what happened outside with Magnolia, probably even who won his Wii game with Danny. (Danny, of course.)

"Yup," he says.

"Michael died."

"I know."

"You do?"

He nods, surprised she didn't know that too. "Magnolia told me."

She sniffs. "He died in his sleep. He had two little kids. He was seeing a doctor about gastric bypass this very week. And I was his dietitian. I could have gotten him in sooner if I'd had it together from the start. I could have saved him. But I didn't. I—"

"Shh," he says, and he reaches out now, unable to stop himself, and touches her shoulder, though cautiously. He waits. Incredibly, she doesn't stop him, so he moves in further: presses his stomach against her back, inches his arms in and around her.

She begins to sob. "He *died*," she says, her body shaking. "He's *dead*. And it's my fault. And I'm just—I'm just *so sad*."

He curls his body around her shoulders, her hips. He can feel her spine, hidden inside her warm flesh. She seems smaller, thinner, almost childlike. His eyes have adjusted to the dark, and he can see her now, or what's visible of her, anyway, smothered in covers and facing away from him as she is. He buries his face in her hair, inches his good leg over hers. "I know," he says. "Shh. It's okay."

She shakes her head, and he holds her tight. "It's not," she says, and she sounds so despairing that tears come to his eyes, too. "It's horrible!" she says. "Do you know, at the funeral, his little boy was announcing to everyone, 'My daddy is safe in heaven now'? Safe in heaven, where even fat people get to live. Can you imagine? And people he'd worked with, so many people. All the ones who wanted nothing to do with him a month ago. His wife, Diane, couldn't be consoled. She was—" She gulps, swallowing her words.

He massages her arm. "It's okay."

"It's not okay, Eric. It's *not*."

She turns to him, finally, and he sees her face, smeared with black makeup, lines creasing her cheeks and forehead. She looks terrible and pitiful and as beautiful as he's ever seen her. He smooths back her hair, wipes her cheeks. "You know what?" he says. "You're right. It's not."

She almost smiles. "Thank you," she says. "I thought you'd gone soft on me."

He shakes his head. "Me go soft? Never."

They are both quiet a moment, looking at each other until she closes her eyes, and then he does too. "But I will tell you this," he says. "It's not okay now. But it will be."

She opens her eyes. "Will it?"

He nods. He is sure of it.

"How, though? How do you know?"

"Because I'll help you. We'll get through it. And then it will be okay." He shifts, just the tiniest bit, to relieve the pressure on his foot. "And then it won't be," he says. "For a long time, maybe, it won't be. And then, just when you think it can't get any worse . . . then it will be again."

Her eyes are closed, but she smiles once more. "When did you get so damn talky?" she says.

18

IN THE MORNING he wakes early: 6:23 on Eve's clock, which means it's probably closer to 6:15. His foot throbs, but gently. Big improvement over last night—and better than he'd anticipated. Perhaps he won't really have to start again at square one. *Maybe square two or three.* He sighs, flips over carefully.

Amazing that after all this time, he's lying here looking at the back of his wife, just like always. He would like to slither close and drape his naked body onto every inch of her—her hot back, her round ass (it's in there somewhere, under all that cotton and flannel), her white neck beneath her mop of hair. But he has a feeling she wouldn't relish that at this point, and he doesn't want to risk it. *In the future,* he thinks, though the truth is, he has no idea what the future will be. He's been gone six weeks, but it might as well be six years for how different things could be now. And yet the smells, the sounds, the woman in his bed are as familiar as the birthmark on his left hand, the bones and bumps on his feet. *We run from our lives,* he thinks, *from the mediocrity and the abandoned plans and dreams and the people we're sick of, including ourselves. But wherever we go, there we are. And so we go back, to the people we love. But you can't really go back, of course. Not all the way. It's never the same.*

Daylight sneaks into the room, slivers of sunlight around the edges of the shades. *And that's a relief, isn't it? Change is good.* It's his mother's line, of course. But she's as happy as anyone else he knows, and happier than many. So maybe there's something to it.

He thinks of the conversation they'd had in the car coming here—many conversations, really. "I'm old!" she'd told him merrily at one point, and when he'd tried to protest, she'd said, "Oh, hush, it's okay. I honestly don't mind being old, other than the usual physical annoyances. I wouldn't turn back the clock even if I could. I've lived a great life! I don't regret any of it."

"Not even the marriages?" From behind the wheel, Eric shot her a sideways glance.

"*Least* of all them," she said. "For one thing, I got you kids."

"That was one marriage. What about the other two?"

She shook her head. "Just because something doesn't last your whole life doesn't mean it's a mistake." She paused, and the sun through the windshield caught a sparkle in her eye. "'Everyone forgets that Icarus also flew,'" she said.

Eric turned to her. "What?"

"It's a line from a poem. I think of it so often, because, of course, everyone thinks of Icarus as the one who fell into the sea after he flew too close to the sun. Remember that myth?"

"I think I was absent that day."

She laughed. "I'll refresh you. Icarus's father, Daedalus, made the two of them wings out of feathers and wax so they could escape the island where they were prisoners. But Icarus flew too high, and the wings melted, and he died." She smiled. "But the poem is about what happened *before* he died. About the glory of the flight, about feeling himself rise and soar. 'I believe Icarus was not failing as he fell,' the poet says at the end, 'but just coming to the end of his triumph.'

Eric nodded. "Nice. I'll look for it." He had never heard her so garrulous.

"Well, I already quoted you the best lines."

"Okay, then. I'll skip it." She laughed once more. He waited a beat, then said, "So, then, you'd marry again if the opportunity came along?"

She shrugged. "Why not? Maybe this time I'd finally get it right."

"Ah, but doesn't that defy your theory that you have no regrets?"

"It does not." She raised her chin proudly. "My life took turns, and I went with them. And I'm as happy as a squirrel in a tree." She looked out the window for a time. "I'm just saying, maybe if I'd met a person from the start who I could spend my whole life with, like you did . . ."

"You think I did?" He turned to her.

"Of course. That's why you're going back. I never went back to mine once I left. Never even thought twice about it."

"Maybe you weren't meant to be married, then," he said. "Maybe it wasn't the men, but you. Or the institution. It's not for everyone, right?"

"No, it's not," she said thoughtfully. "And it *is* a pain. So high maintenance! Like some ridiculous pet, a chimpanzee, or a pot-bellied pig. You're always having to tend to it."

Eric laughed, and then she laughed, too. "Well," she said, sighing, "I did always hate the way I felt in marriage. Not at first, but gradually. I lost myself. Or a part of myself, anyway. Something died, for me, along with the passion—which of course always dies, at least to some extent. Maybe just the idea of being free, or of being able to do whatever I want. Or maybe I didn't like the idea of being responsible for someone else. It kept me from seeing my own needs. That sounds selfish, I know, and the truth is, I never felt that way with you kids—or rather, I felt responsible, of course, but I didn't mind, because you were my babies. But with marriage, I resented that losing of myself. It kept me from feeling real joy, to a certain extent. That's the best I can explain it, except to say that it was always such a relief when I left the marriages and that feeling came back. It was heavenly—that feeling of being able to breathe, or spread out, or mess up, or *something*, again."

He'd nodded, thinking about that. It had been a relief for him, too, to get away—at least at first. Just the idea of not being judged, not being accountable to anyone. But that had faded fast. He missed them. That's what it came down to. All three of them, not just the kids. And he didn't lose himself around Eve. If anything, he found himself through her, and lost himself when she wasn't there to reflect it back to him: to praise his work, to admire what he did. To love him.

But that has mostly disappeared from their marriage, it seems to him. For a long time now, he hasn't felt that from her—no doubt at least partly because he hasn't been able to work. And perhaps for that reason he hasn't been sure what he's felt for her either. It is time to admit this.

Eric shifts in the bed. The physical attraction is still there, and he suspects always will be; they have never lacked chemistry, at least not from his end. (Her end was more complicated, of course. Wasn't it always for women?) But in the early days, along with her vulnerability, he had loved her bluntness and pragmatism—just as she'd loved his dark mystery—and lately "mystery" has perhaps become checking out and "pragmatism" hard edge and bossiness. He has seen all of these traits in their marriage, among other not-so-nice ones. To err is human, of course, but they'd both erred and erred. And a marriage could take only so much.

But then, here he is. Just as his mother pointed out. And maybe if their old way is too damaged to work anymore, they can try something new. Maybe, in fact, if you're going to stay for the duration—and God knows plenty of people don't—you almost *have* to redefine things halfway through. Maybe that's partly why he'd left—and partly why you can never go back: because you're not supposed to. Because there are reasons you left in the first place.

So maybe he can come halfway back, then—and maybe, just maybe, she'll meet him there, at this new place. He is ready to try a different kind of love now, whatever that might be. If she'll let him. If she'll have him.

He inches out of bed, dresses quietly in the dark, finds his crutches and gets himself out of the room, closing the door behind him. He contemplates his next move. There's a noise—ongoing, like a dull radio—coming from upstairs, and he's halfway up to check it out before he realizes it's the sound of a video game. He finds Danny an inch from the TV making shooting noises, his fingers pounding buttons to set off cyberbombs and bullets and blades. The boy's limbs are white sticks bursting out of too-small pajamas; his eyes are puffy and red. Eric reaches out, pulls the plug, literally, on the whole mess. "Dad!" Danny yells, and he turns to Eric for the first time, rubbing one bleary eye. "I was in the middle of a game!"

Eric shakes his head. "It's much, much too early for this, Dan."

"How do you know?" Danny shoots back. "You don't even live here!"

Ouch. Eric stares at him for a long time, trying to formulate an answer. "Do you see me here?" he asks finally.

Danny doesn't answer, just stares, frowning, at the blank TV.

"Do you?" Eric says again, a little louder.

Danny shrugs. "Yeah."

"Then I guess I live here. Right?"

Danny shrugs again. "Yeah."

"Okay, then." Eric takes a breath. "So I'm telling you now, as your father *and* as an adult who lives here, that these are your choices right now. You can go back to bed, or you can come downstairs and make pancakes with me."

Danny looks at him doubtfully. "You don't know how to make pancakes."

"I know. That's why I need your help. But if you choose to go back to bed, I'm sure I can figure it out. Mom has a recipe, right?"

"What*e*ver," Danny says. "I'll help you." It's new, this snottiness; he sounds like his sister. But in the kitchen, after just a few minutes of sulking, the boy finds the recipe, points out where the whole wheat flour and canola oil are, gets out the eggs. "Dad," he says, dumping milk into the bowl for the second time. (The first time they'd forgotten baking powder, so the pancakes came out "flat as pancakes," as Danny pointed out at least six times.)

"Uh-huh?" Eric moves the bowl underneath what Danny's pouring, trying to keep the spillage to a minimum.

"You know when those birds fly in V's, and one side's always longer than the other?"

Eric nods, sensing a riddle. Danny has his riddle voice on.

"Why is that?" Danny cracks an egg, reaches in to pull out the shell that falls in.

"Um—I give up," Eric says, taking the shell his son hands him.

"Because there are more birds on that side." Danny grins.

Eric smiles. "That's funny," he says. "You're a regular—" He is looking up, staring at the shelf where *The Contradiction* used to be. "Hey," he says. "Where's the sculpture?"

"What sculpture? Oh. That one?" Danny shrugs, stirs the mixture. "Mom sold it."

Eric blinks at him. "What?"

"Mom sold it," Danny repeats. "We needed the money, otherwise we wouldn't have any food last month. We got, like, ten thousand for it. That's good, right?" He stops stirring and looks at Eric, a smear of flour on his chin.

"Sure," Eric manages, after a second, and then, casually, "Who'd Mom sell it to?"

Danny shrugs again. "Some dude named Ron. No, Jon. No, Ron. No, wait, it was—"

"Never mind," Eric says. "I'll ask Mom when she gets up."

"Okay. How many pancakes do you want?"

None, Eric thinks. "Five," he says, and he lets his son cook the pancakes, dump them onto two plates. Tries not to look at the empty shelf above the sink. Two days ago, Dria had called his cell phone to tell him her mother died. But she'd sounded okay, and she didn't want him to pity her, she said. Mostly, she had called to thank him. She had gotten to spend the last weeks with her mother purely because he had brought her out there. She would never forget that—or him. *In every gain, there's a loss*, he thinks now. *In every loss, there's a gain.*

"Don't you like the pancakes?" Danny asks, his mouth full of them.

Eric nods and forces in a bite. "They're fantastic."

Eve shuffles in just before eight, in pajamas, her hair falling in front of her face. "Hi," she says, glancing at Danny, and then, briefly, at Eric. She neither smiles nor scowls; it's impossible to read her. She shuffles over to make tea, brings her steaming mug to the table and sits.

Eric looks at her, ready to bring up the sculpture. But he can't do it. Her cheeks are gaunt, her eyes as puffy as Danny's. She looks pained and exhausted. Something stirs in his chest. He has done this to her.

And yet there's a hardness in her eyes too, he sees now—not bossiness, like before, but something different. Defensiveness, maybe. He can hardly blame her. "You're playing Scrabble?" she asks, as if what she sees is an illusion.

"I already got a bingo," Danny says. "I set up the word, but Daddy found a spot for it."

Eric sees the hardness flicker, just the tiniest bit—a melting on the very edges. "Well, that's good," she says, noncommittally. "You haven't played for a long time, have you."

"Not since I was sick," Danny says. "I was, like, six, right?"

"Give or take," Eve says.

Eric puts down a word—*ennui*. "En . . . nyew . . . en . . . ," Danny says.

"En*nui*," Eric says. "It means—um—"

"Boredom," Eve fills in. "Listlessness. Dissatisfaction."

"Oh," Danny says, and then, to Eve, "We're playing Monopoly next. Then Kerplunk. Daddy said I get three games, then I have to read. But I can pick a comic if I want. It doesn't have to be a book or anything."

He catches Eve's face peripherally: again, that slight softening. "That sounds good," she says, though her voice gives away nothing. She won't make this easy. "Not that books are so terrible," she adds, and she gets up again, pops down a slice of toast, stands at the toaster, waiting.

"Eve," Eric says, almost lightly. "Where's *The Contradiction*?"

And now she looks at him hard, for the first time since he's been back. "I sold it."

"See?" Danny says. "It's what I told you. We needed the money to survive."

Eric nods at Danny. "You were right, I guess."

"Sweetie," Eve says to Danny, "can you run upstairs and get my reading glasses? I think I left them somewhere near my bed."

"Oh, Mom, you *always* leave them somewhere!" But he jumps up and runs out of there.

When he's gone, Eve says, "I had no idea where you were, Eric, or when, or even *if*, you were coming home. I didn't have money for the bills without going into savings. Which I wasn't about to do, obviously, at this point. So I did what I had to."

Again, that dagger in the heart—but digging deeper now, and twisting. But he knows he deserves it. "It's okay," he lies. "Who did you sell it to?"

"Some guy who'd expressed interest years ago. His name is Rabinowitz. He's local."

"Do you have his number?"

The toast pops, and Eve takes it out, looks at it as if she's never seen it. "Why?" she says.

"I want to connect with him. Make sure he's happy. See if he wants anything else." It was half true, anyway. Eric would offer to make him something new—either something the guy wanted, or something Eric came up with. And then give him the choice at the end: the new one, or the one he already had. The new one would be even better, he'd tell him up front, because he had that much more experience now. And if he couldn't make that happen, he'd fake it. If he couldn't make it perfect, he'd make it okay. Just okay. He'd do the best he could, and maybe the guy would like it anyway, and no one would know he wasn't a genius. Maybe that was the secret. *Don't let perfect ruin good*, Eve's mother used to say. Lots of people don't care anyway. Some don't even notice. They just like things. They buy them and stick them somewhere, then move on with their lives.

It's a depressing thought, he knows, but oddly, it doesn't depress him. In fact, he feels excited to try. And in doing so, maybe he'll get his old sculpture back. And feed his family. Or at least work in that direction. Because really, what else could he do?

Eve is considering his request. "It's in the Rolodex, under 'Sculpture, Eric,'" she says finally. "His first name is Sam. His daughter used to be friends with Magnolia."

"Thank you."

She nods, then turns away, carries her toast to another counter and begins to butter it. "I charged him ten thousand," she adds, without looking up, and he thinks that maybe, deep down, there's another tiny softening, another fissure in her armor.

"I know," he says. "Danny told me."

She brings her buttered toast to the table, puts it down without a plate, and sits on a chair. She looks at him. "It's appalling, what you did," she says. "Leaving like that. I was terrified, and then enraged, and then humiliated." She picks up the toast, looks at it, puts it down again. Her hands are shaking. "You put me through hell," she says.

"I know." His heart beats hard. "I'm so sorry."

"Then why, Eric? Why did you do it? To me, to the kids . . ." She shakes her head, pushes away her toast and replaces it with her elbows and leans her face on her fists, closing her eyes. She is crying now, and it makes him want to cry too. She is right. How could he do that to them?

"It's complicated," he says. "It's—"

She raises her face and looks at him, nose and eyes red and running now. "If you wanted a divorce, why didn't you just say it?" she says. "If I was such a bad wife—"

"What?" he says, shocked. "I didn't want a divorce! Is that what you thought?"

"Well, what the hell was I supposed to think? That you were just, I don't know, taking a *vacation*? And it simply slipped your mind to tell anyone you were leaving? Or to call along the way? Oh, and you were taking along a cute little escort, too, just in case you got bored, or whatever. Just in case—" She shakes her head, looks up at the ceiling and then back down at him. "Did you have an affair with that girl?"

"Of course not," he says.

Again, he sees that subtle relaxing in her, deep down inside. One more domino in the long black road he'll need to find a way to stand upright again, even just to get to that new place. And then he'll need her to meet him there.

"But she was with you," Eve says. It's a statement, not a question.

He takes a deep breath. "I drove her to Arizona. Her mother is there—or was—not far from mine, and dying of cancer. She had no way to get there. And I—I had to get out of here. I was useless. I couldn't work. I was doing nothing, all day every day. I was losing my mind."

She looks at him, waiting. But listening, at least.

"I felt like a loser," he says. "I'm not blaming you. You didn't create the feeling. But being around you made it worse sometimes. I felt—I *knew*—I wasn't pulling my weight."

"I never said that!"

"You didn't have to. We both knew it. And it made me feel— there didn't seem to be a thing I could do about it, except sit there and watch you get more and more . . ." He pauses, then begins again. "I'd watch you run around, making meals, taking care of the kids, and then selling your book, seeing clients. I didn't know how to step into that. I couldn't help. You didn't let me."

"I didn't *let* you?"

He shakes his head. "You were only doing what you always do. But I couldn't do what *I'd* always done, Eve. I haven't been able to for years. And I felt so left out of the life you had here, you and the kids. I felt like just one more thing you had to take care of."

Again, the softening, deep, deep down. "So why didn't you tell me, then?" she asks. "You came in and out of here, day after day, and you didn't say one word to me about this. We go out to dinner and I talk and talk about myself, my book . . ." She shakes her head. "I felt like an *idiot*! Like I somehow *drove* you away, without even knowing I—"

"I'm so sorry," he says once more, and he reaches out to touch her face, but she shakes him off, backs away. "Listen," he says, trying again. "I wanted to tell you. But I didn't know what to say. I didn't know what to do. I felt like I was failing you in every way."

"You failed me by *leaving*!" she yells. "Michael might not have died if you'd stayed!" She shakes her head. "You left me with everything, Eric. And that's what happened. A man died, a good man, with little children, who was counting on me. And I failed him, because—"

"No, you didn't," he says. "You didn't."

"How do you know? How the hell do you know about any of it?"

She's right again, of course. "I thought you'd be relieved I left," he says finally, lamely. "I thought it would be easier for you, to tell you the truth."

"Are you kidding?" She stares at him. "That's the most narcissistic thing I've ever—"

"Here they are!" Danny says, bursting into the room. "I finally found them, Mom, they were on your floor! You're lucky you didn't step on them."

Eve turns away from Eric, away from Danny. She walks to the sink and splashes water on her face, dries it on a clean dish towel, sniffs hard. When she looks at Danny, she's composed. "Thank you, baby," she says. "I knew if anyone could find them, it was you."

Danny hands her the glasses. "Just be careful next time."

She smiles. "I will."

"Why is your face all red, Mom?" He stares at her. "Is something wrong with you?"

"I'm just tired. I think I'll go back to sleep for a while, and let Daddy take care of you. Okay?" Without looking at Eric, she starts to walk out of the room.

Danny shrugs. His eyes go back to the Scrabble board, but then they jump up again. "Guess what, Mom? Daddy's gonna see if he can teach my kung fu class."

Eve turns around. "What?"

"He's seeing if he can teach one of my classes, after his foot is all better. Because he taught a kung fu class in Arizona, and it was really fun, and he said it would be even more fun if I was one of the kids. He could use me for demos and things."

Eve looks at Eric, and he nods. He would like to do this. He misses teaching those classes. He had called Diego from the road the first night and told him everything, all the things he'd hidden in Tucson: that he'd left his wife and kids back east, because he needed to break out of a rut; that he's not sure if he did, but he's going back anyway. Diego had understood, as Eric guessed he would. ("Listen, man," he'd said. "Everyone interesting has a story.") Eric thanked him profusely, told him the job had saved him. Diego had laughed. "Wish my other teachers felt that way."

He had paid a visit to Natasha and Johnny on the way out of town too. He hadn't seen them since he'd sprained his ankle and plunged to the depths. So he'd looked up their address at the studio (What was she gonna do? Sue him?), and when his mother pulled up at their house, he hopped out with his crutches, planning to leave a note: it was afternoon and he figured Natasha was at work. But he found her and Johnny home, the boy sick with a cough, his mother having taken the day off to watch him. She was cold when she came to the door—"Can I help you?" she'd said, as if they'd never met—but then Johnny ran out, and, nose stuffed, voice nasal, honked, "Sifu! What are you doing here?"

Natasha had opened the door then. She stepped out—barefoot, wearing jeans—and saw his cast. "Oh," she said, appearing surprised. "I heard about that, but I didn't believe it." She looked him in the eye now. "I figured you were tired of the job. The kids."

Like all men, Eric filled in to himself, guessing her thoughts, and he said, "No. I loved the kids. I loved teaching Johnny."

The boy grinned in a way Eric had never seen at the studio. Eric smiled at him.

"Well, I hope you get better soon," Natasha said, and, looking at her son, ordered, "Go in and watch TV." The boy had scowled but obeyed, or at least faked it, and, screen closed, Natasha turned back to Eric. "The new teacher is not good for Johnny. It's a girl. He needs a man."

"I'm sorry," Eric said, and then, dreading the words, "but that's what I came to tell you. I won't be back. I'm leaving town. I wanted to say good-bye to both of you."

She frowned. "You're leaving? Where are you going?" She was tiny without her platforms, he noticed; no bigger than most twelve-year-olds.

"Back east," he answered. "Massachusetts." He took a deep breath. "I have a family back there."

Her eyes widened. "What you mean, you have a family."

"Two kids," he said. "A boy and a girl. And my wife."

"You left them?"

He nodded.

"You're divorced?"

He shook his head. "No. Married."

She frowned, trying to digest this. "Then why did you leave?"

"That's a complicated question. But I can tell you it wasn't about them. It was about me."

She frowned more darkly now, almost glaring at him. "So. Now you decide to go back." He nodded, trying not to feel lower than a worm, lower than a piece of shit, and she said, "Why? Why not just stay here?"

"I miss the kids. I miss my wife. I needed to leave, but—now it's time to go back."

She made a face of disgust. "You men think you can do whatever you want," she said. "You come and go like it makes no difference. You leave when you get bored of it." She shook her head. "It's pathetic. It makes me sick."

Eric nodded. "I don't really see it that way," he said. "But I can see how you do. And I'm sorry. I really am."

Like the first day, he could almost see her body relax with his words. "It's okay," she said after a moment. "Whatever. You are not my husband."

God forbid, he thought, and he laughed a little; he couldn't help it.

Amazingly, after a second, she smiled too. "What's so funny?"

He shook his head. "Nothing. I'm sorry for laughing."

She smiled wider. "It's okay," she said. "I know what you mean. Sometimes I laugh too."

He had bid her good-bye then, wished her good luck with her boy, told her it was great she had him in kung fu. "Try to make him keep going," he said. "It will help him. And give the new teacher a chance. Will you?"

She gave him a look, almost flirtatious now. "I will try. Wait, let me get Johnny to come say good-bye." The boy stepped out immediately (he'd been just inside the screen, Eric was sure, listening to everything) and threw his arms around Eric, almost knocking him down.

Now, in his own home, his own town, his wife contemplates the idea of him teaching kung fu. And she likes it, he sees. "That would be great," she says to Danny. "I hope Daddy does that. I hope you both do."

He will do it, just as soon as he's physically able. He can make that happen, and he will. A dozen dominoes righted right there.

Up in her room, Eve scratches her head. Now that she's here, she doesn't want to go back to sleep.

So she dresses: dark jeans, bright white V-neck T-shirt, nice boots. A leather jacket from her closet, old but slick. She brushes on a touch of mascara and blush, shakes out her hair. "I'm going out," she calls to Eric, heading back downstairs. "See you guys." She closes the door behind her.

Outside, she stands for a moment, breathing. No one stops her. No one calls her or comes after her. Just the cool morning air.

In the car, she turns off her cell phone. Then she drives, without rushing, to Michael Cardello's house. She parks among several cars on the street, walks to the door, rings the bell.

Diane answers, wearing sweatpants and carrying Bella, who sports a diaper and pink paint all over her hands, which are splayed out in front of her. Eve smiles at Bella, then glances at Diane. She looks okay, actually. Better than yesterday anyway.

"Oh—hey," Diane says. She is tentative, but not angry. Another woman appears and whisks the painted child away.

"Hi." Eve takes a breath. "Listen, I'm sorry to bother you at home."

"It's okay." Diane sniffs, pushes back her hair. "Do you want to come in?"

Eve shakes her head. "I just wanted—" She swallows. "I wanted to tell you I'm sorry. I'm so sorry, Diane. Not just for Michael's death but—for my role in it."

Diane wrinkles her forehead. "Thank you. But I'm not sure what you mean by—"

"I should have done a better job," Eve says. "I should have been faster to suggest the surgery, and I shouldn't have made it sound so exciting until he saw the doctor first. I got him overexcited. I—I just wish I'd handled this differently. Maybe I could have saved him." She shakes her head. She's aware that professionally this sort of confession is dangerous, but she doesn't care. "Anyway. I hope it's okay to say all this. I just wanted you to know how sorry I am. And if there's anything I can do, now or ever, I hope you'll call me."

Diane looks at her for a long moment. Then she says, "I appreciate the thought, Eve. But don't kid yourself. You couldn't have saved him."

Eve opens her mouth, but Diane cuts her off. "He had a huge problem—a horrible, unfixable problem. I'm not even sure the surgery would have helped in the end. I mean, I've read about it. You have to be so disciplined."

"They help you with that," Eve says, almost defensively. "They work with you."

Diane shrugs. "The point is, don't blame yourself. It wasn't anything you did or didn't do. It was him. It was how he was born. He had a demon, and he couldn't kick it." She shakes her head. "Others tried before you, you know," she says, and she sounds almost aggressive. "You weren't the first one who couldn't save him."

It is an offer, Eve knows, a priceless gift Diane is extending—and to *her*, of all people, whose husband is back now, at home with her children, while Diane's is gone forever.

And so she takes it. She reaches out, and Diane allows her that too, and for a long time, the women embrace. "Thank you," Eve says finally, stepping away, and then, "He was a lovely man, Diane. A smart, funny, excellent person. I'll miss him."

Diane smiles tearfully. She nods. "Thank you for coming, Eve," she says, and in that moment, in those words, Eve somehow knows that she'll be okay.

Back in her car, Eve feels light with relief, as if a weight has been lifted off her neck, her shoulders, a weight she hadn't fully realized was there. She puts in a CD and drives straight to New York, singing without thinking, barely touching the brakes the whole way. On the West Side Highway, approaching the city, she feels the first thrill of the place. *How long since I've been here?* she thinks, as she watches for her exit. *How long since I've even been out of Bramington, other than to see a client?*

She parks on Riverside Drive around 100th Street. The day is still young, and she feels filled with a vibrant, almost manic energy. She walks east, shedding her jacket, letting the sun warm her arms. On Broadway, people teem by on all sides, and she involuntarily picks up her already brisk pace. As she moves, she takes things in: the storefronts (lavender lace bras, fist-sized chocolate-covered strawberries), the fashions (flouncy skirts and flip-flops), the serious faces and ubiquitous cell phones and general throng of humanity.

The roads in Central Park are mobbed with joggers, parents pushing kids in strollers, people moving to iPods plugged into their heads. Every bench is crammed: hoary old women, fluffy white terriers, exquisite young men. A cop clops by on a horse, ignoring a lunatic with a blanket staggering around babbling. A skinny white guy walks by with a tall black transvestite; a toddler throws a tantrum as a woman kneels talking to him. Eve soaks it in. The playgrounds crawl with kids, fathers, nannies. She passes three Asian girls in tiny skirts, and she smiles, and one smiles adorably back.

A bald, toothless woman asks her for a cigarette. "Sorry," Eve says, shaking her head.

The L train out to Williamsburg is cleaner and faster than it used to be, or at least it seems that way. She climbs the stairs at the other end, comes out blinking into sunlight. Particles of silvery dust float on the warm wind; the air smells of perfume and curry and sugar, vibrates with cars and music and bodies. Two dogs bark back and forth. She heads toward her old neighborhood, carried by the momentum of the people around her.

As she approaches, she sees, with an intake of breath, that it's changed almost beyond recognition. The laundromat is gone; in its stead is a café advertising "steel-cut oatmeal, soya lattes." The video store has been replaced by a tiny boutique with about five pieces of clothing in it. She glances into each store, laughing softly with amazement more than happiness, wondering where all the other people, the old people, went.

Her former apartment building has been renovated. The once grungy entrance is now shiny and sleek, the space next door— which used to be empty but for the junkies and transients artfully draped on the stoop—now an art gallery, full of large abstract paintings (blotches of bright red and gray). Eve stands for a long time just looking at it all. Then she crosses the street and heads back the other way.

People float by, young and pretty, portfolios or expensive cameras or steaming silver mugs in their hands. She veers off the main drag in another direction.

There's an enormous new bookstore this way. A bookstore! Eve wanders around inside it, like a kid in a brand-new indoor play space. Finally she approaches the clerk, an ash-haired young man with thick glasses and very red lips. "I'm looking for a book called *Feast on This,*" she says. "By Eve Adams. Do you know where I can find it?"

He types into his screen, squints a little, types again. "I'm sorry," he says finally. "We don't carry that book. Would you like me to order it?"

"No. Thank you," she says.

So she browses. Picks out a few novels, finds a chair in a corner and settles in with them, slowly turning pages. In one, a girl goes to Nepal. Another is a war novel by a well-known male author she's heard about but never read. In a third, a woman is obsessed with a guy who's abusing her. After a long time, she buys the two she likes best.

Outside again, she is suddenly ravenous. She thinks of a little Polish restaurant she loved so many years ago, wonders if it could possibly still be here. *Surely not,* she tells herself, but she walks that way anyway, just in case. There's a green awning where the old tan one used to be, and her heart grows heavy at the thought that this place, more than anything else, is gone, replaced by a raw juice bar, a Reiki center, a cell phone operation. But as she gets closer, she realizes it's only a new awning. The place is still here, and inside, it's just as it was: same red tablecloths, same waiters, even; older, more weathered, but otherwise just the same.

They greet her like she never left, and she hugs one of them, a slight man with a white mustache who had served her every time she came in. He leads her to her usual corner, and she sits down happily, orders split pea soup, pierogi with applesauce and sour cream, and a bottle of Polish beer. While she waits, a girl walks into the restaurant, goes to a table where a man has been waiting and leans down to kiss him, her honeyed hair spilling over their faces. At the edge of her pants, her sweater rises to expose a tiny tattoo. Eve watches them until her food arrives. She imagines them in a cool, sparse apartment, a sheer red curtain over the window in the tiny, empty kitchen, the fridge shelves bare but for exotic mustard and espresso beans. An old door on cement blocks for their dining room table, a few colorful, mismatched chairs. In the bathroom (tiny, with a small, high window that looks out into an alley) an old claw-footed bathtub with dozens of bottles and jars surrounding it, soaps, oils, candles, body creams. She smiles at her fantasy. *Get real,* she thinks, sipping her beer. *They're probably financial planners or bankers on Wall Street.* Her food arrives, and she eats hungrily, looking out the window as she chews. When she's done, she drops a twenty on her check, finds her jacket, and leaves.

She heads toward McCarren Park; when she arrives, she sits on a bench. More people here: kids walking dogs, tossing softballs, laughing. A couple walks by, the girl in a pleated skirt and two high Dorothy braids, the boy in plaid Bermuda shorts and black nylon kneesocks. The girl is chatting away, and Eve sees that she's about to stumble on a bottle that's rolled into her path—and then she does, lurching forward before the boyfriend, already holding her, rights her again. She bursts out laughing, and then he laughs too, and he picks up the bottle, and Eve smiles, feeling sheepish, because every couple reminds her in some little way of herself and Eric when they were back here.

So long ago. It almost seems like another life, another incarnation. Next to her, a man sits down, smoking a cigarette. He is young and enormous, with long messy hair and huge unlaced boots, jeans splatted with something white: spackle or paint. They glance at each other and she nods at him briefly, then looks away.

She has been angry at Eric for a long time. She sees this now, like a ray of sunlight at the dawn of a day. It didn't start just when he left. She has been quietly angry for years: angry because of the work he hasn't been able to do, because of the way their lives have changed, even because of the mistakes that she herself has made. And maybe that's a little bit of why he left, too. To get away from her anger. Anyway, she's willing to take some of the blame.

But she's not angry now. At least she doesn't think she is. Instead, she feels—light. Blank. Cleansed. And if nothing has turned out quite as she'd thought it would—if her life, if all of their lives were not exactly as she'd once envisioned them—she still picks this life. The exact life she has. She wouldn't trade any of it.

But that doesn't mean there can't be more. *Big dreams are for the young, yes*, she thinks. *But there are small moments, small wishes, too.*

In the distance, to the west and Manhattan, the sun offers its final display of the day: fiery red ball in a bath of mustard yellow, smoky blue, silver gray. Colors filtered through the air of Brooklyn, different even from Manhattan. There is so much out there in the world, so much to fill that new blankness. *So much still to see.* She should get out more. She should come back here. And maybe she will, now that Eric is home. After all, she's here now, already.

She closes her eyes, smells tobacco sweet on the fresh evening air. *Take what you need*, she tells herself. *Take what you want. Figure it out, find it, do it. That's what he's doing. That's what he did.* She opens her eyes. The big man is looking at her. "You have nice eyes," he says.

She smiles. "Thank you," she says.

The subway ride back is long, but that's okay. *There's no hurry*, she thinks. *Take a breath.* At 96th Street in Manhattan, she gets out and heads west. The sun is gone now, Sunday evening having subdued the weekend crowds and smells and colors in its cloak of velvety blue. She gets in her car and drives all the way back to Massachusetts without stopping until she reaches the light in downtown Bramington. It is late, she sees. Almost midnight. She takes out her cell phone, turns it on. Twenty-one missed calls, all from home. She laughs. She tosses her head. Her hair is getting long. Maybe she'll let it grow out. Maybe she won't get it trimmed.

As she pulls into her driveway, the beam from the headlights catching the young sugar maple (swaying in the breeze, showing off its new leaves), Eve thinks, *Open your eyes.* But they are open now, she knows. She is preaching to the converted. She drives the rest of the way in, parks and walks around the house and in the front door. Down the hall, despite the hour, she can see and hear them all at the kitchen table, playing Go Fish: Eric, Magnolia, Danny . . . and someone else. Penelope! Eve smiles, steps into the kitchen. "Hi," she says.

Eric stands, and she sees relief fill his face. The kids wheel around. "Mommy!" they yell, and they stumble toward her and grab her waist, kiss her cheeks, cling to her like a life raft.

"You came home!" Danny yells, taking her hand.

"I told you she would," Magnolia says, but her face betrays her confident tone just a hair; there is relief in her too, Eve sees, and she has to admit, she relishes it. She glances around the kids at Penelope, and the two exchange a look, a slight smile. And then Eve turns back to her children, her big, almost grown babies. "Of course I did," she says. "Of course I did."

Acknowledgments

I AM ENORMOUSLY indebted to my ever-faithful "writing group"—Daniel Jones, Kate Christensen, Amy Hanauer, and Bette Hanauer—who read my drafts quickly and tirelessly and provide wise, honest, and enthusiastic feedback for the price of my eternal gratitude. Judy Spring and Renee Wetstein also offer sharp insight, and Lonnie Hanauer is a wealth of medical information. Additionally, with this book I had generous help from dietitians, psychologists, and/or physicians Wendy Bernstein, Alison Steiber, Robin Blackstone, and David Engstrom, while the adroit Christina Gerrish hooked me into a riveting seminar about bariatric surgery that Dr. Blackstone led. Zachary Dietz and Nancy Rothenberg of Spirit of the Heart Kung Fu graciously provided details about that elegant martial art; Andrew DeVries, on whose work my character Eric's work is based, was exceptionally kind in instructing me about bronze sculpture; Sharon Roffman and Barbara Neulinger advised me on other matters; Phoebe and Nathaniel Jones supplied humor and cultural and language references. (How else would I know all those brilliant "dick" lyrics without teenagers to enlighten me?) Deb-Jane Addis, as always, answered any query I pitched about Tucson. Robbie Myers, Vera Jones, Gretchen Jennings, Ann Barandes, Margot Guralnick, Chris and Gina Russell, Amy Fleishman, and many other excellent people supply frequent encouragement about my writing. Ted Conover and Marjorie Braman offer wisdom and expertise. Cynthia Kling cracks me up during breaks.

Greer Hendricks was helpful in guiding me to my lovely, shrewd, and rigorous editor, Sarah Branham; the rest of the team at Atria could not be more talented, tireless, or great at what they do. Elizabeth Kaplan understands my work and where I want to take it better than just about anyone else. Among other things, she plows through my copious e-mails and drafts and promptly and tactfully offers responses from thoughtful to sage to encouraging.

Finally, I thank anyone who, in this age of iPhones, Facebook, YouTube, Twitter, and Band-Aid-sized movie screens, still takes time to read books. (Extra credit if you buy them in paper/visit an actual bookstore.) Without you, there would be no need for us.

Thank you, thank you.

—ch

Note to the Reader

ON PAGE 300, Nancy Kalish mentions a poem about marriage being like holding up a ceiling. That poem, "A Marriage," by Michael Blumenthal, goes like this:

You are holding up a ceiling
with both arms. It is very heavy,
but you must hold it up, or else
it will fall down on you. Your arms
are tired, terribly tired,
and, as the day goes on, it feels
as if either your arms or the ceiling
will soon collapse.

But then,
unexpectedly,
something wonderful happens:
Someone,
a man or a woman,
walks into the room
and holds their arms up
to the ceiling beside you.

So you finally get
to take down your arms.

You feel the relief of respite,
the blood flowing back
to your fingers and arms.
And when your partner's arms tire,
you hold up your own
to relieve him again.

And it can go on like this
for many years
without the house falling.

About the Author

CATHI HANAUER is the author of the novels *Sweet Ruin* and *My Sister's Bones* and the editor of the *New York Times* bestselling essay anthology *The Bitch in the House*. Her essays, criticism, and reporting have appeared in the *New York Times*, *Elle*, *Real Simple*, *O, The Oprah Magazine*, *Self*, *Glamour*, *Parenting*, *Whole Living*, and many other publications. She has taught writing at The New School in New York and at the University of Arizona in Tucson. She lives in western Massachusetts with her husband, Daniel Jones, and their daughter and son.

Gone

CATHI HANAUER

A Readers Club Guide

INTRODUCTION

Eve Adams's husband is gone. One night, he leaves to drive the babysitter home . . . and doesn't come back. With two children to raise, a budding career, and plenty of bills that need to be paid, Eve has no choice but to hold herself and her family together. In *Gone*, *New York Times* bestselling author Cathi Hanauer presents an honest and compelling story of what it means to grow—both together and apart; what it takes to thrive as an individual; and ultimately, what it means to forgive.

QUESTIONS AND TOPICS FOR DISCUSSION

1. Consider the title of this novel. What comes to mind when you think of the word "gone"? Discuss how the concept of leaving and saying goodbye reappears throughout the novel. Who or what is gone, and in what way?

2. The novel opens with Eve's point of view. Were you surprised when the narrative switched to Eric's perspective? How did the split point of view and change in narration affect your reading of the novel? Did you prefer one to the other? Discuss your answer.

3. "She would not talk to him now. . . . It was after ten, she had a big day tomorrow, and though the ringing hadn't woken the kids, a conversation surely would. *No.* He had made her wait six days to talk to him. She would call him tomorrow." (p. 116) Do you agree with Eve's decision to ignore Eric's phone call? How does this decision impact what happens later in the novel? Do you think things would have been different if Eve did just pick up Eric's call? Why or why not?

4. Discuss Eve's decision to sell *The Contradiction*. Do you think she made the right choice? What would you have done if you were in her position?

5. Minor characters, such as Alexis and Keisha, come and go throughout the course of the novel. Though they don't play significant roles, are there some ways in which they affect the plot or main characters? What do you think *Gone* would be like without these characters?

6. Penelope explains to Eric: "Because for what you give up for marriage—autonomy and sexual freedom, to name two pretty huge things—you'd better get something good in return. You'd better get a *lot*. Financial support, great friendship, a good parenting partner . . . one of them at the very least." (p. 130) How do the other characters define what it means to have a "good marriage"? Discuss the other interpretations of marriage described in *Gone*. Do you agree with Penelope's assessment of marriage? Why or why not?

7. On page 273, Eric reflects on a scene he witnessed in New York City, in which a man fell on the street and was helped up. Read this passage again. Whose reaction to the story do you identify with more: Eve's or Eric's? What do Eric and Eve's different responses tell you about their characters?

8. Discuss Penelope's character and role in *Gone*. How would you describe her as a mother? Do you think she is a mirror or a foil for Eve's character?

9. The notion of forgiveness plays an important role in Eve and Eric's relationship. Discuss how they forgive each other and themselves. Discuss your idea of what it means to forgive. Is there anything that you would consider to be unforgivable? Why or why not?

10. How did you react to Eve's decision to go to New York after Eric finally returns? Do you believe she always intended to return home? How would you classify this decision? Was it brave? Fair? Selfish? What would you have done?

11. Discuss how the characters in *Gone* deal with issues like the overwhelming presence of technology, medication, and obesity in our modern lives. How does the author confront and integrate these issues into the narrative? Did your opinions on these issues change in any way after reading *Gone*? Why or why not?

12. What did you think of the conclusion of the novel? What unanswered questions, if any, do you have? What do you think is in store for Eve, Eric, and their family?

ENHANCE YOUR BOOK CLUB

1. The poem "A Marriage" by Michael Blumenthal is included at the end of the novel in Cathi Hanauer's "Note to the Reader." Take turns reading the poem aloud with your book club members. How do you interpret the poem? How does this poem relate to Eve and Eric's relationship? Do you think this is an accurate metaphor for marriage? Come up with your own metaphors for being married or for being in a committed relationship to share with the group.

2. Reread "Eve's Simple Ten" on page 13. Do you agree with her rules for healthy living? What are some of your own rules? Make your book club meeting a healthy one by serving only health-smart snacks.

3. Cathi Hanauer is also the editor of *The Bitch in the House: 26 Women Tell the Truth About Sex, Solitude, Work, Motherhood, and Marriage*. Choose one or two essays from the collection to discuss at your book club meeting as well. How do these women's experiences compare to Eve's?